"*Between You and Me* is a rich and complex story about faith, love, justice, and friendship you don't want to miss."
—*Bustle*

"Complex, beautifully wrought, warm, and surprising as only Susan Wiggs can do. Two colliding worlds, both fraught with complications and prejudice, spun into a graceful, complex story that will make you turn the pages till the very end. I absolutely loved it."
—KRISTAN HIGGINS,
New York Times bestselling author of *Now That You Mention It*

D0019485

Praise for

Between You & Me

"A big story of love, loss, and honor. Susan Wiggs just keeps getting better and better."

—JACQUELYN MITCHARD,
author of *The Deep End of the Ocean*

"Complex, beautifully wrought, warm, and surprising as only Susan Wiggs can do. Two colliding worlds, both fraught with complications and prejudice, spun into a graceful, complex story that will make you turn the pages till the very end. I absolutely loved it."

—KRISTAN HIGGINS, *New York Times* bestselling
author of *Now That You Mention It*

By Susan Wiggs

SUSAN WIGGS

Between You & Me

A Novel

AVONBOOKS

An Imprint of HarperCollinsPublishers

BETWEEN YOU & ME. Copyright © 2018 by Susan Wiggs. All rights reserved. Printed in the United States of America. No part of this book may be used or reproduced in any manner whatsoever without written permission except in the case of brief quotations embodied in critical articles and reviews. For information, address HarperCollins Publishers, 195 Broadway, New York, NY 10007.

First Avon Books mass market printing: April 2019
First William Morrow paperback international printing: June 2018
First William Morrow paperback special printing: June 2018
First William Morrow hardcover printing: June 2018

Print Edition ISBN: 978-0-06-242554-6
Digital Edition ISBN: 978-0-06-242557-7

Cover design by Amy Halperin
Cover photographs © Matt Anderson Photography/Getty Images (house and background); Frank Whitney/Getty Images (woman); suwatsilp sooksang/Shutterstock (sky)

19 20 21 22   QGM   10 9 8 7 6 5 4 3 2 1

To my beloved daughter, Elizabeth,
who must never outgrow fairy tales—
I dedication this book to you for reasons so profound
we'll just keep everything between you and me.

Prologue

On the day you were born, when you were only a few hours in this world, I tucked you into an old apple crate and left you behind like a piece of my beating heart, like an offering to a god I didn't believe in but didn't dare not believe in. Some might say you were a human sacrifice, but in that moment, I felt as though I was the sacrifice, not you.

Because in that moment, something inside me died.

Though I was too young to know anything, I truly imagined I was leaving you to a better life . . . I didn't want to walk away, but I was scared of what would happen if I didn't.

After all we'd been through that year, I was self-aware enough to realize my youth and ignorance would be a danger to you, yet smart enough to figure out what to do. I didn't know anything about the modern world, about the city, about the law, about the inexorable ties that bind the heart. All I knew was that you'd be better off with a different future. With some other family to guide you. With some other life, far from Middle Grove.

By that time, I understood very well what happens at a hospital. They save people. They saved me. So I took you to a place where I knew you'd be saved.

Of course, that's not how the papers reported it. The news media focused on the most sensational aspect of the case—an abandoned baby, a mysterious puzzle to be solved, a terrible family secret hidden by a distrustful, closed community that walled itself off from the rest of the world.

But the papers got it wrong.

ONE

Harvest

AUGUST

Difficulty is a miracle in its first stage.
—AMISH PROVERB

1

The silver flash of a jet plane glinted in the morning sky. Caleb Stoltz tipped back his brimmed hat and watched it soar high overhead. Against the flawless summer blue, the plane glittered like a rare jewel—precious and out of reach.

"Hey, look, Uncle Caleb. Plane tracks," said Jonah, pointing out the twin white plumes that bisected the sky in the flight path of the jet.

Caleb grinned at his nephew and handed him a galvanized milk pail, half-filled from the milk house. "They're called contrails. Don't slosh it," he cautioned. "I'll be in to breakfast shortly."

Lugging the pail, the boy headed for the white clapboard house, his dusty bare feet leaving shallow impressions in the dry earth. Jonah's skinny legs, browned by a summer of swimming at Crystal Falls up the creek a ways, protruded comically from his tattered black trousers, which only a short while ago had fit him. Now eleven, the kid was growing like the corn in high summer. Caleb would have to get Hannah to sew him a new pair of pants before school started in a few weeks. If not for the way the kids were growing, he would have no notion of the passage of time.

On a farm, the seasons were important, not the years.

Caleb washed down the milking shed, the stream of water hissing on the concrete and misting his work boots. He turned off the hose, reeled it in, and left the shed, glancing up at the puffy trail of clouds dissipating in the sky. The jet was long gone, off to New York or Bangkok or some other place Caleb had no hope of ever seeing. He studied the flight path and then wondered why it was called a path when there was no visible roadway, nothing to mark its way but invisible air. It was only after the jet had passed that its route could be seen.

If Rebecca were with him, she would quirk her brow and scold him for idle thoughts. Then he would challenge her to offer proof that any thought could be idle, and her quirked brow would knit in incomprehension. "I swear, Caleb Stoltz," she would say, and then she'd change the subject. That was her way.

Ah, Rebecca. She was going to be the most difficult part of his day. The problem had been weighing on his mind for far too long. Time to stop putting off the inevitable. They were supposed to have an understanding. She believed that one of these days, she would get her clock from him, the traditional gift of engagement, and she'd present Caleb with an embroidered cloth to symbolize her acceptance. Baptism, marriage, and a family wouldn't be far behind. Though she wasn't keen to raise Caleb's niece and nephew and take care of his father, she was willing to do her duty.

Caleb needed to acknowledge the truth his gut had been telling him since the day the church elders had presented him with the notion that he and Rebecca Zook should marry. And that truth was going to make for a hard conversation. He had a fine, warm affection for Rebecca, but it was not the deep love that would bind a man and woman for life. He wasn't even sure that sort of love existed.

It wouldn't be fair to string her along.

Standing in the yard, he surveyed the farm for a few moments, taking in the sweep of the broad valley that ran down from the Pocono hills. The fields were an abundant patchwork of corn, wheat, alfalfa, and sorghum, spread out over rolling landscape as far as the eye could see. In the distance, Eli Kemp and his sons were cradling wheat. Their scythes swung in tandem to the rhythm of a hymn they were singing, the sound traveling across the valley in the quiet of the morning. They moved along the rows like a line of industrious soldier ants, the forked cradles felling the stalks neatly to one side. Eli's wife trailed behind, bundling sheaves.

That was Middle Grove, Caleb thought. Faith, work, and family, stitched together by the common thread of devotion. Other farmers in the district might breathe the sweet air and offer up a silent prayer. *Thank you for this day, O Lord.* But not Caleb. Not in a long, long time.

From the neighboring farm, the roar of a hydraulic engine broke the stillness of the morning, its mechanical cough obliterating the Kemps' singing. The Haubers were getting ready to fill silo today. The diesel-powered shredder would be used to chop the corn for blowing into the silo.

Caleb would be going over to help after he spoke with Rebecca. In the meantime, he stayed busy. He liked being busy. It kept him from thinking too hard about things. The sun was out, there were chores to do, and the work went fast when neighbors pitched in together.

Taking off his hat, he wiped the sweat from his brow and headed inside. Despite all the open windows, the kitchen was stifling hot. The old iron stove door yawned open with a metallic protest as his niece, Hannah, added fuel to boil the coffee. Smoke and the reek of burned toast layered the room in a misty gray haze.

"Hannah burned the toast again," Jonah announced, unnecessarily.

His sister, who was sixteen and as incomprehensible as an alien life-form in a science fiction novel, planted her fists on her hips. "I wouldn't have burned a thing if you hadn't spilled the milk." She glared accusingly at a blue-white puddle on the scuffed linoleum floor.

"Well, I wouldn't have spilled it if you hadn't called me a *brutz* baby."

"You *are* one," she retorted. "Always pouting."

"Huh. You're gonna get married and have a real baby and then you'll know what it's like."

"Hey, hey." Caleb held up a hand for silence. "It's not even seven o'clock and you two are squabbling already."

"But she called me a—"

"Enough, Jonah." Caleb didn't raise his voice, but the sharpness of his tone cut through the boy's sass. The brother and sister bickered a lot, but a deep bond held them close. Orphaned by a horrendous disaster, they shared a sense of vulnerability that made them cling together, closer than most siblings. "Did you get something to eat?"

"He made grape slush out of his cornflakes again," Hannah said. "It's disgusting." Jonah's strange habit of putting grape jelly on his cereal never failed to gross her out.

"It's better than burnt—" Catching Caleb's warning look, Jonah snapped his mouth shut.

"Go on over to the Haubers'," Caleb said. "Tell them I'll be along shortly."

"Okay." Jonah jammed on his hat and headed for the door.

"Be sure you watch yourself around the machinery, you hear?" Caleb cautioned, thinking of the shredder's sharp blades and the powerful auger at the bottom of the silo.

"Don't worry, I've been helping out since I was knee-high to a grasshopper," Jonah said with a cocky grin, the one that never failed to chase away Caleb's annoyance. "Oh! Almost forgot my lucky penny." He scampered to his room and returned with the token. It was a coin flattened in a penny press machine at the old water-powered sawmill over in Blakeslee, a souvenir of Jonah's only trip away from Middle Grove. He tucked the coin into his pocket, then yanked open the screen door.

"See you at lunchtime," Caleb said.

"All right."

"And don't slam—"

The door banged shut.

"—the door," Caleb finished, shaking his head.

Hannah was still mopping up the milk while Caleb washed at the kitchen sink. Through the window above the basin, he could see Jonah racing like a jackrabbit across the field to the silo. Jubilee, the collie mix that followed the kid everywhere, loped along at his side. With a sudden leap, Jonah launched himself into the air, then planted his hands on the ground as his legs and bare feet flew overhead in an exuberant handspring. This was the boy's special skill, his lithe young body's expression of pure joy, perhaps his way of embracing the perfect summer morning.

In the kitchen, an awkward silence hung as thick as the smoke. Lately, Caleb didn't know what to say to his sullen niece. She had been so young when he'd left Middle Grove under a glowering shadow of disapproval from the elders. He'd had every intention of finding a life away from the community. But he had returned, reeled back in by a hideous tragedy. By that time, Hannah had turned into a skinny, nervous twelve-year-old, haunted by nightmares of her murdered parents.

Now his niece was a stranger, the lone girl in a household of men, with no woman's hand to guide her. Just Caleb, who was ridiculously ill-equipped to deal with her, and his father, Asa, a man who clung with iron fists to the old ways. Already, some of Hannah's friends were getting baptized and promised to young men. He could scarcely imagine his little niece as a wife and mother.

He finished scrubbing his hands and dried them, then fixed up a tray with his father's breakfast and left it on the table as usual. Asa always got up early to read *Die Botschaft* in the quiet of the toolshed adjacent to the house. Caleb opened a cupboard and took a wad of cash from the coffee can, folding the bills into his wallet. After chores, and after his talk with Rebecca, he planned to go up to Grantham Farm to bring home a new horse. Baudouin, the sturdy Belgian, was old. He'd given his all and had earned a fine retirement in the pasture, and now Caleb needed a replacement. He ran a yoke of draft horses to make extra money to keep up with the bills on the farm. His team was in demand, especially in winter, when cars got stuck and fallen trees needed to be dragged out of the way. It was remarkable how much hauling English folks needed.

Glancing out the window again, he saw Jonah scrambling like a monkey up the conveyor belt to feed the bound corn shocks into the grinder. The kid loved high places and always volunteered for them. Caleb had always liked that chore too. The world looked entirely different when viewed from the high opening of the silo. He used to imagine the tower scene from *Lord of the Rings,* a forbidden novel that had once earned him a caning from his father when he'd been caught reading it. While feeding the stalks to the shredder, Caleb used to pretend that the mouthful of whirring, glistening blades belonged to a fierce dragon guarding the tower.

"Sorry about the toast, Uncle Caleb," Hannah spoke up, taking the charred remains out of the wire rack.

"Not a problem." To lighten the moment, he grabbed a piece and took a huge bite, closing his eyes and pretending to savor it. "Ah," he said. "Ambrosia."

She laughed a little. "Oh, Uncle Caleb. Don't be silly."

He choked down the rest of the toast and grinned, showing his charcoal teeth. "Who's being silly?"

"What's ambrosia, anyway? You're always using big words, for sure."

"It's what the gods of Greek myth ate," he said. "So I reckon it means something good enough to feed to the gods."

She gasped at the mention of Greek gods—another forbidden topic—then whisked the toast crumbs from the counter. "You're so smart."

"Knowing the meaning of a word doesn't make me smart."

"Sure it does. I heard Rebecca say you went away and came back smarter, and that's why you still haven't joined the order—'cause your head's all full of prideful English nonsense."

"Rebecca likes to hear herself talk." At the mention of her name, Caleb felt a trickle of sweat slide down his neck. Rebecca's notion that his time away had made him proud was yet another reason they weren't a good match. Getting an education didn't make a man proud. Instead, it was humbling.

In his time away, Caleb had done the unthinkable. Against all Amish principles, he had attended college classes. The traditional eighth-grade education had left a thirst in his soul, and he'd sought out books and knowledge the way a man seeks cold lemonade on a hot August day. He used to ride his bike thirteen miles each way to take classes at the community college, soaking up lessons in history, philosophy, logic, calculus, and the kind of science that had nothing to do with crop yields or tending livestock. It was humbling to discover how much he didn't know about the world, how much he had yet to learn. He had just been starting out when he'd had to come back. These days, he imagined the world he'd discovered beyond Middle Grove shimmering like a chimera on the horizon, out of reach, yet tauntingly real.

Hannah finished tidying the kitchen in her negligent, haphazard way. When Caleb's father came in, he'd likely point out the crumbs on the floor and the dish towels left out on the counter. He'd probably also scowl at his breakfast tray and remark that a proper Amish family broke bread together around the table, their scrubbed faces lit by the inspiration of silent prayer before they dived into hotcakes with berry preserves and thick slices of salty ham.

But they weren't like other families. Caleb could only do so much.

"Uncle Caleb?"

At the tentative note in Hannah's voice, he turned to her. To his surprise, her cheeks shone a dull red against the loose strings of her black *kapp*.

"What is it, *liebchen*?" He used the old endearment, hoping the familiar word would sound soothing to her ears.

"There's, um, a singing Sunday night at the great hall," she said. "I was wondering, um, could I go?"

"I reckon you could do that," he said. The singings took place on a church Sunday after services. The adults would leave for the evening so the kids could gather around the table and sing—not the slow morning chants meant for devotion, but the faster ones, meant to get the kids talking. And "talking" actually meant sizing each other up, because the goal was to get the young folk started with their courtships. It seemed contrived, but no more so than a high school dance in the outside world.

"All righty, then," Hannah said, all fluttering hands and darting eyes.

"Anything else?" he asked.

"Can I get a ride home in Aaron Graber's buggy?" she asked, all in a rush.

Caleb felt an unpleasant thud of surprise in his gut. *Aaron Graber,* he thought. More like Aaron *Grabber.* Caleb wasn't so sure he liked the idea of little Hannah running around with a boy, particularly that one, who looked at girls the way a fox eyes a hen.

A distant, frenzied barking sounded through the window, but Caleb gave his full attention to his niece. This was kind of a big deal. She wanted to go courting. His little Hannah, *courting.* It seemed like only yesterday he was showing her how to get a hit in slow-pitch softball and making her giggle at his stupid jokes. Where was *that* Hannah now?

"Well," he said, "I don't think—"

"Please, Uncle Caleb," she said. "He asked me special."

Before he could reply, the kitchen door slapped open with a violent bang. Levi Hauber's face was the color of old snow, and his shoulders shook visibly. Even before he spoke, the sheer horror in his eyes froze Caleb's blood.

"Come quick," Levi said. "It's Jonah. There's been an accident."

2

"Oh, fuck me sideways," muttered Reese Powell as her work phone buzzed rudely against her side like a small electric shock. God. She'd just closed her eyes for a much-needed nap. Checking the screen, she saw that it was a summons from Mel, her supervising resident, in the ER. With brisk, mechanical movements, she put on her short white lab coat, looped a stethoscope around her neck, and headed out of the break room.

The long, gleaming corridor was littered with equipment and gurneys, the occasional patient slumped in a wheelchair, a rolling biohazard bin or two. Nurses and orderlies swished past, hurrying to their next call.

Reese blinked away the last of the foiled nap and took a deep breath. *I will do right by my patients.* This was her mantra, the one she'd adopted as a fourth-year medical student. *I will do right by my patients.* She had spent three years studying, cramming her head full of knowledge, memorizing, observing, but this year, the year she would earn the title of doctor, she set one simple, powerful task for herself: do the right thing.

One of the things she liked about working in the ER was the element of surprise. You never knew what was coming through the door next. Her parents had been appalled when she'd informed them of her interest in the ER. They had been pushing her toward pediatric surgery, and they expected her to explore something closer to that field. But for once, she had dared to inch a little to the left of their proposed path. She wanted more experience in emergency medicine. And Mercy Heights had a level-one trauma center, the best in Philadelphia.

Patients, family members, and personnel were clustered around the admittance center, the nucleus of the ER. As she scanned the area for Mel, a nurse stuck her head out of an exam room.

"Oh, good, you're here," she said. "We need someone who speaks Spanish. We've got a one-woman shitstorm."

Reese hurried into the small room. "What have you got—oh." For a second, she just stood there, trying to take in the scene. The patient was a young dark-haired woman in a stained dress, crouched on the bed, her posture defensive and her eyes cloudy with fear and distrust. Someone was asking her what she took, when she took it, but she recoiled from the questions.

"They found her wandering on the street," said the nurse. "All we know so far is that she's pregnant. And probably altered. She told the EMTs she was intoxicated. We're trying to find out what she took."

A security guard stood ready, restraints in hand. Mel shook his head. Reese knew he feared things would escalate if they tried to restrain her.

"This is not a place of healing," the woman said in rapid-fire Spanish. "This is a place of death, a place of eternal curses." Then she lapsed into a muttered prayer.

Reese's Spanish kicked in. She spoke the colloquial version she'd learned from Juanita, her childhood nanny. Growing up, she'd spent more time with Juanita than she had with her busy, ubersuccessful parents. Putting on a warm, professional smile, she slowly walked toward the woman. "*Hola, señora,*" she said softly. "*¿Qué pasa?*"

At the sound of her native tongue, the woman stopped speaking and glared at Reese. "I'm Reese Powell," Reese continued in Spanish, never losing eye contact. "My colleagues and I would like to examine you, and make sure you're all right."

"Get away from me. These are bad people."

"We want to help you," Reese said. "Do you understand English?"

"No. No English."

"Please, may I ask you some questions?"

"My secrets are mine to keep."

"Sometimes it is best to share a secret. Is this your first baby?"

"Yes." The woman unfurled a little, dropping her arms from her drawn-up knees.

"What is your name, ma'am?"

"My name is Lena Garza."

"How old are you, Lena?"

She hesitated. "Nineteen."

"Ask her what she took," someone said. "We heard her say she's intoxicated."

Reese studied the drawn, olive-toned face. The girl looked older than nineteen, her deep brown eyes haunted and scared.

"You were wandering around in traffic," Reese said, rapidly translating for one of the EMTs. "Why were you doing that? Did you take something?" She had been taught to practice empathy—direct eye contact, a physical touch—and at first, reaching out to a stranger in this way had felt strange to her. Now that she'd been at it for a while, the gestures felt natural. It was gratifying to see the woman relax slightly, taking a deep breath before she spoke.

Lena Garza twisted the band of silver she wore on her forefinger. "*Estoy intoxicada.*"

"Ask her what—"

"Wait," Reese said. "*Intoxicada* just means that she

ingested something. Could be food, a drug, anything that makes a person sick." She turned to Lena. "Can you tell me what you took?"

"My mother told me I will burn in hell," she whispered. "I am not married. That is why I took the herbs."

Reese's heart skipped a beat. "She took something," she told Mel in English. "What did you take, Lena?"

The girl reached into the pocket of her faded dress and drew out a crinkly cellophane bag. "She said this would cause my period to start."

Reese grabbed the bag and showed it to Mel. "Angelica. Said to have abortifacient properties."

Mel sniffed the yellowish-brown herb. "Also called *dong quai*. When did she take it? Was it within the last four hours? How much did she take?"

Reese asked the patient.

"I don't remember. I will burn in hell," she moaned.

"Only if you die," Reese said in Spanish. "And we are not going to let that happen, not today."

Mel said, "We're going to need a gastric lavage, stat."

While the techs prepared the lavage tray and measured activated charcoal into a beaker, Reese coaxed a bit more information from the patient—When did she have her last period? Had she seen a doctor? Where did she live?

Reese reported the answers, then convinced the woman to lie back and be connected to monitors. "I'm going to have a listen to your baby, all right?" She gently lifted the dress and slid the gel-slicked Doppler wand over Lena's flat belly, trying to detect heart sounds.

"Ay!" the patient yelled. "That is cold. You torture me."

"I'm sorry," Reese said. "We need you to be still and be quiet. We're trying to hear your baby's heart sounds . . . There it is," she said as the Doppler emitted a rhythmic *wow-wow-wow*. "That's the sound of your baby's heart."

Lena went limp on the table and laid her forearm over her eyes. "Yes," she said. "I hear it. I can hear it. My mother says it's a sin to have a baby before I'm married."

Reese let the moment stretch out a few seconds longer. Then she said, "Mothers aren't always right about everything." She offered a brief conspiratorial smile. "Mine thinks she is, though. Let us take care of you, and when you're feeling better, someone will talk to you about your options."

She explained the lavage process and convinced the girl to cooperate by swallowing the gastric tube. The girl gagged and fought, but Reese kept up a soothing patter, the way Juanita used to when Reese was small and scared of the dark.

A short time later, Lena's eyes were closed, and her hands lay slack on the sheeting. Mel gestured, and Reese followed him out to the corridor. "You did a good job in there," he said. "She'll be ready to turf out before you know it."

Reese thought about the disturbed young woman, her frightened eyes and the strange, deep knowing that lived in her like an old, old soul. "Before you turf her, let's get someone to talk to her about her choices. I'll be the interpreter."

"That's a great idea," Mel said. "I'll call social services and OB/GYN."

Moments like this gave Reese a feeling of satisfaction. An overachieving fourth-year at the end of a long rat race, she was full of plans, but full of questions, too. Her parents had their own plan for her—acceptance into an elite residency program, a path to join their carefully built practice. But sometimes, the wall of her armor cracked open to reveal a glimpse of something else—another dream, maybe. A different dream, not her parents' goals.

At the end of the hallway, the double doors burst open and Jack Tillis, the chief of trauma, swept through. His lab coat wafted open like a set of wings. He was surrounded by his team of devoted acolytes—the residents, nurses, support staff, and technicians who made up the trauma team.

"What've you got?" Mel asked, perking up.

"Just had a red phone pre-alert. Major trauma, coming in by life flight," another resident said. "ETA twenty minutes."

Reese exchanged a glance with Mel. She felt a twist of anticipation in her gut. "Can I help?"

The resident nodded. "You don't want to miss this one. Some kid had his arm ripped off in a farming accident."

The helicopter descended from the sky like a huge metallic insect, its giant rotors beating the cornstalks flat against the dusty field. Kneeling on ground soaked by his nephew's blood, Caleb instinctively leaned forward over the boy's body, which lay on the rescue workers' shiny yellow board. The shadows of his neighbors and the rescue workers fell over him, blocking out the morning sun. Above the violent rhythm of the chopper blades, he could hear crackling radios and shouts, but all his attention stayed focused on Jonah.

Only a short time earlier, Jonah had been racing across the field to help fill silo, something he had done dozens of times before. Now he lay broken and bleeding, his left arm and his boyish face slashed by the vicious metal teeth of the shredder. And despite the injuries, Jonah was sweetly, horrifyingly conscious.

White-faced, blue-lipped, his eyes dull with shock as his life drained away, the boy tried to speak through chattering teeth. "Cold," he kept saying. "I'm ssso . . . cold."

"I'm here, little man," Caleb said, his voice a rasp of panic. "I'll keep you warm."

The rescue workers had immobilized the arm with an air bladder and enclosed his neck in a stiff collar. They covered him with every blanket they had, but it wasn't enough to keep Jonah from shivering like a leaf in the wind. Then they prepared to load the stretcher into the helicopter.

"You cannot take him in that . . . that thing." Caleb's father stepped forward, thumping his hickory cane on the ground. "I won't allow it."

From the moment the county rescue crew had declared that Jonah's only hope of survival was to be airlifted to a trauma center in Philadelphia, there had been a division in the community. Dr. Mose Shrock, who supervised the emergency services of the local hospital, had been contacted by phone. He'd confirmed the rescuers' plan, and Caleb had approved the transport without hesitation.

Now his face felt carved in stone as he glared at his father. "They're taking him," he said simply. "*I'll* allow it."

"Sir, you'll have to step aside," a man shouted, jostling in front of Asa. "We're going to load him hot, while the chopper's still going."

"These people will take care of you," Caleb said to his nephew, climbing to his feet. "I love you, Jonah, don't ever forget I love you."

"Uncle Caleb, don't leave me."

Despite the noise of the beating rotors, Caleb heard his nephew's faint plea, piercing his heart.

The nurses and paramedics of the life flight lifted the board as the pilot did a walk around the helicopter, checking the landing area. Jonah was lost amid a pile of blankets and gear. His blood stained the ground everywhere.

"I'm going with him," Caleb said loudly. "I have to go with him."

A nurse in a utility vest looked at him, then over at Jonah.

"Please," Caleb said. "He's just a little boy."

"It's the pilot's call. I'll see what she says about the fly-along."

Caleb turned and found himself face-to-face with his father. Asa held his hat clapped on his head to keep it from being blown away by the rotors. His straight-cut coat and broadfall trousers flapped in the wind. He stood flanked by the neighbors, forming a somber wall of fear and disapproval.

The last thing on Caleb's mind was Amish Ordnung. Clearly it was uppermost in the minds of his father and the elders.

"If it's God's will that the boy is to survive," Asa stated, "then he will do so without being lifted into the sky."

Caleb didn't trust God's will, and he hadn't in a long time. But he didn't argue with his father. He hadn't done that in a long time either.

Hannah rushed to his side. Her face was pale gray and awash with tears. "You have to go, Uncle Caleb. You have to."

Alma Troyer stepped forward, her mouth set in a firm line. She cut a quick glance from Asa to Hannah. "You go, Caleb. I'll keep Hannah with me while you're away."

The flight nurse touched his arm. "You're in. The pilot said you can come."

Caleb nodded and turned to his father. "I'll call." The Amish families shared a phone box in the middle of the village, its use limited to necessary business and emergencies. Without waiting for a reply, he turned on his heel and followed one of the EMS technicians to the chopper.

In a tangle of tubes and monitors, Jonah was being loaded into the side bay of the shiny blue helicopter. "Whoa, you're a tall one. Keep your head low," a technician cautioned Caleb, pointing upward. "Stay to the front and left of the chopper."

Hardwired to her radio equipment, the pilot glanced at Caleb. "You're a big fella," she yelled. "What do you weigh?"

Caleb never weighed himself. "Two hundred pounds," he estimated, aware of the broad blade swinging overhead. He was nineteen hands tall, judging by the draft horses he worked with. Well over six feet. He was definitely at risk of having his head lopped off by the rotating blade.

"Our weight limit's two-twenty," the pilot said. "Let's do it."

The technician kept his hand on Caleb's shoulder and guided him aboard. Someone tossed his hat to him. They showed him where to sit and how to strap himself in. In the cramped space, he was close enough to Jonah to reach the boy, but he couldn't figure out a place to touch. He rested his hand somewhere—the kid's foot. Even through layers of thermal blankets, it was cold as ice.

"Jonah," he said, "I'm with you. Hear me? I'm coming with you."

He was given a set of headphones with spongy earpieces. Radios crackled and screeched. Monitoring equipment beeped, straps and clamps were locked into place. A mask was put over Jonah's nose and mouth, and one of the workers squeezed an air bag at regular intervals. In minutes, the doors were pulled shut. The pilot rattled off a series of orders, simultaneously checking things in the cockpit and snapping a series of switches and levers. With a roar of increasing power, the chopper lifted straight off the ground.

Caleb's stomach dropped, and the breath left his lungs. Through a rounded glass opening, he saw the people gathered near the landing site. Neighbors and friends, his father still holding his hat to his head, growing smaller and smaller as the copter ascended into the sky. They looked like a black-and-gray cloud against the golden fields. Hannah lay crumpled on the ground, her skirts surrounding her like an inkblot. Someone should go to her, put a hand on her shoulder to reassure the girl. But no one did.

The helicopter passed the silo in the blink of an eye, but in one glimpse Caleb could see the conveyor slanting up to the opening, the shredding machine positioned at the top. And on the ground, on the green-and-brown earth where the farm had stood for generations, he saw the livid stain of his nephew's blood, oddly in the shape of a broken star.

The helicopter nurse was yelling information into a radio, most of which Caleb barely understood. Jonah's BP and respiration, absent pulses distal to the injury site, other things spoken in code so rapidly he couldn't follow. He did catch one word, though, loud and clear.

Incomplete transhumeral amputation.

Amputation.

The helicopter lurched and careened to one side. Caleb pressed his hand against the hull to steady himself, and his stomach roiled. Another feeling pushed through his terror for Jonah, a feeling so powerful that it made him ashamed. Because in the middle of this devastating trauma, he felt an undeniable thrill. He was up in the air, hovering above the earth, *flying.*

All his life he had tried to imagine what it was like to

fly, and now he was doing it. So far, the experience was more amazing and more terrible than he'd ever thought it would be. The land lay in squares made of different hues of green and yellow and brown, stitched together by pathways and irrigation ditches. Shady Creek was a slick silver ribbon fringed by bunches of trees. There were toy houses connected by walkways and white picket fences, a skinny single-lane road with a canvas-topped buggy creeping along behind a horse. Caleb could tell it was the Zooks' Shire, even from the sky. He knew practically every horse in Middle Grove.

The chopper moved so fast that the view changed every few seconds, sweeping over the Poconos. The nurse finished punching buttons on some piece of equipment. "Sir," she said to Caleb, "I need to ask you some questions about your son." Her voice sounded tinny and distant through the headphones.

No time to explain that Jonah wasn't his son.

"Yeah, sure." At her prompting, he reported Jonah's name, his age, the fact that he didn't suffer from any allergies Caleb knew of. She wanted to understand the nature of the accident and he did his best to explain how the equipment worked, how the blades shredded the corn and blew it into the silo, how sometimes a piece got fouled up and needed an extra push with the next stalk in line. From the look on the woman's face, he could tell his explanation was as incomprehensible to her as her medical jargon was to him. Another thing he could see on her face was the real question, the one she would not ask.

How could you let a child work around such danger-ous equipment?

Caleb couldn't even answer that for himself. It was the way things had always been done on the farm. From the time they learned to walk, kids helped out. The tiniest ones fed chickens and ducks, weeded the garden, picked tomatoes and beans. When a boy got older, he helped with plow and harrow, the hay baler, sheaves, fetching and carrying from the milk house, anything that needed doing. It was the Amish way. And the Amish way was to never question tradition.

He tried to check on his nephew, but there was little of Jonah to see amid the tangle of tubes and wires and the guy squeezing the big plastic bulb into the boy's nose and mouth. The chopper veered again, and the landscape quickly changed. Philadelphia was a bristling maze of steel and concrete giants arranged along the wide river and other waterways. The city had its own kind of strange beauty, made up of crazy angles and busy roads. Atop one of the buildings, a series of markings seemed to pull the chopper from the sky like a magnet.

"They're going to do a hot unload," the nurse explained. "They'll get him out even before the chopper stops. You just wait until it stops, and the pilot will tell you when it's safe to get out."

"Got it." Caleb was startled when he looked down and saw that his hat was still clutched in his bloody hand.

His other hand lay on the blanket covering Jonah's bony bare foot. *Please, Jonah*, he said without speaking. *Don't die on me.*

The Amish never prayed aloud except at meeting. They were a people of long, meditative silences that made folks think they were slow-witted. Caleb begged, with wordless contemplation, for mercy for his nephew.

He's only a little boy. He sings to the ducks when he feeds them in the morning. He sleeps with his dog at the foot of his bed. Every time he smiles, the sun comes out. His laughter reminds me that life is beautiful. I can't lose him. I can't. Not my Jonah-boy.

Caleb was praying for the first time in years. But for him, prayer had always been like shouting down a well. Your own words were echoed back at you. Only the truly faithful believed someone was actually there on the other end, listening.

3

In Philly, traumas were plentiful and Reese had attended her share. Gunshot wounds, stabbings, and automobile wrecks accounted for most of them. But every once in a while, something new and unexpected came through the heavy doors of the trauma bay—a guy crushed in a log-rolling contest. A window washer who had fallen from a scaffold. A skydiver whose chute hadn't opened properly in midair and who had hit the ground at seventy-five miles per hour.

The dramatic, over-the-top traumas had a peculiar effect on the team. Everyone felt the sting of the razor's edge, reminding them that anyone could be a hair's breadth from death. The sole purpose of the team was to reel the victim back from tragedy.

According to the advance reports coming from the life flight crew, this boy, too, balanced on the edge. On the one hand, he was young and strong and in good general health. But on the other, he had suffered a devastating injury and had lost a lot of blood. If the shock didn't kill him, sepsis or secondary injuries could.

"They're bringing him down now," the lead trauma nurse reported.

"Get ready, people," Jack added. The trauma chief worked the team like a drill sergeant, preparing the high-tech bay with painstaking attention to detail—airway, IV, monitoring equipment, essential personnel, lab and radiology backup. With everything in readiness, the area resembled the inside of a strange, futuristic cathedral, the bed in the center like an altar where victims were brought forth to appease a pantheon of wrathful gods.

The last moments were silent, team members' minds weighted by the tension of expectation while their bodies were physically weighted by the heavy purple X-ray vests. Everyone was alone with their thoughts—the team leader, primary physician, airway team, nurses and patient care techs, radiology tech, CT, pharmacy, recorder, support staff, chaplain. Reese imagined that some were praying. She herself clung to her mantra: do right.

The team members stood poised in their designated positions. Reese felt a surge of adrenaline course through her, starting in her chest and spreading like a drug through her neck and shoulders, arms and legs. She understood the physiology of the human body, but no textbook could adequately describe certain things—the heady rush of anticipation, for one thing.

Stone-cold fear, for another.

During this rotation, she was learning that in a trauma situation, there was almost no time to think. Though her head was crammed with facts and procedures, she shut down everything except that which would help the patient. In a trauma, she didn't feel hunger or fatigue or even the need for the bathroom. She got so focused that she didn't even feel emotion, which worried her.

Mel said it was a good thing. When a patient was coded, the doctor needed cold algorithms, not empathy. He'd told her to consider a residency in trauma, but she had dismissed the suggestion. That wasn't where she was headed.

But in moments like this, she caught herself reconsidering.

"Keep an eye on Jack," Mel murmured in her ear. "Watch and learn. He is the maestro."

Reese nodded. There were a few more moments of breath-held anticipation, tingling with the awareness that everything was about to change. Then the wire mesh doors exploded open with a loud thud, and the patient arrived.

"Coming through," someone said, walking backward and pulling the gurney along a hallway marked with a red line on the floor and the words *All Trauma.* "Clear a path." More paramedics ran with the stretcher between them, preparing for the transition into the trauma bay. Reese craned her neck but couldn't see the boy amid the cluster of personnel and equipment—just an oversize C-collar and two vacu-splints painted with fresh blood.

Behind the stretcher was a man so large he dwarfed everyone else. His shirt and hands were covered in blood. Beneath a dramatic wave of golden blond hair, his expression was a mask of agonized worry—a guy facing every parent's worst nightmare.

The stretcher was angled into the middle of the trauma bay and the team went to work.

"How's he holding up?" Jack asked, positioning himself at the foot of the bed.

"Not so hot." Irene, the life flight nurse, stepped back from the rig, consulted dual tablets, and gave a swift MIVT report—mechanism, injuries, vitals, treatment. She stated that the boy had been given blood agents to lower the risk of hemorrhage. Monitors beeped and screeched off-key as the patient was transferred to the X-ray table. In the corner, a server's lights flashed green and gold.

Reese tried to make out his features with the clear

mask cupped over his nose and mouth. Deep lacerations slashed one cheek, as though he'd been clawed by a huge bear. His eyes were blue, darting from side to side.

"Dear God," she whispered. "He's conscious."

"Been that way since it happened," Irene said. "You're an amazing guy, Jonah. You're doing great."

"I'm Dr. Tillis," Jack said, looking straight down into the kid's face. "We're going to take good care of you."

The boy's lips moved inside the mask, fogging the plastic. He wasn't crying. Reese suspected that shock had pushed him well past that point.

"Right," said Jack. "Let's have a look at that arm."

The field dressing was removed and the arm exposed, and even the seasoned members of the team gaped in awe at the injury. It was a ragged horror of a wound, the tissue and bone and bloody dressing so tortured that it hurt just to look at it.

He never even lost consciousness, Reese thought. What the hell kind of kid was this?

"Jonah, can you move the fingers of your left hand, buddy?" asked Dr. Tillis.

The hand lay unresponsive.

"How about a thumbs-up or an okay sign," Tillis suggested. "Can you do that?"

The boy's eyes narrowed in pained concentration, but there was still no response. Everything had been shredded or severed. "Completely ablated," someone nearby murmured. "Oh, man . . ."

"Get in here, Powell," said Dr. Tillis. "Move in closer. This is something you don't see every day. Let's have you remove the lower-extremity clothing and do the blood draw."

Most of the kid's clothes had already been removed, cut or ripped off by the EMTs, or maybe in the accident.

His skinny chest and pelvis looked as pale as marble. He wore jockey shorts, plain white turned gray from laundering, which she scissored away, looking for further injuries to report to the lead doctor. "No sign of bruising or trauma to the pelvis," she said.

Then she prepped the site with Betadine and palpated the femoral artery with her fingers. "You'll feel a pinch, Jonah," she said, then felt ridiculous warning him about a pinch while his arm was hanging in shreds. She inserted the needle at a right angle. The slender curl of tubing filled with bright red blood, filling the syringe. While another student applied pressure to the site, Reese carefully labeled the blood draw and handed it off to a lab tech.

Jack rapped out orders for further assessments and pain management along with X-rays, piles of warm blankets, a Foley for urinalysis. Reese had a powerful urge to touch the boy—somewhere, somehow—but focused instead on following instructions. IVs were connected, and the surge of fluids and drugs worked quickly. Reese wasn't sure whether or not she imagined it, but she thought the boy looked directly at her as she leaned forward to check a line and a monitor. Then his eyes fluttered closed. She wished she'd touched him.

The work of prepping Jonah Stoltz for surgery was done swiftly, each member of the team playing a part. They debrided and dressed wounds, scanned and tested the slender, broken boy, stabilizing him as best they could and seeking secondary injuries. Three floors up, the surgeons of the OR scrub team were already gearing up for the most likely outcome—amputation. The mobile bed was pushed out into the gleaming stainless-steel maw of the elevator.

With a rubbery squeak, the doors whisked shut and silence filled the trauma bay again. In a vacuum of silence, the adrenaline rush subsided.

People in the emergency department, and especially members of the trauma team, had a brief but vital relationship with the patient. It was like a missed encounter on a bus—they had minimal details about what preceded the trauma, an intense flurry of total focus and attention, during which the patient was the center of their universe. And then, once the patient was rushed off to surgery, everyone moved on. There was no closure. They glimpsed a single page from the narrative, never the whole story.

The room emptied quickly. The once-pristine suite now resembled a bloody field in the aftermath of battle. Orderlies appeared to clear the area. Reese glanced around the room. She spotted something on the floor—an elongated penny that had been flattened on a train track, or maybe in one of those machines. The words *Old Blakeslee Sawmill* had been pressed into the copper.

She slipped it into the pocket of her lab coat. Then she went out to the garden adjacent to the emergency department, where there was an outdoor seating area favored by the staff. From here she could see the river, its banks flanked by long green swaths of parkland populated by kids playing Frisbee and shooting hoops, people lying on the grass in the sunshine, strolling tourists and cyclists rolling by.

She thought of the boy being rushed to surgery, and a shiver passed over her. At the far end of the garden, one of the trauma nurses stood alone, smoking a cigarette and staring into space as she blew a thin stream of smoke into the warm, unmoving air. Reese didn't judge her for the habit, nor did she remind her of the property's ban on smoking. After a major trauma, everyone involved seemed to deal with it in their own way. Some were chatty, expending the excess adrenaline in conversation, while others stayed quiet, floating in some placid reflection pond in their mind until balance returned.

Reese was still discovering what sort of trauma team member she was, but this rotation would probably end before she figured it out. She stood mulling over the incident, putting it into the context of her long-term plan.

For as long as she could remember, she had been focused on this career. She didn't even recall choosing it. Perhaps it had chosen her, or more accurately, it had been chosen *for* her. Sometimes she felt like a stranger in her own life, like Rip Van Winkle waking up twenty years in the future. She blinked and looked around, wondering, *How the hell did I get here?*

On paper, the journey was as clear as a road map. Her parents were physicians, hugely successful in their fields of infertility and neonatology. Her father had an endowed chair at Penn. Hector and Joanna Powell were known for their groundbreaking work. Reese was their most successful experiment of all. She had been a test-tube baby, the result of her parents' in vitro fertilization. She owed her very existence to their efforts and expertise.

It wasn't anything she thought about too often, but every once in a while it made her feel . . . different. On the one hand, she knew she had been so desperately wanted that her parents had gone through an amazing medical ordeal to bring her into the world. On the other hand, the idea of having started life in a petri dish was downright strange.

Her parents had sent her to the best schools in the country, financed by their work for other infertile couples. That she would be a doctor was a foregone conclusion. There was never any other decision to be made. After completing her BS in premed, she went straight into the

MD program and was now aimed like a straight arrow toward a career in pediatric surgery, the perfect complement to her parents' practice. A five-year surgical residency followed by two years of peds surgery would bring her into the fold.

Sometimes thinking about the journey ahead gave her a migraine.

Mel came outside, his affable, slightly disheveled presence a welcome interruption. He was a good doctor and a good teacher, and he was happily married, for which she was grateful. No danger of come-ons or late-night gropings in the on-call room, something she'd dealt with far too often in medical school.

"So what did you think of that?" he asked. "Pretty intense, huh?"

"Yes. That team is incredible." She shook her head. "Poor kid. His life will never be the same."

"The flight nurse said he's an Amish kid."

She frowned, digesting the info as she pictured horse-drawn buggies, bonnets, barefoot children. "No shit. So how did he get mangled by a piece of machinery? I thought the Amish did everything by hand."

He shrugged. "I guess not everything. But the nurse said some of the neighbors and family made a big stink about the chopper. They didn't want him to fly. It broke one of their rules."

"I'm glad the father went ahead and broke the rules, then. Is that why the media showed up?" She gestured at the parking lot. News vans from the local affiliates had already disgorged cables, gear, and primped on-air reporters. This was what was known in the hospital as a "drama trauma"—an unusual and often tragic event that drew the local press and created a storm on social media.

"Probably," said Mel. "A hospital spokesman will handle it."

"Good. The last thing the family needs is the local news hounding them." She glanced through the broad windows into the building. In the ER consultation rooms and waiting area, people huddled in worried clumps or paced the floor. A tall blond man, as upright and still as a tree on a windless day, stood looking outside, his face seemingly carved in stone.

Reese frowned. "Isn't that the father?"

"Yeah, I think so."

"Why isn't he up in surgery?"

Mel shrugged again. "Maybe nobody told him."

Reese felt a hitch of irritation. A big hospital was a wonder in many ways. But sometimes things slipped through the cracks. "Damn. I'll go tell him where the surgery waiting area is," she said.

Mel nodded, and she went back into the building. The boy's father looked wildly out of place in the high-tech trauma center, with his pinned-on dark clothes and a flat-brimmed hat clutched in his hands. There were smears of blood on his shirt and hands and boots. This man had set aside his principles to save the boy, but clearly at a cost, for he looked miserable.

She felt a well of sympathy for the guy. Thanks to her parents' profession, the hospital had always been a familiar environment, the place where they worked. For most people, it was an alien world—and not a friendly one.

"Excuse me," she said. "Are you Jonah Stoltz's father?"

The man turned. This one didn't have the big U-shaped beard she associated with Amish men. Blond guys always seemed to look younger than they actually were, and special, somehow, a breed apart. He had the same clear blue

eyes as the boy. His mouth was set in a grim line of suppressed fear.

"I'm Caleb Stoltz," he said in a rich, slow voice. "Jonah's uncle."

"My name is Reese Powell." The guy inspired a welling of sympathy within her, perhaps because he seemed
so alone. "Will his parents be coming soon?"

"His parents are dead." The blunt words fell into the
silence between them.

"Oh . . . I didn't realize," she said, the warmth in her
throat turning into an ache. She wondered if some awful
farm accident had taken them. Were such things common
in an Amish community?

"I'm raising Jonah now." He focused briefly on her
name and school embroidered on her lab coat. "Is there
news? How is he?"

"Mr. Stoltz," she said, "has someone given you a report
on Jonah's progress? Has a social worker talked to you?"

"They said he needed surgery. I already signed the
papers."

Hadn't anyone bothered to explain things to this man?
Reese's irritation returned. "The trauma team stabilized
him, and he was taken up to the surgical unit. It's in a
different part of the hospital. If you like, I'll show you to
the waiting area."

"Yeah," he said. "Okay. I'll wait there for as long as
necessary." As he spoke, she noticed two things about
him. He maintained a curious stillness in the way he held
himself. And when he looked at her, his gaze was rock
steady, never wavering.

She walked with him to the elevator. People glanced
at him and some did a double take, noting his height, his
bloodied clothes, the hat of woven straw he held in his
large hand. He was wildly out of place here. But then,

maybe it wasn't such a bad thing to be out of place in an emergency ward.

She pressed the button for the elevator and a moment later the doors cranked open. She thought he might hesitate before stepping inside, but he didn't. She pushed the fourth-floor button and the car glided upward.

At a loss for words, she cast a surreptitious glance at him. He had put his hand against the wall as if to steady himself, and his gaze focused on the lighted buttons. She knew very little about the Amish, but their clothes were distinctive—flat-front trousers, a plain shirt with rolled-back sleeves, suspenders, a brimmed hat, and work boots.

Reese felt something she didn't recognize. Surprise, maybe, and a funny warm sense of compassion. He was absolutely striking. He had a face she knew she would never forget, as perfectly made as a sculptor's masterpiece, with square jaw, high cheekbones, piercing eyes.

He caught her staring, and she felt a flush rise in her cheeks. "My colleague told me you're Amish."

"That's right."

Amish. What did she know about the Amish? Quilts and bonnets, the Plain people. "Where do you live? Over in Lancaster County?" The area was known for its Amish population. People from the city took weekend trips to poke around the markets and craft shows there, to sample the homemade goods and stay in cozy inns. Reese had never visited. Her spare time was mostly devoted to studying or networking with people her parents thought she should meet. Every once in a blue moon, she found time to go on a date.

She'd read somewhere that a blue moon occurred twice a year.

That was about right.

He shook his head. "Not Lancaster. We live north of here and a little west, in a place called Middle Grove."

"So, um, the flight nurse said you came in the helicopter," she ventured. "Was that your first time to fly?"

"It was. The Amish have rules against flying in the air," he said. "I understand that. But I have rules against a little boy bleeding to death."

Reese winced at the anguish she heard in his voice. "I'm sure everyone would agree you made the best choice for Jonah."

"I'm not sure of that at all," he said, sending her a dour look.

The conversation was going brilliantly, thought Reese. Well, she had better things to do than make small talk with this guy. When the elevator whispered to a stop at the fourth floor, she led him past the nursing station and to the waiting lounge, furnished with green sofas, low tables, hopelessly dog-eared magazines and books. A large monitor displayed coded updates of the ongoing procedures.

"You can have a seat here," she said. "I'll let them know at the nursing station that you're here for Jonah."

"Okay. Thanks." He made no move to sit down.

"Well," she said, backing awkwardly away. "I know they will take excellent care of Jonah. The surgeons here are the best in the country."

He sent her a curt nod. She couldn't blame him for being skeptical of such a common platitude. Ask anyone at any hospital, and the likely answer was that this was the best in the country, and the patient was in good hands.

She hurried to the nursing station. The three nurses present were lined up at the counter, all staring dropjawed at Caleb Stoltz. Under different circumstances, Reese would have laughed at their transparent lust.

"That man is—"

"—grade-A eye candy," said one of the nurses.

"Mr. Stoltz," she said, lowering her voice. "Caleb. He's the uncle and legal guardian of Jonah Stoltz."

One nurse, whose name tag read ALICE, glanced at a monitor. "The boy is in OR seven." She gave Reese a dismissive glance. Med students were distinguished by their short white coats and afforded no special privileges.

"So somebody keep him filled in, okay? I found him still waiting around in the ER, lost. Show him how to track his nephew on the big monitor board."

"Will do."

She turned quickly to head back to the elevator and nearly collided with Caleb Stoltz. He was so close that she caught his scent of sweat and blood and sunshine, and the intensity of it flustered her.

"Um, the staff here can answer any—"

"I want to give blood," he said quietly. "For Jonah, in case he needs it."

They had already given him many units in trauma. The attending had declared him stable, but anything could happen in surgery. She glanced at the nurses, each of whom sent her an *I'm busy* look.

"I can show you to the blood bank," she offered.

"Thank you," he said. "I'd appreciate that."

On the way back to the elevator, she hesitated. "Wait here a moment. I'll get you some clean clothes to put on."

She went to a supply room and found a set of scrubs, size extra large.

"You can wear these for now," she said, gesturing toward the men's room. "Put your clothes in this bag."

He hesitated. Then he stared down at the hopelessly soiled shirt and pants. "I reckon I look like I just slaughtered a pig."

"I wouldn't know about that, but you'll be more comfortable in these."

While he was changing, she checked her messages. A reminder about dinner tonight with her parents. Study group at nine—Step Two of the medical licensing exam was right around the corner, a test of her medical knowledge and diagnostic and clinical skills. If the ER stayed quiet, she might be able to grab a quick nap in the on-call room.

Caleb emerged from the men's room. In the borrowed scrubs, he looked only slightly less like a fish out of water. She took the plastic bag marked *Patient Belongings*, which contained his bloodstained clothes. "I'll have these cleaned for you." The offer just popped out of her, as if she were his valet. *It would be a kindness, though*, she told herself. Given what was happening to his nephew, he had more important things to deal with.

So do you, said an inner voice that sounded suspiciously like her mother.

She led the way through the winding hallways to the blood bank and introduced him to the technician there. "This is Mr. Stoltz," she said. "His nephew is in surgery and he wants to give blood."

"As much as you're allowed," Caleb said. "My blood type is O negative."

She was surprised he knew. Most people didn't know their blood type.

"You're a universal donor. Excellent," said the technician, a laid-back type named Klaus with a ponytail and a small hoop earring. "Right this way, Mr. Stoltz."

He was calm and compliant as he took a seat in a one-armed lounge chair.

Klaus handed him a clipboard. "Some standard screening questions."

Reese's phone vibrated with a message from Mel: *Get yr ass back down here and detox this drunk pls.*

Lovely. "I have to go," she said. "Can you find your way back to the surgical waiting area?"

"I can, yes."

She wished she could stay with him. Or at least say something comforting. He looked so lost and confused and scared. "Uh, okay. I wish you and Jonah the best." Lame. So fricking lame. The best what? The best outcome of an amputation? The best way to deal with a little boy who now had to go through life with one arm? She tried to think of something more to say, but nothing came to mind, no words of comfort or reassurance.

He didn't reply, simply nodded and started filling out the screening form.

And with that, their association ended. It was the way things worked in the emergency department—once the emergency had been passed on to the next team, the patient and his family were history. The residents and attendings who worked in the department liked that aspect of the job. Sometimes Reese wasn't so sure. Sometimes she wanted the story to continue.

As she stood in the elevator, she looked down at her hand and realized she was holding the bag with Caleb's soiled clothes. And she'd never been so pleased to be stuck with someone else's dirty laundry.

4

C'mon with me, baby. I'll drive you all the way to heaven," roared the drunk, clinging to Reese's hand. "You're one red-hot babe, that's just what you are."

Reese breathed in the scent of Mastisol. She'd popped an ampule and put a few drops on her surgical mask as an odor blocker, a trick she'd learned from a helpful floor nurse. "You'll be fine, Mr. James. Get some rest. Here are your discharge instructions. The program we talked about can work, but you have to show up. I'll make sure you have a ride later."

He serenaded her with "Ride Sally Ride" while she washed at the sink.

"You're good with him," commented the nurse who had assisted her. "He's not everyone's fave."

"And his vomit looks so attractive on me." Reese peeled off the mask, gloves, and disposable paper gown and added them to the waste bin. Actually, she didn't hate the ER, even in moments like this. She didn't even hate treating patients like Mr. James—frequent fliers who had a way of drawing compassion from her even as they destroyed themselves. Perversely, she found herself nurturing the hope that a guy like that might actually get clean one day. There were things she loved about primary care, and sometimes she couldn't help comparing those moments to tedious hours in surgery—a rotation she secretly did not love.

She hurried away to the staff room and went to her

locker. Inside was a jumble of textbooks, binders and clip-boards crammed with notes, a tangle of charging cords, a makeup bag, and a change of clothes. She glanced at herself in the small mirror on the back of the door. Her dark, short hair lay in random wisps around her face, and the ever-present bruised circles under her eyes marked her as someone who had been on call for too many hours. *Shit.* She wished she had time to go home and shower before dinner—her parents were meeting her at Urban Farmer, one of the city's best restaurants. But as usual, she was running late and would have to make do with a quick once-over in the ladies' room.

There, she fluffed out her hair and applied makeup so old she couldn't even remember buying it. She wad-ded up her lab coat, now soiled from her encounter with Mr. James, and added it to the bag with Caleb's clothing. Something pinged on the tile floor—the coin she'd found in the trauma room.

With a quick motion, she stuck it in her pocket, smoothed her hands down the front of her skirt, then faced the mirror and took a deep breath. She wondered if other people got nervous at the prospect of having dinner with their parents. She wondered if others felt the bur-den of family expectations pressing like a weight on their chests. *It's just dinner*, she told herself.

Except with Hector and Joanna Powell, it was never just dinner. Tonight's elegant meal at the trendy spot was more than that. They wanted to discuss her prospects for several elite residency program matches. The stakes were sky high, and her parents wanted to make sure she landed right where they were aiming her. She couldn't remember if they'd ever asked her whether she was on board with the plan.

On her way out, she encountered Mel and his young

son greeting each other in the foyer. With a grin of delight, Mel offered the kid a high five, their hands slapping together in friendly fashion.

"Look who got sprung from day care," Reese said. "How was your day, Frankie?"

"Good," said the little boy. He was four years old and adorable in his Phillies T-shirt—as if there was any other way for a four-year-old to be. "I fed the hamster. It was my turn."

"Cool. What do hamsters eat?"

"Carrots and alfalfa kibbles."

"Yum. And I'm impressed that you know the word 'alfalfa.'" They walked outside together. The air was gritty from the heat of the day, and redolent of exhaust from the traffic surging along the boulevard between the hospital and the river.

"Big plans for the night?" she asked.

"The biggest," said Mel. "Backyard wiener roast."

"Yay!" Frankie danced a little jig.

Reese said goodbye and went into the laundry service she always used. She dropped off her lab coat along with Caleb Stoltz's clothes, asking for a rush job. Outside again, she hesitated. Stuck her hand into her skirt pocket. Her fingers brushed the little token she'd picked up in the trauma room. She took it out, turned it over in her hand. Blakeslee Sawmill. It probably belonged to Jonah Stoltz. The image of a precision saw popped into her mind. She'd never observed an amputation. Christ, that poor little kid.

On impulse, she went back into the hospital and pressed the elevator button.

Compared to the mayhem of the ER, the surgical intensive care unit was an oasis of ominous quiet, punctuated by the artificial hiss and thump of ventilators, monitoring equipment, and life support gear. The waiting area was empty. She approached the nursing station and asked about Jonah Stoltz.

He'd made it through surgery and was recovering in the SICU. She found him in a high-tech suite there, his small form looking even smaller in the steel cocoon of the hospital bed. A nurse stood at a computer terminal on a rolling cart, keeping track of all the monitors; she glanced up and Reese acknowledged her with a nod. Beside the bed, on a wheeled stool, sat Caleb Stoltz.

The big man had his head bowed and his eyes closed. Reese wondered if he was praying, or sleeping. A bandage held a cotton ball in the crook of his arm.

"Mr. Stoltz?" she asked softly.

He looked up at her and blinked, then instantly turned his gaze to the boy.

"I came to see how he was doing," Reese explained, a little awkwardly.

"He woke up once, but he wasn't really all there, know what I mean?"

"That's normal under the circumstances," she said with more authority than she felt. From the corner of her eye, she saw the nurse nod again in agreement. "He's been through a major trauma, and the deep sleep is part of his recovery."

"That's what the other doctors said too."

"I, um, found something." She handed him the flattened souvenir coin. "I thought it might belong to Jonah."

Caleb Stoltz took the coin in his big workman's hand. "His lucky charm. Guess it didn't bring him any luck today." His hand hovered between the side bars of the hospital bed. He seemed unsure of what to do; then he let his fingers rest on Jonah's knee.

The gesture made her heart ache. There was something so piercing about the two of them, strangers ripped away from their quiet existence and thrust into this frightening, sterile world. Her throat felt tight with compassion. "Mr. Stoltz, has anyone spoken to you about accommodations while you're in the city?"

"No." He kept his eyes on Jonah. "I hadn't really thought about it."

A now familiar twinge of annoyance flared up in Reese. "I'll see if I can find someone to help you out with that." She took a step toward the door, and something else occurred to her. "I'll bet you haven't eaten a thing all day."

"Hadn't thought about that, either."

"Let me show you where the cafeteria is."

His long, sun-browned fingers curled around the boy's knee. "I'd best stay here."

"He's going to be asleep for a while, I estimate. You won't do him much good sitting here." He shot her a look, and she added, "The cafeteria is close. We won't be gone long."

He stood up, his long body unfolding from the small stool. "All right," he said simply.

In the elevator, Reese couldn't help herself. She glanced at her watch.

"You late for something?" he asked.

Her cheeks heated a little. "No, it's fine," she lied.

The cafeteria of Mercy Heights was a linoleum and Formica emporium of instant gratification. Rows of salads, floating in a sea of chipped ice, led to long steamer tables of casseroles and overcooked meats in salty sauces. The desserts ranged from thick banana pudding surrounded by bland vanilla wafers to pies crowned with six inches of meringue.

Seeing his hesitation, Reese guessed that he didn't have much practice eating at a cafeteria. She took the lead by selecting a brown plastic tray and gliding it along in front of the salad bar. Though she had no intention of eating, she selected a random salad, an entrée, and a dinner roll and helped herself to a tall, syrupy Coke from the beverage dispenser. Following her lead, he chose exactly what she did. Except on his tray, for a man of his size who hadn't eaten all day, the food looked woefully meager.

"You need to eat more than that," she said. "Otherwise you'll be back here hungry again in just a couple of hours."

With quiet compliance, he loaded up his tray with main dishes, a macaroni salad, and banana pudding, then followed her to the checkout line. Reese paid with her staff debit card. Briefly she considered picking up his tab but decided against it. She knew next to nothing about Caleb Stoltz, but she already sensed that he had his pride.

He took out a worn billfold and counted out the amount in cash. She led him to a table and sat down, resisting the urge to check her watch once again. Having dinner with a patient's family member wasn't exactly a breach of policy, but neither was it standard procedure. Certainly Reese had never done anything like this before.

But then again, she'd never met anyone like Caleb Stoltz before.

Just to have something to do with her hands, she took a napkin from the napkin holder and spread it over her lap. "So I guess—" She broke off, noticing that he had fallen silent and still, his head bowed as he perused his dinner tray.

A moment later, he looked up. "What's that?"

"I guess it's been a rough day for you. Please, go ahead and eat." She toyed with her salad, swirling her fork in the wilted leaves.

He dived in, eating mechanically but probably not

tasting the meat and potatoes, the green beans, the dinner roll shiny with butter. Reese kept trying to figure out what it was about him. An otherness. He seemed to be surrounded by some sort of invisible bubble or cocoon. Though he sat across the table from her, he inhabited a world she couldn't touch.

"I'm afraid I don't know much about the Amish community, Mr. Stoltz," she said, feeling somewhat abashed by her own ignorance. She'd taken a seminar in the cultural competency of physicians, meant to help a doctor understand the patient's perspective. In the class, they'd covered far-flung cultures like Samburu tribes and Tibetan nomads, yet they hadn't touched on a group right next door. "My impressions are based on things I've seen in *National Geographic* and on PBS."

"That's pretty much all most folks know." He took a few more bites of food. "If you don't mind, I go by my given name, Caleb."

She vaguely remembered hearing that it was an Amish custom to use people's first names rather than titles. Simplicity ruled their way of life, that much she knew. *I wish I knew what you were thinking*, she silently told him. He seemed so placid and calm, yet she sensed something more going on.

"So . . . Middle Grove?" She took a small bite of her salad and chewed thoughtfully, picturing rolling hills, painted houses and barns, quilts pegged on clotheslines. "I've lived in the city all my life," she said. "Not right here in Philly, but in Gladwyne, about twenty minutes away." She turned her wrist to check her watch again and then caught herself.

She was surprised to look down at her plate to discover that she'd eaten most of the salad. With a shrug, she started in on the dinner roll. It had been a long shift today, and she hadn't bothered with lunch. "Is it true you don't use electricity or phones?"

"Each community has its standards," he said patiently. "On our farm, we don't use electricity or have a phone. If there's an emergency, like there was for Jonah, there's a phone in a shed we share with the neighbors."

"Is everyone in your community Amish, then?"

"Most folks are, yah. We do get plenty of tourists coming through," said Caleb. "More than our share, though it's not as busy as it is down in Lancaster."

She flashed on the news vans camped out in front of the hospital. "Do the tourists bother you?"

"Not me personally. I reckon it bothers some to have outsiders watching us going about our business, harvesting corn, or plowing a field, or our kids walking to school."

She took a sip of her Coke. "It would bother me."

They finished eating, and the silence between them was oddly companionable. She hadn't meant to eat at all, but she'd just sort of done it without thinking. He had the oddest effect on her, this big, quiet Amish man. Time seemed to slow, moments slipped by, unnoticed.

A nasal sound came from her purse. He started, the first sudden movement she'd seen him make. "Sorry," she said, fumbling in her handbag. "It's my phone." She took it out and checked the screen.

Her mother, of course.

"Shit."

"How's that?" he asked.

Shit. She'd completely lost track of the time. That wasn't like her at all. "Would you excuse me for a moment?" she said to Caleb. Without waiting for his assent, she left the table and stepped over to the side of the cafeteria near the garbage cans. "Mom, I'm really sorry, but

I'm not going to be able to make it tonight. I'm tied up here at the hospital."

"Your shift was over forty-five minutes ago," Joanna Powell pointed out.

How many other adults had a mother who memorized their work schedule?

"I know, but there's a sort of . . . interesting case I'm involved in." She cast a glance at Caleb Stoltz, who had managed to put away a dinner that would have satisfied three regular-size men. "I'm so sorry. I was really looking forward to getting together with you and Daddy tonight."

"I guess there's nothing else to be done," her mother said. "We'll just have to reschedule. In the meantime, I'll email you some things about the residency interviews."

"Thanks, Mom," Reese said. "You're the best."

She got off the phone quickly and hurried back to the table. Caleb finished his large cup of Coke.

"Would you like something else to drink?" she asked. "There's lemonade, iced tea, or—"

"I'm okay. Just not used to the taste of a Coca-Cola. Been a long time."

Reese wasn't quite sure why she'd stood up her parents in order to linger at the hospital with this man, a stranger whose nephew had passed through the emergency room. Ordinarily patients came and went like leaves floating down a smooth-flowing river. Often, that river flowed with blood, but it continued on as regularly as the janitorial staff that cleaned each exam room and curtain area after each successive patient.

Something about this man and his injured little boy took hold of Reese's heart. She simply wasn't ready to sign off on him yet. It happened that way with patients sometimes. The residents and attendings she worked with talked about the fact that a certain case or patient or family member caused a peculiar resonance in the doctor, for a variety of reasons.

Reese sheepishly acknowledged that a few of the reasons might have to do with an unusual man with piercing eyes, and a sweet, broken boy.

She accompanied Caleb back up to the SICU, stopping at the nurses' station to see when the doctor would be by to talk to him again. Outside Jonah's suite, they stood together, looking at the boy through the thick safety glass of the window.

"He's still sound asleep," Reese said.

"Any idea when he'll wake up?"

"You can ask the doctor when he comes on evening rounds."

"Aren't you a doctor?"

"Almost. I'm a fourth-year med student. I was with the trauma team when they brought Jonah in, but he's not my patient. I just thought you might want somebody around in case you have any more questions about Jonah."

He leaned his hand on the upper frame of the window and kept his eyes on Jonah. His whole body tensed. "It's good of you to take the time for us, Reese."

It felt strange to hear him call her Reese. Patients and families often addressed her as "Doctor," unaware that she hadn't graduated yet.

She pressed her forehead to the glass and gazed at the small, still form amid the tubes and monitors. The huge bandage on the elevated arm stump dominated the scene. There would be nothing simple about this boy's life now.

"Did anyone talk to you about what you might say to Jonah when he wakes up?" she asked.

"No. But I've thought about it plenty. How do you tell a little kid that he's lost his arm? How do you tell him he'll never throw a baseball with that hand again or hold a sandwich in his fingers, or pick up a tool to work? How do you tell him he'll never properly shake hands with his bride's father or pet his dog on the head with that hand?"

She winced at the pain she heard in his voice. "You just tell him. I wish there was another way, or a different outcome, but there's not. You'll simply have to tell him, directly and honestly, that he's lost a limb and he'll learn to get on without it. It's terrible, but the worst part is over and he survived. A different sort of life is waiting for him now." She felt surprised to hear herself speaking to him with more confidence than she felt. Speaking like the sort of doctor she hoped to become.

"What sort of life will that be?"

For the first time, Reese sensed anger in him. "With proper therapy and prosthetics, he'll manage," she said. "The technology is so advanced nowadays that a prosthetic arm with a properly fitted artificial hand can function very much like a natural one." She bit her lip, wishing the words could be more reassuring.

"So you're saying he's going to get an artificial limb?"

"That's the recommended protocol. It's the best way to give him the most functionality," she said. "The stump will need time and therapy to heal properly to accept a permanent prosthesis. Once he's fitted with that, he'll undergo more therapy to learn how to use his new hand." She turned to him. "I know it's hard. That boy's life changed in an instant. But kids are incredible. I've worked with many of them in my rotations. They're amazingly resilient. They can adapt to almost anything." She resisted the urge to put her hand on his arm. "The ones who do best are those with a supportive family. Judging by how devoted you are, I'd guess Jonah has that."

When he didn't answer, a disturbing thought occurred

to her. "Don't tell me an artificial limb is against your religion," she said.

"As far as I know, it's not."

"Good," she said.

They stood together for a few quiet moments, then stepped into the room. The nurse at the computer terminal acknowledged them with a nod. Reese tried to picture Jonah playing in a baseball game, helping with farm chores, petting his dog.

"Do you feel like talking about the accident?" she asked.

"I already told everything to a woman from some agency. She wrote it all down and made a voice recording, too."

She was probably from Child Protective Service, Reese guessed. "It's standard to get a detailed report of an accident."

"I see." His face was somber. He was practically radiating guilt.

"Well, if you ever want to talk—not for a report or anything—I'd be happy to listen."

To her surprise, he nodded slowly. When he spoke of his nephew, his reserve fell away. "I was in the kitchen when it happened. I was with Hannah—she's Jonah's big sister. We were just washing up after breakfast. I could see him across the field working at the neighbor's silo, and everything seemed to be going just fine. He's helped fill silo dozens of times. All kids pitch in with chores. Then I guess I got busy with something else, and a bit later, the neighbor came running over, said there'd been an accident." His hand curled into a fist. "The way they told it, something got hung up in the shredding machine. Jonah was trying to push a stalk through when the blades caught him. It all happened fast. Real fast."

Reese kept her gaze fixed on the red and blue monitor

lights that gave a constant readout of Jonah's vital signs. She was beginning to understand that even a boy Jonah's age played a vital role on a family farm. He had lost more, perhaps, than a non-Amish boy.

And suddenly her cheeks felt hot with a deep sense of outrage. With all due respect to the Amish ways, she seriously questioned the practice of letting a boy do the work of a man. She wondered if there would be any further investigation, if Caleb would be questioned for putting a child at risk.

Then she bit her lip to keep herself from speaking out. Now was not the time and she was not the one to judge or comment. She reminded herself of the things she'd learned in her medical compassion classes. Even after the worst of accidents, a doctor must never point the finger of blame at the patient, or at any friend or family member. That was the role of social services. And more often than not, an accident was exactly that—an accident. In her ER rotation, she'd seen any number of adored, protected children who'd suffered accidents. A bad landing in a gymnastics competition. A cupboard door slammed on a finger. A fall down the stairs.

Guilt was a powerful force. It didn't need any help from an outsider. No doubt Caleb Stoltz was feeling plenty guilty already.

Glancing sideways at him, she noticed the tension in his clenched fists and angular face, and in the way he held his neck and shoulders. She tried to imagine the sudden shock of an ordinary day turning into a nightmare.

Finally he spoke again from a place of deep anguish; she could hear it straining his voice. "I yelled at him this morning," he said in a quiet, flat tone. "I yelled at him for teasing his sister. I told him to get on over to the neighbors' to fill silo."

"What would you have done if he hadn't been teasing his sister?"

Caleb looked down at his fisted hands and flexed them open. "I would have sent him over to the neighbors' to fill silo," he conceded.

"Then you can probably quit trying to claim responsibility for an accident. As awful as this is, you should understand that things like this happen."

"I'm his guardian. I love this boy more than my own life. But I failed him. I didn't keep him safe."

"Don't keep torturing yourself about Jonah's accident," she said, though she knew words of comfort didn't always allay the guilt. "Lots of people seem to do that in the ER, and it's not helpful. Things happen. It's awful, but the only choice is to go on." An idea occurred to her. The Amish were a people of deep, abiding faith—or so she assumed, since they had created an entire way of life around it. "I'm sorry, I don't know much about your church. If you'd like to pray, there's a chapel."

"I'm not a prayerful man."

She was surprised to hear him say that, having assumed his faith was what bound him to the Amish community. Not a prayerful man . . . and behind his reserved expression she detected a peculiar sadness. He represented a world so different from her own. She wondered what that world was like.

He stood unexpectedly close, and his nearness flustered her in a way she wasn't prepared for. She detected no danger from him, it wasn't quite like that; yet she felt something profoundly physical that she hadn't experienced in a long time, maybe ever. And something spiritual as well; yearning mingled with hope, as though he represented a long-buried desire. Despite her exhaustion and the fact that she had canceled dinner plans with her parents for his sake, despite the fact that she had a policy against connecting too closely with a patient or his family, she felt drawn to this man with a strange affinity that was more than curiosity. When she looked at him, a gentle, peaceful feeling settled over her. Her vital signs seemed to slow down; the relentless pressures of the ER ebbed away.

She wished the social services counselor or someone from the chaplain's staff—anybody—would show up. She left another message at the extension on the house phone.

The charge nurse came in to do a routine check on Jonah. Though she worked swiftly and efficiently, Reese could see her sneaking glances at Caleb Stoltz. Women seemed to stare at him the way people stared at a work of art, or an exhibit at the zoo. He appeared to have no notion of the feminine interest he sparked. Negligently handsome, with a body sculpted by hard, honest work, he looked far more intriguing than the doctors and staff who populated the halls of Mercy Heights.

She shared a look with the nurse and realized they understood each other perfectly.

Oh, for fuck's sake. What on earth was she thinking? Hospital fatigue must be getting to her. Maybe she was experiencing some sort of end-of-rotation ennui. She had absolutely nothing in common with an Amish farmer. Maybe, though, the unbreachable differences between them actually piqued her interest. She found him as exotic and baffling as he seemed to find the big-city hospital.

She tamped down a barrage of nosy questions. Her schedule was crammed, and she needed to sleep at some point. It was time, past time, to move on, to re-establish that professional distance. "Well," she said, unsettled by her own thoughts, "I should go." She made a point of checking Jonah's chart. "Your nephew's stable but still critical," she said.

Caleb pressed himself as close to the bed as he could get. He eyed the bandaged stump of Jonah's arm, and the look on his face made Reese's heart freeze.

"I'm sure in the next few days, you'll learn a lot more about the therapy and prosthetics I mentioned," she tried to reassure him. "Really, Jonah will be able to live a normal life."

He was silent for so long that she wasn't certain he'd heard her. Then he looked up. "What's a normal life?"

"I suppose it's different for everyone. Jonah will have to find the answer on his own."

"That's a big question for a little boy."

Another long silence. Reese had no idea what more to say. She was rescued from having to respond when someone from the chaplain's staff stepped in. She said a reluctant farewell, and on her way out she took a shortcut across the skybridge that led to the maternity ward, which was called, not incidentally, the Powell Pavilion. It had been named in honor of her grandfather, a pioneer in human fertility in his day. She had a thought of her parents and their high-stakes, high-tech world, playing God and bringing miracles to life. What would Caleb Stoltz think of doctors whose daily work involved chemically freezing a woman's uterus to force her to conceive?

And why should she care what he thought?

5

When Reese got to her apartment that night, she stepped inside, locked the door, turned, and realized she wasn't alone. Something strange and intrusive hung in the air—an unfamiliar energy, a sense of things out of place.

Muttering under her breath, she made her way to the kitchen. The man she was expecting to see sat at the scarred maple table, drinking a glass of wine and reading the latest issue of *Vanity Fair*, the Young Turks of Hollywood edition she'd stolen from a hospital exam room. It was the closest thing she'd had to an actual date in six months.

Her intruder was a slender, handsome man several years older than her, with soft eyes and a cheeky grin.

"Hey," she said. "You know, I gave you that key to use in case of emergency."

"It *is* an emergency," said her across-the-hall neighbor, Leroy Hershberger, who had been steadily nudging his way toward a true friendship with her since he'd moved in the previous year. "I ran out of wine."

She grabbed the bottle and poured herself a glass. "Very funny." She clinked her glass against his and took a sip.

"I was pretty sure you wouldn't mind," Leroy said. "I signed for this package that came for you." He indicated a thick clasp envelope from Johns Hopkins in those large gentle hands that made him a gifted physical therapist.

"Another residency program for you to go into a cold sweat over."

"Thanks," she said and drank more wine, eyeing him over the rim of her glass. He had a fresh haircut from the expensive salon he frequented, and he was dressed in Abercrombie & Fitch, indulgences he claimed kept him sane by reminding him that he had a life beyond scrubs. "You look nice. Plans for the evening?"

"I got stood up. Hence the drinking."

"No way. Who was the culprit? And how dare she stand you up?"

"Some girls have all the nerve." He stretched his legs out, looking nonchalant, though Reese knew he was struggling with disappointment. Leroy was single and lonely. Though the two of them were not a match romantically, they often commiserated over their uneventful love lives.

"Spending a quiet evening at home is underrated." She glanced around the room. This apartment had potential, but it didn't feel like home. Her place had a transitory atmosphere, as if someone were just packing to leave. She'd never gotten around to hanging a picture or two on the wall, or properly shelving her collection of textbooks and favorite novels.

A few touches of her personality lingered here and there, glimmers of a need for more depth and permanence. There was a quilt made for her by a former patient, draped over a painted wooden chair, and a cuckoo clock that had once belonged to her grandmother. Her kitchen tools included an embossed rolling pin and a pie fluter, which she'd never had a chance to use. She had a working fish tank with nothing but water and plastic plants in it.

She kept meaning to make the place feel more lived in, but work and studying kept getting in the way. If she followed her parents' plan for her, she'd eventually be able to afford a fabulous house on the river, or a high-rise condo, or maybe a colonial tract mansion in the suburbs. The trouble was, she didn't seem to fit into the picture of her own life.

Like Caleb Stoltz didn't fit, she thought, remembering the image of him standing hat in hand in his nephew's hospital room.

She took another quick sip of wine. How much would the Amish man tolerate of the therapy Jonah was going to need?

Leroy stood up and walked around behind her, using his gentle, talented hands to massage her neck and shoulders. A skilled physical therapist, he had a way of digging into the source of tension. "I think rigor mortis has set in," he said. "You're stiff as a . . . stiff."

"Very funny."

"Rough day?"

"You could say that. Strange day."

"I thought you were having dinner with your parents tonight," he said.

She glanced at the calendar stuck to the refrigerator. "Nosy." Every single day, it seemed, had something written in it. *Interview with Jacobson. Study group, 6:00 P.M. Board review, 6:30 A.M.*

"Jesus," Leroy said. "Look at the way you schedule yourself. It's not normal. I bet you schedule your bowel movements."

She finished her wine. "Who has time for that?"

"There's one thing missing on that calendar," he said.

"Yeah? What's that?"

"A social life. A life of any kind at all. In case you haven't noticed, it's something most people aspire to."

"I'll get a life once I get through the Match."

"Sure you will. Except once you get yourself placed in the first residency, you have to make it into the next one, and once you find that, you have to apply for another, and after that you need to concentrate on your specialty, and then your subspecialty, and then—"

"All right, all right. You made your point." She went over to the refrigerator, picked one of the few dates that wasn't taken, and scrawled *Get a life* in the empty space. "At least I wasn't stood up by—who was it this time, Roberta the caterer, right?"

"Roberta, yes. And yes, she's a caterer. The rest of my day was fine. Two stroke patients, some back therapy, an accident victim with a major chip on his shoulder. He was no picnic, but I made him channel his rage into getting around in a wheelchair."

She sat back down, poured more wine into her glass. "Have you ever worked with an amputee?"

"Sure. I have a certification in prosthetics."

"There was an amputation in trauma today," she said. "A little boy lost his arm."

"That sucks. Poor kid. What happened?"

"It was a farming accident. He stuck his hand in a grinder or shredder of some sort. Amish kid," she added. "I'd never treated an Amish kid before today. I've never even met anyone Amish."

A funny look came over Leroy's face. "I wouldn't be too sure about that."

She didn't get it at first. And then, all of a sudden, she did. "Holy crap, Leroy. Do you mean to tell me you're Amish?"

"I was. Not anymore, obviously."

In an odd way, Reese felt betrayed. "How can you be Amish and never have told me? You're my closest neighbor. I'm supposed to know everything about you."

"I knew you for six months before you told me you were a test-tube baby," he pointed out.

"I didn't think it was important," she said with a distracted wave of her hand.

"Oh, right. Being the result of your parents' medical specialty has defined you, princess. The petri dish princess."

"And being Amish has obviously defined you. Why the hell didn't you tell me?" She stared at him as if regarding a stranger. Leroy? Amish? How could Leroy be Amish?

There was nothing remotely Amish about this man. Yet now that he'd said something, a few facts became clear. Since she'd known him she'd never met anyone in his family. When she'd asked about it, he'd said his family shunned him because he'd refused to marry a girl he was promised to and had moved to the city.

"You weren't kidding," she said, "about the shunning you once told me about. Your family really did shun you. In the Amish way."

A bitter laugh escaped him. "Nothing like a good old-fashioned Amish shunning. They're better at it than a group of seventh-grade teenyboppers."

"Does that mean you never see or speak to your Amish friends and family?"

"That's the general idea. It's complicated. Those who've been baptized aren't allowed to speak to me or share meals. Folks who haven't been baptized yet have a little more latitude. But for all intents and purposes, I'm persona non grata in the community where I grew up."

"I can't believe you were Amish," she said thoughtfully, still studying him. Clean-shaven, with soulful eyes and manicured hands, he looked every inch the modern male. "I keep trying to picture you Amish, but the picture just won't form."

"Oh, I did it all." That edge of bitterness still sharpened his voice. "The bowl haircut and flat-brimmed hat, the drop-front trousers and suspenders, not a zipper within a five-mile radius. I have nine brothers and sisters, nieces and nephews I've never met. I haven't been in contact with my family in years."

"That must be so heartbreaking for you," Reese said. "And for your family."

"They got over it. There's not a doubt in my mind that they got over it. It's the Amish way."

"Did you?"

He emptied the bottle of wine into his glass. "So tell me about this kid today." His change of subject was deliberate and unbreachable. "He was probably filling silo, wasn't he?"

"How would you know that?"

"It's that time of year. The Amish year is determined by the seasons and the farm chores that go along with them. The corn and other grains are ripe and need to be harvested. On an Amish farm, the whole community gets involved."

"I'm hearing a decided lack of affection and nostalgia in your voice," Reese said.

"Let's just say my experience with the Amish would not fit in the pages of *National Geographic*." He drummed his fingers on the tabletop.

"Was your family cruel to you? Did they neglect you? What?"

"I'm through talking about it, princess. Where did you say the kid was from?"

She forced herself to drop the subject of Leroy's upbringing. "A place called Middle Grove. Do you know it?"

"Actually, I do. It's up on Highway Fifty-Seven, same area as my hometown of Jamesville. Beautiful part of the state, near the Poconos. The Amish of Middle Grove are super restrictive. I remember they wouldn't fellowship with our community because we were a bit more liberal."

"I hope they're not restrictive when it comes to Jonah—the amputee. But he might be in for rough times if they prohibit a prosthetic arm. Do you think they'd do that?"

"Hard to say. The Amish take care of their own. I guess it depends on the support he'll get."

Reese thought of Caleb Stoltz and the way she'd felt, watching his face as he stood over his injured nephew. "I don't know about the whole family," she said. "He's got a loving uncle who's raising him. An incredibly loving uncle," she added. "He came in on life flight with the boy. The flight nurse said it was a near thing, with some of the locals at the scene claiming it was against their religion to fly."

"But not against their religion to let a boy bleed to death. I'm glad the uncle was reasonable."

"He was," Reese said, propping her chin in the palm of her hand. "He is definitely reasonable. The boy's parents are dead, and Caleb—that's the uncle—is raising Jonah and . . . he mentioned that there's a sister." She pictured the big man and the life he'd described, somewhere out in the country, and the image brought a sigh to her lips.

"Oh my God," Leroy said. "Can this be? You're smitten."

She pushed away from the table. "Bullshit. The guy's kid is suffering a major trauma."

He laughed at her indignation. "The hunky Amish farmer and the urban-American princess. It's too precious."

She scowled at him. "How do you know he's a hunk?"

"I know your type. You like ridiculously good-looking guys."

"Don't you have somewhere you need to be?"

"Nope, I've been stood up, remember? You're supposed to help me hobble through the evening. But for once, your life is more interesting than mine."

"You just accused me of not having a life."

"That was before I found out about the Amish guy."

"There's nothing about the Amish guy," she said defensively. "Quit with the Amish guy."

"Tell you what," Leroy said expansively. "I'll drop in and visit with the kid and his uncle tomorrow. Is he in the SICU?"

Nodding, she picked up their empty wineglasses and carried them to the sink. "That would be good."

"See? I'm nice."

Caleb awakened to the quiet sucking rhythm of hospital machinery. A bitter smell hung in the air, mingling with the coppery scent of blood. Although he came fully awake, he didn't move, not right away. Instead, he sat very still in the hard, too-small chair made of molded plastic and crammed into the corner of the small cubicle where Jonah slept. A chaplain had offered to find him a bed for the night, but Caleb had declined, preferring to sit close to Jonah. The ever-present nurse stood in the dim glow of a computer monitor, gazing steadily at the screen. By looking out the display window past the nurses' station, he could see the gray glimmer of a new day.

His hat sat on the floor beneath the chair. He hadn't found anywhere else to put it. The glass, linoleum, and steel cage allowed no extra room for personal items.

"Good morning," said the nurse at the computer.

"How's he doing?" Caleb asked.

"He's stable. He had a quiet night." The Asian woman peered at him, her hands constantly busy on the keyboard. "Can I get you something?"

"Thank you, no."

Caleb stood and went over to the bed. Jonah didn't appear to have moved in the night. Throughout the dark, endless hours, nurses, health aides, medical students, and at least one doctor had come in to check Jonah or, more accurately, to check the equipment hooked up to his poor, broken body. Through it all, the kid hadn't stirred, hadn't even blinked an eye as far as Caleb could tell.

He rested the palm of his hand on the cold steel bars of the bed's guardrail. Something had happened to Jonah in the night. The lost hours had diminished him, sucked the spirit out of him. The boy was smaller, paler than he had been only a short time ago. There was simply . . . less of him.

Maybe that was what a place like this did to a person. Drew things out of him, turned him into a ghost. Of course, Caleb told himself, Jonah would be dead if they hadn't brought him to this hospital.

Looking down at the smooth, gray-white face, Caleb felt a painful surge of terror and love pushing at his chest. They had shaved Jonah's head on one side and repaired the gashes with what appeared to be string and glue. His face was mottled by bruises and flecked with tiny cuts. A bit of blood had pooled and dried in the hollow of one ear. Caleb resisted the urge to clean it out.

Did I do this? he wondered. *Did I let a terrible thing happen to an innocent little boy?* He felt eaten alive by guilt.

In the wake of his brother's death, Caleb hadn't been sure he'd be able to raise Jonah and Hannah properly.

And maybe he wasn't doing such a good job, but right away he had learned how to love a child. It was the easiest thing he'd ever done. He loved Jonah with all his heart, and every second of the boy's suffering belonged to Caleb, too.

Under such extraordinary circumstances, a man of faith would surely pray. He'd pray for this beautiful child to heal; he'd thank the Lord for sparing Jonah's life. But Caleb Stoltz wasn't a man of faith, not anymore. Maybe he'd never been one.

He found himself thinking about John, his older brother, Jonah's father. John's faith had been as deep as a well, as endless as the sky. He would have known how to pray for his son.

"I'm sorry, John. I'm real, real sorry about your boy," he quietly murmured. "I'm going to do the best I can, the best I know how. I hope it's enough." But even as he spoke, Caleb feared it wouldn't be.

His stomach rumbled, the noise loud and profane in the unnatural hissing quiet of the hospital room. He felt slightly embarrassed by the urges of his body. When something this terrible happened, it just didn't seem right that Caleb would feel hungry, that his whiskers would grow, that he'd have to take a piss. And yet, that was the case.

He went to the men's room down the hall, relieved himself, and washed up with thin, watery soap from an old wall dispenser, drying off with flimsy brown paper towels. He was startled by his own reflection in the mirror above the row of sinks. There were no mirrors in an Amish household, of course. Mirrors implied pride and vanity, which had no place in an Amishman's character. He rinsed the taste of sleep from his mouth, snapped his suspenders into place.

But there were no suspenders. He was still wearing the green shirt and loose trousers Reese Powell had given him.

He hurried back to Jonah's room. Another hospital worker stood by the bed, marking things on a glass tablet device. A dark-skinned fellow. He smiled politely when Caleb came into the room. "Your son's been stable all night," he said. "That's a good sign."

"When will he wake up?" Caleb asked.

"That's up to him, mainly," said the man. "The doctors can tell you more during rounds. But you can go ahead and talk to him. He'll be groggy at first, but if everything goes well, he'll be awake and chattering away in no time."

When the health aide left, Caleb returned to his vigil beside the bed. "Jonah." He spoke the boy's name a few times, just Jonah, and nothing more. Then, since the nurse seemed absorbed in her monitoring, he spoke some more. "Jonah, it's me, your uncle Caleb. I'm here waiting for you to wake up, because we've got lots to talk about. Can you hear me, Jonah? Can you?"

The boy lay as still as a rock. He resembled a graven image carved into a gray headstone like one of those stone angels the English favored in their cemeteries.

"Jonah, can you hear me?" Caleb tried again. "It's me, Uncle Caleb. Can you feel my hand on your leg? It's right here on your knee. I'm sure worried about you, Jonah. I sure do wish you'd wake up so we could have a talk."

He kept standing there, gazing down, his big thumb absently circling Jonah's knee. Then he saw it. The tiniest flash of movement. The flicker of a shadow on the boy's cheek.

"Jonah?" Caleb leaned a little closer. "Come on, little man. You can do it."

The boy blinked again, then opened his eyes. He stared

up, then squeezed his eyes shut as if to hide from the glare of the ceiling lights. Caleb kept saying his name, gently touching his knee and right shoulder, taking care not to focus on the thickly bandaged truncated arm. Jonah opened his eyes again—a squint of confusion. This time, he didn't look at the lights, but at Caleb. He moved his lips, his bluish cracked lips, but no sound came out.

"You can give him a little water," the nurse said. "He can have sips of water and ice chips if he wants, until the doctor says it's okay to eat and drink again."

Caleb grabbed a paper cup from the tray by the bed. "Here you go," he said, angling the straw to Jonah's lips. He shifted to their German dialect. "Easy there. Take it easy."

Jonah drew weakly on the straw. Most of the water trickled out the sides of his mouth and down into the hospital pillow under his head.

"You can raise the bed with this." The nurse handed him a remote control on a cord.

Caleb fiddled with the automatic controls until he figured out the button that caused the head of the bed to slowly raise up. Jonah looked almost comically startled by the motion, but when he saw what was happening, he relaxed. Caleb raised the bed only a few inches, just enough so the boy could swallow rather than spill. Jonah took one more sip then and finally whispered, "Uncle . . . Caleb."

"That's me," Caleb said too loudly and too cheerfully. "I've been sitting around wondering when you'd wake up."

"How long have I been asleep?"

"All night long, and then some." Caleb looked right down into Jonah's bewildered eyes. "Do you know where you are?"

The boy's gaze darted to and fro. His poor face looked as though it had been slashed by vicious claws. "No."

"We're at the hospital," Caleb said. "You got hurt bad, Jonah. Real bad. You had to have an operation. Do you remember getting hurt?"

"Um, not so much. I'm having trouble remembering," Jonah said.

A nurse had warned Caleb about this. Victims of trauma often lost all recollection of the accident. Sometimes they never regained their memory of the specific event. It was a protective reaction. The mind didn't want to remember a pain so deep and harsh.

"Do you remember going over to the Haubers' to work?"

"Sure I do."

Caleb was ashamed to realize that he'd been wishing Jonah would forget the entire morning. "Then you probably remember how I yelled at you," he said. "I shouldn't have yelled at you, Jonah. I should know better than yelling."

"Your yelling doesn't bother me, Uncle Caleb."

"It bothers me that I yelled." Caleb took a deep breath. "Do you remember the shredder?"

"The shredder?" Jonah frowned slightly. "I know how to work it. I know how to work all the equipment. You taught me yourself."

The trusting expression on his face pierced Caleb's heart. "Something got fouled up in the blades."

"It happens," Jonah said. "And I know how to fix it, too. I grab a longer stalk and push it real hard—" He stopped abruptly. His frown deepened and then softened. He shut his eyes. His lower lip trembled. "Uncle Caleb?"

Caleb would have given his own life to avoid speaking the next words. "A terrible thing happened, Jonah. You got hurt bad, *liebling*. Real bad."

The boy's eyes opened very slowly, as if he knew somehow what he was about to face. With an even slower motion, he lifted his right hand from beneath the blue blanket. Blood had dried in the seams of the short, stubby fingernails. He opened and closed his hand.

Caleb took hold of it, cradled it between both of his big hands, and carried it to his lips. "I'm so sorry, Jonah. I'm so, so awfully sorry." He felt resistance as the boy tried to free his hand from Caleb's grip. And with shattering clarity, Caleb knew why.

He felt an urgent need to intervene before Jonah discovered the unthinkable all on his own. "Jonah, son, look at me."

The serious blue eyes settled on Caleb's face. There was bewilderment in those eyes, and a sense of betrayal. Jonah was a child; he'd given a child's trust to those charged with looking after him, and he'd been betrayed.

"Your other arm's gone, son," Caleb said quietly. "It got cut off."

They both fell silent. Caleb imagined the realization sinking like poison into the boy's mind. Jonah didn't move. He didn't blink. He didn't speak a word for several agonized moments while he looked at his bandaged stump, wrapped in layer after layer of cream-colored gauze. There was a cap or spigot of some sort protruding from the bandage.

"Gone?" he asked, his voice cracking.

"It got all mangled in the shredder. There was so much damage that it couldn't be fixed. They had to cut it off in order to save your life."

"Gone?" Jonah said again. "It's my arm. How can it be gone?"

"It's a lot to take in, I know," Caleb said. "I'm still . . . I can hardly believe it myself, except that I was there. The emergency workers saved your life. They came out right away, did what they could to stop the bleeding, and then they called a rescue helicopter. Life flight." It had all happened just twenty-four hours ago, yet it seemed as though a lifetime had passed. "They brought us here to the hospital in the helicopter," Caleb added. "You and me both."

"We flew."

"Yeah, we flew. Right up into the sky, like a bird or a dragonfly."

"Isn't that against Ordnung?"

Caleb pushed up one side of his mouth, an attempt at a smile. "Just like your daddy, you are," he said. "To tell you the truth, I was more worried about you bleeding to death than I was about church rules."

Jonah flinched and pulled his gaze away from the terrible, bandaged limb. His face was a picture of dull, uncomprehending shock. He had that look you might see on the face of a mother who'd just lost a child. Miriam Hauber had worn that look long after she'd lost a baby just hours after its birth. That same dazed, hollow nothingness, as if the world had suddenly become a place he didn't recognize.

"Then what happened?" asked Jonah.

"Everything went real fast," Caleb said. "I'm not even sure I remember everything right myself. They took you off the chopper while the blades were still going around, and they rushed you down to the emergency ward. Then it was like flies at a picnic, and you were the main dish. I had no idea such a crowd of folks could swarm all over a little old tadpole like you. They hung blood, and put in lines, and yelled stuff at each other, stuff I couldn't begin to understand. Everyone worked real hard to save your life, Jonah. What happened was, the folks in the trauma center, the doctors and nurses and interns and so forth, they got you stabilized. What that means is they made sure your heart was okay and your blood pressure, and your breathing, so they could take you up to surgery." It felt strange, speaking of such unfamiliar things, but Caleb saw no point in hiding anything from Jonah.

Jonah looked at the ceiling. "Where is surgery?"

"It's . . . it's a place where they took you to do an operation to save your life."

"Is it where they cut off my arm?"

Caleb pinched the bridge of his nose, surprised to feel the throb of a headache. He didn't often get headaches. "Yes, son. Yes."

Jonah turned his attention back to the bandaged arm. "Were you there?" he asked. "I mean, when they were cutting off my arm, were you with me?"

"What? *No.*"

"I wonder if they used a saw, like Eli Kemp when he's doing the butchering."

Good Lord almighty. "I was in a waiting room, thinking about you the whole time. When the operation was done, they put you here in this place called the surgical intensive care unit. Hospital folks have been checking on you all night long. I reckon the doctors will be real pleased to see that you're awake and talking."

Caleb left a gap of silence for Jonah. Sometimes silence was needed, not more talking. Caleb had learned this when, in a single terrible moment, he became responsible for Jonah and Hannah.

Yesterday, though, when they'd rushed the boy off to surgery, he had been grateful for talk. He remembered pacing the waiting area of the emergency room, wondering what was going to happen next and not knowing whom to ask. That was when Reese Powell had approached him. Caleb could not remember what had been going through his head when she'd arrived. But he remembered turning to her, and feeling a small but noticeable measure of relief when she offered a change of clothes and then helped him navigate his way through the labyrinthine hallways of the hospital.

He wasn't sure why she had taken an interest in him. Everyone else in the emergency room seemed to race from crisis to crisis, darting and feinting through an obstacle course of equipment, coworkers, frightened patients, and families.

Reese had looked very young to Caleb, though she projected an air of confidence. She was different from anyone he'd ever met, man or woman, in a way that tempted him to stare, like he'd stared at Niagara Falls or a shooting star. Her short hair was as black and shiny as the wing of a raven, framing a face he could look at all the livelong day. Of course, he had no call to be noticing the beauty of a woman, especially at a time like this, but noticing her like that wouldn't change what had happened, no matter who was bleeding on the operating table.

When she'd started talking to him he had realized the source of that beauty was something simple yet powerful—compassion, combined with a fierce and earnest intelligence. She had this way of looking at him as if she knew how scared he was for Jonah and how much he needed to understand what was happening to his nephew. As she'd explained the terrible injury, Caleb had sensed the smallest glimmer of hope. He knew a medical student was only at the beginning of the practice of doctoring, like an apprentice carpenter learning from a master craftsman. Yet there were things that she knew, things he couldn't even imagine. Things about the human body and the way it worked or failed to work. Through yesterday's endless hours, Reese Powell had seemed absolutely determined to stick with him, answering not only the questions he asked but also those he didn't even know how to.

All this seemed to be a lot to notice about a woman he'd only just met. But Caleb was like that sometimes. He'd meet someone and see exactly what that person was like based on a few minutes' conversation.

It hardly mattered now. He probably wouldn't see her again. She was one of the many strangers passing through. Yet for some reason, his thoughts kept drifting back to Reese Powell. In addition to her fierce, intimidating intelligence, he also sensed something sterile and lonely about her. When they'd gone to the cafeteria, she hadn't talked to anyone along the way. It was probably out of character for her to take the time to help him through his first night in the city.

Jonah gazed at him in silence, and Caleb felt guilty for dwelling on his encounter with a woman. Jonah's face took on a soft, sleepy look, his eyes half-lidded. "Where's Hannah?" he asked softly.

Caleb pictured Jonah's sister, crumpled in a tragic heap as the helicopter bore her brother away. "Back home in Middle Grove. I left word with Alma at the phone box that you were going to be all right. And you are, little man, I swear."

"How can I be all right if my arm's gone?" Jonah's voice was the tiniest whisper.

"Because you're Jonah. My best good boy. And I swear by all that I am that we'll get through this."

His throat felt thick with the lie. There was no getting through a loss like this.

"Hannah knows about my arm? Did you tell Alma to tell her?"

"I told Alma you're going to be all right," said Caleb. "She'll let Hannah know." He had not said anything about the arm, only that Jonah was going to get better. Given what Hannah and her brother had already lost, he owed her the full story, but not until he could see her, hold her hand, and reassure her.

"You're wearing funny clothes," Jonah said.

Caleb looked down at the borrowed shirt and trousers. "A lady named Reese loaned these to me." He didn't want to explain that his other clothes were covered in Jonah's blood. "They're called scrubs, which is curious, since they don't seem to be used for scrubbing anything."

Jonah nodded, then yawned. His eyes fluttered shut.

"You rest now," Caleb said, gently stroking his brow. "You rest as long as you like."

Caleb, too, shut his eyes, but he didn't sleep. Instead, his mind wandered back over time, touching on moments forever enshrined in memory.

When he was a boy about Jonah's age, Caleb used to loiter around the village phone box, hoping against hope to hear the phone ring and his mother's voice on the other end. Hoping she would explain why she had walked away from him and his older brother, John, never to return.

Of course, it never rang. Caleb had tried to find her name in the phone book, a slender paperbound directory with scenic pictures of the Poconos on the cover. He remembered sitting on the floor of the small shelter and methodically reading every name in the book, searching for Jenny Stoltz or Jenny Fisher, her maiden name. Finally, John had come along and explained that the book only listed folks who had their own telephones.

"Mem could be a million miles away," John had explained. He was seven years older than Caleb, and he knew things. "You won't find her name in any book around here."

Some time afterward, Caleb recalled, John had made the big leap, determined to end his life by jumping off the hanging bridge at Stony Gorge. Until that day, no one had understood the terrible demons that haunted John, tormenting him to the point where he wanted to end his life. Caleb hadn't grasped the connection between their mother's absence and John's desperation.

But that day, a miracle had occurred. Despite falling a hundred feet, John had not died. He'd walked away with nothing but bruises and scratches and a broken arm. Folks who witnessed the incident talked about it in hushed and reverent tones.

John himself had been transformed by the fall. A man reborn, no longer an angry rebel, John declared that it was the hand of God above that had saved him. In the time it took for him to fling himself off the swinging bridge, his life had been remade and given back to him. In gratitude, he declared that he was going to spend the rest of his days serving God. And he set himself to the task with a devotion that was almost fanatical. He had returned to the community, accepted baptism with a humble heart, married Naomi, and set himself on a new path.

After the kids came along, everyone seemed to feel the bad times were finally behind them. Caleb still thought about his mother, but time dulled the gnawing ache of missing her. He admired the way his brother had put his life back together after that desperate day at Stony Gorge.

Yet Caleb often found himself wondering about the world. He used to daydream about the jet planes soaring overhead or the cars roaring down the highway. In defiance of his father's edicts, he borrowed books from the county library and read novels about imaginary worlds and far-off places, and people grappling with matters he could only imagine. When he turned sixteen, he knew he needed to go out into the world. His father had forbidden it, of course, but Caleb had been determined.

The thing about being Amish was that kids were not only allowed but encouraged to experience life beyond the confines of the community. There was even a name for it—*rumspringa*. Running around. Most youngsters came running back to embrace baptism and Plain life. Folks thought Caleb would spend his rumspringa the way most kids did—riding around in cars, smoking tobacco and weed, listening to loud music, going to shopping malls and movies.

Caleb had known he would be one of the small percentage of Amish kids who left for good. He knew he'd never join the church, never marry an Amish girl, never raise a family the way his brother was doing. He was forever yearning, one foot out the door, poised for flight. He wanted to see the ocean one day. Wanted to fly in a plane. To learn the calculus and study science and literature and things of that nature. He wanted to experience the world in all its messy, confusing glory.

Most of all, he wanted distance from his father.

Instead of partying, Caleb spent his time at the library. He learned to use books and computers as sophisticated information systems to find out all he could about anything imaginable.

That was how he'd eventually found his mother. A grueling bus ride had taken him to central Florida, where the air was so hot and muggy he could scarcely breathe. The town was nowhere near the ocean or the Gulf of Mexico, but hunched at the side of a highway that bisected the long, narrow state. His search ended at a street lined with modest houses surrounded by scrubby grass and trees decked with little orange bittersweet fruit called calamondin. He still remembered the expression on her face when she had opened the front door. Complete and utter shock had drained her cheeks of color, then blossomed into wonder.

"John?"

"Caleb," he said. For the love of God, she couldn't tell her sons apart.

"Who is it, Mom?" called a voice. A young girl came to the door. She stopped and stared at Caleb. Although he wore English clothes, she stared as if he were an alien from outer space.

Mem leaned her back against the doorframe and tipped back her head, looking up at the sky and then closing her eyes.

He'd scarcely remembered her face. There were no photographs of her. He used to try drawing the image he had of her in his mind, but the picture never turned out. Now he saw Hannah in the curve of her cheek and in the wavy blond hair. He saw Jonah in the bright blue eyes and the busy hands.

She mouthed some words, but no sound came out. Her legs seemed to give out and she slid down to the mat, hugging her knees up to her chest. A dry sob heaved from a place deep inside her, and then the floodgates opened.

He remembered this from his childhood. Mem used to cry a lot. The girl—Caleb later learned her name was Nancy—backed away, her eyes round with fright. "Mom," she said. "Mommy, what's the matter?"

"You'd best pull yourself together, Mem," Caleb said in Deitsch.

Maybe the sound of the old dialect caught her attention. She took in a deep breath and picked herself back up. Caleb pushed open the door. "Let's go inside."

He entered the strange house. It had a vinyl floor and shabby furniture, and it smelled of something damp, like mildew. The girl called Nancy sat on a barstool in the corner, and Mem took a seat at the end of the sofa. Caleb stood in the doorway, waiting. He crossed his arms over his chest. "We woke up one morning and you were gone," he said.

A long silence stretched out. Cool air blew from a vent in the ceiling, a magic wind that turned the hot day cold.

"Nancy, honey, you run along and play outside," Mem said. "I need to speak with Caleb for a bit."

The girl's chin tilted up slightly. "I want to stay."

Mem regarded her steadily. "Run along," she repeated. "I'll speak with you later."

Nancy hesitated for a beat. Then she climbed off the stool and left. The *snap* of a screen door punctuated her exit.

Finally, Mem began to talk, and she seemed to talk for hours. "I couldn't stay. I was drowning—or choking. That's how it felt, day and night. I couldn't breathe, living in fear of what Asa would do to me next. I was so young and naive, I didn't even know what to call the things he did to me."

Caleb hadn't known what to say to that. He hadn't been quite certain of what she meant, although knowing his father's temper, he had an idea.

"I ran away in the night with nothing," Mem continued. "Asa had hurt me bad. I thought I might die, but I didn't. I survived and went off on my own for the first time in my life, and it was awful. But not as awful as staying. At first, I lost the will to live. Wandered out onto a busy highway without a thought for what might happen to me. I was lost. So very lost." She turned her face to the window and stared outside. "I made a lot of stupid mistakes, but I made my way, bit by bit. Found work here in Florida and started over."

"It never occurred to you to take care of your own kids?" Caleb asked. "Did you think it was all right to leave us with the same man you ran away from because you were so scared of him?"

She studied him with pale, tear-filled eyes. "There was no way Asa would have let me take you, and staying was impossible. I didn't have a penny to my name. I knew nothing but Plain ways, and I'd never set foot outside the community. I could only hope you and John would be all right." She stared at him, her eyes swimming with pain. "Did he . . . did your father . . . ?"

"You mean, did he beat me? Yah, sure, until John got big enough to stand up to him."

Their father didn't seem to have the first idea about how to raise two boys. He'd always been strict and stern, with a fearsome temper, but Caleb had no memory of the terrible things Mem had suffered. However, he had witnessed his father's fierce outbursts. John bore the brunt of the beatings. Yes, they were beatings, not spankings— with a belt, a shovel, a hacksaw, or any other weapon their father might grab. Caleb used to cower, shivering, under the cellar stairs when his father laid into John. At night, he'd hear his brother sniffing, trying not to make a sound as he wept, because if their father caught wind of crying, the beatings would start again.

One Sunday, Caleb overheard John asking the bishop for help. The bishop said a man was obligated to discipline his family to achieve the peaceable fruit of righteousness.

Later that same day, Caleb raided the apple bin and ate as many apples as his belly could hold. When his father discovered him, Caleb explained that he was tasting the fruit of righteousness. Asa flew into a rage and dragged Caleb out to the yard for a beating. That was when John stepped in, at fifteen already a full hand taller than their father. He planted himself like a wall between Caleb and Asa.

"You're not to lay a hand on my brother," John said. "Not today. Not ever. If you're going to hit anyone today, it's going to be me."

Now Caleb's mother deflated, curled into herself. "John, he was always the protective one. Knew how to stand up to his father. And look at you. How handsome you are. I knew John would look after you, and you would be all right."

"If that's what you want to think."

"You look wonderful," she said, her gaze devouring him. "It's a miracle, seeing you again, Caleb. I never thought it would happen, but I dreamed of this day. Why, see how tall and handsome you are, just like John. So confident and smart. How is John doing now?"

"John tried to take his own life," he told his mother.

She went completely still. "Oh, dear heaven," she said. "No. *No.*"

"He jumped off the bridge over Stony Gorge—"

"No," she said again, a horrified whisper.

"He was seventeen years old. And he didn't die. He wasn't even hurt too bad. According to folks who saw it happen, he got up and brushed himself off and walked all the way back to Middle Grove. Dr. Shrock set his broken arm. The only thing he lost was his hat." *And himself,* Caleb added silently. After the incident, John was so different. He looked the same—though after the baptism his face had been fringed by a beard. Yet there always seemed to be less of Caleb's brother. Yes, John had latched onto his faith with a powerful fervor, but he was altered, somehow. Not himself. Almost like a clockwork John, mechanically reciting proverbs from *Rules for a Godly Life.*

"My poor darling John." A tear squeezed from Mem's eye and slipped down her cheek. "He wasn't hurt. It's a miracle."

"He's married now. He and Naomi have two kids, Hannah and Jonah."

"I wish I could see him," said Mem. "And those children . . ."

"You're under the Bann," Caleb said. "Now that he's in the church, he won't speak to you. We needed you years ago, and you weren't there. Eventually, we learned to get along without you."

She flinched and started to cry again. Caleb looked around the room, dim and chilly with the musty-smelling air blowing in. There were photographs on a shelf of Nancy at different ages, and another shelf with a collection of books of the self-help variety—*Survival After Abuse. Change Your Brain, Change Your Life.*

Even now, Caleb still flinched at the memory of his father's face, twisted by fury, and John's steadfast refusal to budge. If John hadn't stuck up for his younger brother, maybe Caleb would have been the one teetering on the cable bridge over the gorge, not John. He owed his brother devotion and loyalty. It was a debt he could never repay.

In the mechanical hospital bed, Jonah stirred and opened his eyes wide as he seemed to shake himself awake. His gaze darted immediately to the bandage, then to Caleb. "I wish I still had my arm," he said.

"So do I," Caleb told him. "I was just thinking about your dat, my brother, John. He was the bravest, strongest, kindest man in the world, and you're his flesh and blood. It's going to be real hard, but you'll be just like that one day."

"What if I can't be brave and strong?"

"You can be. I'll help you, the way your dat helped me." Caleb reached out and gently touched Jonah's head. "And that's why I will never leave you."

There was no door on the SICU suite where Jonah lay, just a wide doorway open to the nurses' station. A nurse was always present at the computer in the suite monitoring everything on the screen. At each shift change, the nurse asked Caleb if he needed anything, if there was anyone he wanted to call, but he always politely declined. He did help himself to a book about snorkeling in the Caribbean, and he read it cover to cover by the dim, artificial light in the room.

He was just about to share some of the pictures with Jonah when Reese Powell showed up. She wore loose blue trousers, a shirt to match, and a hip-length white jacket over that. She carried a number of steel and rubber objects in her many pockets, and when she came into the room, she brought with her something Caleb had not expected: the smell of flowers. *Must be the soap she used*, he thought, then felt guilty for noticing the way she smelled at all.

"Good morning," she said. "I came to see how Jonah is doing."

"He woke up a few minutes ago. He's waiting for his breakfast." Caleb's nephew had awakened in a state of fear and anger. Everything about the hospital was strange and new to him, and he was still struggling to accept the loss of his arm.

She fixed her gaze on Jonah, her eyes soft and friendly. "Hi there, Jonah."

The boy regarded her with narrow-eyed suspicion as he mumbled, "Morning."

"I was hoping I would get to meet you," she said. "My name is Reese Powell. I was working in the emergency ward when you came in. Everyone worked hard for the best outcome."

"This is not a good outcome," said Jonah.

"It's not," she agreed. "I'm sorry." She gave Caleb a paper-wrapped parcel. "Your clothes. I had them cleaned for you."

He studied the label on the parcel—CITY WASH & FOLD—and wondered what she would make of the ancient washtub and hand-crank wringer back at the farm.

Jonah glared at her with uncharacteristic anger. "Reese," he said in a caustic voice. "That's not a name. It's a candy."

"At least I never got swallowed by a whale," she shot back.

Caleb stood there, amazed. He was amazed because Jonah had never in his life spoken rudely to a person until now. And he was amazed because Reese didn't seem to care one bit. And in spite of everything terrible that was happening, he couldn't stop himself from feeling a glimmer of amusement.

Jonah settled back against the pillow, and Caleb could see his fear go down a notch. "I always liked that story," he muttered. "Are you a doctor?"

"Almost. I wanted to stop by, because I thought you might have some questions. You've got a super-talented care team. I'm not on that team, because I work in a different department, but I can talk with you about your arm if you want."

"Why is it gone?" asked the boy.

"It was so badly injured. They wanted to save it, but there was too much damage."

"Where is it?" Jonah asked.

She caught her breath. "Your arm, you mean."

The boy nodded.

"It—the part that had to come off was taken away." She shifted her stance and stuck her hands in her coat pockets.

"Taken away where?" Jonah persisted.

"I don't know the exact location, but the hospital has a special way to take care of it."

"What's the special way?"

"Well, there are rules. It had to be incinerated and then disposed of. That probably sounds horrible."

"We incinerate the trash back home."

"Your arm wasn't trash, Jonah."

"I wish I had my hand back."

"We all wish that. Now you have to work with what you've got. You'll get what's called a prosthetic arm and hand. Maybe more than one, depending on what you need. It's going to take a while, because there are lots of steps involved. You have to heal and have physical therapy. I promise, you'll get lots of help from your care team."

"What's my care team?"

"The doctors, nurses, therapists, and all the people who are going to help you. It's a different world today than the one yesterday, that's for sure. Eventually, you'll be stronger than ever. I know it doesn't seem possible right now, but it's true. I've seen it."

"How do you know?" Jonah persisted.

She folded her arms and looked him in the eye. "I know stuff."

"What kind of stuff?" Jonah asked her, narrowing his eyes in suspicion.

"When they move you to the ward, I'll introduce you to some kids who are going to amaze you with their superpowers. Do you know what a superpower is?"

"Course I do. And I know they're just made-up stuff in books."

"Ah. That's where you're wrong. There's one patient who had a heart transplant, and he still comes in every week to make balloon animals for the other kids, just to see them smile. If that's not a superpower, I don't know what is."

"The surgeon said I was lucky," Jonah said. "Do you think it's lucky to get your arm cut off?"

She looked from side to side, then bent toward him. "Let me tell you something about surgeons. When they say you were lucky, you weren't. What it really means is they thought you were going to die and you didn't. So maybe your superpower and the surgeon's superpower were working together."

Jonah's eyes widened. Caleb could see his fear go down another notch. Could be Reese Powell's blunt honesty was what the boy needed. He liked her compassion, and the way she spoke plainly to Jonah, not trying to sugarcoat the troubles he faced.

She turned to him and seemed a little flustered at the way he was staring at her. "How did you do last night?" she asked. "Did a social worker come, find you a place to stay?"

When Caleb didn't answer right away, Jonah angled his gaze at the molded plastic chair in the corner. Caleb's hat still lay beneath it. "I bet he was right there all night," the boy said.

"You were, weren't you?" she asked Caleb.

He didn't want to get anyone in trouble, so he merely shrugged and said, "I wanted to be here in case Jonah woke up."

She bit her lip. She had very white, straight teeth and soft-looking lips he had no business noticing. "You're not going to be good for anything if you don't eat and sleep properly," she said, her female bossiness reaching across any and all cultural lines between English and Amish. There was much to admire about this woman—her thoughtful gestures, taking the time to help him through his first evening in the city. And she had a clear, honest way of explaining things to Jonah.

He wondered what her world was like outside the hospital. Did she spend time with her family and friends? Did she live nearby? What did she do when she wasn't working?

He pictured her in English clothes, driving a car, getting her fingernails polished by someone in a salon—a concept so foreign to the Amish it was almost inconceivable. Did she go out to bars with friends? Surf the Internet? Study her phone as if it held the secrets of the universe?

One of her pockets emitted a buzzing sound. She took out a flat mobile phone with a shiny screen. "I have to go," she said.

"I wish you could stay," Jonah said.

"That's nice to hear. But I work in the ER, not surgery. I just came up here to see how you're doing."

"Oh," said Jonah, clearly not understanding the difference between emergency and surgery.

She backed toward the door, still talking. "Tell you what. At the end of my shift, I'll come back to see you again. If they move you to the ward, I'll find you. And you know what else? We'll figure out a place for your uncle to stay. Maybe get him a more comfortable chair."

That drew a flicker of a smile from Jonah. "Yeah, that would be good, Reese."

She gave him a look that even a wounded boy couldn't resist. "You're going to be okay, Jonah Stoltz," she said. "That's a promise. And you know what?"

"What?"

"Keeping promises is *my* superpower."

6

For a place of healing, the hospital was a cold, noisy institution. Folks were so busy working that they barely noticed the visitors and bystanders. As they rushed about their business, most of them skirted around Caleb as if he were a piece of furniture. He didn't mind so much, though. He didn't feel like fending off what the English referred to as "small talk"—a habit of filling the silence with pointless chatter.

The Amish had no equivalent Caleb could think of. If there was silence, they let it be. No one felt obligated to fill the void.

In this world, if there was no one present to talk to, people talked to their phones, which they connected to with headphones, or tapped the screen, shooting text and pictures back and forth. They did so even while they walked, barely watching where they were going.

Patients were referred to by their afflictions rather than their names. Sometimes they were called a "code" or "that liver biopsy in room ten" as if their illness defined the sum total of who they were. The hospital staff members didn't seem to want to acknowledge that "the aneurysm" was somebody's grandmother, or that "the bypass" had worked at the public library for twenty-seven years.

Jonah drifted in and out of sleep as the hours crept by. When he was awake, he seemed like a boy Caleb had never met before. He was hollow, joyless, with the look of someone being punished for a crime he hadn't committed.

While Jonah was napping, Caleb went to the men's room and washed up, using a kit given to him by a nurse, with soap, a toothbrush and toothpaste, and a plastic-handled razor. Then he changed into his newly cleaned clothes, which had been washed and pressed and folded into a neat packet. His plain shirt had never been so crisp at the edges, better than brand-new. In his own clothes, Caleb felt slightly more like himself and was grateful for the bossy, thoughtful Reese Powell.

Slightly refreshed, he inhaled the manufactured air blowing through the hallway. At the end of the corridor was a window framing the blue sky and the tall, modern buildings. He told Jonah's nurse where to locate him, then made his way down the stairs and out the door. He had discovered a garden on the hospital grounds, and during Jonah's naps he would step outside, trying to find his balance in the chaos. He sat on one of the wrought-iron benches and stared at the grass and trees, taking refuge from the glaring lights and manufactured air of the hospital's beeping, hissing wards. Jonah had to endure that every second of the day; there was no escape for him. Caleb felt vaguely guilty for escaping the strange and harsh environment, even for a few minutes.

There had been further questions from Child Protective Services. Different people had asked him the same question a dozen different ways to determine if the accident was caused by negligence, either Caleb's or the Haubers'. He talked to a half-dozen folks with clipboards and laptop computers and name badges, but after all the questioning—or "interviews," as someone called them—it was determined that the incident was exactly what Reese Powell had said it was—an accident. No one's fault.

But Jonah's to suffer.

As the day wore on, and Caleb met with doctors and other staff members, one thing became clear to Caleb. Reese had been right about something else—Jonah's recovery was going to take a long time.

It was going to cost a lot of money, too. Various staff members had asked for information about his "status," which Caleb soon discovered was their way of trying to find out if he could afford Jonah's care. It was probably well known to the hospital folks that the Amish almost never carried insurance, as purchasing commercial insurance violated the rules. The notion behind this was that the people in the community took care of their own, fiercely independent of outside help. Middle Grove had an aid fund overseen by a committee, and when a huge medical expense came along, the community banded together to raise money, holding fund-raisers and benefit auctions.

But Caleb was a realist. Given what had happened to Jonah's parents, he had been diligent about insurance coverage. Over the strident objections of his father, he had enrolled himself and the children in a comprehensive insurance policy. Here at the hospital, he'd shown them the card he kept in his wallet. He filled out forms, offered the necessary information, and everyone seemed to calm down.

It was one of the few things that had been easy about this ordeal.

In the garden, the shadows of the beech trees and of people strolling along the walkways lengthened, and the traffic sounds from the busy streets increased as folks hurried about their business.

Passersby sent veiled looks of curiosity in Caleb's direction. Amish people were used to being stared at. As far as he knew, they were the only group of people in America who constituted a tourist attraction simply by being who they were. Folks came on tour buses and in their cars to the Amish towns in the countryside. Visitors seemed drawn to the sight of farmers and artisans going through their everyday chores. Most tourists were pretty respectful, treating the Amish like rare, elusive birds, to be spied on from a distance and photographed without their knowledge.

A few were bold to the point of rudeness, poking and prying at the Amish like a cat sticking its nose into a mouse hole. More than once, English girls in short shorts and halter tops had planted themselves beside him for a photograph or a phone selfie without even asking his permission.

Jonah used to think it was funny to posture for the camera lens, even though it got him in trouble with the elders if they caught him at it. Caleb wondered if that laughing, teasing boy would ever come back to him.

A long, slender shadow fell across the grass at his feet. He looked up to see Reese Powell with the sun on her hair and an uncertain smile on her face. "Caleb?"

He stood with automatic courtesy. "Is it something about Jonah?"

"No," she said quickly. "He's sleeping. His nurse said I might find you in the garden. There's someone I'd like you to meet." She indicated the man beside her. He was dressed like a hospital worker, but his scrubs were greenish, not blue, like the ones Caleb had borrowed.

The guy stuck out his hand. "I'm Leroy Hershberger." Beneath a trim mustache, his mouth curved into a smile. "I work as a physical therapist here at Mercy Heights. Reese told me what happened to your nephew. I'm real sorry."

"Yah . . . ah, thanks." Caleb had no idea what he was thanking this man for. His concern, he supposed. He felt a nudge of familiarity when he looked at Leroy and heard a certain cadence in his voice. Leroy Hershberger had what Caleb considered an easy face. Everything was out there, for all the world to see. It was a face that held no secrets. An honest face.

"Leroy's my neighbor," Reese explained. "We live in the same building, six and a half blocks down the street."

"You're going to need a place to stay while your nephew is in the hospital," Leroy said. "Reese tells me you're from Amish country, so I thought a home stay might work better than a hotel. I've got a spare room at my place."

"I couldn't impose," Caleb said, though he was touched by the man's kindness.

"It's not an imposition," Leroy said.

"But if Jonah needs me—"

"We'll get you a cell phone so you can always be in touch."

The offer was tempting, but Caleb shook his head. "I need to be close to Jonah."

"You have to stay somewhere," Reese insisted, "and like I said before, you won't do him much good if you don't take care of yourself. But it's up to you, of course. You do realize the hospital isn't going to let you live here."

Caleb did understand that he couldn't very well keep sleeping in his clothes and washing up in the men's room with thin pink soap and paper towels. "Obliged to you," he said.

"I'm happy to help." Leroy really seemed to mean it.

Caleb looked from one to the other. "Somehow I have the feeling not everyone gets this treatment."

"You're right about that," Leroy said. "There are hotels nearby for patients' families. But Reese here—she said you were special."

Caleb glanced at her and was amazed to see that her cheeks had turned bright red with a blush.

"And by special," Leroy said easily in Deitsch, the German dialect, "I mean she might be sweet on you, but don't let on I told you that."

A short laugh burst from Caleb. "I knew there was something about you, Leroy Hershberger."

Reese looked from one to the other. "It's like you're in some secret club."

"Like a cult?" asked Leroy.

Caleb laughed again. It felt good to laugh, ever so briefly, in the midst of everything. And it felt entirely strange to hear Leroy say the beauteous and exotic Reese Powell was sweet on him. Like a hoax. And a stupid one at that.

"We'll be heading home in about an hour," she said. "Why don't you check on Jonah and let him know the plan."

When Caleb got back upstairs, Jonah was awake and reading a book in the cranked-up bed. "There's a guy who's invited me to stay with him while you're laid up," Caleb told him. "He's ex-Amish."

"Okay," Jonah said, barely looking up from the pages of the book.

"It's real close by the hospital, so if you need me, I can be here in just a couple of minutes."

"That's good."

"Or I can stay here if you don't want me to go," Caleb said.

At last Jonah looked up from the book, and in the boy's eyes, Caleb saw his brother. "You can't sleep in a chair all night," he said.

Their gazes held for a few seconds. Then Caleb gave his nephew a card with Leroy's phone number. "If you need anything at all, even if you just need to tell me something, you get the nurse to help you call me."

"All right," Jonah said. "I'll see you when you come back around."

As Caleb and Reese and Leroy walked away from Mercy Heights, he felt inundated by the action all around them. Four lanes of traffic surged along a divided road by the river. There were big delivery trucks belching diesel smoke, masses of cars honking their horns. The gnashing brakes of buses and the occasional yip of a siren added to the noise. Kids slouching along the sidewalk and shoving one another seemed oblivious to people trying to get somewhere in a hurry. Boats and barges surged up and down the Schuylkill River, and overhead, jets flashed and drew contrails in the deepening evening sky.

Reese turned to Caleb as he glanced around, not quite knowing what to focus on. In Middle Grove, a traffic jam most often consisted of a gaggle of girls on roller skates or a couple of buggies that stopped in the middle of the road so the drivers could have a chat.

"This must seem pretty chaotic to you," she said, reading his thoughts.

"We're so used to all the noise that we don't even notice it anymore," Leroy said.

"It's a lot to take in," Caleb admitted. "I feel like Mike Smith."

She frowned. "Pardon?"

"Who's Mike Smith?" asked Leroy.

"Valentine Michael Smith."

Reese's frown deepened, but the expression made her

look focused rather than angry. "Wait. Don't tell me." Then she snapped her fingers. "*Stranger in a Strange Land.*"

"You got it."

"Cool that you've read it."

"I haven't read it," Leroy said.

"It's a classic," said Reese. "Do you read a lot, Caleb?"

"Sure," he said. "How about you?"

"Not as much as I wish I could," she admitted. "So you're . . . Nobody restricts what you read, then?"

"Och, there are rules. Some folks think the only thing worth reading is Scripture."

"But not you."

He didn't reply.

She looked at him, and then at Leroy. "I wonder who the 'some folks' are, and if their opinions about what a person chooses to read matter."

In German, Leroy said, "We could fill her ears, huh? I once got a caning for hiding a comic book under my mattress."

Caleb nodded. "My dat would've done the same, but not with a cane." Asa was more liable to use a steel cable or a belt.

"Hey," said Reese. "I'm feeling a little left out here. Tell me a little more about Middle Grove. I don't get out of the city much."

"It's a farming community," he replied in English. "Plenty of Amish and Mennonite families thereabouts."

"And you live on a farm. What's that like?"

Caleb exchanged a glance with Leroy, who spread his hands, palms up.

"She's a hothouse flower, my friend."

Reese elbowed him, pretending to be mad.

"Our place is about forty acres," Caleb said. "Most folks farm eighty or more. A lot of the families around

Middle Grove are big ones, but it's just me, Jonah, Hannah, and my father. During the busy season, I rely on neighbors and hired laborers to work the place."

"Is it going to be a problem for you to be away?" asked Leroy.

"It is, but I don't have a choice. I need to be here for Jonah. I reckon I'll have to hire a labor crew to help with the harvest."

"Crews are expensive," Leroy said.

"Yah. I take an English job now and then," Caleb said, "to make ends meet."

"By English, you mean non-Amish?" asked Reese.

"That's our term for it."

"So what sort of job do you have?"

"I have a team of draft horses for hire, and I work part-time at Grantham Farm, up by New Hope. Each spring, I prepare taxes for folks."

"Amazing. So it's not against your religion to fill out government forms?"

He felt the slightest ghost of a smile haunting his mouth, just for a second. "You've got some funny ideas about the Amish," he said.

She flushed. "Sorry. I really am ignorant. Tax preparation seems so modern. Do you use a computer, or at least a calculator?"

"I figure everything by hand." He almost smiled again at her incredulous expression.

Leroy looked at Reese, then back at Caleb. "You two are going to get along just fine."

Reese felt inexplicably nervous inviting Caleb Stoltz to her place. He was still getting settled at Leroy's apartment, which was across the hall from hers. But since Leroy had to go back to the hospital for a shift, she would be Caleb's host this evening.

She had offered to fix Caleb dinner and was already regretting the impulse. When had she ever made dinner for anyone, other than the Red Bull and cheese doodles she served when it was her turn to host study group?

Glancing at the clock, she launched into a frenzy of activity, rushing around her apartment in an attempt to swiftly straighten up. Her mother kept offering—or threatening—to send Viola over to do a weekly cleaning, but Reese always refused the help. She'd grown up far more privileged than her peers, and having maid service just felt wrong until she could actually earn the money to pay for it herself.

She switched on NPR to catch up on the news, then flung her scrubs into the hamper and jumped into the shower for a quick rinse. After her shower, the news was over and music drifted from the speakers, something soft and alternative. What kind of music did Amish people listen to? Probably not Yo La Tengo. As she was toweling dry, she wondered what exactly one should wear to have dinner with an Amish guy. She settled for a fairly plain but summery lavender dress and strappy sandals. Her hair was short enough to dry with a towel, her chief reason for having short hair. Makeup was a quick swipe of lipstick. She was confident the Amish didn't use makeup, anyway. Not that she was trying to be Amish, for Chrissake. She just didn't want to make him feel more uncomfortable than he already was.

A knock at the door sent her speeding to answer, another sign of nervousness. Why was she nervous? She wanted the evening to go well, but there were so many things that could go wrong.

She opened the door, and there stood Caleb, freshly

showered, wearing a pair of broken-in jeans and a black V-neck T-shirt just tight enough to define his chest and shoulder muscles into a ridiculous female fantasy. As she stared at him, she could feel her brain cells dying one by one.

"Oh, hey," she said and couldn't think of anything to say to make the moment less awkward. Seeing him in regular clothes forced her to realize physical attraction was based on more than the fact that he was so completely different from anyone she'd ever known.

Leroy joined him as they stepped inside. "I got him some English clothes."

"Not bad, right?" asked Caleb.

Given that the last guy she'd dated had worn a sweater vest and kept his cell phone in a belt holster, the bar for male fashion was set low. "You look so different. Where did you find these clothes?"

"The Lab."

"What?"

"You know, the thrift shop in the hospital basement."

"There's a thrift shop in the hospital basement?"

Leroy rolled his eyes. "Not everyone shops at Saks. It's a shop called the Lab, run by volunteers. The proceeds benefit the hospital."

The pointed reference to her privileged upbringing made her blush.

"See you around, princess," Leroy added, then turned to Caleb. "You have the entry code for the door, right? Make yourself at home."

"I will. And thank you again, Leroy." They shook hands, and Leroy took off.

"So do you," Caleb said, turning to her with a brief half smile. "Look different, I mean."

"Yes, under the scrubs and lab coat, there's a real

person. After a long shift, I sometimes forget that." She stepped aside and held open the door. "Please, come in." She bit her lip to keep from making excuses—*Sorry my place is such a mess, sorry I have fake plants instead of real, sorry there's nothing but water in the fish tank because the fish died last year and I never bothered to replace them . . .*

She had no reason to impress this man.

"Would you like something to drink?" she offered. The least she could do was be civil.

"Water's fine." He tilted his head to one side, and his expression softened a little. "That's nice."

Oh. The music. "It's Yo La Tengo, I think. I like it too." She rinsed out a water glass and filled it with ice from the refrigerator door dispenser. He studied her every move, and she realized that almost all of this must be completely strange to him.

"I looked up Amish customs on the web," she said. "Not like, in a stalkerish way. I was curious." God, she was babbling. *Stop talking, Reese.* "I read that Amish households don't have electricity, refrigeration, running water, or clothing that fastens with zippers."

"That's true of some communities," he said. "There's a range. The conservative ones—like Middle Grove—are like that for sure."

She handed him a glass of ice water and poured herself a glass of wine. "So that's my big confession," she said. "I looked up information online." She gestured at her laptop. The screensaver showed a tropical beach with white sand and turquoise water. "I hope you don't mind."

"Nope," he said. "Course, you could just ask me."

"I might do that. Some days, I spend more time staring at a screen than I do with people. That's bad, right?"

He took a long drink of water. She stared in fascination at the ripple of his sun-browned throat, and for a moment, she forgot the world. *Snap out of it*, she told herself.

"Guess that would depend on the person," he said.

"I want to be the kind of doctor who works with people, not data," she said. "The article I read mentioned a teenage rite of passage called rumspringa—am I saying that right?"

"*Rumspringa*," he said. "You're close enough."

"Rumspringa," she repeated.

"Sometimes known as Jerry Springa," he said.

She laughed. "Does that mean the rumors are true? That kids go wild, exploring the non-Amish world?"

"Some do. Kids are kids. They're going to rebel. Strictly speaking, they're supposed to use the time for courting—the goal being to find a mate. But plenty of kids dress English and drive cars, try drugs, and party with the English."

"Did you go wild?" she asked, then realized he was studying her with deep absorption. Maybe she'd crossed a line with all the questions. "What?"

"Just noticing what your eyes do when something interests you."

"What do my eyes do?"

"They kind of show what you're thinking."

She wasn't sure what to make of that, so she repeated the question. "Did you go wild?"

"Depends on what you mean by wild," he said. "And I don't know you well enough to give you more detail than that."

"Obviously you watched TV. Jerry Springer."

"I didn't much care for it."

"No one does. Well. I won't pry anymore. I'm starving. If you want, I can make my favorite thing for dinner."

"What's that?"

"A reservation. You know, at a restaurant." As she scrolled through the options on her phone, she could see him shifting from foot to foot as he stared out the window, looking like a caged lion.

She sensed it might be painfully awkward, bringing him into a restaurant where food emerged from an unseen kitchen and was served by strangers. "I have a better idea. There's a great spot along the riverwalk with food trucks. I go there all the time. We can grab a bite and have a picnic."

"Sounds good. Not sure what food trucks are, though."

"One of the great innovations of the modern age." It was strangely exciting, introducing this man to a world that was so foreign to him. She led the way downstairs to the crosswalk at the corner. The six-lane boulevard was jammed with traffic surging in both directions, in and out of the city. The sidewalks were crowded with rushing pedestrians. A street performer cadged for tips between blasts of his harmonica and acoustic guitar. Luigi, the greengrocer from whom she got most of her food, stood on the sidewalk in his apron, rocking back on his heels and watching the world go by. She smiled as they walked past, then noticed Caleb perusing the display of produce in crates—local stone fruit and berries from truck farms outside the city, and a few exotic selections from the Asian market. She saw him checking out the star fruit and dragon fruit.

"Crazy-looking stuff," she said.

"It is. How's it taste?"

"Let's find out." She bought a couple of samples and handed him the bag. "Something for later. Let me know what you think."

They reached the corner and she gestured toward the river. The promenade area was more mellow than the sidewalk. A large swath of green bordered the river, and the walkways were busy with joggers, strollers, people on skateboards and rollerblades, and tourists. "The river-walk will take us almost all the way to the hospital. Let's grab something to eat, and then go check on Jonah, make sure he's tucked in for the night."

Caleb stepped off the curb, almost into the path of a trolley. She grabbed his arm and yanked him back. "Whoa there," she said. "Jesus, watch out. You nearly got creamed." She kept hold of his arm. His muscles felt like carved stone.

"Sorry. Guess I'd better get used to being in the city."

"You gave me a scare," she said, her heart still racing. "Remember to watch the signal lights. When the red man standing changes to a green man walking, then we can go."

"Got it."

She slowly eased her grip on him. Glancing around, she realized he was attracting attention. Not because he was Amish; you couldn't tell, thanks to the borrowed clothes. No, he garnered attention because he was so big and imposing. If Michelangelo's *David* came alive, he might look something like Caleb—larger than life, myth-ically handsome, perfectly proportioned, and somehow removed from the world. He seemed to have no notion of his effect on total strangers.

"This is Millennium Park," she said. "There are bike and walking trails that'll get you all the way to the Old City in one direction and Penn's Landing in the other. Ever been to the historic district?"

He shook his head. "Cradle of liberty, right?"

"So they say."

"I'd like to see that."

"Then you should. I mean, while you're here."

They stopped at shady Race Street Park in the shadow

of the Benjamin Franklin Bridge. Nearby was a collection of food carts gathered in a loose circular arrangement. "It's like the United Nations of food here," she said, gesturing at the scene. "Each cart flies the flag of its cuisine—Mexico, France, Germany, Australia, India . . . take your pick. Where would you like to go tonight?"

"Bali," he said, pointing out one of the carts.

Other than a peach-colored flag with a symbol in the middle, there was nothing to identify the cart. "How do you know that's Balinese?"

"They're flying the flag of Bali." He half smiled at her surprised expression. "I know stuff," he said.

A few minutes later, they found a spot on a bench, where they savored their ikan pepes—a delicate white fish steamed in banana leaves. "Listen," she said, "I didn't mean to suggest—"

"It's okay. Lots of folks think being Amish is the same as being ignorant."

"That's not—"

"It's okay," he repeated. "Some Amish are ignorant. So are some English."

She spotted a guy in a muscle shirt with a rebel flag on it and nodded. "Point taken. So do you travel much?"

"Armchair travel only. When I was a kid, my folks took us all to Niagara Falls. That was a long while back."

"Oh, brothers and sisters?"

"I had one brother, John. Small family, by Amish standards." He watched a tourist boat gliding up the river.

"So your brother was Jonah's father."

"Yes."

Reese felt all sorts of questions pushing at her. She wondered how much she could ask without seeming completely intrusive. She sensed that this was a man who would reveal himself—or not—in his own time. As a doctor, she was going to have to get used to difficult conversations.

"Your brother, John, and his wife both passed away, then," she ventured. "I'm so sorry. Was it an accident?"

He finished eating and looked down at the river again. "They were murdered some years ago."

"My God . . . What? I mean, I heard you, but . . . Oh my God. Those poor kids. What happened?"

"John and his wife, Naomi, were coming home from an auction one night. Amish are sometimes targets, because we only use cash and we're not supposed to fight back. And we don't prosecute. Anyway, John had sold a hitch of Clydesdales at an auction that night and had a wad of cash on him when he and Naomi were driving home in their buggy. A couple of thugs robbed them. And I guess maybe John did fight back, because one of the robbers was beat up pretty bad. The other shot my brother and his wife so they wouldn't be able to identify them. But John survived long enough to tell the police . . ." He paused, swallowed hard. "I was living away from Middle Grove at that time, but I came rushing back. I gave blood—too late. I promised John I'd look after his kids. I promised I'd raise them in the faith. The killers are both in prison now."

"What a horrible nightmare," she said, her stomach churning. So that was how he knew his blood type. "I'm so very sorry for your family. So that's when you became Jonah's guardian?"

"Yep."

"Oh my gosh, you had to take on two kids. There wasn't anyone else who could look after them?"

He shook his head. "Naomi's family had troubles of their own."

"But your own parents? Couldn't they have helped?"

"My mother left the family when I was little. She had

troubles too." His voice trailed off. "You ask a lot of questions."

"I could claim that's my training as a doctor," she said. "Maybe it is, partly. It's also because I'm interested in you. And in Jonah." She was blushing. Babbling and blushing. "So after your mother left . . . ?"

"John did his best to look after me, and I was too young to understand how hard that must have been. I only realized it when he tried to take his own life. He climbed up to a hanging bridge over a gorge, and he jumped."

"Oh, shit," she said. "My God, that's . . . What a nightmare. But he survived the fall."

He nodded. "Some say it was a miracle, because he walked away, when the fall should have killed him. He walked all the way back to Middle Grove. Went straight to the bishop and prayed on his knees to be forgiven and submitted to baptism right away. After that, he embraced the faith with every fiber of his being. He gave a clock to Naomi—that's what a man does when he promises to marry. They settled down and had their kids and John was known to be a man of powerful faith. He always said the Lord gave him a second chance at life and so he intended to spend the rest of his days following the old laws. And he did, right up until he died."

"That's an incredible story. When your mother left—is that what drove him to want to take his own life?"

"Reckon so. And he had a good deal of sadness all his life. It was just his way. After our mother went away, his sadness took a deeper turn. I figure that was the trigger that led him to do it."

There was likely some kind of undiagnosed depression, Reese thought. "She simply left."

"She had a sadness in her, too. My father . . . I guess you could say he's not an easy man. My mother was a lot younger than him, and she . . . I just remember her crying a lot. She packed her bags one day and walked herself to the bus station. My father warned her that she would be shunned, and that brought her back. But she kept trying to leave, and finally one night, she did it."

Reese's heart ached for Caleb's family. The mother leaving, the brother's attempted suicide, a double murder. How much could they survive? "You've been through so much."

"Reckon so. But there was work to do, and after the bridge incident I had to watch over John, you know, make sure he wasn't going to try something crazy like that again."

"That's quite a burden." She thought about herself as she came of age. School, sports, friends. Parents admonishing her to make straight As, to earn perfect scores on the SAT, to get into an Ivy League school like they had. It was a lot of pressure, sure. But nothing like taking on a suicidal brother and a mother gone AWOL.

"I never considered it a burden."

"After your brother and his wife died, did your father not step up to help with the children?" she asked.

"I couldn't allow that."

And with those four small words, thought Reese, he had told her everything. Every blessed thing. *Not an easy man.*

"Where is your mother now?"

"She lives in Florida. Has another family."

"Are you in touch with her?"

"Not so much, although I'm not obliged to shun her. I've not submitted to baptism, so I'm not bound by the rules pertaining to shunning." He didn't offer more, even though she had questions stacked up in her brain like air traffic over O'Hare. Did his mother think about what she'd left behind? How did she live with herself?

She took a deep breath. "Your family is lucky to have you, Caleb. It all sounds incredibly hard."

"I get a lot of joy from Jonah and his sister, Hannah," he said simply. "Although Hannah is sixteen now, and a great mystery to me."

"She's sixteen and a girl," Reese pointed out. "That's her job."

"I hope she's getting on all right while I'm here."

"Have you spoken with her?"

He shook his head. "The phone is for emergency use. I sent her a postcard letting her know we'd be a while, here in the city."

"I can't even get my mind around that," Reese confessed. "She must be frantic."

"No, frantic is when a call comes in on the phone. If that phone never rings, then there's no emergency." He folded up the empty food containers and stood up. "Let's go see Jonah."

One of the things Reese was learning as a doctor was how to deal with other people's pain. She often met a patient on his worst day and had to absorb his fear and agony—and the terror and uncertainty of the family.

As they walked together along the paved parkway, they passed a horse and carriage rig taking tourists around. Another rig waited at the curb. A couple with a little kid sat in the ornately decorated carriage. The driver, in top hat, white shirt, and black pants with suspenders, was flicking the reins and urging the large black horse to move. The animal strained at its bit but appeared to be balking, holding one of its front hooves cocked at an angle. The driver snapped the reins again. "Bumbles," he said. "*Walk.*"

The horse shifted but didn't go forward. The driver reached for a worn leather crop.

Caleb strode over to the rig. "Excuse me," he said. "Looks like your horse might have an injury."

The driver frowned. "Who're you? And how is this any of your business?"

Caleb didn't reply but went around to the horse, making soft, soothing sounds with his mouth. He ran his hands over the animal's shoulder and down its leg. He palpated the lower limb, and the horse flinched. "Pretty sure Bumbles has a bowed tendon," he said.

"What the hell—" The driver glanced at his passengers. "I'll just be a minute, folks." He jumped down. "Bumbles is fine. He and I have been doing this a long time."

Caleb motioned him over. "Right here," he said, placing the guy's hand on the leg. "He's lame with pain. Feel the heat and swelling?"

"I— Yeah, maybe. It's been a hot day, is all."

"No, it's bowed. Could be the summer heat and fatigue. He could use better trimming, shoeing, and footing, too. It'd be a shame to force him to walk on this."

"Who the hell are you, a vet?"

"I know horses," Caleb said simply.

"Look, buddy, so do I. This is my livelihood. I take good care of Bumbles."

"He's going to need a break or it'll get bad," Caleb said. "He needs rest, cold packs, a pressure bandage, and herbs for the swelling. You got any devil's club or yucca ointment? And add some sulfur compounds to his feed."

"Sure, I'll get right on that," the driver said, making a sour expression.

Reese saw the man in the carriage lean over and say something to his wife. They got down and approached the driver. "We're going to pass on the ride," the man said. "Don't want to make your horse work if he's injured."

"Bumbles is fine," the driver said. "We'll take you for a nice ride."

"No, we wouldn't feel right doing that." The man handed him a twenty-dollar bill. "For your trouble."

"Hey now . . ." The driver hesitated. Then he took the money. "Thanks," he added, then shot a scowl at Caleb.

The little kid whined. The mom brought him over to Bumbles. "Give the horse a pet, Sidney," she said. "He has a sore leg, so we can't have a ride today."

The kid stopped whining and stroked the horse's cheek. "Bye, Bumbles. Feel better."

The driver turned to Caleb. "Hope you're happy now, buddy."

Reese handed him another twenty. "Take care of your horse. Please. We're not trying to cause any trouble."

"Yeah, well, you just did, lady."

"A bowed tendon takes six months to heal," Caleb said, seemingly impervious to the driver's irritation. "If you don't look after it, he could be lame for good."

"That's great," the driver said. "Just fucking great." He tore off his top hat and raked a hand through his hair. Then he looked at the horse and down at the cocked hoof. "Sure. Whatever. I have a good vet. I'll get it checked out."

"Hope so. He's a fine-looking horse."

"Have a nice evening," Reese said. She touched Caleb's arm. God, those muscles. "We should go."

He nodded a farewell at the driver, and they walked together toward the hospital.

"So," she said. "You know horses."

"I run a team at home, and I work at the stables at Grantham Farm up a ways toward the mountains—the Poconos."

Everyone in the city knew about Grantham Farm. Part theme park, part livestock facility, it was one of the places where the famous Budweiser Clydesdales were bred and trained.

"I've heard of it," Reese said, "but I've never been there. What do you do there?"

"I work with the horses, mainly. Training and breeding. From the time I was real little, I've always had a knack for managing livestock. Big draft animals like Belgians or Clydesdales tend to intimidate most English. A lot of Amish are accustomed to them because we use the big fellows for plowing and hauling on the farm."

It seemed so perfectly fitting, Reese thought, that Caleb Stoltz had a special gift, working with the immense Clydesdales. He hadn't said so, but she got the sense he was an expert handler. How could he not be, so big and graceful in a way she'd never seen before. There was magic in this man, she mused, knowing it was fanciful but unable to escape the idea.

"That's . . . remarkable," she said. Everything about him was remarkable. Getting to know him was like studying the changing facets of a jewel. Some things about him were perfectly simple and clear, yet she sensed a depth in his character she wanted to explore. He was guarded, though. She didn't blame him. Based on what he'd told her about his family, she now understood the peculiar sadness that haunted him. What was it like, growing up amid those multiple tragedies? How did he go on? How did the heart heal after a blow like that? It made her own background look like a fairy tale.

He was different in every possible way from the people she worked with, who were all driven, competitive, constantly rushing around. Earnestly handsome, with a body sculpted by hard, honest work, he was far more interesting to her than the slender residents and competitive interns she had dated in the past. This wasn't a date, though. It was so far from a date that she felt silly allow-ing the thought to cross her mind. She had nothing in common with this Amish farmer, though she found him as intriguing and baffling as he seemed to find her.

She couldn't deny that she felt different around him. More present. More centered. Lit up. Then she dismissed the feeling as hospital fatigue. End-of-shift ennui. The lure of forbidden fruit. He represented something natural and undisturbed—something that was beyond her reach.

Caleb had probably shared too much with Reese Pow-ell during supper and the walk to the hospital. For some reason he found her easy to talk to, and he'd never con-sidered himself much of a talker. The words had flowed from him with surprising ease as he told her about the things that had happened to his family.

Still, there were things he hadn't fully explained, such as the reason he was so utterly committed to raising his brother's children as John would have wanted. He hadn't told her the plans he'd set aside in order to help Jonah and Hannah. He didn't hold with whining.

Before all the trouble, Caleb had imagined another life for himself, a far different life. But the world had another path for him. The murder of John and Naomi had brought him reeling back to the farm. For the sake of the family, Caleb had abandoned the dreams he'd quietly nurtured for years. In the time it took for a man's finger to squeeze a trigger, his life had changed completely, radically, and permanently.

At the hospital, Reese led the way to the elevator. "Jo-nah's been moved to the peds wing of the patient care unit," she said. "That's good news. It means he's on the mend."

"Peds wing," he said. "What's that?"

"Pediatrics wing. He doesn't need all the monitoring of intensive care. This is the start of his recovery."

That, at least, sounded positive. As they walked down the wide, brightly lit corridor, Caleb slowed his pace, looking around the unfamiliar place. Rolling computer stations lined the hallway. Some of the doors to the patient rooms were decorated with homemade artwork and colorful get-well cards. Some of the doors, left ajar, offered glimpses of the patients. A few lay motionless and dull-eyed, staring at TV monitors. Others were animated and chatty, surrounded by shiny balloons and visitors bearing gifts. Still others were painfully ill or broken—a kid with a bandaged head, another hooked up to a breathing apparatus. In one room, he spied a pale, hairless child who lifted a thin hand in a wave, his bruised and earnest eyes filled with impossible hope.

Reese paused and turned to him. "This is where Jonah will be for the next several days."

"It's . . . nice, I guess." He studied her for a moment. She was like no one he'd ever met—nosy and smart, helpful and earnest, unapologetically bossy, and undeniably pretty. He couldn't set aside his intense curiosity about her, the urge not just to know her, but to invite her to know him in ways he had no business wanting. It was a cause of deep shame, because he ought to know better than to feel these things for an English woman, particularly when Jonah lay fighting for his life.

A doctor in a long white coat came along. He had a round, shiny face and a genial smile, a stuffed bear sticking out of one pocket and sneakers that lit up when he moved. "Reese Powell, as I live and breathe," he said. "I had to do a double take there for a sec. You're the image of your mother."

"Does that mean med school speeds up the aging process?" she asked.

"Oops, put my foot in it, didn't I, young man?" The doctor stuck out his hand. "Oliver Edwards."

"Caleb Stoltz."

"His nephew's a patient—Jonah Stoltz. We're just heading in to see him."

The doctor nodded. "Good seeing you, Reese. Give my best to your folks." He headed into the room with the bald kid. "Suzannah Banana," he said. "How's my girl?"

Caleb looked away. "I thought that was a boy, poor thing."

Reese started walking again. "Edwards is a great pediatric oncologist," she said. "She's in good hands."

"And he's acquainted with your mother?"

"They're colleagues. My folks are both physicians." She flashed her hospital badge at a passing aide. "They're strict with security here," she explained. "Most people on the floor know me. My parents are well known in this department."

"Because of their work?"

"Doctors Joanna and Hector Powell. A fertility specialist and neonatologist. They help couples who have trouble conceiving, and they help the newborns, too. When I was young, I imagined the babies like tiny embers, needing a miracle to fan the life into them. My parents have been able to save babies who were given the slimmest chances of survival—newborns who came too early or were born with problems." She hesitated. "I was one of those babies, so tiny at birth that I fit in the palm of my father's hand."

When she talked about herself and her family, her deep brown eyes took on an extra spark. "You'd never know it to look at you," he said.

She smiled. "I have my parents to thank for that."

The smile darted away, as if she'd caught herself doing something wrong. "You could say I owe them my life—literally. I admired them so much, growing up. I never questioned their plans for me—to be a doctor, join their practice. But every once in a while, I feel guilty when I catch myself wondering if this is the right path for me. Of course it's the right path. Isn't it?"

She would probably be surprised if she knew how often Caleb asked the same question about his own life. "I reckon you need to answer that for yourself."

Reese gestured around the ward. "One day, these will be my patients, assuming I follow the path my parents have mapped out for me."

"They want you to be a doctor to children, then."

"A pediatric surgeon, to be specific. The plan is to expand their practice to include a specialist in pediatric surgery—namely, me. All it'll take is an extra five years of general surgery residency followed by two more of residency training in pediatric surgery, board certification . . . and then I'll be prepared."

"That's a lot of preparation."

She sighed. "Prepared for what, I sometimes wonder. For my life, or for theirs?"

"Are they two different things?"

"Good question," she said. "I sometimes struggle with my parents' expectations for me. But I do love pediatrics. It's hard, though. Being in these competitive programs is a bit like being dropped into a shark tank with a bleeding wound."

Stopping abruptly, she said, "I think we've found our boy."

No balloons or cards festooned the door of Jonah's room, just a bracket filled with charts with his name on them. There were two beds separated by a pleated blue drape. Bed number one was empty, made up with pains-taking neatness, its tautly pulled linens and blankets awaiting the next patient. Reese pulled the drape aside to reveal bed number two. Also empty.

Caleb felt a stab of alarm. "Where's Jonah?"

She studied the heaped linens, the notes scrawled on the whiteboard. "REC stands for recreational therapy." Stepping outside the room, she indicated a sign pointing to the patients' lounge. "Maybe . . . Let's check that out," she said, leading the way.

They passed a physical therapist guiding a boy with a thick white belt and metal walker. The boy's head was shaved, and there was a thick scar curving over his ear. A weary couple stood outside one of the rooms, the woman sagging against the man's chest. Around the corner was the lounge, an airy open space with tall windows, kid-size furniture, and shelves filled with books, toys, and games. The floor was marked with a hopscotch diagram and cartoon ants marching in a line. Several little ones were curled in the laps of volunteers or family members. Older kids sat at a round table playing a card game.

"There he is," Caleb said, pointing to the far corner. Jonah's haystraw hair stuck out every which way. He wore a type of apron and thick socks, bright green. Caleb touched Reese's shoulder. "What's he doing?"

"Looks like they're playing a video game," she said.

Jonah and the health aide seemed absorbed in the flat screen on the table in front of them. It displayed a super-hero character zooming through a maze of some sort.

Caleb hurried over to him, his heart lifting at the sight of his nephew. "Jonah, you're up out of bed."

The screen froze on a cartoon image. "Hi, Uncle Caleb. They said I can get up if somebody's with me."

The aide stood. "I'm Tammy. Jonah and I were having a game of Dr. Boom."

Caleb introduced himself. "Thanks for looking after him."

"It's real good fun," Jonah said, his blue eyes brighter than they'd been the last time Caleb saw him. The facial gashes—Reese called them lacerations—already seemed to be healing. The thickly bandaged stump rested in a sling. "We're fighting diseases and winning points."

"That sounds cool," Reese said. "Hey, Jonah. Remember me?"

He stood up, nearly losing his balance. Tammy gently steadied him. Caleb reminded himself that dealing with the arm loss was going to take time.

"You were in the ER," Jonah said politely. "With the black doctor who had a gold earring."

She smiled. "That's Jack. I'm impressed you remember."

"And then you came to see me in the other place."

"I did. I bet you're meeting all kinds of new people around here."

"Thanks for playing Dr. Boom with me, Jonah," said Tammy. "I'll see you later, okay? I'll come get you when it's time to go back to your room."

He nodded. "Thank you, Tammy."

After she had gone, Reese gestured at an empty table with some drawing paper and crayons, and they sat down together. In the stubby chair, Caleb had to fold his knees up to his shoulders. "Just my size, neh?" he asked, coaxing a brief smile from Jonah.

"Just *my* size," Jonah said. "Everything here is made for kids."

"What was your day like, Jonah?" Reese asked.

"They brought my food on a tray. They rolled the tray

right up to my bed, and a man called an oatie sat with me to make sure I could eat with my good hand."

"An oatie?" Caleb frowned.

"Yep. The letters were sewn onto his jacket—O-T."

"I think it stands for occupational therapist," said Reese. "I'm glad you're already getting lots of help. Did you like the food?"

He nodded. "There was a sandwich and some berries and some bright green stuff called Jell-O."

"Ah. You probably thought it was an alien life-form."

"Like an alien from outer space?"

"It's very mysterious."

Caleb was glad to see the brightness in his eyes. The boy had a tough road ahead, but for the moment, he was in a pretty good frame of mind.

"I looked at the TV, Uncle Caleb," Jonah said in a confessional tone.

Caleb lifted one eyebrow. "Did you like it?"

"Yes. And when I didn't like what was on, I just pushed a button and changed to another program. I watched a story about Robin Hood. After a while, I got tired of looking at it, though. A lady gave me some more books to read. There's plenty of books here, lots more than programs on the TV."

"You like reading books?" asked Reese.

He nodded. "They gave me a stand I can set the book on so I don't have to hold it in two hands." He cut his gaze down and away as if slightly ashamed.

"How are you feeling?" Reese asked. "Does your arm hurt? Does anything hurt?"

He held himself very still, keeping his eyes downcast. Finally, he said, "I don't rightly know. How can my arm hurt if it's not there anymore?"

"Well, your brain has to adjust to the idea that there's been a big change. While you're here, lots of people will be coming to see you so they can help you with the healing process, and that includes helping you understand your feelings about it. Does that make sense?"

Jonah frowned slightly. "I don't much like talking about feelings."

"Then you don't have to. Maybe give it a try and see if it helps. When people lose a limb, there's a very big shock at first, and then a lot of sadness. And that's normal. But I can tell you it gets better. Just not right away. Not as fast as you wish it would."

Caleb liked her manner with the boy. She was kind without seeming forced. She was honest.

"When can I go home?" Jonah asked, finally looking up at Caleb.

"We have to let the doctors say when. You're doing real good, so maybe it'll be soon," Caleb told him.

"Is home really far away?" the boy asked. "Did you come in the buggy?"

"It's too far for the buggy. I'm staying in the city while you're here. Reese introduced me to a friend named Leroy who is letting me stay at his place. It's a real quick walk from here so I can come to see you anytime."

"What about the farm?" Jonah's brow knit. "Who's looking after Jubilee?"

"I imagine Hannah can manage your dog for a bit." Caleb leaned forward, resting his elbows on his knees. "The neighbors will help with the livestock. It's only temporary, little man."

"I wish I could see Jubilee. And Hannah." Jonah hastily added, "And Grandfather, too."

"How would you like to write a letter to your sister? I bet she'd be glad to hear from you."

Jonah's face brightened. "That's a good idea."

"I'll get some writing paper and a pencil," Reese said.

"You can work right here at this table." She went and rummaged through a bin filled with art supplies and came back with a few things. "So, depending on how you like to write, you might have to make a few adjustments. Caleb said you're right-handed, but maybe you're used to holding the paper with your left hand as you write. Here's some Scotch tape to hold it in place."

He studied the roll of tape. "Why is it called Scotch tape? Does it come from Scotland?"

"Ha! No. That's a good question. I don't know the reason, but I'll find out."

"I can tell you what 3M stands for—Minnesota Mining and Manufacturing," Caleb said.

Jonah shot him a grin. "Uncle Caleb knows stuff."

"Clearly he does." She set a blank sheet of paper in front of Jonah, then placed a bit of tape at the top and bottom. "How's that?"

"It'll do." Jonah picked up the pencil. "Thank you, Reese." He bent over his letter and began to write in careful strokes.

Reese and Caleb went to the window and stood looking out at the rooftops with compressors and terraced gravel surfaces. Beyond those lay the river, and to the east, the city center with its streets laid out in a grid. She pointed out a few landmarks—the riverwalk and university district, the old town with Independence Hall amid a long strip of greenery in the urban park.

"I appreciate you talking to Jonah," Caleb told her quietly. "He and his sister are real close, so this letter will help. He seems a bit more like himself this evening."

"I imagine he'll have lots of ups and downs. He's a fantastic kid, and he'll get through this."

Though she'd mentioned that she was questioning her parents' plan for her to be a children's surgeon, she was good with Jonah. Maybe it wouldn't be such a bad plan after all.

"How do you spell 'artificial'?" Jonah asked, looking over at them.

Caleb spelled the word aloud, and the boy gave him a thumbs-up.

"And how do you spell 'prosthesis'?" he asked a moment later.

Caleb and Reese looked at each other. "I'll give it a shot," she said and spelled it out for him. "Boynton County Spelling Bee champion, two years in a row," she added smugly. "You're looking at her."

"Hannah used to beat everybody at school in spelling," Jonah said. "Even the teacher, sometimes. She got a prize for best speller at her graduation."

"Just sixteen, and she already graduated?" asked Reese. "I bet she's really smart."

"Schooling ends after the eighth grade," Caleb said.

Her eyes widened in surprise. "Oh. That's . . . I'm not sure what to say."

"Too bad?" he suggested.

"I suppose it depends on what a person wants in life," she said.

"In our community, folks don't believe youngsters need a lot of schooling," Caleb said.

"And if they want to continue their education? I mean, I'm not judging, but . . . good lord. Eighth grade?"

She *was* judging, Caleb observed. "Further schooling is not prohibited. Not encouraged, either," he said. He watched his nephew turn the page over and retape it to the table, his one hand working nimbly. "Guess it could have been worse. It could've been his right hand."

A few minutes later, Jonah held up his letter. "Finished," he said. "I drew a picture on the back."

It was a depiction of a robotic arm like the ones in the brochures someone had left for them to look through. Next to the arm was a person with short dark hair, wearing a short white coat and a stethoscope. She had large eyes with long lashes and her mouth set in a straight line.

"Is that me?" asked Reese.

"Uh-huh. I'm not so good at drawing people."

"I wouldn't say that." She touched the paper briefly. "This kind of gives me a twinge in my heart. Do I forget to smile?"

"No, I'm not so good at drawing mouths, either."

"Well, for your sake, I'm going to work on smiling more."

Jonah turned the paper over. "You can read what I wrote if you want."

"Sure," said Reese, looking over his shoulder. "You have very nice handwriting."

"Thank you. I like penmanship practice."

"How about you read it to us?" Caleb suggested.

"All right." Jonah sat up straight in his chair. "'Dear Hannah, my arm got cut off in the hospital. It was so bad hurt in the shredder that it had to come off, all the way off and now there's a big bandage around the stump. I'm getting a new arm called an artificial limb, or a prosthesis. They say it's like a robot's arm and I'll get used to it. How is Jubilee doing? I miss that dog something fierce and I hope I can see her soon. I also miss you and I wish I could see you. And also Grandfather. Sincerely, your brother, Jonah.'" He finished reading and looked up. "Is that okay?"

Caleb felt a deep, almost painful affection for the boy. "It sure is, my man. Hannah will be grateful to hear from you."

"I can put it in the mail for you right away if you like," Reese said. "The post office is closed by now, but tomorrow is my day off work."

"That would be fine, Reese," said Jonah. "I'm obliged to you."

"What do you usually do on your day off?" Caleb asked. "Besides go to the post office?"

She shifted her gaze around the room. "I wish I could tell you I take kiteboarding lessons or cook gourmet meals, but the sad truth is, when I'm not practicing to be a doctor, I'm a very boring person. I study for exams, fill out residency forms, and do errands, including going to the post office. It's kind of pathetic."

"What's kiteboarding?" Jonah asked. "It sounds fun."

"It *looks* fun, but I've never tried it. You stand on a surfboard and harness yourself to a giant kite, and the wind takes you on a ride."

"I'd like to do that," Jonah said. Then he glanced at the thick bandage. "Can I do it with one arm?"

Caleb's heart ached anew. This would always be Jonah's first question from here on out—*Can I do it with one arm?*

Tammy came back to the lounge. "Hey, Jonah. Time to head back to your room. Your supper's waiting. Then evening rounds and then lights out."

Jonah caught Caleb's eye as he stood up, pressing his hand on the table to steady himself. "They never actually turn the lights out," he whispered. "Not ever."

"They'll dim the lights a bit more than they did in the SICU," Tammy explained.

"It doesn't ever get totally dark in the city. Not like it is at home." Caleb thought about the expansive feeling he got, standing in the pitch dark in Middle Grove, looking up at the stars.

Jonah was talkative on the way back to his room. In addition to video games, he had already discovered vending machines, streaming music, Harry Potter books, and televised baseball games. Nearly everything here was new to him. "Ever hear of the Magna Carta?" he asked.

"I have," Caleb said. "What do you know about it?"

"Lots," Jonah said. "I read about it in a book from the lending cart. It's called the Magna Carta Libertatum, and in English that means Great Charter. It's famous because it's a written record of laws and the rights of man."

"You're getting a lot of reading done, tadpole," Caleb said. "That's good."

"You never told me your nephew is a genius," Reese said. "You get smarter every time I talk to you."

Jonah's ears turned red. He wasn't used to compliments, especially from pretty girls.

Reese and Caleb stayed through evening rounds. "See that doctor?" she whispered to him, lightly touching his arm and indicating a group of people coming down the hall. "That's the attending on call. He's a Cuban guy named Jimenez. You can tell he's the attending because he's wearing a full-length coat. The others with him are third-years. Jimenez is a good one. They told you it's a teaching hospital, right?"

He nodded slightly. Her hand rested like a small bird on his arm. He wondered if she could feel the tension in his muscles. And buried deep inside his worry about Jonah was something else—an unbidden attraction he had no business feeling but couldn't deny.

She seemed to notice she was holding on to his arm, and her hand flitted away.

Dr. Jimenez walked into the room with long strides, shadowed by a gaggle of the short-coated third-years. Caleb stepped forward and introduced himself. "I'm Jonah's uncle," he said. "If you don't mind, I'll be staying for the visit."

The doctor called Jimenez gave a simple nod and

said, "Thank you for being here. We're taking good care of . . ." He glanced at the white marker board on the wall. "Of Jonah."

The third-years seemed curious about Caleb, particularly the women. That was something Caleb hadn't been able to ignore since being here. Women tended to stare at him, not in the way of tourists who came to the general merchandise shop back home, but in a way any red-blooded man would recognize.

Reese must have noticed the staring, too, as she gave him a nudge and whispered, "You seem to have a peculiar effect on them."

He felt his ears turn as red as Jonah's. "Don't be a ninny," he muttered. He didn't dislike it, but with Jonah so bad off, all this female attention didn't seem right. At the very least, it was a distraction.

Reese was a distraction, too, but in a different way. In a way that kept him thinking about her, even when his mind was supposed to be on helping Jonah. In the small room, she stood with her back to him, pressing close to make room for the doctors. Her hair smelled like flowers, and there was a stray curl at the nape of her neck, dark against the pale, delicate skin.

He reminded himself of the reason he was here—to listen and observe and try to figure out what was best for Jonah, not to make friends. Not to have thoughts about Reese Powell.

The head doctor called on one of the student doctors to present the case. Grasping his digital tablet like Moses on the mountain, the young fellow pushed his spectacles up his nose as his gaze flickered around the room.

Reese turned to whisper in his ear, "Nerves. He reminds me of me last year, when I was new."

"If he's as smart as you, he'll get over it," Caleb whispered back, bending to speak into her ear. Standing so close to her was an exercise in self-restraint, for sure.

She turned again and looked up at him, her voice just a breath against his chest. "Plunging into the world of medicine is kind of like diving into icy water—breathtaking, barely survivable. Panic-inducing. The stakes are so high."

"I don't want anybody panicking over Jonah," Caleb murmured.

"Dr. Jimenez would never let that happen. But oral case presentations are hard. Lots of pressure to get it right, because it's the way doctors share the patient's story with other doctors. It takes practice. You have to explain the patient's issues, the goal being to find the best way to care for him."

The young man presenting Jonah's case spoke in a nervous monotone and kept referring to the admissions notes on his tablet. "This is Jonah Stoltz, an eleven-year-old boy, hospital day three, being treated following irreparable loss of blood supply and function of the arm following acute trauma from the blades of an agricultural shredder. At twenty-eight hours post-op, the patient was moved from the surgical ICU to the pediatric unit. Patient appears well, states injuries are feeling better."

Caleb clenched his jaw, his mind flashing on Jonah's arm—irreparable loss of blood supply. Those images wouldn't leave him for a very long time.

"He shouldn't look down," Reese whispered. "That's a no-no with Dr. Jimenez. He's letting his nerves get the better of him. I feel bad for the guy."

"Is that a problem for Jonah?" Caleb was interested in protocol, but his main concern was for his nephew.

"Not a problem. He seems to understand the clinical information, but he's struggling to be concise."

". . . vitals are normal, pulse range sixty to eighty beats

per minute, BP one hundred over sixty, O_2 saturation ninety-nine on room air . . ."

"Let's hear from Dr. Grandjean," said the attending, rescuing the previous doctor from the pained recitation.

A woman wearing a neat headband, her scrubs and white coat crisply pressed, stepped forward like a Girl Scout who knew all the rules. "Jonah's health history is remarkable only in the sense that it's unremarkable. He's had no major childhood illnesses and his immunizations are up to date."

Reese glanced at Caleb, a question in her eyes.

"It's not against Ordnung," he whispered.

"He lives in Middle Grove," the woman continued, "an Amish community in Carbon County, north of here near the Poconos. His family observes Amish traditions. He has a sister named Hannah, who is sixteen, and they live with their uncle and legal guardian, Caleb Stoltz." She paused to turn toward Caleb to acknowledge him with a glance. He nodded ever so slightly. Sure, he was Jonah's guardian. "Legal" was pushing it a tad.

"Jonah's parents are both deceased," the student doctor added.

Now they were probably all imagining the entire Stoltz family getting shredded like cornstalks. Caleb wondered how much of this Jonah was taking in. Judging by the boy's somber expression, he was taking it all in.

The attending physician looked Jonah in the eye and said, "Although this young man's history isn't remarkable, his recovery has been." Jimenez enumerated the technical aspects of the case, yet the whole time, he addressed Jonah with a warm smile. "All this nonsense we've been jabbering about, my friend, means you're far ahead of the curve. That's something to be proud of."

Jonah craned his neck and his gaze flicked to Caleb,

who offered a reassuring smile. "That's a good kind of pride," he said, then repeated it in German.

Dr. Jimenez and his followers left, each sparing a smile for Jonah as they filed out of the room.

Caleb walked over to the bed. "You push this button if you need anything at all, neh? Even just to say hello. The folks here know how to send for me and I'll come right away."

"*Ja. Ich verstehe.*" His nephew yawned and snuggled down into the blue cotton blanket. Caleb read to him from the Harry Potter book, but after a few moments, the boy couldn't keep his eyes open. "Good night, my little man," Caleb murmured. He switched to their dialect and added, "Sleep well." Then he placed a hand on Jonah's head, brushing his thumb ever so gently across his forehead. "Sweet dreams."

Jonah's smile was brave and heartbreaking. "G'night, Uncle Caleb."

Reese stayed quiet as they left the hospital. Caleb was surprised to see a sheen of tears in her eyes. "Sorry," she said, noticing his look. "It's . . . this is hard. I know that one of these days, I'm going to have to get used to this—seeing a patient's pain and his family's fear. But today is not that day."

In his community, there wasn't a lot of showing feelings, and even less of talking about them. He wondered if it was the same with hospital folks. Unlike many Amish, he didn't mind a show of emotion, not one bit. It just seemed honest and human.

"It was strange to hear them talking about him like that. They have a lot of information about Jonah, but it's not who Jonah is."

She dabbed at her eyes. "Tell me something about your nephew."

A softness came over Caleb, the familiar wave of sentiment that always struck him when he thought of Jonah. "There's plenty to tell. He's a boy who loves his dog and can whistle louder than a train. He knows how to make a fire with only flint and steel. He has a laugh that sounds like music, and he can do several birdcalls. His specialty is the whippoorwill." He paused, feeling a prickly warmth in his throat as he swallowed hard. "He's a boy whose entire future changed in a split second."

He didn't usually speak in so forthright a fashion, unfiltered and honest in his feelings, but something in her manner invited him to show his heart. She was a hazard to him in that way, for sure.

7

Reese awoke with a start, sitting straight up in bed and pressing both fists to her chest. Mornings happened this way sometimes. A lot of the time. She burst from sleep with a feeling of panic so sharp it felt like a heart attack. She was used to the unpleasantness by now. The panic attacks had started when she was in college and had continued unabated through medical school, intense but unfocused, impossible to escape.

The racing heart, the lungs clawing for air, the cold sweat were familiar demons, erupting from a feeling that she had forgotten something or missed something or failed in some crucial way. Over time, she had taught herself a calming routine—self-talk, yoga, meditation, vile-tasting herbal teas, outright denial—but the techniques didn't always work.

The one thing she didn't do was tell someone. She knew the condition was common and that there were effective treatments, but reaching out for help seemed to be another kind of failure, not to mention a source of worry for her parents. They were so ambitious and so successful. They had given her everything and the moon and then some. The last thing she wanted was to disappoint them.

She got out of bed and dropped into her favorite yoga pose—downward-facing dog—feeling a rush of blood to the head. Closing her eyes, she took a breath deep into her lungs and held it there for five beats of her heart. Then she let it out slowly for another five beats. She repeated the sequence ten more times, bringing herself back into balance.

Shaking off a nagging exasperation, she took a hurried shower, forced a coffee through a sealed pod, and drank it black. Then she scrawled one more thing on her to-do list: *Buy milk.*

What do you do on your day off?

Caleb's simple question had lodged itself under her skin. She had a meeting up in New Hope to talk about a residency program, but that wasn't until much later. Today, she was determined to not be boring. Life was supposed to be interesting, exciting, unpredictable. Some of the best doctors she knew played piano or wrote novels or created pottery sculptures. She should take a glass-blowing class, or go rock climbing in the Poconos, or attend a cutting-edge performance at Jazz Works. Only to herself would she admit that all she really wanted to do was hang out with Caleb Stoltz. He was the most interesting thing she had come across in a very long time.

Her phone rang, and she jumped. Joanna Powell, MD. "Hey, Mom."

"What's your plan for your day off?"

"Funny you should ask. I was thinking of going rock climbing, and then to aerial yoga, and after that I was going to hang out with an Amish horse handler."

Her mom laughed. "Right. So I had a cancellation at lunch. Let's meet at the Flying Dutchman around noon. We can go over your strategy for the Match."

Again. The Match had dominated their conversations for the past year or longer. "When did you stop listening to me, Mom?"

"I always listen."

"But you don't hear me."

"Fine. I'm all ears. What do you want me to hear?"

"That I'm having second thoughts about the Match."

"Whoa, Nellie. Too late for that. You're nearly there. All you need to do is figure out the best ranking for your residency programs."

"I realize that, but—"

"Then we should definitely get together and talk things through. If not lunch, then drinks later? We have dinner plans with the Josephsons. You remember them, don't you? He's a professor emeritus at Drexel. And she's a Guggenheim fellow . . ."

While her mother nattered on, Reese wandered over to the window. She watched pedestrians streaming up and down the avenue, hurrying to and from work. A tall man in black and white instantly caught her eye. Caleb was heading for the hospital. It was not only his height that made him stand out; it was the long strides and focused energy with which he moved that drew her attention. She could hear her mother's voice, but the words blended together, a constant stream of verbiage that she had heard all her life.

During a pause in her mother's monologue, she said, "I can't make it to lunch. Maybe another day, okay? Give my love to Daddy."

She rang off, grabbed her things, and dashed out the door. *Do something interesting.* Fine. She was all over that. First stop, a kombucha bar that featured live sitar music and a meditative chant.

She lasted about forty minutes, her brain refusing to cooperate with the chant, which urged her to free her mind and empty her thoughts. All she could think about was work, and Caleb Stoltz, and the Match, and Caleb Stoltz, and her mother, and Caleb . . . Having failed to find her spiritual center, she stepped outside and took out her phone to call a friend. Yes, she should call a friend and suggest a . . . what? A get-together over coffee? A drive to the country?

Yes, it was a good plan. With a swipe of her finger, she slid through the list of contacts. There was one problem. To her great embarrassment, she was woefully short on friends. She had work people. She had colleagues. Fellow students in her program. She went on occasional random dates that at best left her with a temporary warm glow and at worst served only to magnify her essential aloneness. There simply wasn't anyone she could legitimately call a friend.

Aha. Lorraine Kavorkian, whose singularly unfortunate name had sparked all manner of comment. She'd been a mentor through Reese's first year of med school, and they'd been friends ever since—the kind of friends who were too busy to get together. Reese called her, but—no surprise—it went straight to voice mail. "This is Dr. Lorraine Kavorkian—no relation; it's a different spelling. If this is an emergency, hang up and dial 911. Otherwise, leave me a message."

"It's Reese Powell, no emergency, just wondering if you'd like to hang out today. Short notice, I know . . ." She left her number and rang off, doubtful that Lorraine would call her back.

She thought of another prospect, Didi Cobb, her best friend from middle school, who had reconnected with her recently on a social media site. "So, hey," said the voice-mail message. "I never answer my phone and I don't check voice mail."

"Welcome to the club," Reese muttered. "I don't, either."

"Send me a text, K?" concluded Didi's voice.

Reese moved on. The final prospect was Trini Sizemore, a career librarian who had invited Reese to join her monthly book club, a social circle of well-read women who were passionate about literature and wine. Reese read all the books, but almost never managed to attend the meetings. And it was her loss, because the club members always served incredible appetizers and desserts. When her turn to host had come around, she'd been so appalled at the state of her apartment and kitchen that she'd booked a private salon at the Hotel Geneva and had the event catered. It turned out to be the ideal way to alienate a group of women who often struggled to make ends meet.

But Trini had been super nice, and she had amazing taste in books.

To Reese's surprise, Trini picked up after a couple of rings. "Reese? Hey, stranger. Long time no see."

"Hey, yourself. Listen, this is very spur of the moment, but I was just wondering if you'd like to get together later today."

"Gosh, that sounds fantastic," Trini said. "I would so love to catch up. Wow, it's been a long time, hasn't it? A year at least. But . . ."

The inevitable *but*. "You're probably busy," Reese said.

"I am, like you wouldn't believe. Remember Bill, my barely adequate boyfriend?"

"You mentioned him a few times. Did he get upgraded to adequate?"

"No. He got upgraded to complete asshole and I broke up with him. But he had a friend—Jory—and he's amazing. We fell in love and got married and had a baby, all in the past year."

Reese choked back her surprise. "Trini, that's great. And a baby. Wow, you didn't waste any time."

"When you know it's right, you don't hesitate. Timothy was born at St. Rocco's, and he's great. Five weeks old yesterday. I'm completely overwhelmed—in the best possible way. But all this domestic bliss definitely puts a damper on my spontaneity."

"Well, I'm thrilled for you," said Reese.

"Thanks. It all happened so fast. We had a getaway wedding, just the two of us and our parents in Bermuda, and then I got pregnant right away—who saw that coming, at my age?—and here I am! On top of everything else, we just bought a house out in Wayne, and it's a fixer-upper. I feel guilty about not letting my friends know."

"Don't you dare feel guilty. Seriously, my hat is off to you. Sounds as if the pieces fell into place and you went for it. I'm going to remember that just in case some pieces fall my way. You're a great reminder that there's more to life than studying and work."

"Pieces will fall," Trini promised. "You just don't get to say when, or how, or with whom, so keep an eye out. Makes things interesting. Listen—hear that?" She paused, and the sound of a bleating lamb came through the phone.

Reese sighed. "Hi, Timothy. I hope I get to meet you one of these days."

"Let's make it happen. Sorry, I have to go now. I—"

"Of course. Give me a call when things settle down. Talk to you soon." Reese hung up. "And by 'soon,' I mean probably never."

She studied the kombucha she'd bought. It tasted vile, but she'd paid nine bucks for it, so she choked it down as she walked home in defeat.

Leroy was in the foyer, getting his mail.

"What's up?" he asked. "You look as if you just lost your best friend."

"Worse than that," she said. "I've come to the realization that I don't actually *have* a best friend. I don't really have any friends."

"What am I, chopped liver?"

"You're my neighbor. And a guy. I'm supposed to have girlfriends, and we're supposed to go out for drinks and talk about men and share all our secrets, the way they do on the medical TV shows."

"That's why you became a doctor, because you actually thought it was like *that*?" He gave a bark of laughter. "Joke's on you." He tucked the stack of mail under one arm and gave her a brief hug with the other. "Come on. You're just feeling sorry for yourself. I'm your friend."

"You're my work friend," she pointed out, sinking deeper into the swamp of self-pity. "A best friend is someone you've known all your life, someone you've shared all your secrets with. I didn't even know you grew up Amish."

"Listen, I just finished a shift, and I have the rest of the day off. Let's hang out."

Really? Hang out with Leroy? They didn't hang out; they were neighbors. "You need to sleep."

"You're more entertaining than sleep."

Reese smiled. "I'm whining."

"I'm a PT. I'm used to whining."

She thought for a minute. Looked out at the beautiful day. "I have a brilliant idea. Meet me down here in ten?"

"Now I *know* I want to be your best friend," Leroy said when they entered the remote parking garage, which was located six blocks from their apartment building. "You have a car. How come you never told me you have a car?"

"I generally don't work that into a conversation. I don't drive it much and it's a pain to park."

"Poor little rich girl."

"Knock it off." She walked to her designated space and touched the key fob to unlock it.

"And it's a freaking convertible," Leroy said. "A Mini Cooper. Damn, Reese. If you'd take people for a ride in this rig, you'd definitely have more friends."

"How diplomatic of you to say. Let's hope the battery hasn't died. It's been so long since I've driven anywhere. A car is pretty useless in the city, as I'm sure you know."

"True. But *this* car." He settled into the passenger seat and gave a fist pump when the engine turned over with a healthy chug. With the touch of a button, the convertible top lifted and folded down on itself.

"It's a hand-me-down from my dad," she said, fastening her seat belt. "The perks of being an only child."

"Where are we going?"

"Someplace interesting."

"That narrows it down."

She found her way through the snarls of traffic around the Old City and merged onto the riverside parkway. Philly was an urban patchwork of elegance and blight. The grandeur of the historic district gave way to the Strawberry Mansion area and Fairmount Park, a transitional area reaching for gentrification. The Colonial- and Federal-era brick turned quickly to block after block of exhausted grit, and finally suburban sprawl. There was a charmless uniformity to the areas north of the city, as though a committee had determined what success should look like and patterned the neighborhoods after it—iron lampposts, carriage houses, wrought-iron gates, and tree-lined driveways.

They passed a staid-looking enclave of meticulously maintained neoclassical homes. Each bastion of brick and stone was surrounded by lavish gardens and lawns with placid ponds and self-conscious statuary. "I grew up there," she said, gesturing at the area.

"In Gladwyne? Whoa, that's swanky."

She flashed on a memory of shady autumn walks with Juanita, piano recitals in preternaturally quiet community halls and churches, catered backyard picnics her parents hosted for their colleagues around their perfectly symmetrical, spotless swimming pool.

"I don't know about swanky, but it's my original 'hood." On a whim, she turned down a shady boulevard and trolled slowly past the well-kept homes. "That's our house." She pointed out a sprawling Greek revival home set back on a manicured lawn.

"Looks beautiful here, Reese," said Leroy. "Your folks must be squillionaires. Do they still live there?" He craned his neck, looking back at the park-surrounded mansion.

"No, they're in the city now in a big high-rise. They wanted to be closer to the hospital and their practice."

"It must've been fun, growing up here."

"It was. I remember running around with my friends, riding bikes . . ."

"See. You do have friends," he pointed out.

"Had. We've gone in different directions. It all seems so long ago. My parents sent me off to boarding school for high school."

"Oh," he said. "How was that?"

She wasn't sure how to characterize the school for him. "Ah, the Lawrenceville School. I suppose you could call it a lifestyle choice as much as an education. Is it bad that I actually liked it better than I liked living at home?"

"You tell me."

"I used to feel guilty about that, but I don't anymore. It's the sort of place where people send their kids so they'll get into Ivy League colleges."

"Did it work?" he asked.

She'd earned her BS degree from Princeton and was about to get her MD from Penn. "Yeah," she said. "It worked. How about you, Leroy? Where did you go to school?"

He chuckled. "Higher education wasn't a priority for my family. Amish, remember."

"Yes, Caleb told me the Amish typically finish school after eighth grade."

"That's right. Lucky me. I'm from a large family, so the quicker we went to work, the better for the family."

"I used to fantasize about belonging to a big clan, like the Swiss Family Robinson."

"Trust me," he said. "It's not all it's cracked up to be. Not in my family, anyway."

"What was it like, then?"

He was quiet for a moment. Then he said, "Life centers around farming, family, and faith. There's a low tolerance for dissent. I was a misfit. I wanted to be out in the world, and I knew it would be impossible to have it both ways. I had to choose between the life I want and the family I love. They keep me at arm's length."

"Leroy, I'm so sorry. You must miss them."

"Sometimes. I'm okay now. Where are we going, by the way?"

"New Hope. About an hour's drive from here."

"Oh. Why? What's in New Hope?"

"It was either there or Jim Thorpe. I thought New Hope sounded nicer."

"Oh," he said again. "Nicer for what? Besides a *Star Wars* movie."

"For doing something interesting on my day off," she explained.

"Why the sudden preoccupation with being interesting?"

"I had a wake-up call. I've been on a treadmill for years—school and work, reaching the next rung on the ladder." Reese felt funny saying so aloud, but she couldn't deny the sense of discontent that had been creeping up on her for far too long. She was growing disenchanted with urbanized, mechanized, high-pressure medical care—and that was just in her professional life. Her personal life had emptied out as well. Dating and sex had become as rote and routine as daily rounds. "I want the magic back," she told Leroy. "And how bad is it that I'm jaded so early in the process?"

"It's the battle fatigue of med school," he said, ever the voice of reason. "Once you get through each rotation and find the right residency match, your attitude will improve and you'll discover a Zen-like calm. Trust me, I've been around docs long enough to know."

"I want you to be right," she said. "My whole career is focused on healing people so they can live their lives. And in the meantime, I worry that I forgot what Zen-like calm looks like."

"Let's see if New Hope delivers, then." He tipped back his head and smiled up at the summer sky. "This is some ride, Reese. Your life does not suck."

"Glad you think so." She hesitated, wavering about whether or not to level with him about her plan. Yes, she thought. If he was truly her friend, he'd understand. "I have an ulterior motive for going to New Hope."

"Aha. I'm not going to like it, am I?"

"There's a rural residency program at the regional hospital there. I set up a meeting with the two preceptors who run it."

"So it's a work thing. On your day off."

"But it might be a really excellent work thing." She told him what she'd learned about the residency program.

It had been founded by an elderly family practitioner, Dr. Mose Shrock, a preceptor with deep Mennonite roots. The program's mission was to raise the standard of care in rural areas. As a resident at the small level-one hospital, she could live and train in a remote, rural community, learning the old ways of a country doctor in a practice with endless variety.

"Rural medicine? Seriously? Your parents will disown you."

Her stomach twisted. "You're probably right. It might not be right for me, but I won't know unless I check it out."

With the radio playing hits from the nineties, they rolled into a tiny town loaded with charm. There was a main street filled with cafés and antiques shops, an ancient canal lined with paths for bikes and pedestrians, all surrounded by a brilliant canopy of summer foliage. They parked and got out of the car, surveying the scenery.

Families and couples were strolling about, enjoying the sunshine. "Wow, I really do need to get out more," she said.

"What do your folks do for fun?"

"They go to seminars. Save lives. Win awards. Fellowships. That sort of thing. When I was a kid, we used to take two vacations a year. One to a decadent place like Capetown or Paris, and the other to a place in the world that needs help, like a hospital in Lesotho or Bhutan."

"Sounds amazing to me."

"It is. My parents are good people and good doctors. They gave me every advantage, and I know how incredible that is. Sometimes, though . . ." She let her voice trail off.

"Sometimes what?"

"I don't know. Sometimes I feel as if I'm going for their dream. Not my own. They exert incredible influence on me, and I'm so enmeshed in their world that I'm not even sure what my dream is. I know what it's not. I don't dream about a brick tract mansion and well-behaved kids who are scheduled down to the last minute of the day."

"There. I heard it. You want kids."

She thought for a moment. Watched a little boy running around and laughing with a stick in his hand. "I do. I should probably go on a date first. But when? I've got exams and work and interviews for the Match and a million other things to do. I have no idea when that part of my life gets to happen."

"Maybe you don't get to pick when. Could be it's happening right now and you're too busy to notice."

"That's depressing." She stopped to watch a plein air painter working at an easel. Wearing a straw hat and a smock, the artist faced a stone bridge that arched over the canal. He seemed to be in a dream world, totally absorbed in his art, creating an image with deliberate, unhurried strokes. "See, he probably knows what he wants," she pointed out. "Not that I'd ever be a painter. I'm terrible at art. But it would be great to have a passion besides work and medicine. I'd love to get lost in some pursuit that has nothing to do with my goals, or my parents, or just . . . anything."

"Then get lost in it," Leroy said. "It's not that hard. I get lost when I run. In my mind, that is."

"Exactly. That's what I'm talking about. I'm no runner, though. I've gotten lost after too many tequila shots."

He smiled. "You're a mess, you know that?"

"You're right. I'm a mess. And I'm no fun at all. No wonder I don't have any friends. I dragged you all the way out here to rant about my stupid life."

"What's with this soul-searching all of a sudden?" he asked.

"I don't know."

"It wouldn't have something to do with a certain person built like a lumberjack with big shoulders and blue eyes, would it?"

She blushed. "Certainly not."

"You don't need to explain. I already know what's really on your mind."

"You do, do you?"

"Caleb Stoltz, that's what. And what does he have that I don't? Oh, that's right—he's unavailable. You seem to like that in a guy."

"Give me a break." Then she slid a side-eyed glance at him. He had a point. If they were going to be friends, then she should level with him. "Fine. Okay. I seem to be a little preoccupied with him. He is the one who asked about my day off, and I had no answer that didn't sound completely boring. And it got me thinking about having a more balanced life."

"So what's the attraction? Is it his giant shoulders or his giant intellect?"

"Now you're being mean." She sighed. "It's just that I've never met anyone like him before. Haven't you ever met a person who totally changed the way you look at something?"

"I can go one better. I met someone who made me want everything in the world. She's the reason I left the Amish community. The reason I'm shunned."

Reese felt a jolt of alarm. "Wow, I hope she's worth it. Who is she? Do you still see her?"

"Her name is Gabrielle. Gabby. I loved her more than life itself. We're not together anymore, obviously."

"Aw, Leroy. I'm sorry."

"Thanks. I miss her, but I can't be sorry we met in the first place. I lost the girl, but I ended up with a better life. It's a life that never would have happened if I hadn't been with Gabby, if I hadn't fallen head over heels for her. Love is tricky that way. It's hard to know if it's meant to last. When we broke up, I thought the world had ended. Then I picked myself up and moved on to a better life."

"I'm glad you can say that," she told him. "I'm glad this is a better life for you."

"I could never have this career if Gabby hadn't nudged me away from the Amish community. In the English world, there are ways to heal people or make things better for them. A lot of the techniques and interventions I use are forbidden by the Amish. So I ask myself, do I want any part of a society that allows a person to suffer, when a safe and simple intervention would help? And the answer is no."

"That's a good point," she said. "In my rotations, I've definitely seen instances where faith and reason seem to part ways."

"There was a girl in my community suffering from a bad knee injury. She didn't have a diagnosis, but I'm convinced it was patellofemoral pain."

"She could be helped with intensive PT, then."

"Assuming you're okay with electricity," he said. "When I was doing my practicals, I saw a similar case. An almost identical case. In a clinical setting, we used electrical stimulation, and the patient was completely transformed. That's when I knew I'd be staying English, with or without Gabby. It's rare, you know, to leave the community. I've read that there's a ninety percent retention rate. Meaning ninety percent of people choose to be baptized and join the church."

"Pretty impressive," she agreed. "What's the appeal?"

"It's safe. And for the most part, simple. You spend your life with familiar people and in familiar surroundings. So most folks follow what their parents want them to do. We stick with things out of fear or inertia, I suppose."

"I've been doing what my parents want me to do since . . . Oh, forever. When I was small—maybe six years old—I wanted a poster of all the Disney princesses on my wall. Instead, my parents put up pictures of great women of science. Dr. Ann Preston, Mary Edwards Walker, Mary Putnam Jacobi . . ."

"I'm familiar with the first two, but not Jacobi. What'd she do?"

"She's my fave. In the nineteenth century, doctors believed women couldn't menstruate and think at the same time. So she did an extensive research project to disprove it. On the poster my parents hung in my room, there was a quote from her—'There is nothing in the nature of menstruation to imply the necessity, or even the desirability, of rest.'"

"Your parents wanted you to know that," he pointed out.

"I was six years old. I wanted to look at Jasmine and Mulan, not menstruation quotes."

"Disney princesses. You're a romantic, then."

"You think? I figured I was just shallow."

"Or just six, like you said. How about you?" he asked. "Ever been in love?"

She hesitated. "I'll have to get back to you on that."

They ended their canal-side walk by stopping at a quaint sidewalk café for lunch—lemonade and a caprese salad with thick slices of heirloom tomatoes, creamy homemade burrata cheese, and thin ribbons of fresh basil.

Leroy wouldn't be distracted by the lunch. He was like a dog with a bone. "It's a simple question."

"I can't give you a simple answer. Okay, here's what I think. Maybe I've been in love, but it was never life-changing. Not the way it was for you. There was a guy in college . . . and another during my third year of med school. Both times, I thought I was in love. I did love them—that's what it felt like, at least. But the feelings didn't last and it wasn't hard for me to move on. Does that mean it wasn't true love?"

He dipped a piece of fresh bread into his salad. "I'm no expert."

"It makes me wonder about myself. Maybe I'm not cut out for romantic love."

"You're too young to draw that conclusion. So am I. Let's not be pathetic. I'll find someone, and so will you. I keep thinking I'll know her when I meet her, but I've been wrong before."

"Well." She touched the rim of her glass to his. "Here's hoping."

"In New Hope. I'm buying lunch." He signaled for the check.

They poked around a couple of antiques shops. She bought a small green glazed pot with herbs growing in it. "In case I decide to cook something," she said. At his skeptical look, she added, "Could happen."

"And God forbid you spend sixty cents on parsley at the market," Leroy added. He picked up a round painted hex sign with a compass rose and colorful birds. "The tag says this is an Amish sign, but it's not."

"How can you tell?"

"The Amish don't use them. They're Pennsylvania Dutch folk art, though, so people assume they're the same." He picked up an embroidered sampler, also labeled Amish. "Now this is probably the real thing. It's a song we learn in school, sung to the tune of 'Twinkle Twinkle.' *In der stillen Einsamkeit, Findest du mein Lob bereit* . . . There's more, but I won't torture you with my singing."

"What does it mean?"

"Let's see . . . 'In the still isolation, you find my praise
ready. Greatest God answer me, for my heart is seeking
you.'"

She examined the stitching and detail. Then she
looked at Leroy's face. He was studying the sampler with
eyes gone soft with nostalgia, his mouth quirked slightly
in a sweet, sad smile.

"There must be things you miss," she said.

"Some, yes. Not enough to go back. But oh, the sounds
of the farm at daybreak. Eggs fresh from the henhouse,
milk and cream straight from the cow. Of course, then
I remember it was my job to wash down the milk house
every day, even when it was freezing out. In the winter, I
had to carry a pail of hot coals out to the well just to get it
going. Do you know what a luxury it is to have hot water
straight out of the tap?"

"I'm sure it's one of the thousand things we take for
granted every day."

"The Amish don't take anything for granted. They
know how to be thankful for their blessings. They're better at it than the English." He checked his watch. "You
need to get to your interview. I'm going to grab some
things from the farmers' market to bring back for dinner."

Reese expected to feel like a fish out of water the moment
she entered the Humboldt Division Regional Care Center. Instead, she stepped into the foyer of the aging building, and a feeling of excitement washed over her. There
were familiar elements shared by hospitals everywhere,
but the small size of the place made it seem more personal and accessible. After spending the past two years
getting lost at the massive hospital in the city—to this

day, she still did sometimes—this slightly old-fashioned building was a confidence booster.

Doctors Penelope Lake and Mose Shrock met with her in a sunny office that might have been a scene out of a Norman Rockwell illustration, with a hand-pieced quilt on one wall, an old-fashioned washstand, and a spindly wooden chair, painted red. She had a seat on the chair and set down her bag, facing her interviewers across an antique desk. She realized she was clutching her phone, so she quickly stashed it away.

Dr. Lake was willowy and intense, and she got right to the point. "We train only four residents at a time," she said. "Why should you be one of them?"

Reese was prepared for the blunt question, because she knew she'd be asked. "During third year, I did a rotation at the Upper Appalachia Medical Center. The variety of procedures—C-sections, colposcopy, M-Is, endoscopy, setting fractures, running traumas—it was the best rotation I've done so far."

Dr. Lake had apparently memorized Reese's background, asking about her medical education, her goals, her role models. Dr. Shrock was older, bearded and bespectacled, with a quirky way of speaking. "That chair you're sitting in," he said. "Tell me about that chair."

A trick question? She touched the wooden surface. "It looks handmade. And it's a few inches lower than normal."

"It is," he said. "It was once used for powwowing. Are you familiar with the practice?"

Shit.

"Sorry—powwowing? No, I'm not. But it sounds like some of the granny doctoring I came across during the rotation in Appalachia."

A glimmer of approval. "It's something you'll need to be familiar with if you work in this community. The chair is imbued with symbols—the red color for the blood of Christ, the double rail for the two tablets of Moses, the vertical stiles for the pillars of the church, the spindles for the Holy Trinity . . ." He glanced at Dr. Lake. "What am I missing?"

"Judas the Betrayer is in there somewhere," she said.

"And the low seat is to humble the patient."

"Trust me," said Reese, "I feel humble right now. So 'powwowing' is a thing? Folk healing?"

"*Braucherei* is an old practice. You'll still encounter it from time to time. As a boy, I got rid of warts with a potato and a penny, but only when the moon was waning. The point is, you'll find these practices among our patients. I was raised in the Mennonite faith," he said. "In my younger, wilder days, I lost my way and turned to drink. Nearly lost my license. Eventually, I found redemption and fulfillment in the medical arts."

She wasn't sure how to respond to that. "I can't say I'm looking for redemption. Fulfillment, yes. When I first started med school, I thought I'd be a surgeon." Her parents still thought that. Expected that. "I love the practice of medicine," she told them. "I love seeing patients. Doing procedures. A rural program wasn't something I considered until I realized that primary care is what I want to be best at. What I love."

Dr. Shrock smiled. "That's the magic word. Love."

As Leroy and Reese drove back to the city, she fretted about the interview. "It's the one option I haven't discussed with my parents," she told Leroy.

"Oh boy. If I discussed every decision with my parents, I'd be harnessed to a plow being dragged across a field," he said.

"I feel as if I'm deceiving them by not telling them. It's silly, I know. But they've supported every aspect of my education—my life. They're entitled to know."

"And you haven't told them because you don't want them to talk you out of it."

"You're pretty sharp, for a guy."

"I know you better than you think."

Her face heated. She knew he was thinking of Caleb Stoltz again. "I wonder what will happen to Jonah when he returns to the community with a prosthetic arm."

"Caleb and I spoke of it. He favors the prosthesis, and he loves that kid like crazy. But Jonah has to live in the community, so it could be tricky. One thing that would help would be to get Jonah back home sooner rather than later so he can adjust to his new circumstances in a familiar place."

"Will he get the therapy and training he needs?"

"I'm looking into it and making some calls. A three-hour bus ride to the city isn't the best option."

"It's really nice of you to take a special interest in Jonah."

"Let's stop by the hospital when we get to the city," he suggested.

"My thoughts exactly."

In the lobby of Mercy Heights, workers and visitors rushed to and fro. In the middle of the bustling crowd stood a lone, still figure of a young woman in Amish clothes. She held a bus ticket in her hands, turning it over and over with nervous fingers.

Reese nudged Leroy. "I bet that's Jonah's sister. She looks lost. Let's go talk to her."

Leroy spoke to her briefly in German mixed with English. She regarded him, wide-eyed and fearful, as she mumbled an answer.

"Reese, you were right. This is Hannah Stoltz," Leroy said. "Jonah's sister."

As they approached the girl, Reese noticed a subtle likeness to Jonah—similar features, blue eyes, a sprinkling of freckles. Yet where Jonah was skinny and wiry, the girl seemed heavyset, though it could just be the shapeless clothes she wore in uncomfortable-looking layers. She looked very plain, which was probably by design. In a different outfit with a different hairstyle, she could be any teen. She was very pretty, with blue eyes and pale skin, a sweet constellation of freckles across her nose, just like Jonah's. She wore her blond hair in a coiled braid, a small, wispy black bonnet pinned to the back of her head, the untied strings hanging down past her shoulders. She was completely covered in a long-sleeved, shapeless dress of dark blue. The hem skimmed the tops of her scuffed brown boots.

"Reese was part of the team that took care of your brother when he was brought in," Leroy told her.

"Can I see him?" Hannah asked, her voice soft and timid, with the lilting accent Reese now recognized.

"Of course," said Reese. Questions crowded her mind. "Did someone call you? I mailed a card from Jonah, but that was only this morning." She'd sent the card via express mail, unable to fathom the sense of uncertainty his loved ones must be feeling, but it couldn't have been delivered the same day.

"I've been so worried about my brother," she said. "I came as soon as I worked out how to get here on my own."

Leroy said something else in German, and Hannah nodded. He spoke again, and she dropped her gaze to the floor, shaking her head.

"This way," Reese said, and led them to the elevator. Hannah seemed to shrink from the glare of the elevator lights. When the car surged upward, the girl gasped. Her eyes shone—not with fear, but with wonder.

The moment they reached Jonah's room, a gusty sigh and a stream of German erupted from Hannah. Propped up in his bed, Jonah smiled at her with a sweetness that touched Reese's heart. He was such a lovely little boy, beautiful in the most natural sense. Nothing about him ever seemed to be artificial or forced.

Hannah approached the bed and stood there, shoulders shaking. "Look at you," she said, and then said it twice more. "Look at you. Look at you." Cradling his face between her hands, she kissed him with such tenderness that Reese had to glance away. These poor motherless kids, thrust into an alien environment. They must be so scared.

"Where is Caleb?" Hannah asked.

"He went to get me another book, because I finished the last one," Jonah said. "I'm reading Harry Potter. Say, maybe we can read them together."

"Hannah," said Caleb from the doorway. "What are you doing here?" He held out his arms and she rushed to him.

Reese realized he shared that genuine trait with his nephew—his face hid nothing. His expression radiated love as his generous hug all but swallowed the girl up. He was looking semi-Amish today in his plain trousers and white shirt, the collar open and sleeves rolled back. Hannah visibly relaxed against him, and he murmured something to her in their language, his big hands gently cupping her shoulders. After an emotional moment, he stepped back, holding her at arm's length. "Did you come on the bus, then?"

"I had to, Caleb. I couldn't stay away. Don't be mad."

"I'm not mad."

Leroy pulled in a couple of rolling stools. Together, they told Hannah what had happened to Jonah and what to expect. She listened quietly through most of it, and in the end, she asked the expected question. "When can Jonah come home?"

"We're working on that," Reese said. "He has a care team helping him. First his arm has to heal, and then he'll learn how to use a prosthesis. Your brother's really smart and strong. He's going to do all right." She felt Caleb's gaze on her and caught a glimpse of warmth in his eyes. Then, noticing Jonah's lengthy yawn, she added, "One of the most important things is rest."

Caleb stood and stroked the boy's head. "She's right. You get lots of rest, little man."

Reese and Leroy waited outside as Hannah and Caleb told the boy good night and tucked him in with his new book. Leroy wore a thoughtful frown. "What is it?" she asked.

"There's something . . . Caleb's different."

"In what way?"

"Just an observation. The Amish aren't usually demonstrative. You don't find parents hugging their kids the way he does."

"Meaning?"

"Probably nothing. It's just . . . curious."

After Jonah was settled for the night, they walked through the ward.

On a whim, Reese routed them across the skybridge to the maternity wing. A few family members lingered outside the nursery, focused on the new arrivals. "Most of the babies room in with their mothers these days," Reese said, "but the nursery is still used for procedures. Do you like babies, Hannah?"

"Oh, yes." She stood in front of the display window, gazing at the bassinets with their tiny, precious bundles. "Nine babies," she whispered. "They're all safe and sound here, aren't they?"

"Sure," said Reese. It seemed an odd observation to make. Hannah leaned close to the glass and held herself very still. She seemed guileless as she watched the babies with wide-eyed wonder.

A couple nearby, the new mom in a wheelchair, gazed lovingly through the glass at a tiny bundled infant.

"Your first?" Reese asked.

The woman shook her head. "I have four kids."

On purpose? Reese wondered, but held her tongue. She had to resist becoming the world's judgiest doctor. "Congratulations. Your baby is so cute."

Behind them, Caleb and Leroy were murmuring to each other in German. She turned. "Everything all right?"

"There's no bus back to Middle Grove tonight," Caleb said.

Hannah whirled around to face him. "I don't want to go back anyway." She stared down at the floor. "I didn't bring hardly any money."

"You can stay with me," Reese said quickly. She didn't know what else to do. She couldn't foist the girl on Leroy. And there was no way Hannah was going to a hotel. She led the way to the elevators.

"It's a great imposition," Caleb said.

"Not at all," she said. "Okay, a small imposition, and I'd consider it a privilege to help."

Caleb gave her that smile again. The one that melted her in all the right places. "Well, then. Thank you, Reese."

"I have my car today," she said. "Is that . . . I assume you're all right with riding home in a car."

Caleb and Hannah exchanged a look, and both broke into wide grins. "That'd be just fine, Reese," he said.

It was a singular experience to drive everyone back to the parking garage. They'd missed the evening rush hour and now the sun was going down, and the heat of the day lingered in the air. With the top down, she took the road along the river. Caleb and Hannah sat in the back seat. Hannah, in her long skirt and black bonnet, looked as if she'd wandered off the set of a movie. With her seat belt in place and Caleb beside her, she looked around with shining eyes.

"A car with no top," she said. "It's wonderful."

"It's called a convertible," Caleb told her, then said something else in German.

Reese drove slowly, not wanting to alarm them. She was surprised when Hannah leaned forward and said, "We wouldn't mind going fast."

Reese glanced over at Leroy, who shrugged. "As you wish," she said, her favorite quote from her favorite movie. She pressed the accelerator and the car surged forward. Hannah let loose with a laugh of delight. Glancing in the rearview mirror, Reese saw the girl throw her arms into the air, tilting her head back as if she were on a roller coaster. The bonnet flew away like a small black bird.

"Oh, sh— gosh, your hat," said Reese, slowing down.

Hannah clapped a hand on her head. "My *kapp*."

"Should we go back for it?" asked Reese, watching the wisp of fabric swoop through oncoming traffic.

"It's gone for good," said Leroy, twisting around in his seat. "No point getting killed over a *kapp*."

"If you're sure . . ."

"Leave it," Caleb said. "Wearing it is a custom, not a commandment chiseled in stone."

Reese glanced at Hannah again. The girl looked the opposite of distressed as her long braid uncoiled and flew in the wind. She watched the scenery whipping past— pedestrians and buses, modern buildings, statues and fountains.

"It's good that you came for Jonah," Caleb said to Hannah. "But tomorrow you will have to go back to Middle Grove."

She cut her gaze away. "I wish I could stay."

"You can't. You're needed at Alma's shop, and there's no place for you here."

She flinched. "But—"

"Hannah . . ." He lapsed into German. She exhaled a loud sigh and was silent for the rest of the ride.

Reese parked the car and opened the trunk, which was filled with their parcels from earlier in the day. Hannah's hair stuck out every which way, long blond strands escaping from her waist-length braid. Her cheeks were flushed. Her eyes, the same cornflower blue as her uncle's, sparkled with pleasure.

"Thank you, Reese. That was my first ride in a car."

Reese could hardly get her mind around that—a sixteen-year-old who had never been in a car. "You're kidding. Wow. So you liked it."

She nodded emphatically. "I surely did."

"And how about you, Caleb? Have you ridden in a car?"

"Not in a long time," he said simply.

"My grandfather said Caleb got in trouble driving a car when he was younger. Didn't you, Uncle?"

"It was a long time ago. I was a foolish boy."

"That's what Grandfather says too."

Reese smiled at the rapport between them. "You'll have to tell me more about your foolish uncle," she said to Hannah.

"So it's good news," said Leroy, unloading shopping bags from the trunk. "When we were in New Hope today, we bought everything we need for dinner. So no one has to do any work."

They walked to the building together. Hannah regarded everything with wide-eyed wonder. Sheltered in a tiny community, with only an eighth-grade education, no TV or media, living on a rustic farm, the girl marveled at everything—the car, the busy neighborhood, the keypad on the door, even the apartment itself, messy as it was.

"Such a beautiful place to live," she said.

Reese smiled. "Thanks. I sometimes wish it was more homey, but I never seem to have time to do anything about it." She saw Hannah studying the quilt draped over the back of a wooden chair. "That's from a former patient, and it's one of my favorite things."

"It's a very nice one," Hannah said.

"Quilting is Hannah's superpower," Caleb said.

"Really? I'd love to see your work one day," Reese said.

"There's a mercantile in town that sells my quilts," Hannah said, simultaneously blushing and beaming. "And at the mud sales in the springtime."

Leroy caught Reese's clueless expression. "A mud sale takes place before the spring planting, when the weather makes for muddy roads."

It was hard to believe such a different world existed only a couple of hours' drive from here. "Mud sale," Reese said. "I'm going to have to check that out."

Leroy gestured Hannah over to the table. "Give me a hand here?"

"Sure."

He handed her plates and cutlery. As she laid the table, Leroy asked, "Do you like cooking, Hannah?"

Her cheeks turned red as she looked over at Caleb, who regarded her with a teasing grin. "Not so much, to tell you the truth."

"There are worse things than not being good in the kitchen," Reese pointed out.

"It's women's work," Caleb said. "And she's the only girl in the household back home."

Reese bristled. "Women's work is still a thing at your house?"

"Nah," he said easily. "I just said that to get a rise out of you."

"Congratulations. You got a rise."

"Work is work," he said. "The supper doesn't care who burns it."

Hannah blushed again. "Most girls learn to cook and clean from their mothers."

Reese washed up at the sink and opened the cartons of food. "Caleb told me what happened to your parents. I'm so very sorry."

Hannah kept her head down. "Thank you for your sorrow. That's all I know to say about it."

"It must be really difficult. My mother and I are close," said Reese. "I'm an only child. I don't know what I'd do without her."

"Something tells me you would figure it out," said Leroy.

"Did she show you how to cook?" asked Hannah.

That drew a short laugh from Reese. "All my cooking skills were taught to me by the housekeeper. Mom never had the time to cook, let alone to teach me. She and my father are both physicians. One day, I'll be joining their practice. That's the plan, anyway."

"Then it's not so different from the Amish custom," Hannah said. "We're supposed to follow in the footsteps

of our elders." She grew more chatty as they set out the
food. "It's not a law or anything. More like a tradition."
She glanced at Leroy. "Some folks go their own way."

"They do," he agreed. "But there's always the chance
to change our minds."

Reese cleared the table of clutter—mostly paperwork
related to exams and the residency match—and they sat
down. The meal from the farmers' market was a feast of
summer's bounty—a salad of corn and peppers, fresh-
baked rolls and potted cheese, a bowl of greens and thick
slices of tomatoes, and for dessert, Indian pudding that
had been slow baked in maple syrup.

She was about to dig in when she noticed that Hannah had bowed her head. Caleb and Leroy followed suit.
Reese couldn't remember the last time she'd said grace.
A bit of eyes-closed silence before a meal was probably
a very good thing, no matter what thoughts might pass
through her mind—gratitude, regret, contemplation, or
nothing at all.

Her attending during a rotation in general surgery had
been a practicing Buddhist. His advice before cutting into
living human flesh had been nearly identical to a silent
prayer. *Be still. Be silent. Find the center of yourself.* He'd
been one of her favorite mentors. Under his supervision,
she'd scrubbed in on her first kidney transplant.

"Lemonade?" asked Caleb, nudging her back to the
present.

She flushed, realizing how inappropriate it was to be
comparing a surgical procedure to a meal. "Sure. Thank
you. Bon appétit, everyone. That's my fancy way of saying eat up."

"*Mahlzeit,*" Hannah said. "That's how we say it at
home."

Reese smiled and repeated the phrase. "How's that?"

"Pretty good for an *Englischer*," Caleb said.

After dinner, Caleb and Leroy cleared the table and loaded the dishwasher. "Thanks for doing the women's work," Hannah said in a teasing voice.

Caleb grinned. "No one is doing any work at all. It's all done by the machine." He and Leroy finished up quickly.

Reese noticed Hannah trying to stifle a yawn. "What time did you start out this morning?" she asked the girl.

"Plenty early. I rode my bike to the bus station just as the sun was coming up."

"You must be exhausted. Come on," said Reese. "Let's make up the sofa for you."

At the door, she looked up at Caleb. "Don't worry," she told him. "I'll look after her."

"I know you will."

She closed the door gently behind them and stood there for a moment, struggling with the now-familiar sense of incredible yearning, which bumped up against an even stronger sense of utter impossibility. She was entrenched in the culture of the hospital and her world, yet Caleb's arrival had thrown her off track. She caught herself reacting differently to situations. In unguarded moments, she looked beneath the surface of her life and felt a desperate unhappiness.

Yet the things that anchored her to this life exerted enormous pressure—not just her parents' expectations, but her own. Patients she yearned to help, a future she was pursuing with relentless determination.

"Reese?" Hannah's quiet voice broke in on her thoughts.

Flustered, Reese turned to face her guest. "Sorry, just thinking about . . . organizing my day for tomorrow."

Hannah tilted her head to one side. "But it's still today."

The simple words brought Reese up short. She was

so entrenched in the culture of the hospital, yet something about Hannah—and her uncle and brother—threw her off. When Reese was around them, she acted differently in familiar situations, seeing things from a different angle. Seeing, sometimes, that she was desperately unhappy underneath all the busywork.

She nodded. "You're right. It's still today."

8

Despite Hannah's reminder, Reese began to tally up all the things she needed to do in order to prep for the following day. The list was already a mile long, and it grew even longer after she listened to multiple messages from her parents and colleagues.

She was beginning to hate the list. With a huff of defiance, she turned off her phone. She had company tonight. "How about a shower, Hannah? It'll feel nice after that long bus ride."

The girl glanced around the apartment, knotting her fingers together. She focused on the open door to the bathroom. "Yes, sure. Thank you."

"I've never met an Amish girl before," Reese said. "You'll have to tell me how I can help. Do you have running water back home?"

Hannah shook her head. "Some do, but not in our house. There's a hand pump in the kitchen. When it's bath time, we carry pails of water to a big copper boiler that sits on all four burners of the oil stove. Then we pour the hot water into a big round steel tub from the cellar and set it on the rug in front of the woodstove in the keeping room."

"That sounds . . . effortful," Reese said, trying to imagine going through the process every day.

It made her to-do list look like a haiku.

"We're used to it. Bathing's easier in the summer 'cause we can jump in the creek behind the house. There's a deep eddy that makes a natural swimming hole. Caleb put up a rope swing there. Jonah can swing himself clear out to the middle and—" Hannah's voice cracked. "I'm so scared for him. What's he going to do without an arm?"

"He's going to get a lot of help figuring it out," said Reese. "He has a long road ahead. There are lots of adaptive devices to help him. When the time comes, he'll have an extremely advanced artificial limb. Maybe more than one, including something that works great in the water. I don't know about a rope swing, though."

Hannah shuddered. "An artificial limb is not the same. He's just a little boy."

Reese touched her shoulder. "I know this is awful, and I don't blame you for feeling sad."

Hannah drew in a shuddery breath, using her sleeve to wipe her cheeks.

"How about I show you how to work the shower." Reese stepped into the bathroom and demonstrated the light switch and the hot and cold water. She gave Hannah towels and a big terry-cloth robe, fresh from the laundry service. She was fascinated to see that Hannah's long skirt and blouse were secured with nothing but straight pins. "Do you need anything else?"

Hannah shook her head. "No, thank you."

The girl's shower lasted forty-seven minutes. Reese timed it. She imagined the teenage girl indulging in the endless stream of warm water, not needing to worry about boilers or tubs or what to do with the water afterward. The Amish ways seemed incredibly labor intensive. Yet at the same time, there was something appealing about the uncomplicated nature of life in a community like Middle Grove. According to articles Reese had read online, the simple rhythm of the days and seasons kept the heart open to one's faith. Maybe that wasn't such a bad thing.

By the time Hannah reappeared, bundled in the thick

robe, Reese had the sofa made up with a set of spare sheets and a light summer blanket.

"Everything all right?" she asked.

Hannah nodded eagerly. "Yes, thank you." She regarded the sofa with almost comical amazement. "That was all folded up inside, then."

"Yes." Reese patted the pillows. "It's not the most comfortable bed in the world, but . . ."

"It's just perfect," Hannah said quickly. Then she touched the mass of wet golden hair that fell in a tangle down her back. "I forgot to bring a brush."

"No problem. There's a comb and a brush in the drawer under the sink."

Hannah returned to the bathroom, leaving the door ajar. She buried the brush in her thick hair, tugging hard enough to make Reese wince.

"Let's use some detangler," she suggested. "There's some in the cabinet there."

She noticed Hannah staring into the fogged-up mirror. The girl reached out and smeared the fog with her hand, a look of fascination on her face. "We don't have mirrors," she said. "My grandfather says it's a sign of vanity."

"No one's going to think you're vain." Reese handed her the spritz bottle.

Hannah frowned at it. Then she said, "Oh. That's the detangler."

Reese couldn't imagine having all that long hair with no help combing it out. "You're going to like this stuff," she said, taking the bottle back. "May I?"

Hannah nodded. Reese spritzed her hair and gently worked the comb through it.

"When I was really little," Hannah said, "Mem used to do the braiding. With only Grandfather, Caleb, and Jonah, I don't get much help with that."

"Mem . . . Your mother?"

She nodded.

Reese separated the strands, methodically untangling each section. Once again, her heart went out to the girl. Motherless, and the only female in a house full of men who probably didn't have the least understanding of her, Hannah seemed awkward and unsure of herself.

"I hope you keep that memory close," Reese said. "And I hope you have lots of nice memories like that."

Hannah offered a slight smile. "I do. Mem wasn't so gentle, though. For sure she didn't use the detangler. But she was a regular expert when it came to the braiding, that's what I always believed. I can still remember what it feels like, her fingers so fast and light on my head, and the braids taking shape like two shiny ropes."

"I hope there are women in your community who help out," Reese said.

"Oh, yes. Alma Troyer, I work with her on the quilting, and she's wonderful to me. I've been staying at her place while Caleb's away."

Reese furrowed her fingers through the long, golden strands. "Your hair is lovely—so long and thick."

Hannah sighed, watching the motion of the comb in the mirror. "It's never been cut. Sometimes Alma trims up the ends for me, is all."

"I had long hair when I was younger," Reese said. "I'm not sure my mom knows how to braid, though."

"I think you're so pretty," Hannah said, flashing a shy smile over her shoulder, "even with short hair."

"What a nice thing to say. I keep it short now to save time."

"Time for what?"

"For . . . well, everything else," she said. "Studying and work, mostly. There—we got through all the tangles.

Let's head into the living room. You can have a seat while I try my hand at braiding."

While Reese carefully plaited the silky blond hair, Hannah perched on a kitchen stool and perused her bookcases, which were crammed with textbooks and study guides as well as classic novels and the latest bestsellers. "So many books," she said. "Have you read all of these?"

"Almost," Reese said. "I like keeping my favorites close at hand, in case I want to revisit them. Do you like reading?"

"I love it. There's a whole world inside a book. In our community, there are rules against reading certain books—the worldly ones—but I'm not sure what the rules are. Uncle Caleb doesn't restrict what we read, even if it's not *Martyrs Mirror* or *Family Life* magazine." She paused. "Mem and Dat used to scold me for reading English books."

Reese had no idea what to say about that. She didn't want to speak ill of the dead, but restricting a kid's reading choices made no sense at all. "I'm glad you get to read anything you want," she said. "Do you have a favorite?"

"No, it's too hard to choose. I love *My Ántonia* and *Little Women*. The librarian in Stephensville gives me modern books as well, like *The Hunger Games*."

"Librarians are amazing. Many of the best moments of my childhood were spent between the pages of a story. You can borrow any book you see. I love sharing books."

"Thank you. I'd like that." She got up, selected a novel from the bookcase, and studied the cover. It was *Speak* by Laurie Halse Anderson. "What's this one about?"

"That's about a high school girl who stopped speaking because she was afraid to talk about something bad that happened to her. I won't spoil it for you by saying what the something bad was."

Hannah put the novel on the table. "Maybe I'll borrow it."

"Sure, of course." Reese smiled. "You're more talkative than your uncle."

"Am I? Could be that comes from the quilting circle. We talk the whole day long. Uncle Caleb, he's all day with the horses." She paused and looked around the apartment. "He was going to leave Middle Grove for good. The only reason he came back was to look after Jonah and me."

"You mean he was going to leave the way Leroy did?"

"Yes."

Reese was stunned. He'd had a completely different life in mind for himself but ended up back in the community he wanted to leave. To do what? She was dying to know. She tried to imagine what that would be like—to abandon your plans for the sake of family. Did he accept it? Embrace it? Resent it? Did he think about what his future would have been like if his brother had lived? "He seems devoted to you and your brother," she said.

"Yes. He's so very good to us. And now Jonah is going to need him more than ever. And I . . . well, I'm sixteen now. I'll be married and away pretty soon, so I won't be around to help."

"Whoa, wait a second. Soon? I hope you mean, like, ten years from now?"

Hannah smiled, her mouth and cheeks as soft as a child's. "Where I come from, I'd be considered an old maid. By that age, girls have a home and family of their own to look after."

Reese gritted her teeth. *Don't judge.* "When I was sixteen, I fell head over heels in love with a boy named Troy Decker. The only thing in the world I wanted was to marry him and have his babies."

"Well, that's a nice thought—going head over heels. But we're more practical. I want a boy who's a good provider, a good partner. A good friend."

"You're a lot more grounded than I was at your age."

Hannah hesitated, then said, "Caleb, now, he's not in such a hurry. My grandfather wants him to get baptized and marry Amish."

"Is that what your uncle wants?" Reese felt nosy asking, but she couldn't help herself.

"I don't know. Caleb's not one to talk about wanting things. There's a girl . . . Rebecca Zook, a neighbor in our community. She wants to marry him. Everybody knows she's wanted that forever." She looked up at Reese's cuckoo clock, a whimsical item Reese had rescued from her grandmother's estate sale. "When a man wants to marry," Hannah added, "he gives the girl something practical in nature, like a clock."

Reese gave a short laugh. "Seriously? Your uncle mentioned that to me but I didn't realize it was a thing. It would take more than a clock to win me over."

"And then the girl, if she wants to accept him, she makes a sampler for him. It's an embroidered cloth—she gives that to the man to let him know she wants him."

"Because nothing says 'I love you' like a tea towel," Reese said.

"Oh, you English. You have your own funny ideas about love and marriage, neh?"

Reese had many more questions about Caleb, but she didn't want to put Hannah on the spot. "What about you? Do you really want to marry so young? Have a family?"

Hannah flinched and looked away. "There's someone special. A boy. Aaron Graber . . . He's sweet on me."

"Are you sweet on him?"

Hannah's gaze skated away. "My friend Miriam, she

already got her clock. She's the same age as me. They'll be courting until she's eighteen, and then she'll be baptized and they'll marry up."

"So you're saying you'd like to be married?"

Hannah shrugged. "I'd like to be gone." She spoke in such a low murmur that Reese wasn't sure she'd heard correctly.

Reese finished up the braid. "Where would you like to go?"

"I'm . . . nowhere. It was a silly notion. Middle Grove is my home, the only one I've ever known or will ever know. I have another friend who had her first baby last month." Hannah hugged the thick robe tightly around her middle. "I wouldn't know what to do about a baby. Such a big, enormous responsibility. Maybe if I was married."

"You're so young. You don't have to know anything yet. I'm no expert, but I think it's usually best to take your time when it comes to major life decisions." Even as she spoke, Reese asked herself if she'd done that—contemplated her path to being a pediatric surgeon. Had she taken her time, or had the decision been made so long ago that she couldn't remember making it?

"I'll have a big think on it." Hannah absently smoothed her hands over the robe. She seemed flustered by the talk about babies and marriage.

"Thinking big is good. There are days when I get so busy I forget to do that. Other times, I think so big I give myself a headache." Reese put away the comb. "Now. What would you like to do tonight? It's been a long time since I've had a sleepover."

Hannah's gaze darted around the place, taking in all the modern electronics and gadgets, which probably seemed bewildering to her. "I don't rightly know."

"Have you been to a sleepover before?"

The girl flashed another smile. "I bet it's nothing like you would imagine."

"Try me."

"Ever heard of bundling? That's when kids have sleepovers together . . . I mean boys and girls together. In the same bed."

"Seriously? Sounds like a golden ticket to an STD or unwanted pregnancy."

Hannah's gaze veered off to the side. "That's why we bundle—sleep side by side on the same bed, but in bundling bags under different covers. We stay up talking all night. It's a way to get to know one another."

"Okeydokey, then. I can't promise you that level of entertainment, but . . . We could give each other a mani-pedi. Do you know what that is? Have you ever had one?" She held out her woefully neglected hands.

"You mean manicure and pedicure, yes? I've never done that. It's not Plain."

"Oh. Sorry." She snapped her fingers. "I've got it. Popcorn and a movie. How does that sound? Have you ever seen a movie?"

"No. But I like popcorn."

"I have the perfect thing in mind," Reese said in sudden inspiration. "It's the best movie ever made. We might as well start with the very best." She picked up the remote and accessed the streaming service. "Brace yourself. I'll make the popcorn."

While Reese busied herself in the kitchen, Hannah stared at the big flat screen on the wall, and she didn't move a muscle as the opening images came up. With the first soft strains of the theme music filling the room in surround sound, the girl sank back onto the sofa, entranced. "What is the name of this movie?"

Reese smiled. "Wait for it."

The screen lit with the title: *The Princess Bride*.

When the movie ended, Hannah felt herself melting with emotion so powerful she didn't know what to call it. The words on the screen rolled upward while a beautiful song drifted from some invisible source. Tears pressed at the backs of her eyes, and she glanced over at Reese to see her swiping at her cheeks.

"Gets me every time," Reese said, smiling and sniffing.

"I wish we could watch it again," Hannah said. "It was truly a wonder to behold, like looking at a dream."

Reese picked up the empty popcorn bowl and took it to the sink. "I agree. It's late, though, and I've got some reading to do for work."

"All right. Good night, Reese." Hannah used the bathroom again, just because she could. Back home, she tried to limit her visits to the outhouse, disliking the trek across the yard, the spiders in summer, and the cold in winter. It was a terrible sin of pride to be so enamored of indoor plumbing, but there it was. She liked a hot shower and a flush toilet.

And she deeply loved the movie Reese had watched with her. Settling on the sofa bed with her borrowed linens and pillow, she gazed at the blank screen. Where did the pictures and sounds come from, and where had they gone? Were there other things happening on the screen that weren't visible until the remote control button was touched?

She wondered if it was like real life, where the people you couldn't see were still going about their business. She thought about Aaron Graber, trying to picture what he might be doing at a particular moment. Lately, her head was filled with Aaron, Aaron, Aaron.

Did he think about her, too? Did he love her enough to do battle for her heart, the way Wesley did for Buttercup? Did he lie awake at night and relive the moments they'd shared at the singing and the bundling? Was he having regrets about how close they were getting?

She had a think on what Reese had said about the bundling. Had she gone too far a time or two? Moved too close during the cuddling? Other girls had their mothers and big sisters to ask, but not Hannah. There was Alma and the quilting ladies, but Hannah couldn't imagine bringing up such a personal topic. They weren't plain-spoken about it the way Reese seemed to be. Hannah had to take it on faith that her courtship was a proper one. She wondered if it would lead to marriage. Her friend Ruth was already married. She had a baby, and she was overwhelmed, working all the time. Hannah wasn't sure she was ready for that.

She sighed, wishing she could see into a boy's heart the way the movie camera seemed to whenever it focused on a character. Instead, she opened the borrowed book and sank into the story. According to the bishop and to Grandfather, reading was supposed to be strictly confined to devotionals, religious tracts, and the Bible. But Caleb said she should read whatever she wanted and make up her own mind. She loved books of all kinds, and the librarian at the county library was always eager to give her something new.

The borrowed book, *Speak*, was about kids in high school, which was something Hannah often wondered about. She'd never been to high school, and she didn't know anyone who had. Girls were expected to help out around the house and farm, learning the crafts and skills necessary to become a wife and mother one day.

That thought swirled around her brain like a bothersome gnat, and mentally she brushed it away. Some of her friends found domestic work keeping house for nearby English families, but that was not an option for Hannah. Grandfather had forbidden her to work in a non-Amish household. Hannah didn't push back, since she knew very well her cleaning and cooking skills were sorely lacking.

Despite her struggles with all other domestic work, she did have one superpower, as Reese or Jonah would call it. She was the best quilter in town.

Fabric and needlework had always fascinated her. When she was five years old, Mem had given her a pair of faceless rag dolls in typical Plain dress. The dolls were faceless to emphasize the notion that everyone is the same in the eyes of God.

At such a young age, Hannah didn't have an opinion about that, but she did become obsessed with making clothes for the dolls. With almost no help at all, she pieced together scraps and snippets, ribbons and bows, from Mem's sewing basket, creating unique outfits for the pair. Grandfather muttered about what a waste of time it was for a girl to labor over doll clothes, but Mem ignored him and encouraged Hannah to keep at it.

And she did, thinking up designs and stitching every night after supper. Even now, years after Mem was gone, needlework made Hannah feel closer to her. At Alma Troyer's quilt fabrication, she felt valued, a part of something greater than herself. Hand-stitched Amish quilts were popular items at the town mercantile, which was run by Mr. Jolly, who was English but who loved the Amish ways and dealt fairly with the Plain folk. Alma was kind enough to let Hannah design and stitch her own original creations. After mastering the typical starbursts, triangles, rings, and log cabin patterns, she became interested in color and design as a way to express herself. Often, a quilt came to her as if in a dream. And like a dream, it wasn't orderly and symmetrical.

Hannah's quilts evolved into free-form bursts of light and shadow, mysterious undulations in the shapes and patterns. There were those in the community who said her designs were scandalous, rich with forbidden colors, much too fancy for a girl in the faith. But others, including Alma, praised Hannah's diligence and creativity, especially when she stitched hidden messages into the piece. Mr. Jolly called them avant-garde quilts and told the tourists who came to the shop that they were genuine original works of art.

Hannah didn't know about that or even care. She just knew she was happiest when creating beauty and daydreaming about boys.

Fresh from the shower, Caleb scrubbed his hair dry and had a shave in the steam-filled bathroom of Leroy's apartment. He could easily get used to a warm shower, that was for sure. He stood looking out the window at the morning. The summer was nearly over, but in the city, the changing of the season didn't seem to matter the way it did on the farm. Here, people rushed back and forth, going about their business regardless of the weather.

A sense of things undone weighed on his mind. His absence was leaving vital chores and duties neglected. While he was away, the neighbors were looking after his place in Middle Grove, but that was only temporary. He could count on the Zooks to keep the cows milked and the horses fed. The Haubers would look after the chickens and ducks and crops—for a time. But there were other obligations only Caleb could fulfill—property tax bills, clients needing their bookkeeping, the folks up at Grantham Farm wanting his help with the horses. He was going to have to get back to work soon, but he felt torn. He couldn't imagine leaving Jonah alone in the city.

Nor could he imagine bringing that broken boy home. Not yet.

And now there was Hannah to worry about. He finished getting ready, putting on his Amish clothes, crisp and clean from the laundry service. Then he knocked at the door to Reese's place. It opened, and there stood Reese, fresh as the morning. Her dark hair was damp, and she seemed a little breathless, as if she was hurrying or startled. Or both.

That first smile from her flashed like a ray of sunshine. Her gaze flitted over him, eyes widening slightly at the traditional clothes. "Oh, hey. Want some coffee?"

"Thank you," he said, and stepped inside. She gestured toward the kitchen, and he helped himself to a cup from the electric machine. "Is Hannah ready to go?"

"Almost," said Reese, stuffing papers and electronic devices and cords into a backpack. "She's been enjoying a hot shower for, oh, the past forty minutes or so."

He grinned. "Spoiling her already. Now vinegar won't save her."

Another smile from Reese. Another beat of Caleb's heart. "I think she had a good night," said Reese. She darted here and there, putting more things in her bag. The woman was almost never still. "Are you taking her to the bus station?"

"I'm taking her back to Middle Grove."

Reese's smile wavered. "You are? I see."

But she didn't. He could tell. "I'll be back here as

quick as I can. Tonight, if that's possible. Just doesn't feel right, leaving Jonah in the city."

"I understand. It can be a challenge, having to juggle work and family, I imagine."

"Yes." If only she knew. His mind cut from the hospital to Grantham Farm to Middle Grove. No way to be in all three places at once.

She stopped rushing around and joined him at the kitchen counter. "From what I can see, Jonah is doing well. They're keeping him busy almost all day with his therapy sessions. You don't have to be there every moment."

She was right. Caleb had already spent many hours at the hospital simply waiting. Jonah was looked after by an ever-changing parade of doctors and therapists, hospital volunteers, nurses, and aides. When he wasn't working on getting better, he was resting, eating, playing in the lounge, or devouring books.

"I don't want him to be scared or lonely."

"Is he scared? Lonely?" she said. "Have you asked him how he feels?"

So simple a question from an English girl. *Have you asked him how he feels?* In the Amish community, and particularly in the Stoltz family, people didn't ask about feelings. And they didn't offer to disclose them. Sometimes Caleb wasn't sure they even felt them.

"I have not," he told her. He savored a sip of the hot, smooth coffee. It never turned out this good at home. Neither he nor Hannah had mastered the technique of brewing it in the old speckled enamel stovetop percolator.

"Ask him," she said.

Caleb shook his head. "It'd confuse him. He's never known anything but Amish ways."

"And the Amish don't talk about their feelings?"

"Not so much. Not directly. We don't even have a way of saying 'I love you' in our language."

"Seriously?"

He had learned that Reese used "seriously" as a way to demand a further explanation. "*Lieve* is the word for love, but it's a thing, not something that happens. A noun, not a verb. A person doesn't say 'I love you.' If he's backed into a corner by some girl at a singing, he might admit, 'I have a love for you.'"

"I can't even get my head around that."

"Actually, nobody would say that. A fellow might say, 'I think a lot of you.'"

"Pretty roundabout way of telling someone they're important," Reese said.

"I reckon it's not in the telling," Caleb said. "But in the doing."

"Then Jonah knows you adore him," she stated with confidence. "You've been incredibly loyal and attentive."

Her words settled in Caleb's heart. He appreciated hearing that. He appreciated *her.*

"I know you're worried about taking care of things here and at home," she said. "Maybe Jonah can manage without you now and then. Sometimes kids worry about their parents a bit too much."

"You got that right. Jonah, he's always thinking about other people."

"When he's supposed to be focusing on getting better, you don't want him to worry. Tell you what. I'll check on him while you're taking Hannah home," she said.

The tightness in his chest unfurled with relief. "I'd be obliged, Reese. Thank you."

Her smile glowed even brighter. "I'm glad to help. Remember that."

Hannah appeared from the next room, all dressed for

the day, though she was missing her *kapp*. Her eyes were sparkling with excitement. "Good morning, Caleb. I saw the most wonderful thing last night."

He caught himself looking right at Reese. "Did you, now? And what would that be?"

"It was a movie called *The Princess Bride*."

"A movie. And you liked it, then."

She gave an eager nod. "It's about a girl named Buttercup. She's a bride *and* a princess."

"Some girls have all the luck." He grinned at Reese.

Her cheeks turned a pretty color of pink. "I hope it's all right that we watched a movie."

"Sure seems like it was all right with Hannah," he said.

"Oh, yes," said his niece. "It was the best thing in the whole world. It's a story about true love. I never knew what true love was like until I saw that movie."

"Is that right?"

"Yes. I know it's only a made-up story, but it felt so true in my heart. One of these days, I'm going to find that for myself—the *Princess Bride* kind of love." Hannah let out an elaborate sigh. "It's exactly what love must be like."

Reese and Caleb exchanged a look.

"Well, let's find out what a bus ride home must be like," said Caleb. "We're going to say goodbye to Jonah at the hospital, and then we'll go to the station."

Jonah got himself into the wheelchair. Somebody had parked one out in the hallway, and after Caleb and Hannah had left, he was bored and he wanted to do something. Anything. He was angry, too. Pissed off, one of the kids in Group had called it. Back home, a boy would get a caning for saying pissed off. Not here, though. Here, they let you do stuff and say stuff, probably because the kids in the ward were sick and hurt and scared and everything else.

He unlocked the brakes of the chair and looked up and down the hallway. Nobody seemed to be paying attention. He turned the push ring of the right wheel, and the chair turned. He couldn't make it go forward, though.

Because he didn't have an arm on the left side.

He didn't have an arm. It had been incinerated. Now all he could do was go in circles.

That made him even more pissed off. Pushing with his good arm—his only arm—he made circles in the hallway, over and over again, faster and faster until the sweat ran down his face. Faster and faster until he crashed into a supply cart. Down went the cart with a terrific, satisfying clatter, and stuff went skidding all over the floor of the hallway.

And down went the chair with Jonah in it. He reached out with his imaginary left hand to break his fall. The hand wasn't there, and his head banged on the floor. A terrible pain screamed through him and he gritted his teeth, his breath chuffing in and out, in and out.

"Jonah! What happened?" The aide named Tammy came running. She must have pushed a button, because an orderly came right behind her. "Hey now, buddy," Tammy said. "Let's get you up and back to bed."

"I can get up myself," he said, jerking away from her. He saw her trade a look with the orderly. She sent a message on her device. Jonah scooted away from her. His not-there arm screamed with pain. Phantom pain, they called it. Like that made it easier to take. His arm was a ghost. A ghost that hurt like the devil.

Within a few minutes, Reese showed up. She was

breathing hard, as if she'd run all the way. "Looks like you had a little too much fun here," she said, then turned to Tammy. "How can I help?"

"I don't need help," Jonah said.

"Cool," she told him. "So are you going to sit there on the floor or do you want to get up?"

"I can do it," he spat.

"Can I watch? This is a teaching hospital, remember?"

He couldn't get up. It was so embarrassing. He kept losing his balance and plunking back down.

Tammy and the orderly picked up the stuff that had spilled from the cart. Reese sat on the floor beside him. She didn't offer to help.

Again and again, he tried. But the flaming not-there arm kept making him unbalanced. He was covered in sweat. Breathing through gritted teeth. "Fuck this," he said. "Fuck it. Fuck all. Fuck. Fuck. Fuck." It was the first time he'd said the word aloud. He wasn't a hundred percent sure what it meant, but he knew it was bad. It was so bad that he sneaked a glance at Reese to see if she was shocked, but she just sat there. Waiting. "*Fuck*," he said again.

"That's actually one of my favorite words," she said. "It's pretty rude, but I catch myself saying it all the time. So, remember how I said I know things?"

He didn't reply. He tried not to listen but couldn't help himself.

"I know your arm weighed about six pounds, give or take," she said. "That's about the weight of a big bag of sugar. That means your center of gravity is a lot different now. You have to learn what they call adaptive techniques. I'm right-handed, like you. So if I put my left arm away as if I don't have one"—she wound her arm behind her head—"I have to figure out a different way to move."

She rolled around on the floor. Jonah bit the insides of his cheeks to keep himself from smiling.

"I'll try getting to my knees," said Reese. She keeled sideways.

"Not like that," he said. "Put your feet on the *right* side, not the left."

"Oh. Right." She got her knees under her. "Hey, that's better."

He grumbled, knowing he'd been had. "You're pretending just to make me feel better."

"Is it working?"

"No."

"Well . . . fuck," she said.

He hid a smile, then got to his knees and managed to stand.

She made a fist of her right hand and pointed it at him.

He scowled. "What?"

"Fist bump. It's something you do after an accomplishment."

He did the fist bump with her, even though it was a dumb accomplishment. Then he turned his back on her and shuffled back to his bed. He lay down on his right side, facing the window. He heard her come in, heard the sigh of air as she sat on the vinyl-cushioned rolling stool by the bed.

"What do you miss about your arm?" she asked.

"Doing handsprings," he said.

"Wow, I have two arms and I can't do a handspring."

"Neither can I, now." His voice sounded small and peevish. "I can't eat with a knife and fork like I used to."

"Not at the same time. I bet your OT has something for that. Maybe a tool that's a knife and fork in one. A knork. Or a fife."

"You're not as funny as you think."

"I don't think I'm funny at all. I think losing an arm sucks for you. Tell me something else you miss."

"I miss my dog. I miss playing baseball. I miss pie."

"Dogs, baseball, and pie are three of the best things in the world," she agreed.

"Can I go to sleep now?" he asked.

"You betcha." A cool hand smoothed over his head. He didn't say anything about banging it on the floor, because if he did, she'd fuss over him too much. "I'd better go. I helped a lady in the ER who was having a baby. It was an emergency because she didn't even know she was expecting. I want to check on her."

"Okay," he said. A baby was a big emergency, for sure. Very slowly, he turned to her. "See you later."

She spun around once on the stool. "You will. Stay woke, Jonah."

9

Though he'd been away for only a few days, Caleb felt as if he'd been gone forever. He and Hannah got off the noisy, diesel-smelling bus at the highway junction marked by a shed-roofed shelter, where the locals caught the bus when a big trip was necessary. The highway was never busy here, just a two-lane country road that linked up with the poorly paved single track leading to the center of Middle Grove.

Hannah's bike was where she'd left it leaning against the back of the bus kiosk. She wheeled it beside Caleb as they walked toward the farm. The familiar sounds of the countryside surrounded them—birds chirping, the wind shushing through the trees, dogs barking. After the clashing and grinding noises of the city, the softness was sweet music to Caleb's ears. As they neared the town, he heard the clop of hooves on pavement.

At the sound of the approaching buggy, they stood aside and waited. The buggy belonged to Jacob Zook—Rebecca's father. Caleb recognized the Morgan horse in front.

"Climb in," Jacob said. "I got room."

"Thank you kindly," Caleb said. He hooked Hannah's bike on the back, and they took a seat on the bench inside.

Jacob eyed Hannah with a slight frown. She touched her hair and blushed. "I lost my covering," she said, staring at the floorboards of the buggy. "It was windy in the city."

"What's the news on Jonah?" Jacob asked.

"He's in the hospital, but he's going to be all right." Caleb realized the story would likely reach everyone in the community before the day was done, so he'd best be frank and plain with his words. "They had to take his arm clean off. His left arm. It was too damaged to save."

Jacob rubbed the U-shaped beard that outlined his jaw. "*Mein Gott.* That's a terrible harsh thing, then."

"It was a terrible shock, for sure," Caleb said.

Beside him, Hannah trembled. She'd cried off and on during the bus ride home, aching in her heart for her brother. Caleb patted her knee briefly. "He's doing pretty well, under the circumstances. The doctors, they say he's getting better fast, and he's in pretty good spirits."

Hannah said, "They're going to let him come home soon."

"That'll be a great relief to us all."

Caleb hoped it wasn't wishful thinking. They rode in silence for a time, past stubbled, newly harvested fields, another reminder of all the chores that needed doing. "Where've you been, Jacob?"

"I had to bring Rebecca home from her visit with Mose Shrock."

As a Mennonite, Mose had earned the trust of folks from the Amish and Mennonite communities. He was known far and wide for his compassion and practical ways as well as his healing skills.

"Is she sick again?"

Jacob stared directly ahead between the pricked ears of the horse. "I reckon Mose figured that out and we'll hear about it later. Rebecca'll be sorry she wasn't here for your homecoming."

Caleb shifted uncomfortably on the bench, remembering what had been on his mind the morning of Jonah's accident. He'd been planning to have a difficult—but overdue—conversation with Rebecca that day. He'd had the discussion all framed in his head—he wanted to tell her she deserved a devotion he would never be able to offer her. The kind that Hannah had been nattering on about during the bus ride, the *Princess Bride* kind of love.

He still needed to speak with Rebecca, and soon. But if she was sick, it would have to wait.

A modest sign marked the township of Middle Grove. They passed the small white-painted shed that housed the community phone, a reluctant concession to modern conveniences. At the Middle Grove Mercantile, Alma Troyer was hanging out some of the new quilts for sale. Caleb gave Hannah a nudge. "I can always tell which ones are yours."

She smiled. "I might not be so good at cooking and cleaning, but I can quilt."

It was true. Even Caleb, who had no eye for needlework, knew his niece's quilts were something special—vivid abstractions, sometimes incorporating unexpected elements—a shiny river stone, feathers, embroidered words. Her quilts were so different that they attracted collectors from all over.

"I want to make something special for Jonah," she said.

"I reckon he'd like that."

She smiled again and shook her head. "Jonah? He wouldn't notice if I gave him a saddle blanket. It'd be more for me than him."

The buggy rolled to a stop at the lane leading to the Stoltz place.

"Thank you for the ride, Jacob," Caleb said. "We are obliged."

The older man nodded. "Rebecca would be pleased if

you would come calling," he said with a none-too-subtle wink.

"You take care now." Caleb jumped to the ground, went to the back of the buggy, and hoisted down Hannah's bike. She got on the bike and rode along the lane toward the farmhouse.

His father was waiting for him on the porch, thumbs tucked into suspenders, his brow shadowed by a black hat. Flinty blue-gray eyes flashed from beneath the brim. "It's good you're back," he said, "good to hear Jonah's all right."

"He survived," Caleb said. "His arm didn't." He quickly explained the situation, as he had for Jacob in the buggy.

His father took off his hat and furrowed a splayed hand through his hair as he scowled off into the distance. "That's a damnable shame. It surely is. How will the boy get on with only one arm? He's going to be useless on the farm."

Caleb crushed his back teeth together to hold in a retort. "I'd be obliged if Jonah never hears that from you."

"No point in hiding from the truth."

Caleb stayed quiet. Arguing with his father was like talking to a wall.

"It's time for him to come home," Asa pronounced. "We can take care of him here, with his friends and family."

"He's not ready," Caleb said, mounting the steps to the front porch. "Excuse me. I have some packing to do."

His father followed him through the house. "Packing."

Caleb nodded. "I left here in a hurry, you'll recall." *And over your strident objections*, he silently added. "I'm going to need some things for the city."

"The city's no place for you or Jonah. I want you to bring the boy home."

"I said he's not ready." Caleb tried to keep his tone—and his temper—even as he went to his room and took out a few belongings.

"Hannah said he's alert and talking like a jaybird," Asa said, glaring at him from the doorway. "No need for him to malinger at the hospital, surrounded by strangers. What's done is done. There's nothing but trouble for him in the city. He needs to be here with the people who care for him."

Caleb stuffed an old canvas rucksack with several changes of clothes. "He stays where he is until the doctors say it's safe to move him."

"I know more about keeping a boy safe than any English doctor," Asa retorted.

Caleb pivoted around to face him. "The way you kept John and me safe? I don't think so."

He watched the color rise in his father's face like mercury in a thermometer. They almost never mentioned the past, though Caleb's soul was stained with memories. He had long since stopped expecting any sort of acknowledgment, let alone contrition, from his father.

"Excuse me," he said. "I've got a bus to catch." He buckled the bag and brushed past his father, heading outside. Setting the rucksack on the front stoop, he whistled for Jubilee. The dog came frisking down the slope behind the house, sneezing and wagging her tail in welcome. Caleb patted his thigh and walked with the dog across the freshly mown field between their farm and the neighbors'.

Levi Hauber was loading sacks of grain into a cart. He stopped and jumped down when he saw Caleb.

"Your boy," he said without preamble. "He's all I think about." Genuine tears welled in his eyes.

Caleb filled him in on Jonah's progress. "I'm going back to the city to stay until it's safe to bring him home."

"I understand. We all want to help."

"You are, by taking care of the place while I'm gone."

"For as long as you need us. Your team is the best," he added, referring to Caleb's harness of draft horses. "I swear, I've never seen such a fine team. Even old Baudouin is looking lively."

"I'm obliged to you, then."

"We've been looking in on Asa, too," Levi assured him. "Every day."

"Thanks for that, Levi," said Caleb. The Haubers and the Stoltzes had been neighbors for decades, and the neighbors knew Asa's ways.

Caleb and Levi shook hands. Just as Caleb was turning to leave, someone came out of the house.

"Caleb, wait."

Rebecca. She always looked willowy and slightly fragile to him, with pale eyes and wispy blond hair. He knew from experience, however, that she had an iron will. She hurried across the yard toward him. "I was over visiting the Haubers."

Like fun she was. More likely her father had let her know Caleb was back in town. He honestly wished he could be happier to see her. Rebecca was a fine person, kind and devoted. But she wasn't the one for him, and he couldn't force himself to feel that way.

"How are you?" he asked. "Your father said you went to the doctor."

She waved a hand in a vague gesture. "It was nothing. I'm glad I got back in time to see you. And it's wonderful good news that Jonah is all right. Will you and Asa come to supper, then?"

"I can't stay," he told her. "I'm off to the city again to be with Jonah."

"How long will you be gone?"

"For as long as it takes. A number of weeks, at least."

"Oh. I see. Well. I'll miss you. I'll keep Jonah in my prayers."

"You take care, now." He took a step back.

"Caleb. I wonder . . . I think we should have a talk."

Oh boy. Maybe he was more transparent than he realized. "How's that?"

"About us," she said. "I fear you're having second thoughts."

And third, he reflected. *And fourth.* When her family and the bishop had first promoted the courting, he'd believed it might be a way to provide a stable home for Jonah and Hannah. But as time went on, he'd questioned the plan. Yet whenever he'd tried to discuss the matter with Rebecca, she deflected to a different topic. Finally, though, she seemed open to having the difficult conversation.

"I appreciate you bringing that up," Caleb said, holding his gaze steady. "I think you're a fine person, Rebecca, and you deserve the love and safety of a fine family."

"Yes," she said, her voice soft and breathy. "I do want that."

"And everyone wants that for you. But I don't think you'd be so happy with us. We couldn't be right for you."

"But—"

"John's kids are a handful. And will be even more so after Jonah's accident."

She hesitated, then said, "Hannah will be married and away in a year or two. And as for Jonah—well . . . I must do my duty."

It bothered Caleb that she regarded Jonah as a duty. He was a joy, every day.

"It wouldn't be fair to subject you to such a difficult situation," he suggested.

"I embroidered the cloth, Caleb," she said, ignoring the suggestion.

She meant business. She was telling him she was ready for him to follow through with her family's plan—baptism, marriage, babies, following the path of their ancestors.

"Something keeps holding you back," she continued. "It's not just Hannah and Jonah."

"Growing the beard will give me an itchy rash," he said, trying to lighten the tone. He could tell from her expression that she was not having it. "I'm sorry. This warrants a much longer conversation, but I have a bus to catch." He reached out and gently touched her shoulder, giving it a squeeze. "Rebecca, I'm so sorry. I realize you gave up other opportunities, and I never should have let you do that."

"I'm not interested in other opportunities," she said, taking his hand. "I'm interested in you, Caleb Stoltz."

He felt a wrenching sense of guilt as he carefully extracted his hand from hers. "It wouldn't be right. It most truly wouldn't, and it was wrong of me to let you think that."

She pursed her lips, then took a deep breath. "You go," she said. "Go to Jonah. All else will wait."

With a wave of her hand, she turned back toward the house. Strangely, she staggered to one side, and Caleb leaped forward reflexively, taking her arm. "Hey now. Are you all right?" he asked.

She didn't speak for a moment. Then she looked at him strangely, her eyes filmed by confusion. "Caleb. No, I'm just . . . I've been so clumsy lately."

"What's the matter? Do you need help?"

"Oh, it's nothing. A headache, is all. Mose Shrock gave me some tablets. I'll just go inside, then." She held the rail and mounted the steps to the Haubers' kitchen.

He watched her go, then shook his head, wishing it could be a simple thing, to untangle himself from the situation. Wishing he'd never agreed to a courting in the first place. Promising his brother to raise the kids in the faith was one thing, but forcing himself to live in the faith—he hadn't promised that. He signaled to the dog, and they walked back across the field to the house. Hannah was there, waiting to say goodbye.

He handed her a slip of paper with his temporary mobile phone number. "If you need anything—anything at all—you ask Rachel Hauber or Alma Troyer. Levi'll look after your grandfather, don't you worry."

"I won't."

"You call me if you need anything. It's all right to use the phone box."

"As you wish." She offered a quick smile. "That's from *The Princess Bride*."

10

Caleb hadn't done any hard work in days, yet he felt exhausted the next morning. Back at Leroy's place, he had a strange sense that he'd been around the world and back. Matters that pressed on his mind wore him out far more than backbreaking farm chores or wrestling with huge draft horses.

He didn't regret his decision, though. Jonah was his family, and a man didn't balk at making sacrifices for his family.

As he opened the door to the sunny morning, the message board in the lobby of the apartment building fluttered with paper flyers—people seeking jobs, roommates, furniture. Stuff for sale. Complaints about noise in the building. There was a grim-looking Community Watch notice warning folks about a gang of thugs jumping people in the neighborhood. The city was gritty and dangerous and strange, and Caleb was fascinated by it all.

Reese came clattering down the stairs. She was holding a paper cup of coffee in one hand and a Danish pastry clamped between her teeth. "Hey," she said when she saw him, her voice muffled by the pastry.

"Hey," he replied, holding the door and taking the coffee cup from her. "You're in a hurry."

"Late," she said, then wrenched the Danish out of her mouth. Even with mussed-up hair and crumbs down the front of her, she lifted his spirits with just the mere hint of a smile.

"I'm a fast walker." He strode toward the riverwalk.

"You're back," she said, taking her coffee as she hurried alongside him. "I mean, that's obvious, but I didn't know if you'd be making a round-trip so quickly."

"Would have been here sooner, but I missed the bus coming back," he said. "Got a ride with a milk tank truck that was heading this way." Last winter, that same truck had slid off the road in a snowstorm, and Caleb had used his team of horses to pull the rig out. The driver had vowed to return the favor anytime Caleb needed one. Yesterday, he'd called in that favor.

"I decided to stay until it's time to take Jonah home," he told Reese. "Just couldn't imagine not seeing him every day. There are things to figure out, though. I can get myself up to Grantham Farm every day to put in some hours there. It's a lot closer to the city than Middle Grove."

"Welcome to the modern world," she said, "where you get to be pulled in several different directions, and you have to figure out how to do about a dozen things simultaneously and well."

"Yes," he said. "It's awesome."

She tossed her empty cup into a painted recycling bin. Even such a small gesture accentuated the differences in their worlds. In Middle Grove, every discarded item had to be dealt with, either by reusing it, putting it in the compost rack, or sending it to the burn pile.

When they got to the hospital, Reese went off to work somewhere and Caleb headed straight up to the peds ward. He watched Jonah through the therapy session to condition and tone his muscles and to learn new ways to move without his arm. It was both heartbreaking and inspiring to see the boy's concentration and determination as he did the exercises. "He's doing so well," said the physical therapist, giving him a high five. "Jonah, you're my hardest-working patient."

"Did I work hard enough to earn a round of Bird-brain?" That was his current favorite video game.

"Sure, you did. See you later, kid."

"Come on, Uncle Caleb, I'll show you how it's done." Jonah scampered over to the patient lounge.

As the boy happily introduced him to Birdbrain, Caleb reflected on worldly things and wondered what the future held for Jonah. What would life be like for this boy after such a devastating injury? In his darkest moments, Caleb caught himself wondering if Jonah carried the same troubled soul as Caleb's mother, and his brother, John. What if the boy tried to harm himself? How could Caleb keep him safe?

Maybe Jonah would cling fiercely to Old Order traditions the way John had done after the suicide attempt. Or would he feel more like Caleb, buffeted between two worlds? *Be ye not conformed to this world.*

"What're you thinking?" Jonah asked, startling him out of his troubled thoughts.

"Thinking about you, little man," he said, forcing a smile.

"That's funny, so was I." Reese walked into the lounge area, all curly hair and smiles, and that way of looking at Caleb as if he were the only person on the planet. She was a fresh-plucked daisy, even in her doctor clothes, with a pin on her collar that read I WORK THE "ALWAYS" SHIFT.

Jonah smiled broadly, and Caleb's heart lifted. "Hello, Reese."

"I'm on a break," she said. "I heard a rumor about you, young man. I heard you're everyone's favorite on the floor."

"For real?"

"For real."

"That's nice." Then his smile disappeared. "What if it's because folks feel sorry for me on account of my arm?"

"Trust me, no one feels sorry for a boy who can beat Dr. Parmenter at chess *and* Parcheesi."

The smile returned. "Yeah, okay."

A few minutes later, an aide came to get him. "Time for your group counseling," she said.

"What's that?" asked Caleb.

"We sit around in a group and talk about our feelings," said Jonah. "It's pretty fun."

Caleb couldn't stifle a laugh. "Since when do you know how to talk about your feelings, Jonah Stoltz?"

The boy grinned. "See? Making progress." He gave Caleb a brief hug, then made a fist and bumped it against Reese's clenched hand. "Stay woke," he said to her.

"Will do," she said.

After Jonah had gone, Caleb turned to her. "A fist bump? Really?"

She shrugged. "It's a thing."

"'Stay woke'?"

"An expression. Jonah's really quick to pick things up."

He nodded, then glanced at the clock. "There's a bus up to Half Moon Junction—that's the closest station to Grantham Farm. I've got to go to work."

"I should get back to work too." She paused, looking up at him. "Are you busy this evening?"

His heart skipped a beat. "What did you have in mind?"

"It's not a date," Reese said to her mother. Joanna Powell had stopped by unannounced, a whirlwind of energy and motivation. Reese was in the middle of getting ready for her evening with Caleb. "It's a . . . an outing," she said.

Her mother swept around the apartment, focusing on dog-eared test manuals, unopened mail, and stacks of paperwork related to the residency match. "I'm surprised you have time for an outing, let alone a date. Now, who is this person?"

"Just someone I met at the hospital." She bit her lip, reluctant to go into detail. She couldn't explain her attraction to Caleb to herself, let alone her mother. He was like a magnet to her. She often caught herself trying to run into him, seeking that ineffable thrill of warmth that coursed through her each time she saw him. While dozing in the on-call room, she dreamed of him, and awakened with visions of showing him around the city. His sense of wonder at ordinary things was contagious, awakening her to so much she took for granted. She tried to tell herself the feelings would pass once the novelty wore off. Instead, the yearning intensified. She wanted to spend more time with him. She liked the way she felt in his presence—calm and centered, a welcome break from her usual state of anxiety.

"So he's . . . what? A resident? An attending?" her mother persisted.

Her mom couldn't get her head around the idea that Reese might be friends with a guy who wasn't in the same field.

"None of the above. He's the uncle of a patient. The boy's arm was amputated, and Caleb is his guardian. I was in the ER when the kid came in, and Caleb was . . . well, during the surgery, we just . . . connected."

"I see." Her mother's mouth tightened. "You would have learned more by observing the surgery instead of hanging around with the uncle. I worry about you getting distracted."

Reese refused to take the bait. "Sometimes I think I need a distraction."

Her mother's gaze skimmed over her. "You're wearing that?"

Reese smoothed her hands down the form-fitting dress she'd picked out, a bright red print with a flaring skirt. "Apparently so."

"Then *he's* going to be distracted."

"I'll take that as a compliment."

"Well, I suppose you can use a little fun." Joanna set down a folder of information. "Take a look at this program at Georgetown. I think you should add it to your list of options."

"I will, Mom. Thanks."

Her mother checked her phone. "I have to go. Your father has a lecture tonight. Remember, I told you about it."

"Okay, cool." Reese's stress level rose a notch. The truth was, she took enormous pride in her parents' accomplishments, and she knew they loved it when she attended their events.

"So where are you and this mystery man going?"

Reese swiped a lipstick across her mouth and tucked it into her bag. "Salsa dancing."

Raised eyebrow. "Indeed. Well, have fun, then."

Reese let out a sigh as her mother left. She told herself not to feel guilty for skipping her father's lecture. He was brilliant and famous. He didn't need her in his audience.

A few minutes later, Caleb appeared at the door. At the sight of him, worries about her parents dissolved and a different sort of flutter rose in her chest. "Hey," she said, admiring his well-fitting trousers and fresh white shirt, his blond hair slightly damp from the shower. "You look great."

He focused on her, and his gaze warmed. "You're not so bad yourself."

"Thanks. I hope you don't think I'm crazy for dragging you out to salsa night."

"I hope you don't think *I'm* crazy for accepting. It's only fair to warn you that I've never danced a step in my life."

"Don't worry. You'll be in good company. It's amateur night at the salsa club. We're going to meet up with Leroy and his new date, Cheryl, and a few others from the hospital." A social life. What a concept. Caleb motivated her to actually get outside and do something besides study, work, and plan for the Match.

They walked a few blocks to an area full of outdoor cafés, buzzy restaurants, and clubs. It was a golden late-summer evening, and crowds spilled out onto the pedestrian-only street to enjoy the last of the day's warmth. Reese and Caleb met up with Leroy and the others gathered around a bar table outside the club.

Reese introduced Caleb all around, watching the reactions of Cheryl; Misty, a lab tech; and Misty's date, a guy from Australia named Stuart. Predictably, Misty and Cheryl regarded Caleb with clear appreciation. "Welcome to Friday night," said Misty. "We work hard. Time to play hard. Have a beer, you two." She poured them each a glass.

The talk drifted to hospital gossip and patient cases. Reese glanced at Caleb, who listened in polite silence. He was already an outsider, and shop talk only sharpened the contrast.

"Let's not talk about work," she suggested. "We spend too much time working, anyway."

"Good point. I know a game we can play," Cheryl said, picking up a container of small cards from the table. "It's called Never Have I Ever."

Reese took a big gulp of beer. "Not my favorite. I always embarrass myself."

"Then we should surely play," Caleb said, eyeing her.

"Isn't there a trivia game or something?"

Caleb ignored her and turned to Cheryl. "How does it work?"

"Simple," she said. "You hold up your hand with five fingers raised, and if the statement doesn't apply to you, then you put one finger down. You're out when you run out of fingers."

"Isn't there usually a drinking component to this game?" asked Stuart.

"Might be," said Reese. "But it's not mandatory."

Leroy drew the top card. "Never have I ever . . . dyed my hair with a color not found in nature."

Each of the women lowered a finger. Reese had streaked her hair with neon pink, more than once, mainly to annoy her parents. None of the guys had. Caleb looked mystified.

"Next card," said Leroy. "Never have I ever . . . lied to get out of trouble."

Everyone except Caleb had to put down a finger. "All guilty," said Reese. She turned to Caleb. "I can't imagine you never told a fib to avoid trouble."

He grinned. "I didn't even know lying was an option."

Actually, she wasn't surprised. He wasn't a liar. One of the first things she'd noticed about him was his honesty.

"Next one," Leroy said. "Never have I ever ridden a horse."

Caleb lowered a finger. Of course he'd ridden a horse. So had everyone else, except Reese.

"I had a deprived childhood," she said.

"Right," Leroy teased. "You were so deprived."

"Never have I ever used makeup to cover a hickey" was the next challenge.

Reese blushed, but gamely lowered a finger—and she

was the only one. "Seriously?" she asked, looking around the table. "Come on."

"What's a hickey?" Caleb asked.

"You should show him," Misty said.

"Next," Reese said, turning over a card. "Never have I ever . . . multitasked while having sex."

"Well, that's just dumb," said Cheryl. "Let's skip that one. If you multitask while you're having sex, you're doing something wrong."

"No, *he's* doing something wrong," said Reese. "Moving right along. Never have I ever . . . had sex in a moving vehicle." Great. She was going to have to cop to that one as well. Junior year abroad, a microbus trip with a group of students down the Costa Brava in Spain. She barely remembered the guy, but the wine and the sex . . .

"Does a boat count?" asked Stuart.

All of them except Caleb had to lower a finger. Reese was dying to know about his romantic and sexual past. Maybe one of these days, she would get close enough to ask.

"Never have I ever . . . woken up to someone whose name I didn't know," Leroy read from the next card.

Oh boy. Reese had to lower her finger in shame, knocking herself out of play. "It was just the one time, okay? New Year's Eve when I was in college." She could barely look at Caleb. "I'm going to start calling this the don't-judge-me game."

The others dropped out one by one, on much less provocative questions about eating a bacon doughnut or pretending to be a foreigner. In the end, Caleb prevailed, admitting only to riding a horse, building something out of wood, and shooting a gun.

"Hey, the dancing started," Cheryl said. "Let's go inside."

Reese breathed a sigh of relief. She wondered what he thought of her now that she'd had to admit to some of the highlights of her college days.

The salsa club was dark and crowded, pulsing with music and excitement. Reese glanced at Caleb. He surveyed the glittering lights and dance floor with a bemused expression.

"Let's grab a table and watch for a bit," she said. "Then we'll give it a go."

"Sounds good, Reese."

They found a spot near the busy dance floor and ordered the house special—white sangria with bits of fresh fruit. Caleb tasted his. "I like it," he remarked and drained his glass in a few gulps.

"Whoa there, cowboy," she said. "This stuff packs a punch."

"I'm going to need a punch to get me out on the dance floor."

She laughed. "Point taken. I'm not very good, but the basic steps are pretty simple."

As they watched, his knee went up and down in time with the music. There was a lead couple on a raised platform, demonstrating the number. Misty and Stuart, then Leroy and Cheryl joined in, with mixed results but a lot of laughter. After a second glass of sangria, Caleb held out his hand, palm up. "Shall we dance?"

She put her hand in his. "I thought you'd never ask."

His grip was sturdy and strong, as she'd expected. What she hadn't expected was the thrill that coursed through her as he placed his hand on the small of her back and led her out to the dance floor.

"There are only three simple steps and eight counts," said Reese. "Watch the couple onstage. The rest is all showmanship."

"Do you know the three steps?"

She demonstrated—one, two, three, pause. Five, six, seven, pause. He watched her legs and feet with an intensity that felt like a caress, bringing a flush to her cheeks. "There," she said, pretending not to notice the way he was looking at her. "Watch again, and then give it a try."

He stood facing her, and she felt a little thrill as he moved his hand to her upper back, imitating the closed hold demonstrated by the lead couple. "How's this?"

She tingled everywhere. "Uh, yes. That works just fine. Let's practice the steps."

After a few false starts, he picked up the simple pattern. "Where did you learn this dancing?" he asked her.

"I took ballroom dancing for beginners for a PE credit one year."

"A PE credit."

"Physical education. For a college credit."

He offered a half grin. "Physical education. Not a concept we have in our community." Yet he continued practicing the steps, matching the rhythm with surprising panache.

"Hey, you're good for a first-timer. You picked up the moves in no time."

"I go to a lot of horse shows."

"Either that's a non sequitur, or I'm insulted."

"Don't be. My horses win prizes."

"Now I am for sure—" The breath left her as he caught the rhythm of the music and moved with a grace she hadn't expected. By the middle of the number, she noticed several nearby patrons watching them. In the plain white shirt and dark trousers, he cut a striking figure. There was just so much of him—the height, the shoulders, the hair, and his complete unselfconscious delight in dancing.

"For the love of God," Misty said in her ear during a break in the action, "if you don't take him home right this minute and shag him, I might have to do it myself."

"It's . . . We're not like that," Reese protested, but not loudly enough for Misty to hear. Because the truth was, she did want him. This pure attraction was something very new to her. With other guys she'd dated, there was always an element of speculation—*Are we compatible? Do our schedules mesh? Do we work in the same field, have similar goals?*

When it came to Caleb, none of that mattered. He was a mysterious and powerful enchantment, and she had no idea what to do about that except to hope it would eventually go away, like a virus.

She pondered this as they made their way home. Starting something was a bad idea, yet it also felt like the best idea she'd had in a long time. While they walked side by side, their hands brushed, more than once, and she found the casual touch ridiculously provocative.

Leroy and his date were a bit tipsy, laughing and flirting with their arms around each other. At the front door, he took Caleb aside and murmured something, then went upstairs with Cheryl.

"He's going to get lucky," Caleb said. "And yes, I know what that means. It also means I'll need to sleep on your sofa. If that's all right."

Her skin tingled all over. "And if it's not?"

He grinned. "Oh, but it is. I know you, Reese. I know that look."

She preceded him up the stairs. "You do not know me." As she unlocked the door and they went inside, she turned to gaze up at him. "But okay. You can have the sofa. I'll get you a pillow and blanket."

11

As the days of Jonah's recovery passed, Reese and Caleb fell into a pattern. Each morning, he took an early bus up to Grantham Farm, where he worked with the horses. Late in the day, he returned to visit with Jonah through supper and up until bedtime. If Reese's schedule lined up with that, they would do something together. She told herself she spent so much time with him because he was so alone in the city, trying to balance his responsibilities to Jonah, to his work, and to the distant farm in Middle Grove. But kindness wasn't the only thing that drove her.

She took unabashed delight in sharing her world with him. Everything startled him—wall-to-wall carpeting, a restaurant menu, the fact that people could bring food to the table and earn a tip for doing so. She introduced him to pizza one night and sushi another, roaring with delight at the expression on his face as he watched the sushi chefs at work with their knives and blowtorches.

"Back home, we'd probably use this for fish bait," he said, eyeing a portion of unagi and a roll covered in bright orange roe.

"Try it," she said. "You'll never look at fish bait the same way."

He fumbled with the chopsticks, but managed to get a roe-covered morsel into his mouth. His eyes widened and then teared up. He swallowed hard, grabbed for a glass of water, and downed the whole thing.

"Not your cup of tea, then," she said, suppressing a grin.

He gamely stabbed at another bite, this one from a vegetarian roll. "I'll keep trying to like it."

She gazed at him across the table. "Is it hard then? To like being in this world?"

He set down his chopsticks and gazed back at her. He seemed to be looking at her lips. "Sometimes it's altogether too easy."

Her mind lingered on his comment as they went for an after-dinner stroll back to the apartment. "By too easy, do you mean convenient?"

"Could be it's just an adjustment, getting used to the way things work. Like someone brings the food ready-made, then takes away the dishes. Or you need to do the bookkeeping and there's a program to tally everything up."

"You say that like it's a bad thing."

"No, it's just a thing, as my friend Reese would say." As they passed a trendy gym that was crammed with exercise machines, he shook his head. "Now *that* is something you won't see in an Amish community—devices to make a body work harder."

"Lots of people slave all day at a desk job. When you're doing taxes, you probably sit around too."

"Not all day. All night. During the day, it's the farm or the horses. No need for the gym."

It shows, she thought, unable to keep herself from checking out his muscular arms. In the deepest part of herself, she knew it wasn't just attraction she was feeling. Deep down, she sensed an oh-so-satisfying flash of defiance—this was not her norm. It was something wholly new and different and unexpected. She could easily imagine her parents' reaction if she said she had a crush on an Amish guy. It would probably surprise them less if she told them she was dating a traditional Inuit.

Yet even deeper down, at her very core, she felt apprehension. A better person would feel totally confident and open to pursuing this relationship, but she was not that better person. So for her, apprehension was the only possible thing to feel at this moment.

There was no future with Caleb Stoltz, and though they had never discussed anything of the sort, they both knew it. She had been doggedly on this path to a medical career for years and could not let herself falter. Any distraction—and he was highly distracting—was bound to make her feel apprehensive.

Looking around the riverwalk, she noticed an interracial couple on a park bench, a black executive in an expensive-looking suit, carrying a couture briefcase, with his arm around a white woman in a fast-food restaurant uniform. His entire focus was trained on his mobile phone while she blew bubbles with her gum and looked bored. *Those two*, thought Reese, knowing nothing else about the couple. *They'll never work out.* She wondered what people thought when they saw her and Caleb together.

"Yes, but you have to admit, some of the conveniences are amazing," she commented, dragging herself out of her own head.

"I never said they weren't. Being able to hear any music you want with a nap on your phone is incredible."

"Did you just say 'with a nap'?"

"I did. No idea why you'd want to sleep through the music, though."

"App," she said.

"How's that?"

"You mean 'an app,' not 'a nap.'" She showed him her phone screen. "These are programs called applications—apps."

"That makes a little more sense, then." He took the phone from her and studied the screen, then lifted an eyebrow. "Booty Call?"

She flushed. "I never use that one. I forgot it was there."

She grabbed for her phone, but he held it out of reach. He tapped another icon called Favorite Places. "Now, this is nice."

"Other people's travel pictures. You can see the world without ever having to leave your house." She studied his rapt expression as he gazed at an idyllic beach scene. A thought struck her. "When was the last time you went down to the shore?"

"Never been. Never even seen the ocean."

"Well, that's just wrong. So guess what?"

He looked her straight in the eye, and that niggling apprehension dissolved. "Are you thinking what I think you're thinking?"

Caleb admired Reese's persistence. Once she got a notion in her head, there was no stopping her. She was absolutely convinced that he needed to see the ocean for the first time, and on a hot September day, she made it happen. After his morning visit to see Jonah, Caleb met her at the parking garage where she kept her car.

She was already there, looking like a butterfly in a gauzy white dress and a wide-brimmed straw hat with a pink scarf around it. He couldn't keep from staring at her legs as she loaded things into the trunk and back seat. Then he cleared his throat to alert her before he got too riled up.

When she turned to him, her face lit with a smile he thought about all too frequently. "Ready?" she asked.

"I am. You need help with something?"

"Not yet. I will when we get there." She put the top down, and he settled in the passenger seat. He had borrowed a pair of shorts and flip-flops from Leroy and wore a plain white T-shirt. When they stopped at a traffic light, he caught Reese staring at him.

"What?" he asked.

She jerked her gaze away. "Nothing."

"You look at me like that and you see nothing?" With a chuckle, he propped his elbow on the window ledge.

"I just noticed you have a suntan."

"Happens every summer."

"I thought Amish guys wear long pants only."

"Not when we go swimming."

"Oh. You wear shorts, then. Swim trunks?"

"Nah. Never owned a pair of shorts."

She turned back to face him and lowered her sunglasses. Her eyes were wide with dawning comprehension. "Oh."

"It makes no sense to put on dry clothes and then go in the water."

"When you put it that way . . ." The light changed, and she turned away. "Grab the sunscreen from that bag behind you," she said. "It's my duty as a doctor to warn you about sun damage. Do yourself a favor and put some on. We'll put on more when we get there."

He gamely spread the coconut-scented lotion on his thighs and arms.

"Don't miss the tops of your feet," she said. "Very vulnerable."

"I never wore shoes in the summer until I was old enough to work the fields."

"I'm curious. You make the simple life sound so idyllic. Why would anyone want to leave?"

"Everybody's got his reasons. It's complicated."

"I can do complicated." She flexed her hands on the steering wheel. "Hannah told me you intended to leave but came back when your brother was killed."

He squinted at the road ahead. "I was away on rum-springa . . ." He still remembered the heady, unfettered sense of freedom and possibility of those times.

"And how did it go? Like Jerry Springa? Did you hang out at the mall and get high?"

He grinned. "You must've seen that documentary on the TV."

"Parts of it, I admit. So is that what it was like?"

"Maybe for some. Not for me, though."

"You weren't such a rebel, then."

"That depends on whose opinion you're asking for. Some folks would say I was the worst kind of rebel. In the eyes of the most conservative members of our community, anyway."

"Oh. So what's the worst kind of rebellion?"

"I went to school." He could tell from her expression that she didn't understand. "To college. Community college. The owner of Grantham Farm paid my tuition and I took classes."

"And people in your community objected to this?"

"Oh, yah." Worldly knowledge inspired a hint of fear—always that. Fear was the thing that poked the beast awake. Asa had stood with his fists pressed to his sides, clenching and unclenching in silent rage. "Education is considered a more powerful lure than 3-D movies or rock 'n' roll music," Caleb told Reese. "The more a person learns, the more he wants to experience the world."

"And yet you went back to Middle Grove."

"I did."

"Because of Jonah and Hannah."

"That's right."

"Have you ever thought about leaving the community with the two of them?"

"Nope. John wanted them to be raised Amish. Honoring my brother's last wish is the least I can do." He paused, then unearthed one of his most painful memories. "John didn't die right away when he was shot. He survived long enough to tell the bishop and me his final wish."

"That his children be raised in the faith. Yes, you told me that. You're very loyal," she said. "And the kids are lucky to have you."

He was more grateful than loyal. He owed John so much. There had been times when the one thing that stood between Caleb and his father's fists had been his fiercely protective brother. For that alone, Caleb would be forever in John's debt. Now more than ever, given what Jonah was going through.

She glanced over at him as they left the city behind. "You're a good guy, Caleb Stoltz. And your big teenage rebellion was going to college. I still can't get over that."

"What was yours? Assuming you had one."

"The usual. Sex, drugs, rock 'n' roll. It didn't really rattle my parents, though. They started talking to me about safe sex before I even hit puberty. They gave me a chart about recreational drugs and made me memorize the risks and antidotes. And they played arena rock all through my childhood—Pearl Jam, Nirvana, Soundgarden. If I really wanted to shock my parents, I would have *refused* to go to college."

"Guess we both failed in our mission to rebel," he said.

The highway swept them away, and the stream of traffic thinned to a trickle. She followed signs to a state road. Soon they would cross into New Jersey. Caleb had never been to New Jersey before. The stretch of road leading due east was all but deserted—one of the perks, Reese explained, of coming out on a weekday.

"Ever driven a car?" she asked him. "Hannah said you did."

"A time or two. One of my buddies kept an old Chevy in a shed back home. We managed to get it up and running. Took turns driving it until my buddy's father caught on and sent the thing to the junkyard." He decided not to elaborate on his father's reaction to the situation.

She pulled off to the side of the road. "Switch places with me."

He didn't need any urging. He jumped out and went to the driver's side and fastened his seat belt. His knees were cramped awkwardly against the dashboard. "How does this adjust?" he asked her.

"There's a switch on the side of your seat." She leaned across him, took his hand, and guided it to a small lever near the floor. The soft weight of her against him, the smell of her hair, the feel of her sun-warmed skin made him dizzy. He held himself immobile, trying not to react to her nearness and her touch.

He managed to adjust the seat and then refastened his seat belt. "I got it," he said. "Okay then. All set."

"Same here," she said. "It's pretty straightforward. Let me know if you have any questions."

He angled the rearview mirror, trying to remember the last time he'd driven a car. Hiram Voss's old Chrysler, maybe ten years before. The occasional tractor or truck at Grantham for work or chores. That was about it, though. And a convertible sports car? Never.

His mouth curved upward as a sense of anticipation spread through him. He shifted into drive and checked the road—still empty. Then he eased out onto the highway. The car lurched a little until he got the hang of driving something so responsive. Smooth, steady acceleration and braking, that was the key.

Reese switched on the radio. A song about a bad habit and looking for a stranger was playing, the heavy beat thumping from invisible speakers. "The Kooks," she said. "An oldie from the nineties."

He liked the way the music felt as he drove along the arrow-straight road toward the shore. The flat pavement bisected an area of lowlands, passing scrubby marshes and occasional side roads leading to small settlements here and there. When he was a kid, he used to be obsessed with maps, tracing his finger along the lines marking roads and rivers, imagining places he knew he'd never see.

Glancing at the speedometer, he accelerated up to the speed limit, feeling the power of the engine carry them along. He relaxed and sank into the pleasure of freedom flowing through him. The warm sun and the wind, the radio playing, the coconut essence of sunscreen, a pretty girl beside him—all these elements combined into a singular sensation that was so heady he almost didn't have a name for it. He tipped back his head and laughed aloud.

"I'm glad you're enjoying this," said Reese.

"Enjoying is an understatement. It feels like freedom and joy and exhilaration all at once."

"We can all use more of that."

"Yeah?"

"I have this problem. I tend to forget to have fun because I get so busy with studying and work and trying to plan ahead."

"That's quite a problem."

"I'm working on it." She turned slightly in her seat. "This is helping. How do you like driving?"

"This car doesn't handle like a tractor." He pressed on

the accelerator and with a growl of power, the car surged even faster. Caleb allowed his worries to peel away like leaves on the wind. He could do anything. Anything was possible. Jonah would heal and be as good as new. Hannah would find her own happiness, somehow. And he—

A high-pitched yip crashed into his thoughts.

"Oh, shit," said Reese, looking back over her shoulder. "Pull over. Shit. Shit. *Shit.*"

He glanced in the rearview mirror. Sure enough, the blinking, flashing, colorful lights of a Highway Patrol car filled his vision. He eased the convertible over to the shoulder of the road and shut off the engine.

"Do you know what to do?" asked Reese. She looked ghostly pale, as though bracing herself for disaster.

"What I'm told, I reckon."

"Damn. *Shit.* Quick, let's get our story straight."

"What's wrong with the truth?"

"The truth will get you a giant expensive speeding ticket."

"Crime doesn't pay," he murmured. "Neither does lying."

He heard the crunch of boots on gravel as the cop approached. She had on a Highway Patrol uniform. A badge and gun in a holster gleamed in the sunlight. She wore dark glasses and a hat, hair in a ponytail and her mouth pink with just a hint of lipstick.

But no hint of a smile.

"License and registration, please," she said.

Reese looked slightly nauseated as she rummaged in the console and extracted a printed page. Caleb took out his billfold, produced his driver's license, and handed it over. Reese looked as if she might faint with relief.

The patrolwoman took off the sunglasses and studied his license, front and back. Then her gaze swept over the car. "Mr. . . . Stoltz," she said. "Do you know how fast you were going?"

Like the wind. "No, miss. I was watching the road."

She looked at him, then back at the license card, and something about him seemed to catch her eye, because her expression changed a bit.

"You were going seventy-six miles an hour," the cop said. "Do you know what the speed limit is here?"

"Last signpost we passed said fifty-five," Caleb admitted.

"What's your hurry?"

"I'm going to see the ocean," he said. "I've never seen it before."

Her eyes narrowed. "Sure." Then she snatched the registration paper from Reese's hand. "Wait here," she ordered. "I'll be right back." She pivoted sharply and went back to the patrol car.

"Thank God you have a license," said Reese.

"I got it when I turned sixteen," he said.

"Is it still valid?"

"I renew it every five years, whether I need to or not."

"God. Seventy-six in a fifty-five. I can't even . . ." Reese took off her hat and fanned herself. He couldn't help but notice the single trickle of sweat slowly wending its way down between her breasts.

The patrolwoman returned. She handed over the registration and Reese put it away. Then she looked down at Caleb, keeping hold of his license for a stretch of silence. "You're in the database," she said.

Reese took in a quick, audible breath.

"I don't know what that means," Caleb admitted.

"It means I looked up your records."

"You have a record?" asked Reese, looking faint again.

"Oh," Caleb said. "Is that a problem?"

"The milk truck incident. There's a record of it. It was a viral video on the Internet." The officer paused. "I guess, being Amish, you don't watch Internet videos."

"You're right about that."

"But you remember the incident, don't you?"

"That I do." A winter morning, the roads covered in ice, dragging himself out of bed to help a fellow out.

"There was an incident?" Reese asked, fanning herself with her hat again. "What kind of incident?"

"There was a milk tanker stuck in a snowbank, and the tow trucks weren't having any luck, so your friend's team of Clydesdales pulled it out. Somebody filmed it on a cell phone and put the video clip up on the Internet, and it went viral."

"I didn't realize that," Caleb said. He had only a vague notion of what a viral video was. The whole process had lasted maybe half a minute. He couldn't imagine why folks would look at thirty seconds of horses at work.

"You pulled a tanker truck full of milk out of the ditch with your horses?" asked Reese.

"He did indeed." The woman handed back his license card. "I'm sorry about your brother, too," she added. "That's also in the records."

He put the card back in his wallet. "I appreciate that, miss."

"You take care," she said. "No more speeding."

As he started the engine, Reese sighed and put away the registration papers. "Must be nice."

"What?"

"Talking your way out of a ticket. I've never been able to do that."

"Seems to me the patrolwoman did most of the talking."

"She was totally smitten because you hitched up a team of horses and pulled a massive truck out of the snow." She took out her cell phone and tapped her way through a search. When she found the video, they looked at it together. It was the first time Caleb had ever seen the images. Despite the wildly blowing snow, the picture clearly showed his team pulling the eighteen-wheeler out of the ditch. Though his features were indistinct under his hat and heavy coat, Caleb recognized himself on the buckboard, maneuvering the powerful horses. There was no sound other than the wind and, at the end of the half-minute video, an anonymous person saying, "That's something you don't see every day."

It had been snowing all night and was still coming down thick and hard the next morning. The tanker had come to collect milk from the local farms, which was usually a routine operation. In the foul, icy weather, though, the truck slid off the road, and the tires spun uselessly, digging a trench. Caleb had hitched up his team of four, hook-and-chained the rig to the truck, and the big horses went to work. Within a few seconds, the rig was out, and Caleb discovered he'd made a friend of the grateful driver.

When he finished explaining the circumstances to Reese, she simply looked at him, her mouth in a soft smile. "You never stop surprising me."

He eased the car out onto the road, thinking that he could say the same of her. The way her mind worked was a surprise—her thoughts about everything from healing to salsa dancing. The words she used were a surprise— the frequent curses at odds with her kindly way with Jonah. The feelings she inspired—now, those were not a surprise. He had trouble keeping his eyes and his mind off her.

The highway brought them across New Jersey's eastern flatlands, and then to a beach town called Sudbury

Park. He got a little nervous negotiating the narrow streets lined with bustling shops and traffic.

"I'm impressed at the way you maneuvered into the parking spot," she said.

"Guess it comes from dealing with a team of Clydesdales. Seems easy compared to that."

The air smelled different here. Briny. Tang of salt. These were things he had read about in books, and it turned out they were real.

She opened the trunk and saddled him with towels, a boxed picnic, a cooler of drinks, and some books and magazines. She glanced at her phone screen and then said, "Screw it." She locked the phone in the trunk. He staggered slightly as they crossed the parking lot and followed a long boardwalk at the edge of the beach.

"I know why you brought me here," he said. "You need someone to carry all your gear."

"Ha, guilty as charged. You won't complain when you see what's for lunch."

"I'm not complaining."

"Good. Thanks for helping out, by the way."

They descended the boardwalk to a long flat stretch of amber-colored sand. Kids ran around laughing and playing in the waves. People of all sizes, shapes, and colors were on the beach, some lying out on towels, some walking along where the waves met the shore, others sitting in groups on blankets and lounge chairs under shade umbrellas.

Caleb stepped onto the sand and took it all in. The smells and sounds. The newness.

Reese led the way to a blue-and-white-striped umbrella stuck in the sand at the edge of the breaking waves. "We can set down here." She spread a plaid blanket on the sand. An attendant came along and she gave him a fee for the umbrella. Then she organized everything in the patch of shade.

"There," she said with a satisfied smile. "Our day at the shore can begin. Kick your flip-flops off. That's always my favorite moment."

He slipped off the sandals and sank his bare feet into the sand, reveling in the smooth texture of it. "Oh, yeah," he murmured. "That's nice."

"Isn't it? What would you like to do first? We can take a walk, go for a swim—"

"Yes," he said immediately. "Let's do that." He pulled his shirt off over his head and dropped it onto the blanket.

"Keep your trunks on," she said. "This isn't Amish country."

He grinned. "Got it."

She untied the bow of her flimsy white dress and let it slip to the ground. What she wore beneath took his breath away all over again. It was a tight red suit that hugged her curves like a lover's hands, outlining a shape he knew would haunt his dreams. On her thigh, just at the outer curve, she had a tattoo—a simple line drawing of a bird.

Caleb's knees felt weak. And he wasn't the only one who couldn't stop staring. Several other fellows nearby were checking her out as well. She bent down to grab the sunscreen lotion, giving him an even more enticing glimpse of her backside.

"We both need plenty of this," she said, slathering her arms, legs, neck, and shoulders. "You do my back and I'll do yours." She swiveled around, presenting herself and handing him the plastic bottle.

"Sure, okay." He squeezed the lotion in a pale line across her shoulders and set the bottle down. Then, with far more pleasure than anyone would deem proper, he ran his hands over her shoulders and down her back, then up again to her neck. Her skin was impossibly smooth and warm from the sun, and he took his time, covering her delicate, silky skin with the lotion. He focused on a curl of dark hair at the nape of her neck, thinking about how small and vulnerable she was. Sometimes it was easy to forget that about Reese.

After a few minutes, she turned so they stood face-to-face, their bare skin touching. "Thanks," she said in a soft, slightly husky voice. "Now, I'll do you."

"I'm all yours," he said, turning around. He felt a warm coating of lotion. Then her hands glided over his shoulders and back, and he shut his eyes and clenched his jaw to keep from moaning. "I have a confession to make," he told her.

"What's that?"

"I'm enjoying this a lot more than I should."

Her hands slowed but didn't stop. "I have a confession to make too," she said.

"What's that?"

"So am I."

He stood still while she finished, gritting his teeth as he fought for control. "Now about that swim . . ."

She nodded. "Let's go."

The waves rushed up to the shoreline, swamping his bare feet in the swirls of cool water. The ocean was vast, as endless as the sky. He stepped into the surf, and the whole world shifted.

He looked over at Reese and grinned. "Wow."

She walked backward into the deepening water, and the waves foamed up around her thighs. "You like?"

He couldn't take his eyes off her as he followed her deeper and deeper into the water. "I like," he agreed.

"I wish I could remember my first time in the ocean,"

she said, "but I was too little, and—" A big wave rose up like a giant hand and inundated her. With a squeal, she went under. Then the waves came for him, slapping him backward with unexpected force. The salt water filled his nose and mouth, an elemental sensation flowing through him. He found his footing and pushed himself upright. He spotted Reese nearby, gently treading water, her dark hair sleek and plastered to her head. She was smiling, her face sparkling with beads of moisture.

He found her mesmerizing, and the motion of the waves amazing. The force was muscular in nature, stronger than any man, stronger than willpower.

He took her hands, pulling her toward him. Momentum carried her right up against him. Without a single thought or hesitation, he planted a firm kiss on her mouth. Grabbing a woman and kissing her was the last thing he expected himself to do, and yet the impulse was so swift that it was happening even before he knew what he was doing. It was unlike him. His entire existence since the accident was unlike him.

As a kid, he'd once been swept away by a current he couldn't fight. John had plucked him out a ways downstream, hollering at him for being an idiot, but all Caleb could do was grin unapologetically. Getting carried away in the white water had been the ride of his life. And this . . . Sweet heaven above. She tasted like the ocean—elemental, unforgettable. He reluctantly lifted his mouth from hers. "Thank you," he said. "Thank you for today."

She gasped and paddled backward. "Um, sure."

He couldn't figure out what that reaction meant. Was she startled? Offended? Repulsed? He instantly raised his hands, palms out. "I got carried away. Sorry about that."

"I'm not sorry," she said and playfully swam away.

He couldn't figure that out, either. All women, Amish or English, were a mystery.

He tucked her words away to take out and ponder later. *I'm not sorry.* They bobbed and floated, and Caleb made a raft of his body, gazing up at the blue sky, enjoying the feeling of weightlessness. Reese showed him ways to catch the incoming waves and body-surf to the shallows. Folks were skimming along with the waves on small rafts Reese said were called boogie boards.

A man and his son, in matching orange swim trunks, were laughing as they raced on their boards, again and again. Caleb wondered what it would have been like to have a father like that, playful and easy, not just allowing enjoyment but seeking it out.

Farther out, a guy on a board, who was harnessed to an arched parachute, went aloft with a yell of excitement. As Caleb looked on, he felt a powerful yearning like an ache in his gut.

"Kiteboarding," said Reese. "I've been meaning to try it."

"What's stopping you?" he asked. "I swear, it looks like a dream."

"Maybe we could try it together sometime," she said.

He sank a little, realizing "sometime" was not likely to come for them. He could still taste that kiss. It would never leave him.

After a while, she knifed through the water toward him.

"I'm starving," she said. "You?"

He hesitated, waiting for his brain to catch up to his words. "I can always eat."

They wrapped themselves in towels and sat together on the blanket. The salt on his skin and hair formed a light dust that felt incredible. Everything about this day felt incredible.

Reese slipped on the white dress and opened the lunchbox. "From the Big Belly Deli," she said. "You're going to love their food."

There were egg salad sandwiches on seedy bread, pickles, and wedges of chilled watermelon. They washed it all down with ice-cold Nehi soda, and then walked across the sand to the boardwalk. There, they found an ice cream truck and treated themselves to dessert.

Licking a chocolate-dipped cone, he leaned against the wooden railing and surveyed the beach. Music, laughter, crying seagulls. Saltwater taffy. Warm sand beneath his feet and a beautiful girl at his side. The smell of ocean air riding a balmy breeze. The way she tasted when he kissed her.

Perfection.

They lazed together on the blanket and he thought about kissing her again. He wondered if he should say something. Turning to her, he placed his hand on her soft thigh.

"Help!" A panicked cry split the air. Caleb jumped up, grabbed Reese's hand, and pulled her to her feet.

"Looks like something's wrong over there." They sprinted across the beach, joining a small knot of people in the shallows.

"My dad's drowning," screamed a boy in orange swim trunks, surging into the water. "Out there!"

Caleb and Reese both swam out to a bright blue boogie board that was tethered to a motionless man. Another guy was already there, pulling him toward shore. The man's skin was blue. He wasn't breathing. When they got him back to the beach, a woman who must have been his wife crumpled next to him, keening, "Oh my God. Oh my God. Oh my God . . ."

"I saw a wave crash over him," said a swimmer. "He went down headfirst."

Several people had already called 911. A lifeguard arrived from down the shore with a kit of some sort. "Oh, Jesus," he said. He looked like a kid, barely older than Hannah.

Reese pushed forward and dropped to her knees beside the man. "I can help," she said. She checked his airway, then sought a pulse.

Caleb joined her. "She can," he told the boy. "She's a doctor."

"Somebody tell the EMTs there's no respiration or pulse. Starting CPR," Reese said. "It's the only option until they get here." She pressed her hands rhythmically on the motionless chest, attempting to restart his heart. The boy sobbed hysterically. Without breaking her rhythm, Reese looked up at the lifeguard. "Are you trained in CPR?"

"I am, but I've never—"

"Is that a resuscitation mask?"

"Yeah, I think so."

"You in the Nike shirt," she said to a nearby man, "go out to the street so the paramedics can find us." Reese was soaking wet, her small hands slipping on the man's chest, but she didn't pause. Compressions and rescue breaths in an unflagging rhythm. She instructed the lifeguard to help her, but he seemed frozen. Caleb dropped to his knees next to her. "Tell me how to help," he said.

She showed him what to do and they took turns. The minutes dragged. No one spoke except the boy, who repeated *DaddyDaddyDaddy* in a mindless string. Some of the bystanders filmed the action on their phones.

"I think we sparked a pulse," Reese said. She paused and put her ear to the man's chest. "*Yes.*" Then the guy spat foamy seawater in a fountain that sprayed the on-lookers. He still seemed to be unconscious.

"He's alive," someone said. "Check it out. He's alive."

"Hand me the mask," Reese said to the lifeguard.

Several agonizing minutes passed. A flurry of activity on the boardwalk indicated that help had arrived. A crew of EMTs jogged across the beach, laden with a backboard and equipment.

"No peripheral pulse," Reese said to one of the rescu-ers. "But he has a heartbeat."

The EMTs swarmed the guy as she related what she'd done so far.

"Good work," said a rescuer. "Damn, you saved him. We got this now."

Reese nodded and staggered backward. Caleb caught her against him. She was shaking, breathing hard. "Hear that?" he said to her. "You did good work. Reese, you saved a life." He tightened his hold. "You're doing what you're meant to be doing, and it's a privilege to watch you."

"Caleb kissed me," Reese told Leroy. She had to tell somebody, and he was her self-appointed best friend.

He froze in the middle of sorting berries from a gor-geous flat of blackberries, raspberries, and blueberries she'd bought at Luigi's. "I'm . . . sorry?" Leroy said. "Jealous? Shocked? Not sure what you want me to say here."

"I'm not sure either. Maybe you don't need to say any-thing. I just wanted to tell someone." It was nice, having him as that go-to person in her life, someone with whom she could safely share anything. They'd been across-the-hall neighbors for a good while, yet she was only now getting to know him. And that was her fault, not his. She'd been so focused on work that she'd never bothered to make time for anything else—such as that pesky little thing called living.

"And here I thought saving a guy's life was the biggest thing that happened to you that day," said Leroy.

"Well, there's that," she said. The truth was, she didn't need to talk about the incident at the shore because her feelings about it were unambiguous. For the first time, she had felt utterly right in her own skin. In the aftermath of the drama, there had been a flurry of attention. Word had gone out via tweets from multiple camera phones. For a good five minutes, she was a star of the Internet—"Med student and her hunky blond boyfriend bring drowning victim back to life." She'd received several marriage proposals, along with a few lewd comments about the tattoo on her hip.

Her parents, of course, were bursting with pride. It was more than pride, though. It was triumph. Not so much that they had raised a person who knew how to save a human life, but that Reese now had a perfect topic for her residency applications. She was a public relations jewel in the crown of the hospital.

Reese cared about none of these things. She cared that she had been there, fully present, with the knowledge, skills, and nerve to do what needed to be done. Time had stopped for her. She had no thought of anyone or anything but the man on the ground with no pulse or respiration. She would always see his face in her mind. And she would never forget the name of Mr. Roth. Mr. Howard Roth. He'd taken his son to the beach for the afternoon. He was alive—and this had been verified by the first responders to the scene—solely because of Reese.

Yet she could not escape the notion that *she* was the one being saved. It felt like a kind of salvation.

In the drowning incident, she'd found a private peace. But not in the kiss. All she could think about was the kiss. And her most vivid memory of saving a man's life was the expression on Caleb's face when she brought Mr. Roth back to life.

"You just saved a life for the first time," Leroy said, "and all you can think about is kissing a guy?"

"My feelings about saving Mr. Roth aren't an issue," she said. "My feelings about that kiss are . . . confused," she said, mulling it over for the thousandth time.

"Oh, honey. Confused?"

"Okay, excited. Maybe . . . What? Afraid. Not physically afraid, of course. But . . . you know, *afraid*. As in, apprehensive."

"Sounds like the start of something to me."

"The start of what?" She used the back of her hand to brush a lock of hair off her cheek.

"Falling in love."

"I'm not—"

"That, my friend, is a classic symptom."

"I have no symptoms."

"Denial is a symptom."

"Bite me. Why did I think talking to you would be a good idea?"

Avoiding Leroy's gaze, she consulted the recipe and set two pie plates in the middle of the counter, sprinkling the bottoms with a pinch of cornmeal, a technique she recalled from working alongside Juanita in the kitchen when she was young. Baking was an unlikely hobby for Reese, but she had decided it would be good for her mental health. It forced her to slow down and take her time, to be precise but creative, to focus on the task at hand and nothing else. She planned to take one of the pies to Jonah, who made no secret of feeling homesick.

Handling the dough as gently as possible, she transferred each bottom crust to a pie pan. The soft dough sank into place. She filled the shells with a mixture of blackberries and raspberries, flavored with sugar and almond extract, and the all-important tapioca powder so it would thicken perfectly during the baking.

Leroy watched her work, his mouth set in a bemused expression.

"What?" She dotted the berries with butter.

"You're good with your hands."

"My parents say that's going to make me a fine surgeon one day."

"You're already great at making pies."

She carefully added the top crust to each pie, using a scalpel to create several vent holes. Then she got out her vintage fluter to crimp the edges. A brush with egg wash, a sprinkle of coarse sugar on top, and her creations were ready for the oven.

"An hour in the oven, and an hour on the windowsill," she said in Spanish. Then she repeated it in English. "That's what Juanita used to say. The most common error a person tends to commit in pie making is to fail to let it cool in fresh air. If you cut into it straight out of the oven, the juice runs everywhere. People have no patience when it comes to pies."

She felt his scrutiny on her as they worked together tidying the kitchen. "What?"

"So about that kiss," he said.

"I've thought about it and concluded that it didn't mean anything."

"Don't be daft."

"To us. It didn't mean anything about Caleb and me

specifically. I'm convinced that he was totally over-whelmed by being in the ocean for the first time. He would have kissed anyone in that moment. It was like New Year's Eve, or when the Phillies won the pennant—you just grab whoever's handy and kiss them."

"In that case, remind me to take Cheryl to the shore on our next date. So far, she is the opposite of excited."

"I thought you got lucky the other night."

"I tried, but she said she was too tired from the dancing."

"I'm sorry. Gosh, Leroy, I've been so preoccupied with this Caleb thing that I haven't been keeping up with your love life."

"See, I was right. It's a thing."

She dusted the flour from her hands. "You think?"

"Yes, I do. And believe me, it's a lot more interesting than my love life." He checked his watch. "Gotta go," he said. "Save me a piece of pie."

A couple of hours later, the pies were resting on the win-dowsill in all their golden-baked glory. Reese had show-ered and primped and spent far too long deciding what to wear, changing her mind, trying things on, then discard-ing them.

"This is nuts," she finally muttered to herself. "It's not the freshman formal. It's not even a date. It's just . . ." Caleb Stoltz. He occupied all available real estate in her brain.

She grabbed a blue A-line dress and paired it with es-padrilles and a white cotton cardigan. "Whatever," she said, frowning at herself in the mirror and fluffing out her hair. She resisted the temptation to put on more makeup. She did have a nice pendant she always wore with this dress. It was a dazzling free-form design with a light-catching tourmaline stone in a setting of white gold. It had been a graduation gift from her grandmother, and it looked nice against the plain blue dress—not too blingy, but blingy enough to be noticed.

She enjoyed being noticed by Caleb Stoltz.

There. She admitted it.

She frowned into the mirror. Too much sparkle for an Amish guy?

Then she turned away. Screw it. She wasn't Amish. And that, she realized, was the reason her attraction to him was so nonsensical. She and Caleb Stoltz came from completely different worlds. They never would have met if not for the horror that had befallen Jonah. Their lives had intersected for the briefest span of time. Before long, they would each go their separate ways, never to meet again.

"That's depressing," she said aloud.

That's reality, she told herself. He had his rural community and the kids, his farm and the horse farm where he worked. She had the almighty Match and years of work in front of her. Their lives were going to veer off in different directions, and she doubted their paths would ever cross again.

Maybe that was the reason she felt so different around him. He made her feel brave, and in a state of wonder.

It was oddly liberating to be with a guy who had no stake in her future and no role in her life. Nothing mattered but the relationship.

Of course, there was a catch, she told herself. And the catch was, their relationship would never work. It was unsustainable. And oh so fragile. It could shatter at the slightest upset and ruin them both.

Hannah had hinted that there was a woman back in

Middle Grove who was sweet on Caleb—Rebecca Zook. Something about exchanging a clock and an embroidered cloth. Was Caleb in on those plans? Did they have an understanding? Hannah hadn't said.

Reese knew she should ask him. If she did, he'd tell her the truth, because he didn't lie. But she wasn't sure she wanted to hear the truth from him.

12

Jonah was in his room when Reese and Caleb arrived at the hospital. Reese carried one of the berry pies loosely covered by a tea towel, feeling an undeniable pride of accomplishment.

The first bed in the room was empty, though the covers were mussed, indicating that the bed now had an occupant.

Jonah was so deeply absorbed in the pages of a book that he didn't move a muscle when they walked into the room. She and Caleb exchanged a glance.

"What is Harry Potter up to these days?" Caleb asked, leaning down to kiss the top of the boy's head.

Jonah nearly dropped the thick book onto the rolling tray in front of him. "Oh! I didn't hear you come in. I'm reading something else now—a story called *To Kill a Mockingbird*. It's about a man defending a black man. The whole town thinks he did a terrible thing, and I can't wait to get to the end and see if he really did."

"That's a wonderful book," Reese said. "I'm impressed that you're reading it at such a young age."

"The girl telling the story, she's just a kid like me. Her daddy, he's a lawyer, like I want to be one day."

"An Amish lawyer?" asked Reese. "Can such things be?"

Caleb grinned and rumpled his nephew's hair. "Not according to Ordnung. But there's a first time for everything."

Watching the two of them together, Reese felt a rush of

affection. Their bond was both powerful and effortless. Ever since the kiss and the beach emergency, she'd been more sensitized, somehow, her heart yearning for connection with friends and family. She indicated the bed closer to the door. "Looks like you have a new roommate."

Jonah nodded. "A boy who had an operation. He mostly slept all day, but he seems nice enough."

Caleb lifted the plastic dome on Jonah's dinner tray. "You weren't hungry?" he asked.

Jonah cut his gaze away. "I know it's wasteful, but the food doesn't always taste so good." He sighed. "I miss Miriam Hauber's roast chicken."

"I'll be sure she brings it over for your homecoming. But while you're here, you have to eat so you can get stronger."

The boy looked bereft. "I want to go home now."

"We all want that, little man."

"When?"

"When the doctors say."

Jonah looked over at Reese, and his round, troubled eyes implored her. "When?" he asked again.

She braced herself for a storm like the last one. She could see Jonah struggling, his features strained by emotions he scarcely understood, and she ached for him. "I'm not the doctor who gets to say." She stepped to the opposite side of the bed. "But tonight, there's a bit of good news." She set aside the dinner tray and placed her parcel on the rolling table. "I have a new superpower," she announced and unveiled the pie. It was baked to perfection, the top crust beautifully browned, the sugar crystals glistening on the surface.

A big smile bloomed on Jonah's face. "That looks like a most wonderful pie, Reese."

"I hope so. I mean, I hope it tastes as good as it looks and smells. You see, the thing about a pie is that you don't know if it's wonderful or not until you serve it. There's no sneaky way to have a taste without cutting into it."

"Then we'd better have a slice right this minute," Caleb said. "I brought something too. Ice cream, and we didn't even have to get out the hand crank to make it." He set a pint of gourmet vanilla next to the pie.

Reese served them each a slice on paper plates they'd brought from home, and Caleb added a scoop of ice cream. Jonah watched her every move as she placed his plate in front of him. "Go ahead," she said. "Tell me how I did."

He scooped up a spoonful and wolfed it down. As he leaned back against the bank of pillows, Reese saw a flare of mischief in Jonah's eyes—a good sign. With a smile on his face, he declared, "You do have a new superpower, Reese."

"He's right," Caleb said, making short work of his dessert. "It's delicious. Where did you learn to bake a pie like this?"

"From my—from Juanita. She lived with us when I was growing up. Took care of me while my mother and father were at work. She's an incredible cook."

The occupant of the other bed came in and there were hasty introductions—Dane Rasmussen and his parents and sister. "I had an operation yesterday," said Dane, who looked to be about Jonah's age. "They took out my appendix."

"He was really brave," said his mom.

The sister sniffed. "Huh. He was fast asleep the whole time."

"Any dietary restrictions?" asked Reese. "We have homemade pie. And there's a bit of ice cream left over."

Dane's face lit up. "It looks really good."

"It's the best pie ever," Jonah said, and Reese felt the most absurd sense of accomplishment.

She and Caleb served up the rest of the pie to the neighbors, which they accepted gratefully. "You're right," Dane said to Jonah. "Your mom makes the best pie ever."

"Reese isn't my mom," Jonah said, but he spoke quietly and no one but Reese seemed to hear.

The Rasmussens appeared to be the ideal family, the parents openly affectionate with their kids and with each other. Watching them together, Reese wondered if she would ever find that in her life—a partner she loved, kids to raise together. That ineffable, unassailable feeling of belonging.

From where she was at this point in her career, she couldn't imagine it. Putting it all together seemed so far out of reach as to be unattainable. And she was likely idealizing the family, anyway. The parents probably got on each other's nerves and didn't have sex. The kids squabbled about nothing and made messes wherever they went. Mrs. Rasmussen fantasized about the days when she was single and free to pursue a career.

Lost in thought, Reese was taken by surprise when a group arrived for rounds. The attending, Dr. Jimenez, had only two third-years with him this time. "Jonah's progress has been faster than anticipated," he reported to Caleb.

The students pulled the curtain that separated the beds and earnestly offered their evaluations.

"When can he go home?" Caleb asked after they'd finished.

"There's a team meeting tomorrow," said Dr. Jimenez, consulting his tablet. "They'll be discussing the discharge plan. The recommendation will be for him to go to a skilled nursing facility for a period of rehab and training."

"Is it mandatory?" Caleb asked.

"Nothing is mandatory. The plan is a recommendation for what's best for Jonah."

"And sometimes that's a matter of opinion," Caleb said.

Jimenez studied him for a long moment, his expression inscrutable. Reese knew Jimenez was one of those doctors who tended to look askance at patients who questioned him. "Sometimes," he said. "Other times, it's a matter of medical fact."

"I want what's best for Jonah," Caleb said. Unlike students who had been reduced to rubble by Jimenez's glare, he seemed perfectly at ease with the conversation.

"Sounds as if we all want the same successful outcome." He paused. "Jonah's going to do great. Everyone on the care team has a lot of confidence in him."

"Did you hear that?" asked Caleb after they left. "You're going to do great. If the head doctor says so, then it must be true."

"What's a facility?" Jonah asked.

"That's the place you'll go after you leave the hospital," Reese said.

"And didn't you ask me that yesterday?" Caleb opened the nightstand drawer. "Here's the information about the different places. Did you take a look at it?"

Jonah shook his head. "Atticus Finch and Harry Potter are more interesting."

"There are two that specialize in prosthetics." Caleb opened one of the brochures. "This one—Northwoods Lodge—is closer to my work at Grantham Farm. Or there's this one—it's part of the hospital. You would stay nearby, but in a different building."

"Will I still get my meals on a tray and have books and TV?" Jonah looked at Reese.

"You can read all you want, and I imagine there's TV

time," she said. "No more room service, though. When you're in rehab, they like you to go to the cafeteria. Have you ever eaten in a cafeteria?"

"No, but I bet I'd like it."

"I'll still bring you pie."

He paged through the glossy brochures, which depicted valiantly smiling patients and earnest therapists, seemingly bonding and making progress. "There's a swimming pool?" he asked, noticing one of the pictures.

"Looks that way," Caleb said.

"I've never been in a swimming pool."

"It's super fun," said Reese. "Are you a good swimmer?"

He glowered at his bandaged stump. "I used to be. How would I ever swim with only one arm?"

"In a circle," Caleb said simply.

"Hey." Jonah's scowl deepened. Reese stifled a snicker.

"Hey, yourself. Tell you what, little man. Suppose we visit both places and see which one you like better," Caleb suggested.

"That's a good idea," said Jonah. "I know something better, though. What if I just come home?"

"You could do that. The hospital people said going home would be harder because you won't get as much help as you would from a rehab place."

"Most people make really fast progress at those places," said Reese. "There's a whole staff who organize your stay around helping you get better."

Jonah pushed the table with the brochures away. He looked down at his bandaged arm for several seconds. "I want to get better," he said in a low voice.

"You will." Caleb touched his shoulder. "I aim to make sure of that."

"Why do they have to call it a stump?" Jonah asked, still staring at the bandage.

"You can call it anything you want," said Reese.

He looked up at her, his eyes brightening just a shade. "I can? Like what?"

"Like . . . I don't know. Atticus Finch?"

A smile glimmered. "Maybe not that."

"Jonah's amazing appendage? The titanium titan?"

He shook his head, still smiling. "Nah."

"Tell you what. You have a think on it and let me know what you come up with."

"I will." He reached for the book on his table.

Caleb adjusted his covers and said something in German.

"Yah, okay," Jonah said. "I'll see you later."

As they walked to the elevator, Reese looked up at Caleb. "I just love that little guy," she blurted out. Then she caught her breath, completely surprised at herself. And then again, not surprised. Jonah was incredibly lovable—funny and sweet and vulnerable, with a wide-eyed way of looking at the world that never failed to give her spirits a boost.

"Me too," Caleb said easily. They stepped into the elevator together.

"He's so smart," said Reese. "I mean, reading *To Kill a Mockingbird* at his age."

"Jonah's always sticking up for other kids if he thinks an injustice is being done. Sometimes I wonder if it stems from what happened to his parents. He was so young when it occurred, but I never kept the truth from him."

"He's really special, Caleb. You're lucky to have him in your life." She understood why he had returned to Middle Grove even though he'd planned a different path for himself.

"That I am. So about tonight."

"Yes? What about tonight?"

"There's going to be a full moon. And I have a plan. If you're free, that is."

Reese felt a flutter of anticipation. Then the flutter was crushed by the hard reality of the medical licensing exam, which was staring her in the face. She needed to know the material cold, and she wasn't there yet. Her study group was holding a special session tonight for that purpose. She looked up at Caleb to explain this to him. Instead, what she heard herself say was "What do you have in mind?"

He smiled. "I need to borrow your car."

"I've never been up this way," Reese said as Caleb exited the state road onto a country byway. Philadelphia was forty miles behind them. The sun was setting, and a blanket of glorious color spread in layers across the sky, outlining the broken silhouettes and gentle curves of the hills all around them. She had not one moment of regret about pushing off her studies until later tonight. If she needed to pull an all-nighter, so be it. She was an old hand at all-nighters.

"It's beautiful here," she told him.

He slowed down and turned at a grand river stone and wrought-iron gate. "Welcome to Grantham Farm."

She read the plaque affixed to the stone wall. "Home of the Budweiser Clydesdales. Established 1927. Oh my God. When you said you worked with draft horses, I didn't realize you meant *those* horses. This is so cool."

He pressed a code on a keypad by the wall, and the large iron gate slowly swung inward.

"Security cameras everywhere," she said, noting a couple of them mounted on poles around the entrance.

"The folks here are protective of the horses. Some of the best stock are worth a pile of money."

"I imagine so. But if I was going to steal something

for the money, it probably wouldn't be a two-thousand-pound horse."

"Three," he said, his mouth curved into a smile.

"Three thousand pounds?"

"An adult gelding in his prime. I'll show you a few."

White fences with horizontal rails lined both sides of the road, and there was a row of residential cottages for workers and caretakers. They came to a small stone-and-timber security office with lights aglow and more cameras. A guy came out and Caleb stopped the car. "Evening, George," Caleb said.

"*Dude*. I thought that was your code. Look at you, driving this hot little number." The guy nodded at Reese, and his gaze lingered. "The car, that is. Evening, miss."

"Hi there, George. I'm Reese."

He looked over at Caleb, took off his cap, and scratched his head. "I take it you're not here for work."

"Not tonight," said Caleb.

"Damn, I've never seen you driving a car," said George. "You look so rad."

"My sole aim in life is to look rad," said Caleb.

George checked out Reese again. "Mission accomplished."

"We won't be long. I want to show Reese around a bit." He rolled forward and drove to a big barn. There were signs for visitor parking and areas marked for employees only.

The evening light painted everything with a magical glow—the buildings and mountains, fenced fields and trails, open and covered arenas. A lone worker led a huge horse along the path to the barn.

Caleb pulled into a lot next to a barn, parked, and got out of the car. "Hey, Miguel," he said.

"Caleb." Like George, Miguel regarded him with open curiosity. Apparently the sight of Caleb Stoltz with a car and a woman was cause for speculation. "Just finishing up," Miguel added.

Reese got out of the car.

"*Ay, mujer,*" Miguel said under his breath. "*Huy, qué buena estás—*"

"You don't want to go there," she said easily in Spanish.

"Listen to you two, jabbering away in Spanish." Caleb took hold of the horse's lead. "I'll put Rolf away, Miguel. You have a good night."

"Thanks, man." He slipped a cautious glance at Reese. "See you tomorrow."

With the horse in tow, Caleb walked down the center of the barn. The warm smells of hay and horses pervaded the air. It was an incredible building, almost cathedral-like, its gambrel roof soaring above rows of stalls on either side. Deep amber sunlight fell slantwise through the skylights, illuminating the space with a soft glow.

"Holy shit," Reese said, looking around. "This place is nicer than my first college dorm."

"These animals get the royal treatment, that's for sure." Caleb stopped at one of the stalls and touched another keypad. He slid the door open and settled Rolf into the roomy space with a flowing water trough and a rack of pale green hay. "They travel all over for the beer company events, so they need to be in tip-top shape."

She felt like a kid as she peered into other stalls, admiring the huge, gorgeous animals, with their placid expressions and long-lashed eyes. "The famous Clydesdales. They're even prettier than they look on TV."

"There are a few stables around the country," Caleb said. "New Hampshire, Virginia, Missouri, Wyoming . . .

some other places. I don't travel with the hitch, though."
He went to the end of the aisle and opened a door marked
with his name and title: SENIOR HANDLER AND BARN
MANAGER.

"That's your job here, then?" Reese asked. Another
surprise. He had a job title. An office.

He nodded and held the door for her. His office was
small and spare, with a plain wooden desk, trays neatly
stacked with files, and a large wall calendar covered in
hand-lettered notes. The bookcase was filled with manuals and journals about horses. There was no computer or
phone, just a hand-crank adding machine. He took a key
from a desk drawer. "The tack room's through here."

"All right," she said, not quite sure what a tack room
was. It turned out to be another beautifully designed
space filled with saddles, bridles, reins, and bits, along
with larger pieces of harness. He took down a slender
loop of leather from a hook. Then he tossed her a pair of
tan stretch pants and a pair of ankle boots. "You're going
to want to put these on under your pretty dress," he said
and stepped outside the door.

She frowned at the pants. They had some kind of re-
inforced seat and silicone dots on the inner thigh area.
Riding breeches? Not a great look with the dress. The
boots were too big, but she shrugged, put on the clothes,
and went outside to join Caleb.

"This is Stanley," he said, indicating a horse in a set of
crossties. "He's going to take us for a ride."

She regarded the enormous animal. "You mean, in a
cart or something?"

"Nope." He pushed a bit in place between the big yellow teeth, then slipped the headpiece of the bridle over
the horse's head. "We're riding bareback."

"On a draft horse?"

"They're not the most common breed for riding, but it can be done."

Her inner kid did a happy dance. "That's wonderful. I've never been on a horse."

"I know," said Caleb. "You said so during that game we played. That's why we're going for a ride." He finished getting Stanley ready, then handed her a helmet. While she put it on, he brought over a kitchen stool and set it on the floor beside the animal.

Reese regarded the horse from his dinner-plate-size hooves to the top of his head, and a thrill of fear went through her. "I, um . . . This is a little intimidating."

"Stanley's the best we've got. I trained him up myself, starting when he was two years old. And even though these horses are huge, this breed is known for being docile. Some folks call them gentle giants. The main thing is to show him you trust him." He stood beside the step stool and held out his hand, palm up.

She looked up at him and placed her hand in his. "I trust."

He helped her swing one leg up and over. She was startled by how broad the horse's back was—she was practically doing the splits. Then she looked down and urgently grasped a lock of the mane. "Holy crap. He seems even taller from up here."

"Nearly nineteen hands," Caleb agreed. "He's a big fellow."

Feeling completely vulnerable, she held on to the horse's long mane with both fists. "I don't know about this . . ."

"I do," he said, unhooking the crossties and grabbing a second helmet. "The hospital's your world. This one is mine."

This gave her an inkling of how out of place he must

feel at the hospital. He seemed completely at home here, moving among the horses with ease and confidence. Watching him, she forced herself to relax. To believe. He knew what he was doing. He wouldn't let her get hurt. She had dragged him to salsa dancing and sushi, and he'd taken it all in stride. The least she could do was let him treat her to a glimpse of his everyday life.

But the moment the horse moved, she squawked, "Shit, I'm scared."

"Hang on," Caleb said calmly. "I'll lead him out into the paddock and we'll go for a ride together. Look ahead, not down. Relax. It's fine, Reese."

Fighting all her control freak tendencies, she took a deep breath and focused her gaze through the pricked ears of the horse. With the lead in hand, Caleb walked outside to a paddock adjacent to a meadow. With each step the horse took, Reese felt wobbly and unbalanced.

Then she looked around at the glorious scenery and felt a glimmer of calm. It really was beautiful here, with the deep twilight shadows of the fields and hillsides. In the distance, the first turning leaves of fall created flickers of color.

"Doing all right?" Caleb asked.

"Sure," she said, trying to get used to the rhythm of the horse's undulating muscles beneath her. "Honestly, riding a horse looks easier than it is." She pictured Wesley and Buttercup on horseback in *The Princess Bride*, flowing like a banner of silk across the landscape. The reality involved a lot more teeth-gritting, swearing, and white-knuckled clutching.

Caleb walked the horse to a mounting block and got on behind her in one easy, graceful movement. She gasped at the intimate contact, but he didn't seem to notice. "Ready for a ride?"

"Isn't that what I just did?" she asked weakly.

He chuckled. "You're going to like this, Reese."

"If you say so."

"I say so." His long, strong arms bracketed her as he reached forward and took hold of the reins. The horse walked on, this time at a faster, more even pace.

She strengthened her grip on Stanley's mane.

"You can relax," Caleb said. "I won't let you fall."

"All right. Just . . . take it easy, okay? Remember, it's my first time."

"I'm glad I get to be here for your first time," Caleb said.

She could feel the brush of his breath on her neck. The pressure of her back against his chest and the dense muscles of his arms awakened nerves she didn't know she possessed. Who knew shoulder blades could be an erogenous zone?

When the horse picked up its pace again, she grabbed hold of Caleb's arms. "Hey, that's fast enough," she protested. "His back is so wide, I can't hang on with my legs."

"Gravity does all the work," he said, "if you let your hips move with the horse. Since he's way bigger than you, your only job is to absorb his movements, not the other way around. It'll feel a lot smoother when I take him up to a canter."

"You mean he has a faster gear than this?"

A moment later, the brisk walk accelerated. Reese caught her breath and held tighter to Caleb's arms. *Relax*, she reminded herself.

Caleb managed the horse with utter confidence, and ultimately, that won her trust. In no time at all, she *did* have the sensation that they were flowing across the field like silk. The horse ran the length of the field, then turned and ran to a line of trees that bordered the meadow. They did a few loops as the sky deepened to purple twilight and a full moon appeared. As they headed back to the barn, the moonlight turned the field to silver, and Caleb urged the horse to a lope and then a full-on gallop.

Best date ever, she thought, tingling with exhilaration when they stopped in the paddock. Caleb got off, then grasped her by the waist and hoisted her down to the mounting steps.

"Wow," she said. "Wow, that was . . . wow." Her legs wobbled, and she grabbed his arm.

"Easy," he said. "Riding's hard on the legs if you're not used to it, especially on a big guy like Stanley."

"I'm in love with Stanley," she said. "Just so you know."

"Then you can help me put him up for the night. We need to walk him a bit to cool down his muscles."

Reese's own muscles could use some cooling down. They walked together in the moonlight, with the horse following like a docile dog. Then they took him inside and groomed him with a sweat scraper and then a curry-comb.

"This might be the worst possible dress for the occasion," she said with a laugh, remembering how she'd agonized over her outfit. "I'm not complaining, though."

"You can clean up in there while I put Stanley in his stall."

She ducked into a restroom, where she peeled off the boots and riding pants and scrubbed her hands clean. Her hair was windblown and there were some smudges on the dress, but she couldn't stop smiling. She rejoined Caleb, and they walked outside together. The evening had grown cool and quiet, and when her arm brushed against his, she shivered a little.

"Cold?" he asked.

"I . . . no."

"Sure you are." He took off his jacket and placed it around her shoulders. The garment held his warmth and scent, and it felt like an embrace.

"Thank you for bringing me here. I like your world. I think I even like horseback riding. This is a really special place, Caleb."

"Glad you think so."

Their arms brushed again, and this time, Reese knew it was no accident. She also knew this was a bad idea on many levels. "Hannah said there's a girl back home. That you have an understanding." There. She'd said it. Yes, she had just opened that door.

He stopped walking and took her hand, turning her to face him. "Everybody supposes that. Everybody except me."

"Really? And how about you? What do you suppose?"

"I suppose that it's okay to kiss you."

Any protest melted against the soft, insistent pressure of his mouth on hers. She lost herself in his taste and warmth, in the way he surrounded her. Everything that had been simmering between them overflowed and she pressed close, feeling the beat of his heart against hers. One kiss from Caleb was more erotic than an entire night with a different guy.

There were things that she knew—that this kiss was serious. That it was going to make her life more complicated, her goals harder to attain. It was going to upset plans she'd been making for a decade. It was probably going to end with someone getting hurt.

Yet despite the flurry of doubts, there was a rush of helpless surrender. If they didn't stop, she was going to explode. If they did stop, she was going to shatter. She gripped his shirt in both her fists the way she'd grasped the horse's mane, holding on to him, holding on to a sense of astonishment the likes of which she'd never felt before, even as she knew she would have to force herself to let go.

13

I've been hearing rumors about you."

Reese gave a guilty start as she looked around the on-call room. At the moment, the only occupants were her and her mother. "What sort of rumors, Mom?" Her mind raced through the possibilities. Her parents' spies were everywhere in the hospital. It was their home turf, after all. The stage upon which they performed. Everyone who was anyone knew them and, by association, Reese. She lived in a fishbowl, which wasn't usually a problem, since she barely had a life. Until lately.

Her mother set her Birkin bag on a chair by the door. "The sort that make me go 'hmmm.'"

"My life is not interesting enough to make anyone go 'hmmm.' What have you heard?"

"That you've taken up with some farmer from the backwoods."

"I'll try to keep a straight face," Reese said, though her heart sped up with a surge of guilt. *Guilt.* Was she still that kid, living in horror of disappointing her parents, pathetically eager for approval? "Where did you hear this?"

"You know hospitals. Everyone talks. So is it true?"

"What? The farmer? The backwoods? Or the taking up?"

"Any of it."

No. Yes. *I don't know.* "I imagine they're referring to Caleb Stoltz. I mentioned him before. His nephew is a patient here, and Caleb's staying with my neighbor so he can be close to Jonah."

Her mother said nothing, which only made Reese more intent on rationalizing. "He doesn't know anyone in the city. And just so you know, there's been no 'taking up.' I've hung out with the guy a time or two. Introduced him to friends. It's nothing."

She hated that she had to explain him. She hated that it made her defensive. She hated that she'd just called her thing with Caleb "nothing."

"In that case," her mother said, "we don't have anything to worry about, do we?"

"Why would you worry even if I did happen to be involved with Caleb?"

"Are you saying you might be?"

"Jesus H. Christ, Mom—"

"It's a simple question."

With no simple answer.

Her mother glanced at her watch. "Come to dinner tomorrow night," she said. "Bring your friend."

"But—"

"He's all alone in the city. You said so yourself. I'm sure he'd appreciate a home-cooked meal."

"Since when do you cook at home?"

"I never said I was doing the cooking. But I have a home. And I have a cook. You need to eat. So, I assume, does your friend."

"But—"

"Drinks at seven, dinner at eight. Text me if he has any dietary restrictions."

Reese felt rotten about the conversation with her mother. Caleb was not "nothing." He was exactly the opposite of nothing.

The moonlight ride at Grantham Farm marked a turning point for her, and maybe for them both. The moment he had kissed her was the moment she'd been forced to stop pretending this wasn't a thing. It was the moment she had to face reality and admit to herself that not only was it a thing, it was a big thing.

Which made it a big problem.

She thought about him day and night. She thought about him in the OR when she was observing a neurosurgeon clip an aneurysm. She thought about him in the on-call room when she was supposed to be sleeping. Or working on research. Or eating lunch or meeting with attendings and preceptors.

Her obsession with Caleb was like a chronic condition. One she never wanted to get rid of.

She couldn't stop thinking about his touch and the way his eyes crinkled at the corners even before a smile reached his lips. She couldn't get enough of the deep, assured pitch of his voice and the unique cadence of his speech. She got high on the smell of him alone. The way he looked at her and listened to her as if she were the only person in the world.

Each time she thought about Caleb, everything else ebbed away, including all the other obligations and duties that used to fill her every waking hour.

When they weren't together, she had trouble concentrating on anything other than the next encounter. The feeling she'd had the moment he'd kissed her—that utter bliss, that warm surge of tenderness, that lively tingle of sexual excitement—it was a ridiculous craving, but one she couldn't deny.

A feeling this strong was dangerous. Yes, dangerous, because it was so enormously distracting. She had stopped caring about everything else except the rush of unbidden yearning. She didn't worry about being swept away by passion. She *wanted* it.

She was utterly beguiled. Some people might call it chemistry, but it was more like electricity. Caleb Stoltz had hit the switch that turned on her whole body.

Sometimes she tried to reason the feelings away. She was a woman of science, for Chrissake. She should know better. Attraction was a function of pheromones, a chemical reaction, waist-to-hip proportion according to some studies, human instinct regarding genetic differentiation according to others. She thought she understood her hidden sexual archetype. Yet this defied all logic. No empirical data made sense when she found herself caught up in a moment of wonder at the depth of her attraction.

She kept waiting to discover that he was boring or narrow-minded, that he had no interest in the things that interested her, that his mind was closed to new ideas, his heart to new feelings. Instead, each moment she spent with him revealed more about him—his effortless masculinity, his kindness, his inventive mind and tender heart.

If they were ever intimate, would it be as intense as she imagined?

And she imagined this a lot. She was imagining it when she knocked on the door across the hall the next morning, and Caleb opened it. He was dressed for work, ready to catch the seven o'clock bus to Grantham Farm.

"My parents want us to come to their place for dinner," she said.

"All right," he said simply.

"Is it?"

"Sure. Folks eat supper with their families every day." He closed the door quietly behind him. "I have to get to the bus."

"I'll walk partway with you." Outside, they fell in step together. The pavement was damp and acrid-smelling with a light rain, and the morning held a slight chill, an early hint of autumn.

"So anyway," she said, wishing this did not make her nervous. "About my parents . . . They're kind of intense." She adjusted the shoulder strap of her bag. She flashed on memories of childhood mornings, heading off to school with her backpack, her parents bidding her goodbye. They were always affectionate, but their unspoken expectations made her school bag feel weighted with bricks.

He gave her a slight smile. "I wouldn't have guessed."

She gently slugged his arm. "Hey."

"This worries you a lot," he said.

"No, it doesn't. Yes, it does. I hate that it does. See, my folks have very specific ideas about . . . Shit. They think you and I are— Never mind. Let's just get it over with. Can we meet at the hospital after you visit Jonah tonight?"

"Sure." He stopped walking and studied her intently for a moment. Then, very gently, he reached out and cupped her cheek in his hand. "Don't worry, Reese. I'll behave myself."

"It's not your behavior I'm worried about."

He lowered his hand. "Good to know," he said. "I'll see you later."

The blustery early-fall weather quickened Reese's steps as she walked with Caleb to her parents' place. "It's a fair hike," she said. "If you'd rather go by car—"

"I don't mind walking."

"All right. It's quicker to take the pedestrian bridge. It goes through a kind of rough neighborhood, though. Not exactly the most scenic area."

"Are you saying it's not safe?"

"I'm saying it's rough. If I were walking by myself at night, I'd probably avoid it. With the two of us early in the evening, I'm not worried."

"Then I won't worry either."

The truth was, she felt safe with him, whether or not the feeling was warranted. A brisk autumnal wind swirled through the cracked streets and alleyways of the blighted neighborhood. Abandoned warehouses with broken windows were surrounded by razor wire and warning signs. Dilapidated tenements hunched shoulder to shoulder above hole-in-the-wall convenience stores, payday loan centers with burglar bars, and bail bond offices. Broken-down cars and walls covered with gang symbols lined both sides of the streets. Panhandlers and tweakers loitered here and there, but none of them paid much attention to them—until they reached an intersection at the edge of the district.

"Help a brother out?" asked a hulking guy covered in layers of old clothing and street dirt.

Reese held Caleb's arm. "Sorry," she murmured, trying to brush past him.

Caleb slowed his pace. "What kind of help are you looking for?"

"Whatever you can spare," the guy said, holding out a hand seamed with grime.

"Caleb—"

"Here you go, friend, and good luck." Caleb handed him a few dollars. Then he shook the man's hand, looking him in the eye and offering a warm smile.

"Uh . . . thanks." The guy stepped back, then turned and walked away.

Reese knew better than to point out all the reasons it was a bad idea to give to panhandlers. There was no point. Besides, the way Caleb had given the money—

acknowledging the man's humanity and wishing him well—was above reproach.

She sighed. "You're a good person. So much better than I am."

He tucked her hand back into the crook of his arm. "Handing a fellow money doesn't make me nice. Just means I had a bit to spare."

"It was good of you to speak kindly to him, though. Most people, even if they hand out spare change, don't even acknowledge the person." She sighed again. "The city can be a hard place to live. Sometimes I fantasize about going someplace else, way out in the country. I think I'd like that."

"Then maybe you should try it."

Her mind flashed on the meeting with Dr. Lake and Dr. Shrock. She shook her head. "Not possible. My whole life is about this medical career. Big-city hospitals for the next seven years at least, and after that, I'll join my parents' practice. I swear, every vacation will be out in the country." She saw his mouth lift briefly in a smile. "You don't take vacations, do you?"

He shook his head. "Very foreign concept, for sure."

She was relieved when the distressed neighborhood gave way to the quiet splendor of Fitler Square, a century-old park surrounded by vintage brick buildings, tree-lined streets, and well-tended gardens with fountains and sculptures. At the edge of the old district by the river, her parents' high-rise soared like an obelisk of glass. The level of luxury here was almost embarrassing—the grand entry, the iron-clad security, the understated elegance of the lobby. Every detail of this place was designed to impress, and to highlight the success of its well-heeled residents. She watched Caleb taking it all in with his typical openness and ease.

Their footsteps echoed on the polished marble floor as they crossed to the elevators. She waved her access card in front of the one marked *Private* and they stepped into the gilded, mirrored capsule. She waved the card again, and the elevator floated to the penthouse on the twenty-second floor. The door hissed open, directly into her parents' home.

"Welcome to Casa Powell," she said a tad too brightly as she stepped out of the elevator. To her relief, he didn't look nervous at all. Nor did he seem intimidated, the way some of her friends did when she brought them here. He simply waited with his customary patience.

"Hey, Mom, Dad," she called. "We're here!"

"Come in," her mother warbled, her midheeled pumps tapping on the hardwood floor. She looked picture perfect in a simple couture dress and cashmere wrap, her hair and makeup flawless. "We're just getting drinks on the veranda." She hugged Reese, then greeted Caleb with a handshake. "I'm Joanna," she said. "It's probably standard to say I've heard so much about you, but I haven't. I've heard almost nothing about you."

"Mom—"

Caleb smiled, his blue eyes crinkling at the corners. "In that case, I reckon we'll have plenty to talk about."

The expression on her mother's face almost made Reese laugh aloud. Even Joanna Powell was not immune to Caleb's looks. She fake-fanned herself. "You, young man, are already delightful. Come and meet Hector." Grabbing his hand, she towed him across the apartment, past designer furnishings and museum-quality art, through the French doors to the expansive glass-railed terrace with a lap pool, potted trees, and a full bar. A cocktail-hour playlist drifted through invisible speakers.

"It's chilly tonight, but I wanted you to see the sunset," she said. "I had Quentin fire up the propane heaters for us."

"Hi, Dad." Reese went over to the bar, which was dramatically lit from beneath. An array of bottles were lined up on a shelf behind her father. "Whatever you're putting in that shaker, make mine a double."

"Tough day today?" He gave her a hug.

Tough evening looming ahead, she thought. "This is Caleb Stoltz. Caleb, my father, Hector."

"A pleasure," her father said. "What's your poison?"

She could tell it was one of those phrases that had Caleb flummoxed. He hadn't watched enough cheesy TV shows. "Would you like something to drink?"

"A glass of beer, please."

They brought their drinks to a table under a pair of gently glowing heaters. "Cheers," said Reese's father, lifting his highball glass.

"We're so glad you could come—both of you. It's been nearly impossible to wrangle a visit from our own daughter, she's been so busy."

Caleb offered a pleasant nod. By now Reese knew he wasn't given to small talk. He didn't seem to need to fill silences.

"So, Reese tells us you're from the country." Joanna waited with an expectant smile.

"Yes. It's a town called Middle Grove, up north and a bit west of the city."

"And how are you liking Philly?"

Christ, thought Reese. *He's here because his nephew has been mangled, not to visit the fucking Liberty Bell.*

"It's fine," he said.

"Hector and I love it here," Joanna announced, indicating the panorama with a sweep of her arm. As promised, the sunset was glorious, the clouds shot through with fire to the west. "I miss our home in Gladwyne, but when Reese went away to college, it seemed to be time for a change. We were a bit apprehensive about moving so close in. Then we found this place, and it's the best of both worlds."

Unlike other friends Reese had brought here, Caleb didn't effuse over the magnificent home, the artwork, the mind-blowing views from the floor-to-ceiling windows and rooftop terrace. It simply wasn't his way.

"The main thing is that we got to keep our golf membership," her father said. "Is your beer all right?" he asked. "I don't have much of a palate for it."

"Delicious, thank you," Caleb said.

"This is such a crucial time in your career," Hector said, turning to Reese. "Fill me in on your progress with the Match. Do you have a plan for ranking?"

Great. Let's talk shop in front of our guest. "It's going fine," she said. "And of course I have a plan." She looked around the terrace, hoping to change the subject. "The place looks great. Like a five-star hotel."

"The ranking, for the uninitiated, is the process of matching medical students with their residency programs," said Hector, turning back to Caleb.

Uninitiated, thought Reese. Why did that sound so patronizing?

"Man, I remember those days so well," her father went on. "I lay awake night after night, trying to make sure I did the right thing. Do I put Mass General at the top, or Johns Hopkins? And then there was an opportunity at the Mayo Clinic . . . It was agony."

"I'm not in agony, Dad."

"What's your top-ranked program at the moment?" her mother asked.

"Well, the ones Dad just mentioned, and right here at Penn, of course."

"We'd like to see you taking your life more seriously. With the Match coming up, things are going to get very real very fast."

She flinched at the implied criticism, then glanced at Caleb to make sure his eyes weren't glazing over.

Her dad sent him a sorry-not-sorry look. "Big step for our little girl," he said. "We want the best for her."

"Perelman at Penn is the best for global health studies," Caleb said. "For surgical technology, it'd be Johns Hopkins." He looked from one startled parent to the other. "Been studying on it. On account of Jonah."

"Oh," said Joanna. "That's . . . admirable."

"I interviewed for a rural residency program, too," Reese said. Might as well get that out there now.

"Rural?" Her father swirled the ice in his glass. "They don't train pediatric surgeons out in the country."

Reese tried not to bristle. "They train family physicians."

With an expression of bemused tolerance, Caleb followed the conversation as if watching a Ping-Pong match.

"That's not your chosen specialty," her mother said. "You don't want to spend your time treating earaches and hay fever."

Reese could feel the conversation wandering into treacherous territory. "Hey," she said, "I'm starving. What's for dinner?"

"Ah, I hope you brought your appetite. Quentin went to the farmers' market this morning, and he's been cooking all day."

They went inside and gathered around the table, which was set with bone china and crystal, the water tumblers and wineglasses precisely lined up, the array of silver carefully laid on crisp linen napkins.

Quentin came out of the kitchen. "All set?" he asked.

"Starving," said Reese, and she introduced him to Caleb. She couldn't bring herself to say Quentin was an actual butler. It sounded so pretentious.

"Crostini with prosciutto and burrata," Quentin said, serving the starters.

Caleb leaned over to Reese. "It's a ham and cheese sandwich." Then he smiled at Quentin. "And who doesn't like a ham and cheese sandwich."

Quentin grinned. "Yep. The burrata was made fresh this morning. I have a nice Lambrusco to pair with it. Enjoy." He filled everyone's glasses.

The food *was* delicious, but it was pretentious, too—a salad of fennel and blood oranges, a ragout of foraged mushrooms and farro, a dessert that looked more like a 3-D collage on free-form glass. Throughout the meal, Reese's parents were at their condescending, judgmental best.

"I find it so intriguing—that you're Amish," Joanna said, as if encountering a rare disorder. "We've never met someone who's Amish before, have we, Hector?" She paused for a moment. "No, wait, I have a colleague in Lancaster, remember her, Reese? Lane St. John. She was a professor of genetics studies, and both her sons went to Princeton. Anyway, that's neither here nor there."

No, Mom, you just wanted to bring up Princeton. "Lane had this amazing housekeeper, an Amish girl. And I mean, *amazing*. She did everything—ironed the sheets. Baked bread and pies from scratch. Scrubbed the front walk on her hands and knees. Did all the mending and alterations. Incredible. My colleagues and I were totally envious. We all wanted one."

Reese gritted her teeth. Her mother had not just said that.

Yes, she had.

Caleb, on the other hand, took it in stride. "I reckon we could all use somebody like that," he said with a cocky grin. "Where'd your friend get her, at the Kmart?"

Joanna had the grace to blush. "I only meant, a young woman with that skill set is a rare find. Most girls in this day and age don't focus on domestic arts."

Stop talking. Reese tried to telegraph the message across the table. "I made a berry pie from scratch the other day," she said, almost defiantly. Something about her parents made her feel twelve years old again.

"It was delicious," Caleb said. "Jonah, my nephew who's in the hospital here, is still talking about it. Your daughter's been kind to us since the accident."

"That's nice to hear," said her father. "I imagine it's quite a culture shock to go from your Amish community to the city."

"It's different, for sure. I wouldn't call it a shock, though."

They grilled Caleb with questions designed to discomfit him, to make him feel out of his element, less than. He answered with unflappable honesty, talking easily of farm life, the close-knit community, the history of his family, which had occupied the same home for six generations.

"I wish I had better gardening skills," her mother said. "I've been thinking of adding a garden out on the terrace. Do you think that would work? And beehives. Did you know urban beekeeping is a trend? Maybe you could give us some pointers."

"Just because he's Amish doesn't mean he's a walking, talking *Farmer's Almanac*," Reese pointed out.

He grinned at her. "Could be I am." He turned to her mother. "Bees and butterflies won't venture to the top of the building, so the hives will help with the pollinating."

"Oh, that's smart. I'll get Quentin on it next spring."

Reese gritted her teeth through coffee and digestifs in the lounge room. Caleb politely declined and just as politely gave his attention to the art collection as her mother talked about her favorite pieces.

"Did you take art in school?" Joanna asked.

Caleb offered a fleeting smile. "Didn't go to that kind of school. It's strictly the basics and ends after grade eight."

"Schooling stops at eighth grade?" Her father's eyebrows shot up. "How is that even legal?"

Finally, she was pushed to the breaking point. "For Chrissake, Dad—"

Caleb touched his leg against hers. *It's fine.*

She reeled herself back in. With exaggerated precision, she set down her coffee cup. "We both have to be up early tomorrow," she said. "So we'd better get going."

"I'll call for a car." Her mother reached for the phone.

"That's all right," Reese said. "The walk will do us good."

"The boardwalk is the best route to take, then. Such spectacular views of the city at night. Just make sure you don't take the shortcut. It's dangerous at night, you know."

Reese gave them each a brief hug. *Dangerous.* "Right," she said. "I know."

As they walked away from the Powells' place, Caleb could feel the emotion emanating from Reese like heat from a fever. He didn't say anything. She'd speak up when she was ready to talk. He had complete faith that she would talk. She was a talker, this one.

"Not my finest moment," she said after a few minutes. "Sorry. Why do I let them get to me?"

"Because they care so much about you. They want good things for you. And you want to make them happy because they're your parents and you love them."

They took the pedestrian walkway Joanna had suggested. The river reflected the bright lights and colors of the city at night. The art museum was lit up from below, and it resembled a Greek temple on a hill. In some waiting room or other, he'd read that the urban trail was the pride of the city, one of its newest attractions. Despite the chilly weather, there were folks in stylish clothes and shiny shoes, businesspeople hurrying with their briefcases, kids in groups jabbering away, cyclists and joggers getting their late-night exercise. Such a contrast to Middle Grove, where evenings were spent at home, reading in the soft glow and quiet hiss of a lantern.

"You're right, of course," she said. "I do love them and I want to make them proud and happy. They've given me so much. I'm grateful for that. But . . . I'm worried," she said.

"About what?"

"I'm scared that what I want for me and what they want for me are two different things. If I do what they want, I'll always wonder if it was the right choice. If I do what I want, they'll be disappointed in me."

"What's harder? Disappointing your parents or disappointing yourself?"

"Both options suck."

He felt a wave of affection for her, this woman who'd burst into his life like a spring flower. She thought everything through. And through. And through. "Then choose a different option," he suggested.

"Such as . . . ?"

"You tell me." It was all he could do to keep his hands to himself. Every instinct made him want to touch her, to bring her close and kiss her the way he had at Grantham Farm. And he wanted those kisses to lead them to long, fevered hours of making love. He'd been raised to repress those urges, but kissing Reese felt more reverential than any prayer, and if that was blasphemy, he'd gladly burn for it.

". . . what drives them, you know?"

"Sorry, what?" *Focus.*

"My parents," she said. "Isn't that what we're talking about?"

"Yes, sure."

"I worry that I don't have their drive to achieve. Both of them are so successful. Every memory I have of them when I was growing up is about moving ahead—for them in their work, and for me, in school. Even on weekends and vacations, everything we did was supposed to feed into that. I don't remember ever doing something just for the sake of doing it, you know? If I just wanted to lie in the grass and stare up at the clouds, I was supposed to learn about the types of clouds and how they form."

He didn't say anything.

"You're not saying anything."

When he was a kid, he would have been grateful for someone to have that expectation. To expect him to learn things beyond basic knowledge, to want him to pursue a grand dream. He wasn't quite sure how to tell her that, so he stayed silent.

"Okay, here's another example. When I was little, maybe ten or eleven, I was in a Girl Scout troop. You're familiar with Girl Scouts?"

He nodded. "The cookie merchants."

She laughed. "That's us. Anyway, my folks approved of it, because it was all about setting goals and getting rewarded. Accomplish something—get a badge. I didn't realize it at the time, but I think they were probably more focused on the badges than on the things I did to earn them. One project I remember was planting a garden. I made a tiny plot in the yard. There was a sunny spot by the driveway, and I worked and worked. When the first peas and beans came up, I was so excited. Each day I couldn't wait to see what came up. The peas tasted like candy to me. Then one day I came home to find my garden gone."

"What do you mean, gone?"

"Just . . . leveled. The whole area. My father had hired a crew to build a shed for his golf cart, and they dug out the foundation right where the garden had been. I raised holy hell. Full-on meltdown. Screamed at him and demanded to know why. It's the only time I remember having a meltdown with my parents. And Dad just looked at me and said, 'You planted it for your Girl Scout badge.' Like that explained everything. He figured since I'd already earned the badge, I didn't need the garden anymore. He was, like, 'If you want some green beans, ask the housekeeper to buy you some next time she goes to the market.' He wasn't being mean. Just realistic. Totally clueless about what I really wanted—to the point that I questioned my own judgment."

He touched her arm, directing her to a bench positioned under a pool of light. They sat down together, and with no forethought at all, he slipped his arm around her. "You're shivering."

"The weather's changing," she said softly. "And I'm . . . I guess you can tell this is an emotional topic for me."

"Family stuff usually is," he said.

"Tell me about your family," she said. "I mean, I know the basics—your mom, your brother . . . Tell me a story about when you were a boy. I suspect you didn't expect a badge for planting a garden. What's something I don't know about you?"

Something about her question brought up a rush of memories. He sat motionless, feeling the warmth of her against him.

A lighted boat chugged past on the river. Four guys on bicycles wove back and forth on the trail, veering close to the bench and then away. Teenagers, talking loud and swearing.

When they were gone, Reese nudged him. "Well?"

"It's a pretty loaded question." He glanced at her, and when he caught the way she was looking up at him, it took his breath away. Because what he saw in her eyes echoed what he felt in his heart. "When I was a boy, I spoke with a stutter."

"Oh, gosh. That must have been hard."

He was silent again. Bracing himself. Because Reese was too smart not to connect the dots. He knew she would start digging. And the funny thing was, he wanted her to probe. He wanted her to know.

"Caleb?" Her voice was very soft. "What caused the stutter?"

And there it was. No one had ever asked. "Everything was a weapon," he said. "A shovel. A hacksaw. A horse harness. Whatever my father could get his hands on. Up at the barn, the outhouse, the milk house. I never knew when he'd come at me. He beat me until I prayed for mercy. If I ever dared to complain, I was told to pray harder."

She gasped and pulled away from him, grasping his arms. "Oh my God. Caleb, no."

"John had the worst of it, being older," he said, know-ing her "no" was rhetorical. Never in his life had he told these things to anyone. It was as if someone else were saying the words. It was remarkable how raw the memories were even now, decades later. He still remembered the terror and the pain. The shame and humiliation. "When John got to an age where he was bigger than our father, he put a stop to those things."

"Wasn't there anyone you could tell? It's criminal behavior. Didn't someone notice—a teacher or neighbor?"

"The community prides itself on being close-knit, protecting its own. That kind of treatment—it's not considered criminal. Obedience and submission are demanded, and folks abide by Solomon's rule."

"Spare the rod and spoil the child? *God.*"

"I reckon in some families, it works."

Reese trembled against him. "Oh, Caleb. I don't know what to say."

"I'm okay with silence."

She gave a tremulous chuckle as she wiped the tears from her cheeks. "All right, so you win the awful-parent sweepstakes. I'm ashamed I complained about anything at all. I'm so, so sorry that happened to you. With all my heart, I wish I could hold that little boy in my arms and keep him safe forever."

"That's a sweet thing to say." He touched her damp cheek. "I've never told these things to a soul."

"I'm glad you told me. And for what it's worth, you don't seem remotely like a person who endured abuse from your own father. When I see you with Jonah, I'm constantly amazed at how patient and expressive you are."

"When I came back to raise Jonah and Hannah, I made a vow to myself. I swore I'd be the kind of man I wish I'd had as a father."

"You're incredible. But I have thoughts. And questions."

He smiled. "Of course you do."

"Why do you stay, then? It was horrible for you."

"But not for John, not after he forced our father to back down. After that, after he jumped off the bridge, the Amish community *saved* John. He opened himself up to all that was good about Amish ways—family and community, working the land and living close to God. And it's what he wanted for his kids. Not the life our father gave us, obviously. The life he made with Naomi. They turned the farm into a wonderful home, a truly happy home. I'm doing my best to keep faith with that."

"It's so remarkable—and so admirable—that you recovered from what happened to you when you were a boy. Jonah will probably never know how lucky he is."

"When I look at Jonah and his sister, I feel like the lucky one."

"What a nice thing to say. Family obligations can be so complicated. It's so hard to separate parental expectations from your own."

Caleb was in a similar dilemma and the parallels were obvious. "I wouldn't call this complicated," he said. "It's very clear. I know what I have to do." He used to think about the years to come, after Hannah and Jonah were on their own. Maybe then he would leave Middle Grove. Now that Jonah was hurt so bad, that might not be an option.

Caleb would have to find a way to be more accepting of the good things about Middle Grove, the things his brother had embraced. It was a secure home for Jonah. A safe harbor. The trouble was, Caleb had so much anchoring him that he felt as though he were drowning.

She touched his leg and got up from the bench. "Thank you for telling me. I wish it was a different story, but I'm glad you told me."

"It's easy to talk to you, Reese." They started walking again.

"You never tell lies," she said. "That's something I love about you."

She was wrong, though. And he knew it. The biggest lie he told was to himself. Every day.

Reese resisted the urge to take Caleb's hand as they walked together through the brisk night. It seemed like a natural gesture after the intimate conversation they'd just had, but there was something else they needed to discuss.

"I've been wondering about us," she said. "That's blunt, I know, but it's probably best to be direct about this."

"That's pretty direct." There was a hint of a smile in his voice. She wasn't sure how she knew that. It was because she knew him. How was it that she had come to know him, the small, intimate things about him, so well? Was it because she couldn't stop thinking about him?

She stuck her hands in the pockets of her jacket and studied the vertical shadows of the boardwalk railing. Somehow, it was easier to talk if she forged ahead.

"I don't know how else to approach this. There's something going on between us. It feels . . . romantic and special. And if you think I'm wrong, you'd better speak up now because it's kind of a big deal to me."

"You're not wrong," he said.

A feeling of relief unfurled inside her. They both felt it, then. "I'm going to be very honest here and tell you I probably don't have much in common with an Amish woman. I'm telling you this so you know I really mean it when I say I . . . I think a lot of you. Remember when you explained to me what that means?"

"Yah, I remember."

"Then you know that it means I'm falling for you." There. She'd finally spoken the words aloud. And it was a cringey thing to say, but it was also true, unlikely as it seemed, even to her. "You don't need to say it back to me," she said. "If you don't want to say anything at all, I understand, because seriously, I'm not asking you for anything, and I get that your life and my life are totally and completely different, and there's really no point in—"

He stopped her with a kiss, swift and hard. Right there in the middle of the boardwalk, probably captured by security cams, he grabbed her and kissed her with a long, open-mouthed kiss that made the world shift and change color. The moment went on and on, and it still didn't last long enough. The kiss was like a wave, building to a crest and then subsiding gradually, leaving her dizzy with wonder and delight. *Who knew?* she wondered. *Who knew there was a feeling like this in the world?*

With studied gentleness, he lifted his mouth from hers and smiled down at her.

"Oh," she said. "Well. Wow." She tried to gather her thoughts and find a few words beyond monosyllabic exclamations. "After a kiss like that," she said at last, "there needs to be some kind of follow-up."

"There does," he agreed. "Unless you mean more talking."

"Shit, I do talk too much," she admitted, suddenly in a hurry. "But no, I don't mean more talking." Damn. This was really happening. And she wanted it more than her next breath of air. They were nearly home. She felt exhilarated as they hurried down the access stairs from the bridge to the street.

At the bottom of the stairs, there was broken glass on the pavement from a shattered streetlight. Across the road, a neon sign flashed over a deserted launderette. There were broken bricks and small beads on the ground.

"Careful," said Caleb, touching the small of her back as they skirted around the debris.

A rustle and a movement stirred to life. Four guys on bikes burst from the shadows. One of them nearly collided with her, and she fell back against Caleb. "Hey," she said, "watch where you're going."

"Hand over everything," one of the guys said. He wore a low-brimmed hat and a funnel-necked shirt. Tattoos on the backs of his hands. Glimmer of fire in his neon-lit eyes. "Make it fast."

Whoa. Shit. A robbery. Seriously? Now?

She grabbed Caleb's arm, feeling instantly that the muscles there had gone rock hard. "We don't want any trouble," she said, her voice trembling from a swift rush of terror.

"No," Caleb agreed. "We don't." His voice didn't tremble at all.

Three of the bikes clattered to the pavement. "Then do like you're told," said one of them, swaggering forward. Hoodie and loose jeans. Missing front tooth. "Hand it aaaaall over. Wallets, cash, jewelry, phone . . ."

Caleb calmly took out his stitched leather wallet. As usual, it contained nothing except a bit of cash.

A hand snatched it and dug out a few bills. "Thirty-five bucks? *Fuck*. That ain't shit."

"You gotta do better than that," said one of the others, grabbing Reese's handbag and practically yanking her arm out of its socket. He dumped it on the ground, and there was a scramble for the wallet and phone.

"Jewelry." One of them grabbed her necklace—the pendant from her grandmother. She yelped as the chain cut the back of her neck.

"Don't touch her," Caleb said. "Please." Still calm, but she recognized a new note in his voice—the quiet growl of an attack dog.

She tried to breathe through panic. Adrenaline was firing through her every nerve, yet she felt utterly paralyzed. She saw Caleb's large hands clenching and unclenching.

"Here," she said, removing her cheap earrings with shaking hands. "Take everything and go."

"Dude's got manners," said one of the thugs. "He said 'please.' I think he should say '*pretty* please.'"

"Yeah, make that 'pretty please,' big guy."

"And unlock the fucking phone, bitch." One of them thrust it at her and grabbed her wrist.

"I said, don't touch her," Caleb repeated.

"And I said, you gotta say '*pretty please.*' And while you're at it, cough up the rest of your cash." As he spoke, the guy whipped out a handgun and jammed the barrel under Caleb's jaw. "You hearin' me all right?"

Reese nearly threw up. "Oh my God. Please don't shoot. Please—"

One of the men shoved the phone in her face. "Unlock it! Do it now, bitch."

Her hand shook so hard she couldn't touch the right digits on the screen. The man lost patience and shoved her up against the iron railing of the stairs. He reeked of weed and sweat. "Put your fucking thumb on the fucking button," he yelled, his breath hot in her face.

She couldn't hold her hand still. From the corner of her eye, she saw Caleb's right hand form a hard fist. "Caleb, no," she screamed. "He's got a gun—"

There was a not-very-loud popping sound. And then a sickening crunch as Caleb's fist shot up and connected with the guy's face, hitting him so hard it knocked him to the ground. The gun went spinning toward the gutter and disappeared into the shadows. The other three went for Caleb like a pack of rabid dogs.

Rushing forward, she sank both her fists into the back of a sweatshirt, trying to yank one of them off Caleb. An elbow connected with her chest, knocking the wind out of her. She staggered, but didn't fall.

There was a clicking sound. A blade flashed in the glow of the launderette's neon sign. Caleb grabbed the assailant's arm and twisted. Reese heard the snap of a tendon or ligament, then a ragged scream of pain. She spotted the knife and snatched it up, though she couldn't imagine using it. She heard a strange sound, like a wet thud. It was Caleb's fist, smashing with stunning force into his opponent's face.

One of the men grabbed his bike and raced away into the shadows. The others groaned and swore as they dragged themselves up.

"Fuck my fucking life," howled one of them, clutching his face. "Dude broke my fucking nose."

"I can't move my goddamn arm," said another. It was oddly angled at the elbow, probably dislocated. Still, the guy managed to mount a bike and wobble away.

"I see you again, you're dead, motherfucker." The words lacked authority, though, because they were all fleeing.

Reese dropped the knife—a switchblade—and staggered as her legs buckled. Caleb put his arm around her and helped her sit down on the stairs. "Are you hurt?" he asked.

"N-no." She rubbed the back of her neck. "Scared shit-less is all. You?"

"I'm all right." He bent to the amber-lit sidewalk and picked something up—her necklace.

She barely looked at it as she stuffed it into her pocket.

"They had a *gun*, Caleb. You're not supposed to fight back when someone has a gun to your head. Why the hell would you resist somebody who has a gun on you? Damn it, you could have been shot."

He rubbed his jaw. "I was."

"*What?* Jesus, where?"

He tipped up his chin. "Just here. It's nothing to worry about."

"You were shot? Did it graze you? Oh my God."

He walked over to the curb and retrieved the gun.

She shrank from the sinister black object.

He gave it a shake, and she could hear something rattling like a snake. "It's a BB gun," he said. "I recognized it right away. Looks real, but it's not so hazardous. They must've been shooting it off earlier. I saw BBs all over the sidewalk."

She nearly fainted on the steps. "A BB gun."

"They left your phone." He held it out.

She grabbed it from him. Her hands were still shaking too hard to deal with the phone, but the Emergency option could be activated with one touch.

"Nine one one," said a voice on the other end. "What's your emergency?"

TWO

The Match

MARCH

*In the end, it is important to remember that
we cannot become what we need to be,
by remaining what we are.*

—MAX DE PREE

14

The silver flash of Caleb's blade glinted against the winter sky as he lifted it high overhead. Jonah watched as his uncle swung the long-handled ax in an arc, then brought its blade down deep into the heart of the chunk of wood he was splitting. Against the eye-smarting deep blue above, Jonah spotted the contrails of a jet. The aircraft had drawn a white arrow aiming dead southeast, toward Philadelphia.

Caleb paused in his work and wiped the sweat from his brow. "A man who chops the wood warms himself twice," he said with a grin. "Care to give it a try?"

Jonah eyed the ax. "Maybe later. I got more practicing to do with my arm."

"All right then. I think we have enough for the night." Caleb stacked the split wood in the old canvas carrier. "You warm enough?"

Jonah nodded, though the cold had numbed the fingers of his good hand. His only hand. Winter held Middle Grove in its icy grip deep into the heart of March. At the last Sunday social, he'd heard folks remarking on the brutally long winter. Woodpiles were depleted, and the spring planting would be delayed.

The other hand was made of aluminum and thermoplastic and carbon fiber, and it should have felt nothing, and yet it hurt almost constantly, a pulsing, squeezing sensation. Phantom pain, the orthotics people said. In time, and after more surgery, it would stop.

He patted his thigh to get Jubilee's attention. The dog had been his constant companion ever since he'd come home six months before. She was such a big help when he practiced with his arm that the therapist in New Hope let her come to all the appointments.

"Let's get to it, girl," he said, positioning himself in front of the workbench where he did his practicing.

Start with a breath. Focus. Jonah stared at his robotic arm, not the way kids stared at it in school, but the way he'd been trained. He was supposed to picture his muscles and nerves and their connections inside the socket. The arm had electronic motors and sensors that were being trained to know what his mind was thinking. His orthopedist said legs were stronger, yet arms and hands were smarter.

But only if Jonah concentrated. Today's practice: picking up a dog's squeaky toy that was in the shape of a doughnut. Jubilee was focused on the toy and concentrating as hard as Jonah. She crouched on a patch of ground that was just beginning to thaw and stared at the doughnut as though trying to hypnotize it.

Jonah managed to pluck it from the workbench. *Now lift elbow, close grip.* The arm lifted, but the grip opened instead of closing.

"Keep trying," Caleb said calmly, still bundling the wood.

In the chilly silence, Jonah heard the tiny gears of the arm whirring.

He crushed his eyebrows down into a frown. *Close grip. Close. Breathe.*

And finally, he picked up the doughnut. The toy let out a squeak, which brought Jubilee to her feet. He held it steady, exactly as his mind was telling his arm to do. Then he tried the most complex maneuver of all, throwing the toy for his dog. Flinging it was no problem. Letting go—that was a different story.

He drew his arm back at the shoulder and brought it forward. *Let go.*

The grip opened at the exact right moment. The dog toy flew through the air. Jubilee gave a yelp of joy and bounded after it.

"Good work," Caleb said. He grinned with his whole face. His whole body. He always did, even when the success was just a small one.

"I tossed a toy for the dog," Jonah said.

"With your new arm. That's something."

He was learning to think about muscles he didn't have anymore, like his biceps, so his brain would tell the arm what to do. Bend, flex, contract.

In Philadelphia, they told him the pioneering surgery was only the beginning. He figured out that pioneering meant he was one of the first, like a space explorer. It also meant that the real work was up to him.

He had been very surprised when Caleb made the abrupt decision to come home to Middle Grove. One day Caleb had come to the hospital with his face and his knuckles all banged up from some bad guys attacking him and stealing his money. There was a big meeting with the care team. Even Jonah was allowed to attend. Uncle Caleb had explained that he and Jonah had to go home.

Jonah had been overjoyed. Home to Jubilee and his regular life. Somehow, they worked out a plan so Jonah could be at home but still get the training and therapy he needed. His days were the same in some ways, different in others. He had more time for reading, and Caleb and the bookmobile lady from the county library made sure he always had something new to read. Lately, he'd been reading a series of adventure books about a kid lawyer named Theodore Boone.

"Help me carry this inside," Caleb said. He blew on his hands to warm them.

Jonah couldn't remember what it was like to have two cold hands. He watched his uncle, studying those big hands. They were strong enough to wrestle a stubborn bull. Yet even now, long after the attack in Philadelphia, Caleb's knuckles bore white scars.

"What?" Caleb asked. He must have noticed Jonah staring.

"How did you hurt your hands when the bad men attacked you?" asked Jonah. He swallowed hard, feeling brazen. Until now, he hadn't dared to ask. Back when he was still in the hospital, he'd stayed quiet about his uncle's hands, fearful of jinxing his chances of getting to come home.

"Guess they got bumped or scraped on something." Caleb leaned the ax against the woodshed.

"On what?" Jonah persisted. "Did the bad guys beat your hands because you were trying not to let them take your money?"

Caleb turned to him. He sat on the edge of the workbench. "What do you think, little man?"

"I think you're not lying to me because you never lie. But you're not saying the whole truth and nothing but the truth." Jonah liked quoting his fictional hero, Theodore Boone. The law was the law. It just laid everything out, which was so much simpler than folks arguing about what was right and what was wrong. He leaned down and picked up Jubilee's squeaky toy. "I think you fought back."

"You do?"

Jonah was figuring out that to get the truth out of someone, you shouldn't say what you think. You had to ask questions to see what *they* thought. "Did you fight with the guys who attacked you?"

Caleb looked directly at him. His face didn't show anything. "I did. It's against our principles and I'm not proud of it, and there's no excuse for that kind of behavior."

Jonah noticed that he didn't say he was sorry. He didn't say he wished he hadn't done it.

"Why's it against our principles?" Jonah asked.

"Because the Amish are strict pacifists," said Caleb. "Ordnung prohibits us from raising a hand against another human being."

"Then why did Ray Graber get a caning from his dat yesterday? Right outside the school it was. How is that different?"

"We're out of firewood," said a loud voice. Grandfather came outside with the kitchen waste. As he put it in the bin, his mouth was a macron of disapproval above his bushy beard.

"Jonah and I'll bring some right in," Caleb said.

"Jonah, too, eh?" Grandfather shut the bin and turned. He hated the arm. He claimed it was a tool of the devil. He objected to the electrical plug Caleb had installed in the milk house to power the battery pack. "Carrying wood's a two-handed job."

"I'll thank you to keep your thoughts to yourself," Caleb said. He never raised his voice, but Jonah could hear the anger, like the low vibration in the throat of a dog issuing a warning.

"I got two hands," Jonah said, wanting to break the tension. "Just one of 'em's made of alloy." He hooked the strap of the carrier around the hand grip.

Grandfather wasn't the only one who didn't like the arm. The bishop said it was God's will that Jonah's arm was cut off, and it was a sin to use an artificial limb.

In the house, Jonah stoked the fire in the iron stove. Maybe his prosthesis *was* a sin, but at least he wouldn't burn his hand when he made a fire. Once the lively flames were crackling, he stacked the rest of the wood in the copper bin.

Hannah came home from the quilt shop, her cheeks bright from the cold. She was carrying a basket of something. Jonah hoped it was food. The ladies who worked at the quilt shop made the best cookies and cakes.

"It's not food," she said, reading his mind, something she'd always been able to do. "We made a lap blanket for Rebecca Zook. She's doing poorly again." Hannah slid a sideways glance at Caleb, and Jonah knew why. A while back, folks thought Caleb would marry Rebecca and bring her here to the farm as his wife.

Ever since Hannah had been baptized into the church, she seemed more mysterious and grown up. Jonah had been present for the ceremony, when she and her buddy bunch pledged their faith to the church. The pouring of the water, the serious-sounding questions, and the prayers had transformed his sister in ways he couldn't quite understand.

"Come with me to give it to her," she said to Jonah. "Let's bring Jubilee along for a walk."

"I'm tired from all the practicing and wood carrying."

"You have two perfectly good legs, Jonah Stoltz," she said in a bossy voice, sounding like the old Hannah now. She plunked his knitted stocking cap down around his ears. "Let's go."

She knew him better than anyone. They told each other things. He felt lucky to have her. Caleb worked every day—at Grantham Farm, doing bookkeeping for his English clients, hauling, anything that would bring in more money. Jonah knew it was because the doctor bills were so high. But Hannah, she always had time for him, and sometimes she needed him as much as he needed her. Still, she seemed different these days, somehow. Spent lots of quiet time in her room, made mysterious trips to the outhouse at all hours of the night. She was his blood sister, though, and she would always have his back, same as he would have hers.

They crossed two fields, lifting their legs high over the dried winter wheat stubble. Jubilee raced and cavorted ahead of them, scaring up a flurry of crows.

"Aaron Graber's parents won't let him go to the singing tonight," Hannah said. "Should I go, even if he's not going to be there?"

"You're asking me?"

"No, I'm asking the Oracle of Delphi," she said. "Of course I'm asking you. You're old enough to have a fancy arm, so you must be old enough to have an opinion."

"Why would you stay home just because Aaron's not going?"

"Because we're courting. But I still want to go." She crushed her boot down on a clump of stubble. "Stuff like this is vexing, that's what it is. I wish . . ." She didn't finish the thought, but Jonah knew what she was thinking.

"Do you ever wonder what it'd be like to have a regular mother and father like most folks?" he asked.

She lifted her face to the sky, and the wind blew back her bonnet strings. "All the time," she said. "All the time."

Entering the penitentiary at Forest Hills felt as routine as a church Sunday in Middle Grove. Being searched, scanned, and sniffed by dogs before entering was not so different, somehow, from the scrutiny of church elders. Caleb wasn't sure getting used to this process was a good thing, a bad thing, or just a thing.

Three times a year, all the Stoltzes visited inmates Anthony Frackton and Darryl Krebs. The Amish principle of forgiveness was absolute. These men had murdered John and Naomi, yet doctrine demanded that the survivors—Caleb, Asa, Hannah, and Jonah—find grace through forgiveness. They brought approved reading material and small change for the vending machines. They'd learned early on that homemade food or anything from home could not be given to an inmate, only what dropped from the machines in the visiting area.

Early on, Caleb had felt a killing rage toward the assailants who had stolen two innocent lives. As time went on, he resigned himself to the visits. Rage would not bring his brother back. Bitterness was simply poison.

Yet today's encounter felt different to Caleb. He knew why. Because now he understood what it felt like to attack someone with raw, protective fury pouring through his body. That, he believed, was what John had felt trying to fend off his attackers. Despite the Amish principle of nonviolence, John had fought back. That night in Philadelphia, Caleb had done the same thing. The assault, and the powerful anger that had overtaken him when the thugs had confronted him and threatened Reese, haunted him still, months later.

The attack had slapped him out of the trance he'd been in during his stay in the city. He'd realized that night that he had to leave, not because he didn't like Philadelphia, but because he'd liked it too much—riding in cars and dancing and eating all kinds of food, Reese and her friends, each one so interesting and unique. And Reese herself—complicated and challenging, smart and unpredictable and funny and sexy. She'd woven an enchantment around him until he'd started imagining a life far from the Amish community—a life he couldn't have. Even the fight had been dangerously seductive. He couldn't forget those moments of raw energy he'd felt when the thugs had surrounded him. He'd been raised to submit or, at the most, flee when threatened or attacked. But pure instinct overpowered teachings and traditions.

In the aftermath, he'd felt a strange intoxication, as if he could do anything. And he'd known better than to trust that feeling. He told himself he'd fought off the thugs in self-defense, even though he knew it was against Amish principles. Reese had tried to be reassuring, saying that under the circumstances, he'd done the right thing.

Caleb hadn't worried about right or wrong. He'd worried because he had *liked* the fight. He should not have enjoyed breaking a man's nose and another's arm. Yet he'd taken a sick satisfaction in the violent act. It was as if all the rage at the attackers of John and Naomi had found a secret home deep inside Caleb, festering like an untended wound. Somehow, the Philadelphia thugs had tapped into that rage, causing it to erupt like a volcano.

At the end of the seemingly endless night, Caleb had made himself face the truth. The mesmeric effect of the English world was taking hold of him. He had no business there. He could not set aside the promise he'd made to John as his brother lay dying. John had begged Caleb to raise his children Plain. The Amish took care of their own. They didn't mingle with worldly folks, particularly women like Reese Powell. The time had come to take Jonah home.

He thought he'd find peace, coming back to Middle Grove. Instead, he'd found tension with his father, worry about the children. Peace was a relative thing. It didn't

have so much to do with where a person lived as *how* he
lived.

Anthony was his usual terse self—"Whatchoo
got?"—taking the chocolate bars they'd purchased from
the vending machine. Darryl was the same, too, which
meant an unfocused stare, a string of drool from the corner of his mouth. Caleb hadn't known either man before
the attack, of course, but according to reports, Darryl had
suffered brain damage in the fight. John had hit him so
hard it had fractured the man's skull, and now he was
what some English called "simple."

Asa pressed his work-worn hands flat on the table.
"Let us pray," he said in his gruff voice.

Jonah regarded the prisoners with a steady gaze. Hannah hugged herself around the middle as she did the
same. Over the years, they had learned to look their parents' murderers in the eye. Caleb had to wonder what that
cost them, what it took out of their souls.

Asa cleared his throat. "May the Lord awaken in us
a hunger and thirst for righteousness. Teach us to act
according to the will of God . . ." The familiar words
seemed edged by darkness, delivered in Asa's flat, se-
vere tones. The inmates were quiet, probably not listening. Probably wondering when they could eat their treats
from the vending machine.

After Asa finished, Anthony eyed Jonah's arm. "'Sup
with that?" he asked.

"I had an accident," Jonah said. "My arm got cut off."

"Sucks for you."

"Yah."

"My parents said to come hungry tonight," Reese told
Leroy and Cheryl. "That's all I know."

"Your parents rock," Cheryl said. "I still have impure thoughts about the chocolate silk pie they served last time we came to dinner." Since she and Leroy had become a couple, Reese had brought them to her parents' place a few times.

Although she remembered every moment of the night she'd gone to her folks' with Caleb, it seemed like a dream now. Or as if it had happened to someone else.

In the moments following the attack, neither had spoken of the incident. There was nothing to say. Even the police hadn't wanted to hear about it. Reese had been trying to explain to the dispatcher what had happened when Caleb had gently taken the phone from her hand and said, "Everything is fine. There's no emergency." And then he'd hung up.

She had tried the police again that night, certain they needed to take action. When it was clear to the overworked guy on the phone that no one had been hurt, no property damaged, and no suspects present, he had invited her to file a report, but didn't encourage it.

"Let it go," Caleb had said. "You're safe. That's all that matters."

Back at her apartment, she'd cleaned his abrasions. "I'm so sorry that happened. And so grateful you knew how to handle yourself."

"I didn't know. I just reacted."

"Well, those thugs are in a lot worse shape than you."

"Are they?"

"I heard breaking bones." She saw the torment in his eyes. The Amish were famous for being pacifists, for turning the other cheek. Turning away from a fight. But Caleb had not hesitated. Given what had happened to his brother and sister-in-law, his distrust of English ways made sense. So did the rage with which he'd fought back.

Caleb's voice had been quiet and firm, though filled with regret, when he'd told her, "I'm taking Jonah home."

The outside world had brought heartbreak to his family. She knew she would never convince him that the world wasn't always horrible. Her assurances would surely ring hollow after the attack.

After Caleb and Jonah had left the city, everything had gone back to business as usual—friends who were in the medical field, the endless chase for the right residency placement, untold hours of studying and hospital work.

Except that nothing had felt like business as usual since then.

"I don't know what's on the menu," she told Cheryl, "but the lack of information makes me nervous, especially when it's an invitation from my parents. Especially on the evening before the Match."

"Are you nervous?" Leroy asked.

She smiled a greeting at the doorman of her parents' place. "Nervous about the most important step in my career so far? Nervous about getting the brass ring I've been reaching for since I was in utero? Nah."

"All right," he said, stepping aside to let her and Cheryl precede him into the elevator. "Dumb question. You should be totally confident, though. You're one of the best med students I've ever met."

Her stomach churned as the luxurious elevator whisked them up to the penthouse. The all-important process of finding a residency was finally at its end. The decision was out of her hands now. Letting her nerves get the better of her would not change anything. Except . . .

"I did something," she said faintly.

Leroy frowned. "What?" He must have recognized the queasy expression on her face, because he grabbed her by the shoulders. "Reese, what did you do?"

"Breathe," said Cheryl, a respiratory specialist.

"It was—"

"Surprise!"

As the elevator doors whisked open, a group of people were clustered in the foyer to welcome Reese. In the middle of everyone were her parents, beaming with pride. Surrounding them were both sets of grandparents along with various aunts and uncles, a few cousins, colleagues of the Powells, and some of the other students in her program. Her parents' lawyer, Domenico Falco, was present as well, a silver fox in a bespoke suit.

"Whoa," Reese said, pressing her hand to her chest. In spite of everything, she felt a genuine rush of pleasure. "Surprise is right. Mom, Dad, you got me. Totally."

A live band on the veranda started playing "Let's Get It Started."

"Nice," Leroy said, and swung Cheryl into his arms as everyone moved outside and started dancing.

Reese stepped back and beamed at her parents. "You guys are crazy, you know that? This is all way too much." She greeted her grandparents with genuine pleasure. Their love and pride filled her with affection for her family. She could practically feel the excitement emanating from them. She'd screwed up. She was sure of it. They were going to hate what she had done.

"It's not too much," her mother pointed out. "No one has worked harder for this residency placement than you have. We've all seen it, Reese."

"We couldn't be prouder," said her father. "Come on, baby girl. Dance with me."

On the way to the veranda, warmed by propane heaters and lit with colorful tiki torches, Reese managed to slam a tequila shot, served in a laboratory beaker. "You know I hate surprise parties," she said.

"That's why we put this together. Because you weren't expecting it."

"Hang on a sec," she said before they joined the dancing. "I need another shot." But as the fiery tequila slid down her throat, she knew it wouldn't be enough to quiet her nerves.

In the middle of the dancing, Trent Withers, a cardiothoracic resident she'd worked with on a past rotation, stole her away from her father. "You come from a family of rock stars, don't you?" he asked.

Trent was all teeth, perfect veneered teeth. The moment the rotation had ended, he'd started asking her out. On the surface, he was the ideal match for her—a gifted physician with a fine educational pedigree and a bright future.

"You know," he said, as he pulled her into a close embrace, "I always wanted to go out with you. And I always knew you would say yes one of these days."

"Trent—"

"I don't think that anymore," he said.

She tried to be polite as she leaned away from him. "Okay, then . . ."

"It's not going to happen one of these days," he concluded.

She breathed a sigh of relief.

"It's going to happen tonight," he said.

Oh, brother.

"I like your confidence," she said, wondering if his teeth really were veneered or naturally perfect. "But it's still a no, Trent. You're a good doctor and teacher, but outside the hospital, we're not a match."

He laughed and held her more firmly. He didn't grip hard enough to alarm her . . . yet the suggestion was there. "I have a different diagnosis."

"Dude, you're putting me on the spot," she said. "See, right now, I have to decide whether to pretend this is all good fun for me, or to knee you in the groin and cause drama at this super-special party my parents are throwing for me on the eve of Match Day. And just so you know, I'm not going to pick option one."

He lowered his hand to her butt. "I know you, Powell. You're not going to fuck with your mommy and daddy on their big night."

"I was thirteen when I earned my self-defense badge in Girl Scouts," she said, keeping a pleasant, social smile on her face as she pressed closer, maneuvering him toward one of the tiki torches. "You could take my word for it that I still remember my moves. Or you could call my bluff and find out for yourself."

"You're cute, Powell," he said, giving her butt a squeeze.

At the same moment, she pressed him back toward the tiki torch. "And your pants are on fire, Dr. Withers. Literally."

He yelped and jumped away, swatting at his pants. No one but Reese heard him over the music. She quickly walked away and told someone from the catering staff one of the guests might need some water.

"Having fun?" her mother asked, handing her another drink.

"So much fun," Reese said.

Domenico, the lawyer, handed her a multipage document. "Your folks had me draw this up. It's a partnership agreement with their practice. Congratulations, young lady."

Oh boy, she thought. "Oh boy," she said. "I don't know what to say. Isn't this about seven years premature?"

"We have another surprise for you." Her mother brought her over to a seating area to join her father.

"You guys," Reese said. "Stop it."

Her father handed her a large, flat envelope. Reese set down her drink and opened it to find a glossy trifold brochure for a high-rise called the Lofts. She frowned. "What's this?"

"Unit 4B. Say hello to your new home."

"What?" Reese felt nauseated. "This is a complex in Baltimore. What the hell makes you think I'll end up in Baltimore?"

"Because that's where your top residency match is," her father said. "Look, it's got secure parking, a Whole Foods in the complex, and—"

"Jesus Christ, there's no way you guys can know where I'll match tomorrow." Then she narrowed her eyes in suspicion. "Or is there? Please say you haven't heard anything."

"Of course not. The Match is strictly monitored. But we know you, sweetheart. You deserve this. The sale isn't final yet, but it's all in place. It'll be one thing you won't have to worry about when you move. We haven't signed the papers yet—"

"Don't sign the papers," Reese blurted out.

"Why not?" her mother asked. "We looked at all the options, and this is by far the best—"

"I'm sure it's absolutely perfect." Reese wished she could be as thrilled as her parents looked, but instead, she wanted to curl up and die. These people had organized her entire life for her, and she should be grateful. Yet her parents' hopes and expectations felt like a heavy weight. She had always been their trophy daughter, the one whose achievements added luster to their reputation. And like a trophy, she was hollow inside.

"Trust me, it is," her father said. "Honey, it's impossible to find a better place than this."

"You're probably right. And if you want it for an investment, I wouldn't blame you, because it looks spectacular. But don't get it on my behalf." She took a breath and looked at their eager, proud, loving faces. "I won't be living there. I won't match at Hopkins."

"Nonsense. Of course you will. It's exactly what the Match is all about—putting the right candidates in the right residency programs."

"I understand that, Mom. But . . . I did something," she said quietly.

"You certainly did," said her mother. "We couldn't be prouder."

Reese stared at the glossy brochure until the images blurred. "Please listen. Mom, Dad, I couldn't ask for a better family. A better education. A better anything. All of this—everything you've done for me—is amazing. But I need for you to listen. Please." She wished she hadn't thrown back those tequila shots, because now they were coming up to haunt her.

"You're white as a sheet," said her father.

"It's a lot to take in, I know," said her mother.

"I changed my rank order list," she told them, blurting out the news all at once.

They looked at each other, then at her. "You changed . . ."

"My ranking. At the very last minute in February, just before the certification deadline, I picked a different program for my top residency match."

"What?" Her mother leaned forward, grabbed her hands. "Hopkins isn't your number one pick?"

"No. I chose something else. And I'm hoping like hell I get it."

"And you're telling us this now?" Her father rubbed his jaw as if she'd hit him there.

She took another deep breath. Cautioned herself not to go into defensive mode. She tried to distance herself from the burble of music and laughter out on the terrace. She tried to quiet the noise in her head. "I wanted to make my decision without any input. I didn't want to be talked out of it. That doesn't mean I failed to give it plenty of thought. It came down to deciding how I want to spend not just the next three years, but the rest of my career. And what I want is to work in rural medicine. My top rank is a regional medical center in New Hope."

For a few moments, her parents said nothing. She gave them time to absorb what she'd just said. The expected questions swirled around her in a fog. She had no answer other than "This is what I want."

She gave her mother's hands a squeeze and let go. "During third year, I went to a rural health retreat in West Virginia to observe what a family physician in a rural setting—"

"You hated that rotation," her mother interrupted. "I remember you saying how much you hated it."

"No, I said it was hard, not that I hated it. In fact, the hard parts were the ones I liked best, the ones that made me feel like the doctor I want to be. One minute, you're delivering a baby, and the next, treating the infant's great-grandparents. It was incredibly challenging, but I'm not afraid of a challenge."

"Believe me, you're going to be challenged in the program at Hopkins," her father said.

"Of course I would be. Dad, I know what I'm passing up. I *know*."

"I can't believe you never said anything to us."

"I'm sorry. All my life, I've depended on you for . . . God, for everything. And you've been fantastic. I owe you everything. Then last fall, I came face-to-face with a truth I kept trying to bury for a long time—I realized I didn't want the life I've been aiming for all these years."

"Reese, we can see you're upset," her father said. "Why didn't you talk to us about this? We could have helped you clarify your goals."

"That's just it—you've been doing that all my life. And it's been wonderful. You've been wonderful. But the pediatric surgery specialty—that's your dream. Not mine. I didn't even know what my dream was, because I kept it hidden. I didn't want to disappoint you."

"You should know that it's not about disappointing us," her mother objected. "We simply want a wonderful practice and a wonderful life for you."

"Thank you. If the match comes through tomorrow, that's exactly what I'll have. And if I'm wrong, then I'll only have myself to blame." Her heart skipped a beat. "I don't think I'm wrong. There are just four places in the program, but I really do think I'll match."

"I've never even heard of that regional . . . whatever," her mother said, looking mystified. "And New Hope? Isn't that some village in the Poconos? Whose program is it? Who is the director?"

"There are two preceptors—Penelope Lake and Mose Shrock. I've met with them, and I want to learn from them."

Her father set his jaw in a grim line. "You haven't thought this through. I want you to talk to my buddy Paul Medford. He's the best career counselor I know. He'll help you get to the bottom of your motivation and figure out what's really driving you."

"I know what my motivation is," she said.

"Does it have big shoulders and speak with an Amish accent?" her mother asked.

Reese gasped. "I can't believe you just said that."

"I want you to be honest with us—and with yourself. Do you really want to practice in the back of beyond, or is this your way of rebelling against us?"

"I know what I'm signing up for," Reese said, hating the quaver she heard in her own voice. "I found something I love, and I'm not going to stupidly let it get away."

"Sweetheart, we just don't want to see you get hurt. We don't want you throwing away your talents and your first-class education on working at a walk-in clinic."

"Dad, that's not fair. Not only that—it's insulting."

"My mind is still blown," her mother said, reaching for a glass. "The program at Hopkins is your ticket to a life in medicine most people only dream about."

"I guess I'm not most people. I hate that I've let you down, and I love you for caring so much, but I won't change my mind. If I match with the New Hope residency, it will be exactly what I want."

"And if you don't match?"

"I'll go with the next one on my rank order list."

Her parents exchanged a glance. "Then we'd better hope you don't match with the country doc program."

15

Caleb peeled off his shirt and gave a whoop as he ran down the hill to the swimming hole. He flung himself off the edge of the bank and plunged into the deep eddy of clear water. The creek was cold, but it felt wonderful on the sweltering June day.

He shot to the surface and shook the water from his eyes. Jonah and his buddy Samuel stood teetering on the bank, their skinny bodies silhouetted against the summer sky.

"Come on in," Caleb called, his voice echoing against the steep sides of the eddy. He paddled backward, treading water. "You'll forget you were ever sweating like a pair of rented mules."

Jonah and Samuel looked at each other, then shucked their breeches and jumped together, their limbs splayed like falling starfish. They hit the water willy-nilly, creating a fount of diamond droplets. Then both came up laughing.

"Whoa, Nellie, that's cold," Jonah said.

"Feels really good, eh?" said Samuel.

They paddled around, all three of them grinning up at the sky. Summer days were made for doing chores, but when the chores were done, there was no sweeter reward than a dip in the silky waters of the creek's deepest eddy. Jonah lay back and turned his face to the sun, keeping himself afloat with the paddle attachment on his arm. It wasn't his usual robot arm, but a simple apparatus specially made for swimming. Jonah had mastered it quickly, and the other kids were used to seeing it by now.

Three times a week without fail, Caleb hitched up the buggy and took Jonah to an outpatient clinic in New Hope for sessions with a physiatrist, a physical therapist, and a prosthetist. It was time consuming and caused Jonah to miss a lot of school, but worth the effort for the progress he made. Hannah supervised his makeup work in the evenings. To keep up with the bills, Caleb worked twelve-hour days at Grantham Farm and stayed up late with the bookkeeping work. In between, he looked after the farm. This afternoon was a rare break from the grueling schedule.

"Can we put the rope swing up this year?" Jonah asked.

"I reckon so," Caleb said. "We need to find the right limb for it, though. The old one broke off last winter." He gestured at the thick oak branch, which now formed a bridge across the creek. "Did you know it was your dat who first put that rope in place?"

"I did not," Jonah said.

"Well, he hung it years ago. And he was famous for being able to do a full somersault before hitting the water. He's the one who taught me."

"Can you teach us?" Samuel asked.

"I can, and I will, once we get another rope up there." Caleb paddled to the bank and got dressed, then climbed out along the rock ledges. He inspected the tree, picking out a likely branch or two. The boys played and splashed, spraying each other, their laughter chiming in the stillness of the afternoon. Later, they got out to explore the fallen limb across the creek above the swimming hole, chattering away like a couple of magpies.

As Caleb lay on the grass letting the sun dry his hair

he closed his eyes for a moment and took it all in. There were moments, he reflected, when the sweetness of life was like honey on the tongue, something to savor, even though the blissful flavor was temporary. Jonah was reclaiming himself, growing stronger and more confident every day. Not only was he making progress with the robotic arm, he was learning ways to dismiss the phantom nerve pain. At school, at home, and in the community, Jonah worked harder than anyone could possibly know to fit in and live his life. Caleb was so proud of the boy that sometimes it made his heart ache.

At times, Caleb felt guilty for not staying in Philadelphia, where Jonah could get the maximum intensive therapy he needed. Coming home had been a compromise, but a necessary one. Caleb thought about the city a lot, deep in the night when, despite his exhaustion, he couldn't sleep. Though he knew this was the way things had to be, he couldn't stop himself from thinking about Reese Powell and her fancy bed and Bluetooth speakers playing all the music in the world, and the sweetness of her taste and smell, the gentle sigh of her breath in his ear, and the way she reached for him whenever he was near.

His thoughts were interrupted when Hannah came up the hill, walking with a purposeful stride, her long dress and apron flapping in the breeze. Even though the June day was sweltering hot, she had chosen not to go swimming. "It's too hard for a girl anyway," she'd told him earlier, "having to keep the dress and covering on."

When she was younger, she used to come up with clever ways to pin the dress so it wouldn't billow up in the water, and to tie the bonnet so it wouldn't float away. These days, she was acting more secretive than ever. The one visit to the city had turned her head, that was for sure. She'd gotten hold of a copy of the novel *The Princess Bride* and had practically memorized it. She'd even designed a quilt around the story.

Last fall, Hannah had spent far too much time with Aaron Graber. Caleb wanted to forbid it, but he had no reason. She was a young lady now and had to be allowed to make her own decisions—and her own mistakes. In early spring, she and her gang went on rumspringa, and they'd hooked up with some English kids over in Pine Creek. Then, a couple of weeks ago, she'd stopped the rumspringa. She stopped everything but quilting, reading books, and staring dreamy-eyed out the window.

It was the way of a girl, Alma Troyer assured him, when he'd confessed to her he was worried about Hannah.

The way of a girl. No wonder he didn't understand her.

"Caleb Stoltz, didn't you hear me calling from the house?" she said, her face red and sweaty from the heat.

"You were calling?" He grinned. "Maybe you called the wrong number."

She didn't crack a smile at the familiar quip. "You need to come."

"*Vas is letz?*" he asked.

"I'm not sure what's the matter," she said, answering in dialect. "Something with Grandfather and the bishop. You need to come." With a swish of her hem, she pivoted and went back down the hill.

There was always something with Caleb's father, some infraction or other that was going to lead them all into eternal damnation.

Even so, he returned to the house feeling better. A dip in the clean, cold water on a hot day improved any outlook. Whistling a tune, he went through the back door into the kitchen.

The sound on his lips died when he saw his father

seated at the table along with the bishop and a stranger Caleb didn't recognize—a woman in English clothes. She had a mobile phone and a clipboard, and her mouth was pressed into a seam of disapproval.

Caleb greeted the bishop with a handshake and introduced himself to the woman.

"Victoria Duncan," she said, and handed him a business card. "I'm with Child Protective Services."

"What's this about?" Caleb asked. His mind was racing. Jonah's accident had been investigated months ago. There was no child here who needed protecting. *Where were you when my father was beating the crap out of my brother and me?*

"It's a guardianship issue," said Victoria Duncan. She flipped open her clipboard to reveal a collection of papers. "According to the information we have, you've been acting as legal guardian of your minor nephew, Jonah Stoltz, and your minor niece, Hannah Stoltz."

Caleb said nothing. He could feel his heart like a cold stone in his chest.

"The parents died intestate," said the woman. "Upon their passing, the presumed guardian was not you, but your father, Asa Stoltz. Were you aware of that, Caleb?"

He looked directly at her, though from the corner of his eye, he saw his father sit forward expectantly. "I was," Caleb said.

"Hello. I'm Dr. Powell." The night before her first day of residency, Reese stared at her image in the mirror that hung above an old-fashioned washstand. The floorboards of the old farmhouse that would be her home for the next three years creaked beneath her nervous feet. Weighted down by her new, untried status, she felt like an imposter.

She was utterly convinced that everything she'd learned over the past four years had vaporized into the ether.

She had blown her parents' minds when she'd chosen this residency program. The program here in New Hope, administered by the two deeply experienced preceptors she'd met last fall, was the last place her parents had expected her to choose. Yet the moment she'd walked into her interview with Dr. Lake and Dr. Shrock, she'd known what her decision would be.

She had probably made a mistake, just like her mom and dad had said. But it was her life. Her mistake to make.

Turning away from the mirror, she tried to forget about the disappointment in their faces.

A breeze through the window, carrying the scent of phlox and roses from the garden, reminded her that maybe she wasn't wrong after all. With her newly minted MD degree and a heart full of hope, she had moved to New Hope to become one of four residents in the program. Instead of the high-rise luxury condo her parents had tried to give her, she now occupied a room on the second story of Mose Shrock's house, situated high on a hill overlooking a broad valley. Housing was nearly impossible to find in the town. That was the reality of rural life. There was no place for a visitor to live. You had to board with a local family. The Shrocks had taken her in like a stray.

Mose and his wife, Ida, were too old to get upstairs anymore, so they rented two of the four bedrooms up there to residents. The other boarder was a new doc named Ursula Mays, a second-year resident who would be one of Reese's mentors. Ursula seemed to be as laid-back as Reese was keyed up.

Reese's room overlooked rippling fields, a meandering stream, and a bright patchwork of storybook farms, now gilded by the light of the setting sun. Despite the scenery, she felt a stab of uncertainty. This change was huge. Maybe it wasn't what she wanted after all.

Breathe, she told herself. She took in the panorama of streams and ponds with ducks gliding across the clear water, the new growth covering the hills. No traffic, no city noise intruded. On a distant slope, she spied a barefoot boy on an unsaddled horse, dragging a plow as the father, with a little girl on his shoulders, walked behind, directing it.

She leaned out the window and let the breeze surround her. She absorbed the aroma of the plowed earth, and she felt reluctant to take the next breath for fear of disrupting the perfect moment. She pictured the noisy asphalt-and-metal city that had been her home forever and felt a welling of emotion. This was right. It had to be right.

She turned away from the window and contemplated the days to come. Her schedule would be divided between work at the hospital and clinic days in the outlying areas surrounding New Hope.

It just so happened that one of the towns served by the regional group was a place called Middle Grove.

It just so happened, she told herself. It wasn't *not* a coincidence.

It was no surprise to Reese that Caleb had left after the night of the attack. The surprise was how much it hurt. How much she missed him, day after day. Yearned for him. Leroy said time would mellow the ache, but it hadn't happened. If anything, the pain intensified.

She had tried to convince him to stay, to compromise, to find a way to get Jonah the help he needed. But Caleb had been intractable. The incident with the thugs had shed a glaring light on the fact that he didn't belong in the city. Though he hadn't said so, she believed he felt guilty

about his relationship with her. He was feeling pressure
from the Amish community to return Jonah to his people.

And who was she to argue or object? Jonah was not
her patient. Caleb was not her boyfriend.

After they'd left, she had searched for her own next
step. Finally, she'd forced herself to pay attention to the
insistent inner voice that kept telling her that maybe,
just maybe, she didn't want to be the kind of doctor she
thought she would be. Maybe, just maybe, she needed
to separate herself from her parents' expectations. She
imagined Caleb would be amused to know he'd triggered
all this deep self-reflection.

She imagined Caleb a lot. More than she should.

Agitated, Reese laid out her clothes for her first day as
a doctor—a simple dress and comfortable shoes. At the
hospital, her locker was ready with scrubs and a lab coat
embroidered with her name: Reese Powell, MD.

Dr. Powell. Yet she didn't feel any more like a doctor
than she had the day before her degree was conferred.

She forced herself to stop pacing and sit down in a
wicker armchair with quilted cushions. She tried reading a novel, a high-flown fantasy replete with sex and
violence and political intrigue. Fail. Concentration was
impossible.

Time ticked past, measured by an antique clock on the
shelf. The sounds of the settling house drifted in—Mose
calling his dog in for the night, Ursula gabbing away on her
phone. Reese climbed into bed, settling back on a comfy
bank of pillows, but she couldn't sleep. After an hour, she
got up, checked her email and message boards, littered
with squealy posts from fellow grads. She put on her headphones and danced to Carly Rae Jepsen but stopped when
she caught herself blurting out "Call me maybe . . ." and
then worried that she might wake the household.

After far too long, she drifted off in fits and starts. Then multiple alarms stabbed into her consciousness. She sat straight up in bed, on fire with a familiar state of panic. She wondered why she'd bothered to try sleeping at all. She staggered to the shower and blasted herself with a stream of well water that took its time warming up.

Coffee. Her primary food group. Her residency survival guide advised her to avoid caffeine and alcohol in favor of herbal tea. Fuck that.

Downstairs in the kitchen, she seemed to be the first one up, so she tried not to make noise as she filled the kettle and French press. The dog came scampering in, a friendly ball of taffy-colored fluff, and submitted to belly rubs before running outside. Reese forced herself to eat a bowl of cereal sprinkled with wild strawberries. Yesterday morning, she'd stopped at a sweet little homemade fruit stand and picked up a couple of pints. Ursula had told her to pack a lunch, so she slapped together a peanut butter sandwich and put it in a bag with a banana.

She decided to head to the hospital early to get into her scrubs, study her drug formulary, and try to remember everything she'd learned in her rotations—surgery, neurology, psychiatry, internal medicine, obstetrics, pediatrics, radiology, emergency medicine—in preparation for her thirty-hour shift. While she waited for the morning conference, she peeled the banana from her lunch and sutured it back together.

Warren, a fellow intern, came into the locker room. "Is that banana I smell?" he asked. "Or is it the stench of fear?"

She smiled and showed him her handiwork. "Hungry?"

"Are you kidding?" said another intern, Yvonne, as she rummaged in her locker. "I've already thrown up twice."

When the fourth intern arrived—Riku, from Japan—

they went to a small conference room for their first briefing of current patients, and then it was showtime. The newbies dispersed with their assigned mentors, second- and third-year residents charged with showing them the ropes. Her resident, a guy with the unfortunate name Cain and an annoying habit of quoting Shakespeare, eyed her like meat on the hoof. "Get thee hence, fragment," he said, and instructed her to go write chart notes on their first patient.

It took a special talent to get lost in such a tiny hospital. But somehow she managed to do that.

Eventually she located her first patient—Mr. Drexler, with a troublesome gallbladder. Tubes pulsing with fluids were connected to him, and a sour expression pinched his face. "I'm Dr. Powell," she said. "I'll be taking care of you today."

"This is yesterday's paper," he said. "I need today's paper."

Oh. A paper. She scurried away to the lobby. There were no complimentary papers, so she fished some money out of her pocket and bought one from a box, then delivered it with a smile. Four years of medical school had brought her to this. Paper delivery. Somehow, she managed to make notes about the case, feeling like a fraud the whole time.

"Paging Dr. Powell," came a voice over the PA system. "Paging Dr. Powell to the respiratory clinic."

Startled to hear her name, Reese looped her stethoscope around her neck and hurried to see her next patient, getting lost only briefly this time. A little girl was holding a nebulizer. Reese greeted her and made notes on the girl's asthma. "We just moved here," the mother said. "We thought the country air would be good for her, but her breathing is worse than ever."

The girl had a helpless, glassy look in her eyes. Reese felt helpless too. "I'm sorry you're feeling bad. The treatments we prescribed should expand your airways and make you more comfortable."

"Thank you, Dr. Powell," said the girl in a raspy voice as she left with her mother.

Reese turned to the respiratory therapist. "What a sweet kid. I don't know what she's thanking me for. She seemed miserable."

"Some kids are sensitive to livestock and crops," said the respiratory tech. He put away some equipment. "Funny thing, I never see Amish kids in here. It's like farm life protects them."

She made a note on her phone to check for asthma studies. But that didn't count as an accomplishment. She'd accomplished next to nothing on her first morning at work.

There was another meeting later about cases. A name jumped out at her—Rebecca Zook. Hannah had said Caleb was supposed to be courting her. Reese tried to stay detached as she studied the notes—neurological symptoms of headache, behavioral changes, unusual eye movements. The poor woman. Dr. Shrock noted that the patient was reluctant to follow through with suggested scans and tests. "It's frustrating," he said, "but a patient has that right and we have to respect it."

"What about a blue sheet?" asked a third-year at the table. "Is that an option?"

Reese wasn't the only one at the table who quickly looked up what a blue sheet was—a legal means to admit a patient involuntarily.

Mose took off his spectacles and rubbed the bridge of his nose. "We won't go there. Not now, anyway."

Reese retreated to the call room and sat in the darkness. From the deepest part of her, she felt a welling of uncertainty. Who was she to think she could help people, heal people? Why couldn't she be content to settle down like her friend Trini, make babies and bake berry pies?

Then, as fatigue overtook her, she felt a pure, clear sense of determination. She was here for a reason. She was here because she was going to love the job. She was going to be the job.

16

With a stout rope in hand, Caleb climbed up the big tree over the swimming hole while Jonah and Samuel watched him from the ground. He'd picked out the perfect limb for the new rope swing. It was high enough for a good ride, and it stuck out far enough to be safe.

The warm bark beneath his hands and the sound of the breeze through the leaves evoked memories of long ago. He and John used to race up the hill to swim after chores each day. He knew John let him win, but the race was an essential part of the fun. It was an escape from the heat—and from their father.

And now, years later, Caleb's father was still a problem. After the woman from the state agency had paid a visit, he'd been locked in a power struggle with Asa. It was true that Asa was in fact the legal guardian of Jonah and Hannah. When John and Naomi were killed, there had been a flurry of official paperwork to assign guardianship. It was given to Asa so the children could stay in the home they'd always known.

The family court didn't know about Asa's temperament. His rages, his intolerance, and his cruelty had been a secret protected by the community's strict adherence to Ordnung. Caleb had realized that the only way to protect John's children was to return to the farm and raise them himself, simple as that. Asa had been only too happy to hand the work over to someone else.

But now that Jonah needed the modern world, now that English intervention was the best way to help him, Asa had finally decided to assert his rights of guardianship. He was trying to forbid further therapy for Jonah. There were moments when Caleb saw in Jonah's eyes the hopelessness he'd once seen in John, who had tried to take his own life because of the things Asa said and did to him.

Caleb was mad, and mad made him careless. As he threw the end of the rope from the high branch, he missed his mark and lost his hold. Grabbing at nothing but air, he fell through a lower branch, feeling the jagged broken wood score the back of his shoulder before he hit the water with an enormous splash. Breaking the surface, he heard Jonah yell.

With his shoulder on fire, he swam to the edge and climbed out of the water. Blood coursed down his left side.

"Uncle Caleb!" Jonah rushed forward. "You hurt yourself."

"It looks bad," Samuel said, his face chalk white. "You cut yourself on a broken limb."

"Does it hurt?" Jonah asked. "Should we go get help?"

Caleb wasn't much for swearing, but a few choice phrases came to him as he tried to see the damage.

"It's real bad," Jonah said. "You're going to need stitches."

"No, I'll just have Hannah bandage it up."

Jonah shook his head. "You're not seeing what I'm seeing. You're cut to the bone."

It was clinic day, and Reese, Ursula, and Mose were headed to the satellite facility in Pine Creek. She was still finding her footing as a working doctor, and one of the things she loved about clinic days was that she never knew what might come through the door—a woman in labor, an injured child, an elderly patient having breathing troubles. Despite a rocky beginning, the residency was all she could have hoped for and more.

With the top down, they drove through the glorious summer morning. In the passenger seat, Mose held his hat on his lap. Ursula was in the back seat, her face tilted to the sky. The drive took them along misty country roads, past small towns, pristine farms, and fields clad in summer glory. Old German names marked the mailboxes, and Amish and Mennonite buggies crept along the narrow byways. A few miles from Pine Creek was a milestone pointing toward Middle Grove.

Though she told herself to keep her mind on work, she kept remembering all the moments she'd shared with Caleb, the deep, impossible connection she felt, the exquisite intimacy. She thought about Jonah, too, wondering how he was doing now that he'd gone home to Middle Grove. Mose and the rest of the team were well aware of the boy, having seen him when he used to come for his sessions with the prosthetist. Lately, though, he hadn't been going to his sessions, and it was all she could do to keep herself from intruding.

She parked at the clinic, a low, modern building nestled in the heart of the small town, shaded by old maple trees. Most days were fairly routine, but today they were going to see Rebecca Zook. Clad in layers of plain clothing, her head covered in a bonnet, she was incredibly beautiful, blond and delicate, every hair in place. The fingernails of her dainty hands were chewed to the quick. She sat impassive and expressionless while her mother, a humble-looking woman dressed exactly the same as

Rebecca, said the young woman was exhibiting strange behavior.

"Sometimes she puts her clothes on backward," explained Gretchen Zook, worrying her bonnet strings with nervous hands. "Yesterday, she wandered into a cornfield and couldn't find her way out. It's worrying."

Mose murmured something soothing in their dialect, and the mother nodded. "She gets scared of small things, like leaves and birds."

Ursula gave Reese a nod, and Reese took a seat on a swivel stool in front of Rebecca. The chart was filled with notes from the past several months. "How are you feeling?" she asked, fighting a familiar feeling of helplessness.

"Not so good," Rebecca mumbled. "My head aches all the time. I can't sleep."

"Can I check your eyes with this?" Reese took out her scope, and when Rebecca nodded, shone the light into one eye, then the other. Rebecca's eyes moved rapidly back and forth. "Can you look straight ahead?"

"I'm trying. But no."

Reese did what she could, feeling a mounting uncertainty and bafflement. They tested Rebecca's vision, coordination, and cognitive skills. There were abnormalities, but nothing conclusive. They gave Rebecca something for the headaches, and then the two women left. "She needs a full neuro exam," Reese said.

"For that, she would need to go to the city," Ursula told her.

"And let me guess. She won't go. *Damn* it."

"Neuro will verify what we already know," said Mose. "I've been following this case for a long time. Rebecca knows aggressive treatment would affect her fertility, and she won't hear of it."

Gaining the trust and confidence of the patients in Dr. Shrock's practice was a challenge medical school never prepared her for.

"Not so long ago, a lot of the Plain people consulted a *braucha*—you've heard of this?"

"After our interview, yes. I read up on powwowing," said Reese. "I read enough to know it's quackery."

"It is that," he said. "Some folks think there are certain people who can heal by touch, or by moving around a sick person, or through incantations."

"What's even more frustrating are the therapies that are harmful," Ursula said. "I had a woman last year who actually had an untreated fistula, of all things."

"Trust is a friable thing and an Amish community is a delicate sanctuary," Mose said. "You earn trust by respecting the patient's beliefs, and you have to be careful how you intrude."

Reese studied his face—tired and wise. "Is it hard for you, trying to help people who don't want your help?"

"Of course it is," he replied, taking off his glasses and wiping them on his shirttail. "We do what we're called to do. But so do our patients."

They treated a few more patients—poison ivy, a guy with terrible bunions. Later in the day, there was a summons to urgent care. Ursula led the way to the exam area. Reese's heart skipped a beat when she saw who was waiting there. "*Jonah.*"

He looked wonderful, sun-browned and tousle-headed, inches taller and more filled out than when she'd last seen him. "Are you hurt?" she asked.

"You know this boy?" asked Ursula.

"From Mercy Heights," Reese said without looking away from him. She wanted to hug him and never let him go. But he was off-limits now. "Jonah—"

"Caleb got hurt." He gestured at a curtained area.

Her knees nearly buckled, and her stomach felt like a ball of ice. Caleb . . . hurt. She was supposed to hang back and let the nurse do a preliminary eval, but protocol flew out the window. She swept back the blue curtain to find him sitting on a paper-covered exam table. His shirt was off, and a nurse stood behind him, frowning as she gingerly dabbed at his bare back with gloved hands.

"Caleb." She nearly forgot to breathe. From some small part of herself, she dug out a crumb of professionalism. "I'm Dr. Powell," she said to the nurse. "Caleb's a . . . friend of mine." Her heart pounding, she looked at him. "I'm probably the last person you expected to see," she said. "What happened to you?"

"They say I got a big cut on my back," he said. "I haven't seen it, but it hurts like hellfire."

"Twenty-centimeter laceration," the nurse said. "It's going to need suturing."

"Perfect," Ursula murmured, standing behind Reese. "I'm Dr. Mays," she said, "and it appears you already know Dr. Powell. She'll be taking care of you today."

Thus far, Reese hadn't had a major laceration to treat. "Lucky you," she said to Caleb. She walked behind him, unable to keep from noticing his physique and feeling ridiculously unprofessional.

Focus. Check the wound, assess the patient. It was probably good that he hadn't looked at the gash. It was long and deep, exposing the muscle. She asked the nurse to prepare a suture tray. "Wow, how did you do this to yourself?"

Jonah poked his head through the curtain. "He climbed way up high in a tree to hang a rope swing over the creek," he said. "He fell and got gouged by a broken limb on the way down. I was there. I saw the whole thing."

Caleb nodded. "That's about the way it happened. At least I landed in the water."

That would explain the damp trousers and bare feet.

"I'm going to give you a shot for the pain," she said, noticing the stiffness with which he held himself. "After that, I'll numb the area."

"It looks horrible," Jonah said, peering at the wound. "Was my arm even more horrible than that?"

"Even more," Reese said, administering the pain meds. "Way more."

"He was real brave. He didn't howl or nothing."

"That's pretty brave. I've missed you, kiddo," she said.

Jonah flashed his trademark killer smile, then nattered on. "I couldn't figure out how to do a bandage so I used a couple of Hannah's sampler cloths to stanch the bleeding. She won't miss them, on account of she throws away her samplers if they're not perfect." He held up something from a pink plastic basin. "Look at all this blood."

The cloth was embroidered with the phrase *No Winter Lasts Forever*, and some other words that were obscured by sticky, drying blood.

"Are you going to operate on him?" Jonah asked. "Do you need to stitch him up? How're you going to fix that giant cut, huh?"

Reese gritted her teeth, trying to concentrate.

Caleb said something to Jonah in German, and the boy got quiet. In English, Caleb said, "I bet they have some of those *Highlights* magazines over in the waiting area."

Jonah shuffled over to the waiting area with a stack of well-thumbed magazines. Ursula settled herself at the nurses' station and opened her laptop. The nurse set up a sterile tray, and Reese went to the sink to wash her hands, which were now raw from so many washings, and smarting from the alcohol hand rub. She was ready for this.

That was what she told herself, anyway. In actuality, she stared at the tray of supplies and instruments, and everything she'd learned about wound care and suturing emptied out of her head.

"What was that shot?" he murmured.

"It's for pain and swelling." She had a moment of panic, thinking of the long list of rare but possible side effects. "How are you feeling?"

"Like I'm dreaming. Like I could translate the language of frogs."

She suppressed a smile. "That means it's taking effect." Then she turned to Caleb. Her wounded patient. "I did want to see you again," she said. "Not like this, though. I need you to lie on your stomach."

He nodded, seeming to melt onto the paper-covered treatment table. The lac was relatively clean, though she observed slivers of wood and debris. She glanced over at Ursula, who looked up from her computer and nodded a go-ahead. Ursula was not only the most laid-back resident; she was the most likely to push. She refused to let an intern look for someone who could do a procedure better.

Reese tried to shore up her confidence. If she didn't learn to handle a situation, someone could end up in worse shape than when he'd come in. "Let's get you fixed up."

"I'm all yours," he said.

Though she couldn't see his face, she heard a smile in his voice. "This might sting," she said. "Try to hold still." She injected anesthetic solution along the edges of the wound, watching the flesh around it swell slightly and whiten from the epinephrine in the solution. She'd done this a hundred times or more, but the patient had been a foam roller or a pig's foot. The fact that this was a man's living flesh—Caleb's living flesh—was starting to mess with her head.

She set the syringe on the sterile tray and closed her eyes. Anything less than total focus could harm her patient. *Remember that*, she told herself.

"You got this," Caleb said softly, as if he could read her thoughts.

Her eyes flew open. "Yes," she said simply and picked up the syringe again. She infiltrated the wound itself, since it was so deep, sending numbness through the superficial fascia and all around the jagged edges and corners of the gash, gaining confidence as the syringe slowly emptied. Then she probed with tweezers to make sure he was numb. "Let me know if you feel this."

"Nope," he said simply. "So far so good."

"Can I watch?" Jonah had wandered back over.

Reese exchanged a glance with the nurse, who shrugged. "Okay by me," Reese said.

"Were you there when they sewed up my stump?"

"I was not. They did that in surgery, not the ER." She irrigated the wound, the blood-tinted water soaking the absorbent paper towels under Caleb's torso. The nurse placed a piece of sterile drape over his back, centering the hole over the cut. Reese put on gloves and picked up the first blister pack of sutures for the interior. "I need to close the inside wound first. These sutures will be absorbed gradually."

Glancing briefly at Jonah, she saw him blanch at the sight of exposed sinew deep in the wound. "You should take a seat," she murmured. "We don't want to have to deal with two patients today."

He nodded and stepped back. "I might go watch for babies."

Caleb sent him a confused smile. "How's that?"

"There's a baby box outside the door, like the book drop at the county library."

"Did you give him some of that shot?" Caleb asked. "He's high too."

She watched Jonah scurry outside. "He means the safe haven box," she said. "You should see this cut. I swear, Caleb. Tree climbing?"

"Lost my hold," he said simply. "It happens."

"All set, Doctor?" asked the nurse.

There was a flurry of activity at the admittance desk—another kid with a wheezing, asthmatic cough. Reese glanced at the nurse. "Yes, thank you." The nurse hurried away, and Reese was on her own with Caleb and his gaping wound. "I'm going to get to work now," she said, aware of the time window for the lidocaine. She closed her eyes again, seeking that sense of total focus. Her patient's well-being depended on her. By the time she opened her eyes, she was ready. Everything fell away except this single, driving thought. Willing her hands to stay steady, she sutured the deepest layer of the wound with the absorbable material, probably taking twice as much time as a more experienced physician would.

"It's kind of blowing my mind, seeing you here like this," she said quietly.

"Is that a good thing or a bad thing?" he asked.

"It's just . . . a thing."

"I heard you were working at the regional hospital," he said. "That was a surprise, Reese. I thought you would be working in the big city."

"I changed my mind." You *changed my mind*, she thought. She bit her lip, feeling a deep need to connect to him. Finishing the inner layer of suturing, she switched to the outer repair, using a curved needle with the filament attached. Deep breath again. "This is a jagged cut," she said. "It's not going to be too pretty for a while."

"Never had much use for a pretty back," he said.

A smile flickered. "Good point. But I don't want any scarring. Get someone at home to put some white petroleum jelly on it every day." She put the edges together, matching them like pieces of a puzzle. Ursula came over to check her work, approving it with a simple nod; then she went to look after another patient. Reese used the needle driver to push the curved needle through his flesh and pull the filament through behind it. Stitch and tie, stitch and tie, putting him back together again. She finished the sutures and counted them up. "Twenty-four," she told him. "Are you doing all right?"

"I am." He hesitated. "I didn't expect to see you again, either. Especially like this."

Her heart leaped. With deliberate care, she removed the drape, swabbed the flesh clean, then covered the suture line with surgical tape. "I miss you," she whispered, her voice rough with stark honesty. "I've been missing you ever since you left."

"I feel the same way," he said simply. "You . . . were—I liked spending time with you. But you understand, I had to go."

"I get why you left," she said. "I do, but . . . I miss you," she repeated, finishing with the tape. "And now you're done. Take your time sitting up. You might be light-headed."

He sat up, and she found herself facing his bare chest. She turned away quickly and grabbed a pamphlet from a shelf. "Here's some information about wound care and follow-up. Promise you'll do what it says."

"I promise," he said, stepping down from the table.

"What did you do to yourself, young man?" Mose ambled into the urgent care clinic. "I hear you've been swinging through the trees like Tarzan of the Apes."

"I'm all put back together now," Caleb said.

"You got a shirt to put on?"

Caleb's ears reddened. "Didn't see the point in ruining a good shirt."

Reese found a set of scrubs and tossed him the top. "It wouldn't be the first time you had to wear hospital clothes."

Before Caleb put the shirt on, Mose inspected her handiwork. "Get some help looking after that wound, you hear?"

"I hear." Caleb took his hat from a hook. "Come to supper, Reese," he said. "Hannah would love to see you. Mose, we'd be obliged if you and Ida would come too."

17

"It's not a date," Reese said to Ursula that evening as she got ready to visit Middle Grove. The conversation reminded her of one she'd had with her mother last fall. "It's just supper."

"I saw the way you were looking at him," Ursula said, crowding into the upstairs bathroom they shared.

"Fine. It's a date. A date with my preceptor and his wife and an Amish guy." She wore a cotton dress and sandals, and no makeup other than tinted sunscreen. Though she hoped it didn't show, the prospect of seeing Caleb again electrified her. After so much time had passed, she should have moved beyond this, but she was stuck. Stuck on him.

"So you and this guy . . ." Ursula leaned toward the mirror and lavished on the mascara.

"There is no me and this guy." Maybe if she said it enough, it would be true. "We met because of Jonah, and he stayed with my neighbor in Philly for a while last fall."

"Got it." Ursula applied gloss and smacked her lips.

"You're like that snippy older sister I never had," said Reese. "Where are you heading?"

"Unlike you, I'm not afraid to call a date a date—that radiology resident I was telling you about. We're going to a sweet corn and barbecue festival over in Mountain View. I plan to drink just enough beer to let him have his way with me."

"Nice," Reese said, grabbing her keys and phone.

"I'll be back by lunchtime tomorrow," Ursula added. "My folks are coming up for a visit."

"Even nicer," said Reese. "I miss my parents. I keep hoping they'll get over being mad at me for going with this program."

"Have you told them that?" Ursula dropped a few condoms into her purse. "If not, you should." She was one of those people who made things seem simple. Reese had never been that kind of person. Picking up the phone, she scrolled to their home number and initiated the call.

Voice mail, of course. No one answered their phone anymore. "Hey, parents," she said, her voice a little too chirpy. "Just calling to say I miss you . . ."

"We've known the Stoltz family since, oh, I don't know, do you, Ida?" Mose asked. He was in the passenger seat of Reese's car, half turned as he spoke to his wife.

"Must be twenty years or more," she said.

"I'd say more," Mose agreed. "Asa's wife, Jenny, used to bring the boys to the clinic for their shots. I remember that, because she had to keep it a secret from Asa."

Reese stiffened. "He wasn't in favor of immunizations?"

"Seemed that way. Next time I saw the older boy, John, it was to set a broken arm."

"Caleb told me his brother broke his arm when he jumped off a bridge," Reese said. "It was a suicide attempt."

"It was," Mose admitted. "That family's had more than its share of trouble. I was on call the night John and Naomi were murdered. I hope you never have a call like that, but you have to be prepared for any test."

As they drove through the rolling hills to Middle Grove, Reese tried to tamp down her excitement. Jonah was not her patient. Caleb was not her boyfriend. Yet she had to see them again.

"It's so beautiful here," she said. "It's hard to imagine trouble in places like this. Which is a ridiculous observation, I realize. Trouble doesn't seem to care what it sees out the window."

Mose nodded. "You're learning."

"It's harder to imagine out here," Ida said. "But this community can be just as hard to survive as the inner city. I still think it's magic, though. If I hadn't come here forty-six years ago fresh out of nursing school in New York City, I never would have met Mose. We were a regular Romeo and Juliet, weren't we?"

Another nod. "The city girl and the country mouse. We still have a few family members who don't speak."

"What made you move from New York?" asked Reese.

"A broken heart," Ida said simply. "Some people come here to escape, some to hide, some to heal."

"Which one are you?" Mose asked Reese.

The blunt question took her aback. "Suppose I said I came here simply to find my way past the politics and red tape of big-business medicine? Don't you think I'm young and idealistic enough to want my career to be about patient care and healing?"

"Sure I do. That's why we picked you for the program," he said. "You did bring some baggage with you, though." She opened her mouth to reply, but he forged ahead. "I've been at this for fifty years, young lady. I know when a person is holding in her pain, thinking that if she doesn't acknowledge it, then it'll go away on its own."

She caught herself pushing too hard on the accelerator and forced herself to slow down. "Ida, help me out here," she said.

"Sorry. When Mose goes into psychiatry mode, there's

no stopping him. I've watched my husband teach for years, and one of the great truths of medicine is that the best doctors are the ones who know what to do with their baggage."

There was only one paved road into Middle Grove. They passed a cemetery with trim rows of markers, and Amish homes with green window shades and no curtains. The town was a modest collection of wooden and brick buildings. She tried to take it all in—women in long dresses and bonnets, guys in sweat-soaked blue shirts and black hats; tourists browsing a small open-air market and a big mercantile with signs for homemade jam and sausage and handcrafted furniture and quilts; a bakery and a mill with a waterwheel. This was her first glimpse of Caleb's world, and she felt like as much of an outsider as he probably had in Philly.

The paving gave way to gravel, tufted with grass down the middle. She slowed down over the bumps, looking at the plain mailboxes along the way. A gentle breeze combed through the fields of wheat and rye. "So no phones or electricity," she said, enjoying the lack of electrical lines leading to the houses.

"Folks have their reasons," said Mose. "There's modern plumbing to meet health code standards, so they can sell their dairy products. You might see a computer running on a generator in a chicken coop or milk house. Some Amish will speak on a mobile phone, but only while standing out in a field. They favor the innovations that enable a man to stay home with his family rather than going off somewhere else for a job."

An even narrower dirt road led to the Stoltz place. The house was bigger than she'd expected, white and boxy, with a line of laundry flapping in the breeze. There were multiple workshops and outbuildings, and a red barn that dwarfed everything else.

It all looked so idyllic, almost too beautiful to be real, the sort of place where nothing bad could ever happen. She knew that wasn't the case, though. Beside the barn was a tall silo with a domed top, and she wondered if that was where Jonah's accident had occurred.

As she parked near the house, Jonah and a fluffy dog came leaping down the front steps. "Hey, Reese, you're here!" the boy said. "Hannah, they're here!" he called over his shoulder.

His smile was as warm and infectious as the sunshine. "We found you," she said, leaning down to pat the dog. "Is this Jubilee the wonder dog, the one I've heard so much about?" The dog nuzzled her hand, gazing at her with adoring eyes. "I can see why you like her so much."

Hannah came outside, pink-cheeked and smiling. Reese waved her over. She tried not to do a double take, but was startled to see that Hannah had put on a bit of weight since last fall. Or maybe not. Could be she looked bigger due to the long layers of her dress and apron. Despite the warmth of the evening, she wore a shawl around her shoulders.

"It's good to see you again," she said, giving the girl a brief hug. "Thank you for having us."

"We've brought you a little something," Ida said, indicating a basket looped around her elbow. "Reese made one of her famous pies."

"Hurrah for pie," Jonah said. "Reese, you make the best pies. I remember that one you made for me when I was in the hospital."

"Please, come inside," Hannah said. "Caleb and Grandfather will be finishing chores soon."

The house was shadowy and extremely warm. The

slight breeze through the open windows wasn't sufficient to chase away the heat. The floors were made of wooden planks, and the furniture was sturdy and spare. A folded quilt on a rack off to the side caught Reese's eye, and she paused to study it. The design was startling, an asymmetric design of abstract shapes and colors undulating from dark to light.

"Is that your work?" she asked Hannah.

"It is. I call it sunshine and shadow."

"It's wonderful," Reese said.

"You're very talented," Ida said.

Hannah ducked her head in modesty, then led the way to the kitchen, which was dominated by a scrubbed pine table and a big enameled range with iron legs. A dry sink with a pump was piled with cooking utensils. Here, the heat was nearly unbearable, and Reese was relieved when Hannah announced that they'd be eating outside at the picnic table.

I love electricity, she thought.

"How can I help?" she asked Hannah.

"We just need to carry things outside." Hannah led the way down the kitchen stairs. Jonah was there already, spreading a cloth over a handmade picnic table. He wasn't wearing the robotic arm he'd been fitted for, but a simpler mechanical one, which he used with impressive ease.

Mose lifted an arm and waved at Caleb, who stood with another man—presumably his father—at an outdoor pump, washing up. Caleb took a clean shirt from the clothesline and went behind a shed. A few minutes later, he and his father approached. At the sight of Caleb's smile, Reese's heart skipped a beat. She would never get tired of that smile.

"Thank you for having us," she said when he introduced her to Asa.

He was nearly as tall and broad as Caleb, and the family resemblance was strong in their clean-boned faces and blue eyes. His smile was fleeting as he said, "You're welcome. Mose and Ida, it's been too long." He added something in German and shook Mose's hand. Then he turned to Hannah and said something else—a question, or perhaps a command.

"Yes, of course," she murmured and hurried over to the table to finish laying out the plates and cutlery.

"I'll give you a hand," said Reese, and they worked together. "How have you been, Hannah?"

The girl kept her gaze down, as if setting the table took all her concentration. "Very well, thank you," she said. "I had to join the church, even though I didn't feel ready. If I hadn't accepted baptism, I wouldn't be able to get married."

"You're so young," Reese said. "You should take your time."

"That's not how it's done." She said a word that sounded like *oof givah*. "That means to give up yourself, and in that way, you become part of the community. The way a grain of wheat becomes part of the loaf of bread."

Reese bit her lip to keep from making another comment. She reminded herself that she was a guest here, and her job was to show respect.

Hannah's hands fluttered nervously as she gestured at glass jars lined up on shelves. "It's canning season, and I've been helping out at the neighbors'. Not my favorite chore, I confess, but it's better when we all pitch in."

"What's your favorite chore?" asked Reese. She tried to picture the girl's life here—domestic duties in an endless cycle, subjugation to the men of the community, pressure to join the church, prayer and submission. Was it enough for a girl like Hannah? Was it what she wanted?

"I suppose my favorite would be the quilting," Hannah said. "To me, it's not a chore at all. Alma—she's in charge of the quilt shop—lets me choose any colors I want to put in a quilt."

"I'd love to see more of your work," said Reese.

Hannah darted a glance at the others. "This way," she said, motioning Reese to the house. "I'll show you a few more."

The upstairs of the house was even stuffier, though as tidy and plain as the downstairs. Hannah's room was as spare as the rest of the house, with one window and no closet, just a few dresses and shawls on pegs along one wall. Near the bed was a small shelf with a dish of straight pins and two homemade faceless dolls, not in plain Amish clothes but in bright, edgy outfits.

Noticing her look, Hannah smiled. "My mother made the dolls for me. I created the fashions myself. Mem probably wouldn't have approved."

"Well, I approve. They're so cool," said Reese. "Hipster Amish."

Hannah had a small collection of books, including the one she'd borrowed from Reese. The quilt on the bed had a dramatic conceptual design of a delicate feather, the fronds morphing into a flock of birds in flight. Hannah showed her a couple more—one that seemed to depict a hex sign melting into darkness, and another embroidered with the signature phrase of *The Princess Bride*—"As you wish."

"I'm so impressed," she said. "Hannah, you're really talented. Have you ever—"

"Hey, Hannah." Jonah's bare feet thumped on the stairs. "Grandfather says come to supper *now*."

"Hey, yourself," Reese said, exchanging a glace with Hannah. "That doesn't sound like the nice Jonah I know."

His face turned bright red. "Sorry. Can you please come down to supper?"

"We'd love to."

They gathered around the picnic table under a shade tree. Reese took a seat between Caleb and Hannah. "How is your shoulder feeling?" she asked. "Is it—"

"We'll have a proper prayer yet," Asa said, then bowed his head. There was a good half minute of complete silence. Reese could hear the sound of her own heart beating, and Hannah's quiet breaths. The quiet ended with the clink of glassware and cutlery as everyone filled their plates.

Supper was pork chops with potatoes and sauerkraut, and sweet corn just picked from the field. The pork was dry and tough, the kraut extremely tart. "I'm not so good at cooking," Hannah said.

"The corn is delicious," Reese told her. "So is this fresh-baked bread."

Hannah nodded. "Jonah and I picked the corn this afternoon, and the bread's from a neighbor. Baking's a hard chore in the summer when it's so hot."

"Well, this dinner is a treat, and I'm grateful," said Reese.

It did not escape her notice that Asa hadn't spoken to her directly. He seemed pleasant enough with Mose and Ida, commenting on the weather and the crops, an upcoming auction and a barn they were going to help build for someone in the community. His old-school mannerisms underscored the otherness of the Amish culture and the fact that she was an outsider here. His appetite for the pie was gratifying, though.

"It's wonderful to see Jonah doing so well," she said to Asa. "He was one of the best patients in the pediatrics ward in Philadelphia. You would have been proud of him—"

"Pride is not something we aspire to." Asa's tone was mild, though his stare burned a hole in her.

She literally bit her tongue. In a strange way, she understood this man, probably better than he understood her. Everything he had done in raising his son had been geared to protect Caleb from the temptations of a woman like Reese—a woman of worldly and ungodly ways. Asa regarded her the way her own father had regarded Caleb.

I'm not here to steal your son, she thought. *Or maybe I am.*

After supper, Hannah and Jonah went to the village to join in a game of baseball, a nightly occurrence in summer. "How would you like to take a buggy ride?" Caleb asked.

She looked around and saw that his father was sitting in the shade with the Shrocks. "Yes, please," she said, her pulse speeding up at the prospect of some alone time with him. "I'd love that."

He took her to the barn and introduced her to Arrow, a lovely chestnut horse who stretched his lips in a comic smile as Caleb brought him to the crossties. With practiced movements, he harnessed the horse, his hands flying over the buckles and loops. Then he hitched the horse to a gray-and-black buggy and held out his hand, palm up.

She placed her hand in his, and the merest touch was an electric sensation as she climbed up to the flat bench seat. There was a fleeting moment when their eyes met, and his expression made her heart skip a beat.

"You sure you want to do this?" he asked.

"Yes."

"It's gonna be a bumpy ride."

"I can handle the bumps," she said.

He got in beside her and flicked the reins. The horse

moved forward in a walk and then extended his stride to a smooth trot as they drove along the gravel lane to the main road. The only sounds were the steady clop of hooves and the jangle of the harness. Evening sunlight gilded the landscape, and a sense of enchantment rose inside her.

Seeing Caleb in his own home sharpened the sense that they were worlds apart. Still, the heat of their attraction was as palpable as the warm air flowing over her skin and the touch of his thigh against hers. And it felt even more forbidden here.

"So anyway," she said, "your father."

His mouth twisted in an ironic smile. "My father."

"He was looking at me as if I were his private vision of hell."

"Sort of the same way your father looked at me."

"They're not so different then, are they?"

"They both recognize a threat when they see one."

"Is that what I am? A threat? I'm not sure how I feel about that. Should I be insulted? Or flattered?"

"Asa is very clear in what he believes. Outsiders are supposed to stay outside. The rigid rules are a comfort to him. When you know your place, you know what's expected of you."

"Is that what you believe?"

He shot her a grin. "What do you think?"

"I think you don't need rules to know what's expected." She hesitated, then added, "Jonah seems different. I mean, he seems to be doing well, but he was sort of bossy with his sister."

He was quiet for a moment. The horse's hooves clopped on the road as they passed the playing field where the baseball game was going on. There were a few carts and buggies and tethered horses along a fence. Kids of all ages, boys and girls alike, shouted and clapped their hands. Whistles pierced the air. She spotted Hannah on a bench at the sideline, leaning forward eagerly but sitting out the game. Jonah was in the thick of things, in short-stop position.

"That looks like so much fun," she said. "My summers as a kid were a lot different."

"How's that?"

"Totally structured. I was sent to camps designed to make me better at things—sports, music, Spanish, science—you name it. It was fun, too, but I don't remember moments like that." She gestured at a barefoot boy running home from third base, his hands in the air and a look of pure joy on his face. Had she ever simply played for the sake of playing? In between camp sessions, her adolescence had been a time of grinding academic study and a desperation to excel. She wondered what her life would have been like if she had taken the time to lift her nose from the grindstone.

"Hannah used to be one of the best batters in the village," Caleb said. "She doesn't join in so much lately."

"She mentioned that now that she's joined the church, she's supposed to be thinking about getting married," Reese said. "And I guess I don't have to tell you how I feel about *that*."

He was quiet again as they passed the playing field. He kept his eyes steadily on the road as he said, "I'm in a dispute with my father."

That didn't surprise her in the least. "What sort of dispute?"

"He doesn't want Jonah to have the robotic arm. Thinks it's too modern, and the bishop agrees." He glanced over at her. "And, yes, I do agree with the expression on your face."

"Then why is it a dispute? Jonah should have what he needs. As his guardian, you get to make that decision."

Caleb didn't respond.

"Caleb?" she prompted.

"I'm not his guardian," he said at last.

"But I thought—"

"Everyone thought. The fact is, Asa is Jonah's legal guardian. He has been since John died."

"Wait. What? But at the hospital, you authorized everything as his guardian."

Caleb nodded, turning the rig down a narrow lane, away from the main part of town. "I took charge of things. But according to the law, when John and Naomi died, the guardian would be John's next of kin, and that was Asa. I simply took over when I moved back to Middle Grove. There was never any legal arrangement for me to do that. Now it appears Asa is claiming his authority."

"What will you do?"

"Jonah needs that arm. I'll do what I have to do."

Her heart ached for him. He seemed so torn, wanting to do what was right for the boy while keeping the peace with his father. "I wish I could help," she said, and she covered his hand with hers. "I was raised so differently. My parents are all about high achievement and self-sufficiency. Depending on someone other than yourself is considered a sign of weakness. In a situation like this . . . have you explained the situation to your father? Has Jonah's care team?"

"I reckon that's what Mose is doing right now," he said. "Won't work, though. There's no arguing with a man's faith. He believes the boy will burn in hell if he adopts modern ways, so he thinks he's saving Jonah's soul."

"Shit. Why was your father appointed guardian over you?"

"He was here the night it happened, and I was not. I was living away and working at Grantham Farm when I heard. I showed up the next day. Naomi was gone, and John nearly so. There was just enough time to say good-bye. He told me to raise his kids in the faith, but the judge who assigned the guardianship to my father never knew that."

"Is there a way to have yourself appointed his guardian?"

"I would have to make an appeal to a court. In our culture, we don't use the courts. But I fear my father would do that in order to get his way with Jonah."

"You could get a ruling in your favor," she said, feeling his frustration. "Would you be able to find a lawyer who specializes in medical guardianship?"

"I've been studying up on the law myself. There's a doctrine called *parens patriae*, which allows the state to protect a child's welfare, and it might apply in this situation. For now, we're keeping up the training with the robotic arm."

"That's good, then. Maybe your father will see that Jonah's better off with a better arm." She looked at him, and her heart seemed to swell in her chest. "You amaze me. When do you have time to study the law?"

"I don't. Just quit sleeping so much. Let's talk about you," he said. "I'm sick of me."

"I'm a bit like you. I work and don't sleep. It's harder than I ever thought it would be. And more wonderful. And sometimes terrible and sometimes sublime. I hate myself when I make mistakes. Sometimes I hate my patients when they don't cooperate or refuse treatment or skip their meds or keep smoking . . ."

"Rebecca loves you," he said, though Reese had not brought up the woman's name.

"That's nice to hear. I'm sorry she's so sick. Sometimes I don't know if I can do this," she said. "I know I need to respect her wishes, but those wishes are destroying her."

"Because she won't accept medical treatment."

"Yes. Is it strange that you were expected to marry her?"

"Some still expect that."

"Does Rebecca?"

"I don't know, Reese. I told her clearly enough that it wasn't happening, but . . ." He stopped, taking her cheeks between his hands. "What is it? What are you thinking?"

She trembled at his touch, and she tried to hide the terrible struggle raging inside her. This was one of the challenges most doctors never faced. Here it was, then. The stark contrast between modern patients and rural Amish. She had made this choice and was now forced to change, not just as a doctor, but maybe who she was as a person—more humble, more soulful. Making a sacrifice for her patient.

"Reese?"

She nearly melted at his touch. "If you were her husband, you could save her life."

He took his hands away. "*What?*"

Reese couldn't help what she was thinking. It was terrible, but it was . . . possible. She rushed headlong into the conversation. "As her next of kin, you could authorize treatment. You could make that decision for her."

He held himself completely still. "You're suggesting I marry a dying woman to force her into treatment she doesn't want."

"I'm grasping at straws. She's young and beautiful and I'm her doctor and I'm desperate for a way to keep her from dying."

"And for that, I admire you," he said quietly. "You have a great heart, Reese."

He flicked the reins and the horse sped up. They came upon a covered bridge over a stream. On the far side of the bridge, he pulled the buggy off to a gravel area in the trees. He helped her down and pulled out a rolled quilt from beneath the seat.

Then he took her hand and started walking. She didn't know what would happen. She didn't ask. He brought her to a meadow by the stream and spread the quilt on the ground. The night air was warm on her skin, a light breeze lifting her hair. They were surrounded by the fresh green smell of broken grass, the chirp of crickets.

"Reese Powell," he said, cradling her face between his hands, "I've been wanting you since you swapped my bloody shirt for hospital scrubs, when the only thing I should have been wanting was for Jonah to get better. It was a great shame to me that my body and my heart wouldn't listen to my head. After I left the city, I thought the wanting would fade, but it's only grown worse."

She was stunned by his words. "I'm . . . I don't know what to say."

A grin flashed. "An unusual state for you. Tell me you want this or stop me now," he said, "because if I kiss you again, I might not be able to stop at all."

"I . . . I want . . . yes. Oh my God, yes," she whispered. "But I . . . I suppose I should tell you—it probably won't surprise you to learn I'm not a virgin."

He pulled off his shirt one-handed over his head and dropped it on the ground. "It probably will surprise you to learn that I am," he said. Yet there was nothing tentative about him as he took off her clothes and shucked his trousers and drew her down to the quilt, his hands and mouth and tongue making excruciatingly slow designs on her bare flesh.

His kisses, the shape and pressure of his mouth—she

had dreamed of this for months, and he seemed as rav-
enous as she was. At the same time, his touch was ach-
ingly gentle, yet under the tenderness was a hunger that
seemed to pulse with every beat of his heart. Though his
mouth was soft on hers, his kisses were hard, demanding.
She felt possessed as he groaned and unfurled a kind of
power that from another man might be frightening. From
Caleb, it was simply the stark, honest need held at bay
far too long. He touched her in places that caught fire.
The bite of his teeth drew a gasp from her, surprise and
delight tumbling together. She opened herself to him and
clasped him against her. He lifted her up in a moment of
weightless suspension. It was only a moment but it felt
like eternity. Then she came crashing down and felt herself melting into the earth.

He shuddered, aligning his forehead to hers, his wonder and joy tangible, somehow, even in the darkness. For
long minutes, she glistened with sweat and joy, unable to
move or even to form a coherent thought.

"That was . . ." She couldn't form a coherent sentence,
either.

"Yah," he said. "It was."

They lay together, listening to the night sounds until
the breeze dried their sweat. Caleb kissed her with a lin-
gering sweetness. He anchored her with his arm, holding
her steady, and they dozed for a bit. She loved the sense
of him so close, the way he breathed in and out so evenly,
a man at peace, not tormented by doubt.

"Can I ask you something?"

"Sure, Reese. I'm an open book."

"How could it be that that was your first time?"

"Did I do something wrong?"

"God, no. You were . . . you seemed to know just what
to do."

"I'm a farm boy," he said simply. "I know things." He traced her tattoo with his finger. "I never danced the salsa before, and I did all right."

She laughed and rolled over, propping her chin on his chest. "Here's a harder question, then. What was your original plan?"

"My . . ."

"Before your brother and his wife died. What did you think you'd end up doing?"

A long pause. "I did have a plan, for sure. I wanted the world—more learning, managing the horse farm at a higher level, doing things I'd dreamed about. Flying in a plane, diving in the ocean, all the wonders forbidden to me as a boy. When I had to come back, it was a shock at first. But it was the right thing to do. The only thing. I had to make a new plan—to stay until Hannah married and Jonah . . . Then there was the accident. It means I'll never leave him, or not for a very long time. And now here you are, and I wish to heaven I could make a different plan."

Reese felt dizzy as she looked up at his face in the moonlight. Until now, she'd had no idea about the undiscovered world contained within the warmth and safety of a man's arms. All her life she had focused on achievement and accomplishment, setting goals and attaining them. It was a shock to realize she really had no emotional anchor.

Now she didn't know what the future held. She didn't care. She didn't have a plan, either. She just wanted it to happen.

"Are we going to do this, then?" she asked.

He flipped her over and drew her hand down his chest and lower still, then pressed her thighs apart, smiling slightly at her look of disbelief. "We already are."

18

The internship turned out to be a richer, more meaningful education than Reese had ever experienced. Her whole life seemed to change; every moment seemed charged with importance, whether she was removing a catheter or disimpacting a bowel. The bowel procedure might have been horrific, but the look of relief on the patient's face was worth everything. She found herself dealing with every sort of ailment. She'd been anointed with blood and shit and tears; the cry of a newborn might be followed by the hollow gasp of an elderly patient's dying breath.

For the first time, work was an emotional investment. A labor of love. Sometimes, even when she was doing the most mundane task, she felt an almost spiritual calling. She was meant to do this work.

She made mistakes—chipped a man's tooth while attempting to intubate his airway. Misread a dosage and gave too much potassium to a heart patient. Messed up the placement of a stent. The ways to screw up were myriad, and she lived in fear of doing damage. Mose and Penelope and the residents helped her through the agony of failure, but her softest place to fall was located in the quiet isolation of Middle Grove.

She spent every spare minute she could with Caleb, driving over to see him in a fog of exhaustion after a thirty-hour shift. When they were apart, she felt distracted, even agitated. When she saw him again, she felt so full of bliss that she was like a different person entirely, a person on fire with life, so euphoric that she knew there had to be a catch. Then he would open his arms and wrap her in his embrace, and her worries would fall away. She was utterly seduced by him in every way that mattered. With Caleb, she found something she'd thought only existed in stories and dreams—a grand passion, endless and all-consuming.

She was drawn to Jonah and Hannah as well. Her brightest moments were spent in their company, browsing through the farmers' market, admiring the quilts and crafts at the general mercantile, cheering Jonah on as he worked with his arm.

After one particularly grinding stint at the hospital—her supervising resident, Cain, had assigned her to the ICU and had criticized everything down to her handwriting—she came into the kitchen to find Mose and Ursula sitting together, stress eating. The only way she could tell Ursula was stressed was when she saw her eating Life cereal, and at the moment, she was chowing it down from a mixing bowl.

"What's up?" Reese asked, setting down a bag of things she'd picked up at the store on the way home.

"We need to go to Middle Grove," Mose said.

"Oh, good. I got a soccer ball for Jonah." She took it out of the shopping bag and palmed it. "Thought it would be a nice change of pace from baseball."

"Good thinking," said Mose. "We need to go first thing in the morning to look after Rebecca Zook."

"Oh . . ." Reese's voice trailed off and she sat down slowly. All summer long, they had watched the young woman's condition worsen. The intermittent strange behavior, flashing headaches, and visual changes had intensified, yet Rebecca continued to refuse all but the most basic treatment.

Reese left early the next day with Mose and Ursula. The Zook household was a big one—seven or eight siblings with various spouses and offspring. The women bustled around putting out bowls of stewed plums and pans of cinnamon rolls so fresh and delicious they made her swoon. There were barefoot children everywhere—girls helping out, a little one in a choring kerchief feeding a kitten from a bottle. Some of the women were seated on benches, sewing as they spoke quietly in reverential tones. Reese sensed an indefinable air of settled peace. These women embraced their roles and their places in the world.

Alma Troyer bustled in with a pair of gorgeous pies. "Made with Pocono Golds, my favorite for pies," she said. "Some say they're too sweet. I say they're just right."

Other women had macaroni salad, baked ham, fried chicken. *If food had the power to heal, these people would live forever*, thought Reese. It wasn't a social call, though, so she followed Mose into a room adjacent to the kitchen. Like all Amish homes, it was furnished in a spare, unadorned style, with a railed bed against one wall, a few wooden chairs, a washstand, and a row of pegs along the wall. Above the bed was a sampler stitched with the phrase *And he that doubteth is damned if he eat, because he eateth not of faith: for whatsoever is not of faith is sin.*

Rebecca lay in the bed, her face expressionless, her eyes moving without seeming to see. Mose motioned for Reese to come forward. "How are you feeling?" she asked in a quiet voice.

"So much hurt," Rebecca said.

Reese swallowed hard. *Be here now*, she reminded herself. *Be with the patient now.* "I'm sorry. Is the medication helping?" They'd given her morphine for the pain.

She didn't answer. Reese had spent hours with her colleagues discussing the situation. As doctors, they knew the risks and benefits of treatment. They also knew that when a competent patient refused lifesaving treatment, their options were limited.

"Rebecca, I know we've talked about this before, but I want you to know there are medical interventions that could help you."

"I understand. You've told me and told me I might get better with your treatments. You also said I might not. And I've told you and told you no."

"You could have a longer life. More time in this world."

"More time to be childless. There's no purpose for me in this life if I can't have a child. I know that sounds ridiculous to you, but you don't know my world. You don't know my life. I would be alive, but I would be revolted by my post-treatment life."

There was a stir in the doorway. Reese turned and was shocked to see Caleb, dressed as she'd never seen him before. His shirt was white and crisply pressed, his trousers creased down the middle, his shoes gleaming with a shine. He didn't look at Reese, didn't acknowledge her as he set a wooden clock on a table at the end of the bed.

"Rebecca, this is for you," he said. "I have talked it over with your father and the bishop. I'm offering this and my hand in marriage, if you'll have me."

Rebecca blinked and winced. "*Himmel*, what is this nonsense?"

"There was a time when you wanted us to marry."

"That time is past. I'm going to do you the kindness

of saying no, Caleb Stoltz. I'm not well. I won't last much longer." She took a wispy breath. "I know what you truly need. And it's not me."

Reese felt a jumble of shock and pain and admiration. He had tried. Even though he knew it was wrong, he had tried to find a way to help. And it was she who had put the notion in his head. She nearly drowned in humility as she watched him kneel at the bedside, murmuring in Deitsch as Rebecca drifted.

Other visitors and family members came and went. Hymns were sung, prayers recited. Reese stayed with her patient. She studied the exquisite beauty of the young woman, felt the perfection of her slender hand as she held it. Amid the fear and the sadness, Reese discovered a gift from Rebecca—a sense of peace. Reese had the honor of being with her for the amount of time she had left. She stopped seeing Rebecca for what she might have been and started to see her for what she was in this moment. She didn't have to measure out her feelings so they would last, like a course of antibiotics. She understood, finally, that sometimes the grandest thing a doctor could do was to treat her patient kindly in the hours she had left.

Sitting with Rebecca, she read a favorite short story by the light of a lantern—*The Gift of the Magi*. The impossibly romantic tale brought a faint smile to Rebecca's lips. "That's nice," she whispered. "They both gave away their most valuable possessions and ended up with nothing."

"Well, nothing useful, anyway. A fob without a watch, combs without hair."

"It's forbidden for a woman to cut her hair," Rebecca said. Her features were growing slack, her eyes unfocused.

Reese didn't reply. One of the reasons Rebecca had refused treatment was that it would involve shaving part of her head. A part of Reese wanted to scream, *It'll grow back*, but she knew that wasn't the issue. To change the subject, she picked up a cloth from the nightstand. "Your embroidery?"

"Mm. I started another sampler. Didn't get too far."

One letter, to be exact—*W*. Perfectly formed. "What were you going to stitch there?" she asked.

The tiniest of smiles flickered. "I don't remember."

"It's all right. You don't have to."

More time passed. Rebecca's mother and sisters came and went in silence, their simple presence a loving gesture. Reese got up, thinking Rebecca was dozing. When she stood, the young woman opened her eyes slightly. "You're going?"

Reese nodded. "I have work. I'll come again after." She picked up the cloth. "Do you mind if I try my hand at this? My embroidery's not so good, but I'm excellent at stitching wounds."

"Of course," Rebecca murmured. She motioned with her hand for Reese to come closer. "How will I know when it's time?" she asked in a faint whisper.

"I can't say. You're very wise and surrounded by love." *Do right by your patient*, Reese reminded herself. "When your pain is bad, and your strength is gone, you might start thinking of leaving."

"Leaving. I like that."

While staying with Mose and Ida, Reese rediscovered the pleasures of gardening. She'd helped Ida with the kitchen garden throughout the abundant growing season. Now an Indian summer was upon New Hope, and the garden was enjoying a last hurrah with a crop of big dense squash and pumpkins on the vine. She'd used the best pumpkins to make pies for the funeral.

Rebecca was gone. Beautiful, ethereal Rebecca, who had chosen to live and die on her own terms. The funeral took over the entire community. Women had prepared a mind-boggling amount of food. The line of black buggies stretched for half a mile. During the lengthy service, the processional to the burial ground, and the graveside farewell, Reese had thought about how she and Rebecca had been friends of a sort, and her heart ached.

While in the thick of med school, she had trained herself to face tragedy with philosophical detachment, but she didn't feel that distance anymore. She felt close to Rebecca and her heart ached with sadness. Yet in the midst of that was a sense of gratitude. Learning to work and love in the here and now pulled her away from her old self, the one who was always looking ahead.

Death was a part of life. In a case like Rebecca's, there was nothing Reese could offer, and because of that she somehow found a way to succumb to the inevitability of losing her.

With a sigh that blended in with the autumn breeze, she tidied up the faded foliage and dropped fruits of the summer, loading up a wheelbarrow for the compost bin. Doing the fall chores properly laid the groundwork for the springtime. Death and decay would bring new life, a certainty as dependable as the seasons themselves. Moving aside the rough vines, she found more squash and placed them in a bushel basket. As she was preparing to take the harvest into the kitchen, she heard the smooth whir of an engine and saw a shiny SUV pull into the driveway.

She set down the basket and took off her gloves. The visit she'd been waiting for all summer was finally happening. "Mom, Dad. You found me! How was your drive?"

Her mother rushed forward, effortlessly stylish in jeans and boots, oversize sunglasses, and a silk scarf fluttering on the breeze. "Totally scenic," she said, folding Reese into a hug. "And *long*. But we picked a gorgeous day to come out here."

Reese turned to her father and embraced him, too. "Well, I'm delighted you're finally here." Things had been strained between them since she'd gone rogue and opted for the rural medicine residency. She wanted them to let go of their plans and to see that this was right for her.

"Look at you," her father said, holding her at arm's length and taking in her overalls and gum boots. "You always liked mucking about in gardens."

She flashed on a memory of her childhood pea patch. "Yep. No chance of someone putting a golf cart shed here." He probably didn't even remember the incident. "Come inside and meet Ida." She led the way to Ida's big country kitchen and made the introductions.

Ida bustled around, pouring glasses of lemonade and setting out a plate of iced oatmeal cookies. "Welcome, welcome," she warbled. "Reese has told me so much about you. Two busy doctors and professors. Mose was hoping to join us, but he's delayed at the hospital."

"I can see why Reese likes it here so much," said her mother. "Your home is lovely."

"Thank you. And we love having her. She's already one of our favorites. You must be very proud of her."

"Extremely," her father said.

Ida made a shooing motion with her apron. "Go outside and enjoy the day. Indian summer is so short, you'd best take in the sunshine while you can."

Sending her a grateful look, Reese brought her parents to the sunny back porch and they sat together. "I've missed you," she said. "Thanks for coming."

"We miss you, too," her mother said. "And we have a proposal to make."

Crap, thought Reese. Her guard went up.

Her father laid a sheaf of papers in front of her. "I didn't want to send this by email. Let's look at it together. An incredible opportunity has come up."

Reese felt a prickle of suspicion. "That's what this is about? You want me to switch to a different residency program?" She should have known. Her parents were nothing if not persistent. Even after all that had happened, they still believed they knew better than she did what she needed.

"Keep an open mind," her mother said. "You can start next summer and you won't have to go through the Match again. There's a new pediatric surgery program . . ."

Reese's ears rang as her parents talked. It was like so many other conversations they'd had throughout her life. Her parents explained what they wanted for her, and it was her job to tacitly accept. In a way, she was reminded of the vanloads of Amish elders who went out periodically to chase down runaway Amish, exhorting them to return to the fold or face eternal damnation.

In her parents' case, they wanted her to return to a more conventional training program, the one they had always planned for her. If she didn't, her own eternal damnation would be an unrewarding and undistinguished career.

"It's really nice of you to show me this option," she said, keeping her tone even, although she wanted to scream. "I'm staying here, though."

"If you're worried about switching programs, you shouldn't be," her mother said. "If you act soon, you might even be able to salvage your year and make the move sooner."

"Doubtful, Joanna," her father cautioned. "She might need to stick it out here. It'll take some doing, but we can still get her credit for the first year. We can use our connections and back channels to find an opening. Reese, you'll be there before you know it."

"Switching programs at this phase is career suicide," Reese pointed out. "Even with your connections and back channels."

Her mother didn't seem to hear. "Hector, we can talk to her program director—"

"Maybe you could talk to your daughter," Reese suggested.

"That's why we're here," her father said. "This is just a stellar opportunity, and it could pave the way to the career you've always wanted."

"This *is* what I want. I'm becoming the doctor I want to be, and I'm sorry if it doesn't fit your vision."

"You could do so much more," her father said. "Cutting-edge facilities, clinical trials, high-level studies—"

"I'm working on an asthma study," Reese pointed out. She'd become intrigued by the fact that so few Amish children suffered from asthma and was working with one of the residents to study the phenomenon.

"That doesn't compare to what you could accomplish in a more challenging setting," said her mother.

In that moment, Reese felt an incredible affinity with Caleb. This was what it was like to deal with demanding, manipulative parents, doggedly committed to maintaining their way of life to the point of threatening to shun her.

19

The medical center in New Hope stayed busy, mostly with routine cases. Day by day, Reese gained confidence in her skills working with patients. She was covering the ER on Ursula's service one night, a duty she had come to like a lot. She was energized by the immediacy of it, the instant connection to the patient. It was hard but rewarding to be privy to people's pain and fear, their hopes and joys. And she had to admit—a quiet ER in the midst of a long shift was a chance to catch up on sleep. Housekeeping, pharmacy, dietary, and most support staff went home at seven, leaving a small crew behind.

Tonight, she'd counseled a drug-seeking teen, then treated an older gentleman who had banged his head on a tool hanging in his garage, resulting in a nasty bump and a laceration. After the CT scan, sutures, and tetanus booster, she retreated to the small, closet-like on-call room, where Ursula was already snoring away. Reese had to learn to detach—a survival mechanism—to clear her head for the next patient. At the moment, there was no next patient on deck. She laid her head down and dreamed of Caleb. He worked constantly, trying to keep up with Jonah's bills. In her dream, she could taste him and feel the warmth of his skin against hers, and hear the sound of his voice murmuring in her ear.

Rather than clearing the way for them to be together, Rebecca's death had pushed them apart. The unbearable sadness and its aftermath had laid bare their insurmountable differences. A girl could dream, though. She could visit him in dreams.

When the buzz of a page intruded, she left the dream reluctantly, brushing away the cobwebs of sleep.

"Coming," she muttered. "Shit."

She shrugged into her lab coat, pocketed her phone, and looped a stethoscope around her neck. She hurried but she didn't rush. There was a difference. Not so long ago, she often awakened to a full-blown panic attack. Here at the Humboldt, she never did. One of these days, she would unpack and examine the reason for that. Not now, though. Now she had to find out what was going on in the ER.

After splashing water on her face and raking a hand through her hair, she hurried to the ER. There was a flurry of activity in one suite. Nurses and techs surrounded an infant warmer on an exam table, and the charge nurse was on the phone, speaking rapidly. When another nurse saw Reese coming, she motioned her over.

"We have a newborn. Abandoned baby. Appears healthy, but she's tiny."

Reese felt a jolt of shock. *Abandoned.* This was a first for her, and, judging by the faces of the others, it was a first for everyone on the floor. She washed at a sink, resisting the urge to summon Ursula right away. "Do not disturb the resident" had been ingrained in her.

"Let's have a look," she said, bending over the tiny baby—a girl, the umbilical cord tied with what appeared to be a bit of baling wire. She was streaked with vernix and mewing softly, her eyes slitted against the bright lights. She was perfectly formed, her delicate skin flush with life. A nurse went over the intake assessment while Reese double-checked the airway, breathing, and circulation and took in the general impressions. The disc of her stethoscope practically covered the baby's entire chest—strong peripheral and central pulses. The soft crying sounded normal, and the muscle tone was good as she slowly moved her extremities. The baby's weight was 2,700 grams, on the small side but above the benchmark for preterm.

She ordered a blood gas analysis to check oxygen levels in the blood, tests for glucose, calcium, and bilirubin levels, continuous monitoring of the baby's breathing and heart rate. She decided to wait for an attending to order a chest X-ray. "Who brought her in?" she asked without looking away from the infant.

"We don't know."

"What do you mean, you don't know?"

"She was in the safe haven box in a crate with some towels, quiet as can be. First time the box has ever been used, and it worked just like it's supposed to. The silent alert came through to the ER, and there she was."

Hospitals and fire stations, even some police stations had safe haven boxes for newborns. The device was meant to prevent desperate women from leaving their babies in dangerous places. Infants could be left anonymously and without legal consequences.

"No one saw the drop-off," said a nurse. "The surveillance cameras don't monitor the box."

Reese was astounded. She couldn't get her head around the idea that a woman would abandon a baby, though she knew it happened on rare occasions. While preparing the infant for admission, she stayed focused on the child. As the physician on duty, it was her job to take the newborn into protective custody, a process that felt unbearably crucial. She had to perform a medical evaluation and safeguard the baby's well-being. A call went out to alert other facilities about the birth mother. The head nurse was rapidly following protocol, alerting the local police and county child welfare agency.

Once the baby—Baby Jane Doe—was foot-printed, braceleted, and placed in the nursery, Reese went back to the ER to meet with the police. She and the rest of the staff gave an exhaustive report. During the interview, she watched an investigator evidence-bagging the box that had been found. It was a slightly battered apple crate with a peeling label—POCONO GOLD APPLES, PENNSYLVANIA'S FINEST.

She stood at the periphery of the area. It felt surreal to realize this was being treated like a crime scene. With gloved hands, another investigator catalogued and bagged two faded and threadbare towels. As he was folding the fabric, she saw a flash of . . . something. A line of dark thread at the bottom hem, a bit of embroidery, perhaps.

And her heart turned stone cold with shock.

"You're getting real good at that," Caleb said to Jonah as he came into the kitchen.

With a guilty start, Jonah looked up from the table. "Sorry, Uncle Caleb, what's that?"

"Putting your arm on." Caleb checked the old coffeepot on the stove. "Your sister's not up yet?"

"Guess not." Jonah concentrated on his arm. It was the robotic arm, the one Grandfather didn't want him using. He knew his uncle and his grandfather disagreed about it; he heard them arguing a lot lately but pretended not to hear. He'd discovered it was possible to learn a lot by pretending not to hear things.

"Did you get some breakfast?" Caleb asked.

"I will in a bit," said Jonah.

"You need to eat if you're going to help out at the

Beilers' today." Caleb gave his shoulder a gentle squeeze. "I'm heading over there right away to get an early start on their new barn. You can ride over with the Haubers after breakfast, yes?"

"Yes."

"I'll let them know you'll be there shortly."

"I will. After chores." Jonah's throat felt very tight. It was hard to get the words out. Feelings and doubts were clogging him up. He hoped beyond all hope that he had done the right thing.

Shortly after Caleb left, he heard a shuffle on the stairs and hoped it wasn't his grandfather, whose thunderous frown never failed to worry him. No, it was Hannah.

She looked the way she always did, in her long dress and apron, her braid coiled under her *kapp*. But her face was different—pale skin and sad, puffy eyes.

"It's done," Jonah said. "I did what you told me to do."

She nodded and brought cereal and a pitcher of milk to the table, pouring herself a big serving. "That's good. All will be well, neh?"

"I don't know." His head felt fuzzy with exhaustion. He was hungry, but he didn't feel like eating.

"Tell me what you did," she whispered. She eased down into a chair, moving like an old woman. "I want to know."

He took a deep breath, sorting through the memories. In the middle of the night, Hannah had awakened him from his bed. "I need your help," she'd said. "Leave Jubilee closed in your room and come with me."

There had been a note in her voice, strained and scared, rousing a vibration of fear inside Jonah. His Spidey sense, the kids in Group would have called it, back at the city hospital.

Their bare feet made no sound as they went to her room. An odd smell hung in the air, musky and metallic.

She lifted a hissing lantern, and a bundle on the bed was illuminated.

At first, Jonah hadn't understood what he was seeing. He didn't want to understand. He forced himself to look. A baby. A tiny little baby, making soft, mewing sounds like a kitten. And now he recognized that smell. It was the birth smell, something he knew from the foaling box in the barn, or from the cow shed. He noticed an oilcloth table covering on the floor, with a big bloody thing in a shallow basin.

"*Gott im Himmel*," he'd whispered. "What . . . ?"

"A terrible thing has happened," she said. "I need your help making it right."

Jonah tried to take it all in—the light and shadow, the smell, the strange heaviness of the air. "We've got to wake Caleb," he whispered, turning toward the door as understanding dawned on him.

"No." She grabbed his arm. "I have a better plan."

An icy chill had swept over him. "Hannah—"

"Take it to the hospital in New Hope and leave it there. They'll keep it safe and take care of it."

"I can't—"

"You can. Hitch up the buggy. You've done it a hundred times, so quick with your new arm. I'll help. You can go and be back before it gets light out."

"Hannah, don't make me do this."

"It's the only way. You know what will happen to me and to this baby if I keep it. I'll be shamed and shunned. I'll lose everything and everyone dear to me. And they'll make me marry Aaron Graber, and I can't. I cannot bind myself to him forever. I'd die if I had to do that." His sister took his good hand between both of hers, and he felt the dampness of her sleeves. "Please, Jonah," she said. "*Dabber schpring.*"

Go quickly. He would never forget the expression on her face—the stark, desperate need, the fear.

Now in the bright light of morning, she regarded him with the same desperation, but in her eyes was a glimmer of hope. "Jonah, please talk to me."

The kitchen clock ticked into the silence. "There was nobody on the road," he said. "The little one was just so quiet. I left the buggy a ways away from the hospital and walked up like you told me to, keeping clear of the cameras. I put the box in the haven door and left and nobody stopped me and I came home and it was still dark."

"That's good, Jonah. You're so smart and brave. I knew I could count on you."

"I'm not brave. I'm scared," he whispered. "We did a bad thing."

"No," she said swiftly, her voice quiet but fierce. "It was the right thing to do."

It was not. He felt in the pit of his stomach that it was not. But he had no idea how to fix it.

"Are you all better now?" he asked quietly. "I mean, are you . . . is everything . . ." His voice trailed off. He couldn't figure out how to ask what he needed to know.

She pressed her hands on the table and got up slowly to put the big copper pot on to boil. "I need to see about the laundry," she said.

20

Reese practically broke the sound barrier driving to Middle Grove. Speeding was probably the least of the laws she was breaking. She had signed her statement to the police as the physician on duty, attesting that she had given them all the information she had on the abandoned baby.

But she'd signed the statement before she had noticed the towel.

On the way, she phoned Domenico Falco, her parents' longtime family lawyer, on his private mobile number. "Sorry to wake you," she said when his sleep-thickened voice came through the car's speakers. "It's Reese Powell, and I'm speaking as your client, okay?" She needed to make sure anything she said to him would be privileged.

When she explained what was going on, he was quiet for a few moments. Thanks to her parents' specialties, they were constantly at risk for lawsuits. Domenico also handled partnership agreements, hospital and insurance contract negotiations, Medicare investigations . . . but Reese knew this would be a first for him.

Then his voice was wide awake as he said, "I'm on it."

His confidence made her feel marginally better. She took a few deep, calming breaths as she headed down the gravel drive to the Stoltz place. The sprawling farm was bathed in the golden light of sunrise. A ground mist softened the landscape, giving it the look of a vintage painting. She was mistaken. The crazy story she'd told

Domenico was nothing more than a fairy tale—a dark fairy tale. She wanted to be wrong. *Please*, she thought. *Let me be wrong.*

She burst through the kitchen door and found Hannah alone at the breakfast table, eating a bowl of cereal and a slice of bread slathered with jam. The kitchen was still dim and shadowy so early in the day. Hannah looked up from the table, her eyes wide. "Reese."

"I need to talk to you."

Hannah frowned. "It's so early. Is something the matter?"

Reese scarcely knew where to start. "Where's your uncle?" She looked around the room. On the stove, a copper pot simmered with a load of clothes and lye soap.

"Caleb's gone to the Beilers' for a barn raising, a couple miles down the road." She sighed. "I'm supposed to bring two pies over at lunchtime, but I'm so bad in the kitchen—"

"And Asa?" Reese looked around.

Hannah shrugged. "Probably in the Daadi Haus, reading his papers." The rhythmic cadence of her speech suggested it was simply another day at the farm.

Reese regarded the perfectly ordinary scene before her and felt a flicker of relief. Her suspicions were totally unfounded. She was glad she hadn't come in blazing with accusations. Hannah would think she was losing her mind.

But unease niggled at her. Hannah was polishing off a slice of bread and jam, and when she got up from the table, she caught at the edge of it to steady herself.

"Are you all right?" asked Reese.

"Yah, sure. I need to finish the washing and then see about those pies." Hannah looked directly at Reese, her expression benign, slightly pleasant. "Can I get you something, then? I finished the bread, but there are sticky buns from yesterday."

"No, thank you. I came to check on you." Reese took a deep breath. "We had a big night at the medical center." She paused, watching Hannah's face. "Someone left a brand-new baby and I was the doctor on call. That's a first for me. A first for the hospital, too. It's never happened before. It's very mysterious, and everyone is trying to figure out how this came about. I decided to come and ask you if you might know something, because it's a very big deal."

Hannah raised her chin and folded her arms in front of her. "I don't know what you're talking about."

"I'm talking about the fact that someone made a terrible decision last night. I know you have a few friends who are already married and expecting babies. Suppose one of them panicked and left her newborn at the hospital."

"Why would a person panic? My friends are all happy to be having their babies."

"Well, somebody must not have been, because when a baby is left all alone, it usually means the birth mother is in danger or trouble of some sort. And a baby separated from its mother needs special care."

"Will she be all right, then?" Hannah turned away, busying herself with the laundry pot at the stove.

Reese felt a chill of certainty now. "The baby, you mean?"

Hannah nodded as she stirred the pot with a wooden stick.

Reese walked over to the stove and took the stick from Hannah's hand. "You need to sit," she said.

"I must—"

"Sit." Reese tried to keep her temper in check by reminding herself that the girl was in an extremely fragile state. She brought her back to the table and sat her down. "Let's talk about your baby. I want to help."

"She's not my—"

"I never mentioned the baby is a girl. You did. That's because she's your brand-new baby, and you need to come to the hospital with me and we'll get this sorted out."

Hannah quailed, pressing herself against the table and crossing her arms. "No. I can't."

"Let me put it this way, Hannah. You can let me drive you to the hospital now, or you can stay here and let the state decide the fate of your baby."

The girl gasped aloud and said something in German.

"That's the way it works," said Reese. "Help me understand why you did it, Hannah. I know you. You're a good person. It's not like you to abandon a helpless baby."

"It wasn't like that. And I didn't—"

"We'll talk about it during the drive. I'll explain everything that's going to happen, and I promise I'll be with you every step of the way." She grabbed a pair of oxford shoes from the mat by the door and handed them to Hannah. "Put these on."

Hannah's hands shook. Reese was shaking too. As a doctor, she was obligated to subject the girl to an extensive physical examination. At the moment, though, she knew in her heart that the invasive questions and actions would shatter the fragile teenager. She also knew that failure to do so could result in losing her credentials, or at least being flagged. *Christ.*

"Are you bleeding?"

"I'm . . . I have my monthly pad."

"And the placenta?" Reese asked. "The afterbirth."

"Outside in the bin," she muttered.

Shit, thought Reese. It was important to examine the

placenta to make sure it had been delivered in its entirety. "Was it intact? Did it seem to be torn?"

"It was intact and the cord was attached. I know these things from the cows and horses. I tied and cut the cord myself."

Reese observed the girl closely as she sat down and put on her shoes. Her movements were cautious, but she didn't seem to be in pain, or even in shock. Reese was amazed. Hannah didn't seem like a woman—a very young woman—who had just endured one of life's most arduous, emotional ordeals.

"Talk to me," said Reese. "I can help you, but I'm going to need to know everything that happened."

"It just . . . happened." Hannah finished tying her shoes and stared straight ahead, her delicate profile outlined by the morning sun.

Reese pursed her lips, gathering patience. "Let's start with last night. How on earth did you give birth to a baby, take her to the hospital, and get home, all without anyone noticing?"

"It wasn't . . . I didn't do that."

"Who was with you? The baby's father?"

"*No*," she said emphatically. "I . . . this was all my doing."

"You went to the hospital, then? How the hell did you manage that?"

"I managed. It was my doing," Hannah said. She seemed agitated now, her hands bunching into the folds of her dress and apron.

"So you did go to the hospital. How did you get there? How did you manage to leave the baby without anyone seeing?"

"I don't know. I just did."

"Hannah, there are going to be a lot of questions. You have to explain everything, exactly as it happened."

Now the girl looked up, her eyes welling with tears. "I can't have a baby. I *can't*. Could we just leave her? Make sure a good family takes her in?"

"It doesn't work that way," Reese said. "You do have options, but that's not one of them. Please, Hannah. Tell me what happened. How did you get the baby to the hospital?"

"I didn't. I—"

"Listen." Reese struggled to be patient. She frequently dealt with uncommunicative patients—they gave incomplete information, misreported things, or flat-out lied. Getting to the truth took time. She didn't have time, though. Every moment the investigation progressed was a strike against Hannah. "Just listen," she said. "I need to know what you did so I can help you. And that includes telling me how you brought the baby to the hospital."

"She didn't." Jonah came into the kitchen, his somber expression telling Reese he'd been listening.

"Jonah, don't," said Hannah, extending her hands in a pleading motion. She said something else in Deitsch, her tone urgent.

Reese stopped breathing a moment. A big piece of the puzzle fell into place. "Do you realize what you made your brother do?" she blurted out.

Hannah stared at the floor. "I'm terrible. It's going to be like my grandfather says, I'll burn in hell for all eternity."

"Stop it," Reese's heart ached for the girl, and for the steadfast, loyal boy. Jonah and his sister were so close. They shared everything and always had, ever since she'd known them. She went to Jonah and put her arm around him. "I'm bringing you both to the hospital. We can make this right, but only if we come forward now."

He didn't argue. Instead, he took his sister's hand. "Let's go with Reese," he said.

"I can't." Hannah tried to pull away. "Please, I just . . ." She said something else in their dialect.

"She's afraid to see the baby," Jonah said.

Reese felt a welling of compassion. In a single night, Hannah had endured a terrifying ordeal with only her young brother to help. And this was only the beginning of a reality for which they were completely unprepared.

So much trauma to unwind here. There was a part of Reese that simply wanted to hold Hannah in her arms and soothe her. Hannah had been dealing with an unwanted pregnancy for months, and she had no mother to turn to. She'd just delivered a baby without assistance and was exhausted and weak, surely in need of medical attention.

Yet the task before them forced Reese to be the adult here. Everything about this situation was precarious. As a doctor, she was expected to act with swift decision. She thought about the rigorous questioning she'd gone through at the hospital. She was out of her depth, but hesitation would only compound the problem.

Reese knew Hannah had not thought this through. The girl had acted out of panic and impulse. Maybe she would ultimately decide to surrender the baby for adoption, but not like this. Not in a state of physical trauma and terror. She deserved time to reconsider. Unless she acted now, she would lose that option.

Reese wrote a note on the back of her hospital business card and left it on the table.

"Come, Hannah," she said. "We'll get through this. I'll help you."

A few minutes later, they were on the road. "When did you realize you were pregnant?" asked Reese. "This is important, and it's one of the first things we need to know—the date of conception."

Hannah chewed on her thumbnail and stared out the window. "That would be at the end of January. I . . . I think I realized in March."

Holy crap, thought Reese. She couldn't imagine the pain and stress of hiding a pregnancy, particularly among people who refused to even say the word. "Who's the father? Is it that boy you told me about? Aaron?"

She hesitated. Stared straight ahead at the road racing up to meet them. "Please, he can't know. I don't want to marry him. I can't. I just can't."

"Don't worry about that now."

Within a few minutes, Hannah nodded off. The salty ghosts of tears dusted her pale cheeks, and Reese felt a wave of sympathy. She had only begun to comprehend what Hannah had endured, in secret and alone, with no source of support.

When she called Domenico to give him an update, he was slightly encouraging. "It could be categorized as an emergency home birth. The fact that the brother brought the baby in is consistent with that scenario."

"What about me?" she asked. She could sense Jonah behind her, coiled like a spring.

"You exercised good judgment," he said.

"God, I hope you're right."

"I'll meet you at the hospital," he said. "I'm almost there."

After she rang off, Jonah spoke up from the back seat. "He's a lawyer?"

"That's right."

"And he's going to fix it?"

"He's going to help," Reese said, hoping her stone-cold fear didn't show. By leaving the hospital during the inquiry, she had put her entire career at risk.

Things were quiet when they arrived, though there was a woman in a sheriff's deputy uniform stationed at the ER. Reese greeted the nurse and showed the badge clipped to her lab coat, keeping hold of Hannah's arm as they passed. She brought Jonah to the waiting area. "Don't move," she said. "Don't talk to anybody. If someone asks you a question, tell them to page me immediately."

He nodded and sat down. Reese took Hannah down the hall toward the nursery.

Hannah balked, trying to pull away. "I don't want—"

"We're not dealing with what you want right now. You have a responsibility to take care of, and we're going to see to that immediately." Reese felt like a bully, speaking to Hannah like that, but she was driven by a sense of urgency. Hannah had only moments to step up if she hoped to make a different decision about her child.

The only occupant of the nursery was Baby Jane Doe. Presumably, other newborns were rooming in with their mothers. A social worker and a hospital security guy—one of only three on staff—were seated outside the nursery.

"I'm Dr. Powell," said Reese, showing her badge again. "This is Hannah Stoltz, the baby's mother. We understand the custodial situation, but Hannah needs to see her child." There must have been a certain note in her voice, because the woman and the guard both nodded and stepped aside. For the first time since starting her internship, Reese felt the full power of her self-confidence as a physician. She was trained to act decisively in life-threatening emergencies.

Yet the part of Reese that made her so determined at the moment had nothing to do with medical training. The girl had been dealing with the terror of an unwanted pregnancy for nine months with no mother to confide in. She'd just delivered a baby alone in the dark. She was mentally exhausted by the trauma and physically ravaged by pain and blood loss, needing medical attention herself. Yet Reese knew her most urgent need was to see and touch her baby. She didn't want Hannah to have regrets or to miss out on life's biggest challenge—being a mother.

Hannah's face was ghost pale as she went to the sink, pushed back her sleeves, and stood before the stainless-steel bowl. She touched the faucet handle but couldn't make it operate—yet another stark example of the girl's otherness. Reese hurried over and showed her how to turn on the water. She washed her own hands in the warm stream, then stepped back while Hannah did the same.

Reese gently lifted the sleeping baby from the clear bassinet. "She's made to fit perfectly in a person's arms," she whispered to Hannah. "That's her only job right now. Take a seat."

Hannah gingerly lowered herself to a chair with nursing-height arms. Reese stood in front of her, hoping the guard wouldn't see the sheer terror in the girl's eyes, the tremors in her hands. "Here you go," Reese said, transferring the baby into Hannah's waiting arms.

The girl gasped and shut her eyes. Her arms curved perfectly around the small bundle. Bending low, she inhaled the scent of the downy-headed infant and whispered something in Deitsch. Reese saw the moment the magic took hold—that indelible connection between mother and child. When Hannah looked up at her, Reese could tell the girl's world had changed.

"My heart is hurting me," Hannah whispered.

"It can be overwhelming. All new moms feel that way."

Hannah studied every feature of the baby—the curve of her cheek. The quiver of her lower lip as she floated in some infant dream. The starfish shape of her elfin hand splayed upon the swaddling blanket. The impossibly fragile pulse in the tiny neck.

"She's a miracle," Hannah said. "She's my miracle."

21

Caleb burst through the doors of the hospital in New Hope, having driven a borrowed car from Middle Grove. His father had sought him out at the Beilers' barn raising and had thrust a card with a scribbled note at him. "Your English friend has taken Hannah and Jonah away," Asa had said with a glare of fury.

> Hannah and Jonah are fine. Meet us at the medical center as soon as you can get here.

If they are fine, he'd thought, *why has she taken them to New Hope?*

With the sawdust still clinging to him from the barn raising, he parked at the medical center lot and jumped out of the pickup, shoving the key into his pocket as he strode to the entrance. For no reason he could fathom, a guy with a shoulder-mounted camera and a woman with a smartphone approached him, but he ignored them as the doors swished open.

The hospital folks must have been expecting him, because when he entered the lobby, an administrator introduced himself and brought Caleb to a room with a curtained hospital bed and several people standing around. Jonah sat on a swivel stool, swinging back and forth and staring at the floor. Mose and Reese were present, speaking with a guy he didn't recognize.

When she saw him, Reese rushed to his side. She looked both harried and beautiful, her dark hair mussed and her eyes tired but bright with focus. "Everything's going to be all right," she said.

He clenched his jaw. Though grateful that she'd told him the first thing he wanted to hear, he knew it wasn't the whole story. He glanced over at Jonah. The boy got up and grabbed Caleb's hand with his good one. Reese moved the curtain aside. Hannah was on the hospital bed, wearing her bonnet and a thin tie-on gown. In her arms, she held a wrapped bundle in a posture he saw every day among the young women of Middle Grove.

His gut told him what he was looking at while his mind muddled around, trying to make sense of it. "God in heaven, what is this?" he murmured in dialect.

Hannah slowly raised her gaze to his. "Caleb," she said, also speaking in Deitsch, "I'm so sorry. I pray you can forgive me."

He felt Jonah's grip tighten. "Never mind that," he said. "Tell me, Hannah. Make me understand." Yet as soon as the words were out of his mouth, he realized that the explanation was right here before him, staring up at him with cornflower blue eyes, the same eyes as his brother, John.

It was a shock. And yet it wasn't. This situation played out with predictable regularity—young folk got together, they fooled around, the girl ended up in trouble. In his younger days, Caleb had done more than his share of fooling around, although he'd never been stupid enough to get a girl with child.

Now he was flooded by guilt. His niece had hidden a pregnancy and the birth of a baby from him. He hadn't suspected a thing. How had he let that happen?

"I can't make you understand," Hannah said in Deitsch.

"Never mind," he said, feeling a terrible softness in his chest. "The important thing is that you're all right, neh?"

"I made an awful bad mess of things." She hesitated, her chin trembling, tears forging fresh tracks down her already tearstained cheeks. Ah, his poor little Hannah. *I'm sorry, John. I'm so sorry.*

"Oh, no," Caleb said. "You didn't make a mess. It appears to me you made something precious."

Letting go of Jonah's hand, he went over to a sink and washed up. From the corner of his eye, he saw Mose shooing everyone out of the room.

"Reese, can you stay?" Hannah called. "I need . . . it would be nice for you to stay."

Reese murmured something to the people at the door, then came over to the bed. "Have a seat," she said, indicating a large, vinyl-covered armchair. Once he was seated, she gently took the bundle from Hannah and settled it into the crook of Caleb's arm. He stiffened, and his heart felt as though it surged to his throat. The tiny thing was as light as a loaf of bread fresh from the oven. He looked down to see a round, red face, eyes puffy and swollen, a wisp of colorless hair and one elfin fist poking out of the blanket. The love and wonder that engulfed him were as pure and powerful as a wave of ocean water. He felt nine clouds higher than cloud nine.

"*Mein Gott*," he whispered. "What a little thing to cause such a stir."

"I wanted to tell you," Hannah said. "I was so ashamed, I just couldn't."

Shame. He gritted his teeth, trying not to comment. In their culture, shame was the key to keeping people in check, pushing down the truest desires in their hearts. He felt a sense of wonder, too, that Hannah had endured a pregnancy in secret, right under his nose. "You can tell me now," he said. "What about you start with telling me who this one is?"

For the first time, Hannah offered the glimmer of a smile. "She's a little girl, and everyone says she's just perfect. The hospital called her Baby Jane Doe, but I want to name her Sarah. Sarah Jane." The glimmer shifted to a look that seemed to be made of equal measures of pain and joy. "I have a *daughter*," she whispered brokenly.

"She's wonderful," Caleb said, staring down at the sleeping stranger. Then he stood and settled the baby back into Hannah's arms and sat down again. Neither Reese nor Jonah had spoken yet; they seemed to be holding their breath. "Sarah Jane is a wonderful name."

Hannah held the little one close and began to speak, hesitantly at first, but with increasing openness. She told Caleb she had gone too far with Aaron Graber, then realized too late that she didn't want to be his wife, keep his house, and raise his kids after all. She was so mortified to be pregnant and unmarried that she didn't say anything, just loosened her clothes and tried to pretend it wasn't happening.

None of that surprised Caleb. The shock came when she said she'd delivered the baby in the middle of the night and given it to Jonah to bring to the hospital. Caleb sat forward and stared at his nephew. The boy's actions were epic and heroic—and tragically wrongheaded.

"You never thought to come to me?" he quietly asked.

Jonah stared at the floor. Then, remembering his manners, he looked directly at Caleb. There was a glint of defiance in his eyes, and for a moment, he looked far older than his years. He and Hannah had lost their whole world the night their parents were murdered. They had only each other. It was no wonder they clung together, just the two of them. "I did it for Hannah," he said.

"I don't fault you for wanting to help your sister," Caleb said. "But do you understand, this was very dangerous, not just to the baby, but to Hannah as well."

Jonah offered a somber nod, though the defiance remained. "I kept her safe. I was so careful, and I used the box just like you're supposed to."

Caleb steepled his fingers together and took a deep breath. "That you did."

"Am I gonna get walloped?"

"When have I ever walloped you?"

Jonah turned away. "Just asking."

A new worry for Caleb. Was Asa . . . ? He pushed that worry aside for the moment and turned to Reese. "Thank you for helping," he said.

"Of course." As exhausted as she looked, she offered a smile of encouragement. In that moment, he loved her so much he couldn't see straight. That he could even feel such a thing at a time like this was extraordinary. And frustrating, because he needed to focus on Hannah and a thousand other matters.

"I'd best get to it, then," he said, standing up. He leaned down and kissed Hannah on the forehead and spoke in Deitsch. "All will be well. I promise you."

Reese didn't know what to wear to an emergency judicial hearing. She opted for dark slacks, a cream-colored sweater, and a plain blazer. Minimal makeup, no jewelry. Deep, calming breath. There was a moment when she reached for her phone to call her parents. *I did something. . . . I'm in trouble.*

She resisted. Her parents would likely have all kinds of advice. They'd come riding to the rescue, but she needed to deal with this on her own.

The county courthouse was a painted Greek revival building from the nineteenth century, with a cupola and clock and a bell that rang on the hour. It was the sort of building that adorned postcards of yesteryear, especially in the autumn, framed by maple leaves aflame with color. At the moment, a gaggle of reporters and news vans had gathered there.

She flashed on a memory of Jonah's trauma last year—the rubbernecking media intruding into a family's pain. The press seemed to have a special fetish for all things Amish. Was it their otherness? The perception of unclouded simplicity—faith, family, and farming? It made Hannah's fall seem all the more dramatic—an Amish girl doing something so patently un-Amish as abandoning a baby.

With a cold chill of apprehension, Reese kept her distance from the cameras and microphones. She ignored the hurried questions of the reporters. Domenico arrived, armed with a stuffed briefcase and clipboards. "This should go all right," he said, heading inside. He stopped and checked in with the clerk, then led the way to the circuit court. The judge's bench was empty, though a court reporter was in place. Somehow, Domenico had managed to get the judge to ban the media from the courtroom.

Caleb and Jonah were seated at a bench in the back. They stood when Reese and Domenico came in. Both were dressed in the sort of outfits worn on church Sundays, black trousers and plain blue shirts, and both looked equally ill at ease. Reese's stomach churned and her mouth felt dry. The only thing that kept her in balance was the sight of Caleb, looking impassive yet sure of himself. Everything had happened so quickly that she hadn't had even a moment to speak to him in private. If she had, she would have told him . . . what? That she'd guessed that Hannah was the birth mother and confronted her without telling him? That she'd possibly violated hospital policy and put her credentials at risk? That she'd have done the same thing over again if given the chance?

Domenico shook hands with Caleb. "This will be quick. It's an emergency hearing, meaning the judge will only hear facts related to the emergency. Everything else—what you've decided going forward, what Hannah's rights and needs are—we'll deal with all that later."

"I understand," Caleb said. Jonah pressed closer to him, as though trying to hide in his shadow, and Caleb said something to the boy in German.

Mose and Ursula arrived. As the attending and resident on call when the baby was discovered, each had made statements and responded to questions. Domenico asked everyone to take a seat behind the bar, then went on the other side to the table. The only others present were the hospital counsel and two administrators.

"All rise," said the bailiff. "Court is now in session. Judge Orville Rucker presiding. Please be seated."

The judge swept in through a side door, still fastening the top of his judicial robes. His hair looked damp, and he had what appeared to be a bit of shaving cream on one cheek. "I was getting a haircut," he said, "but I had to cut it short."

Reese glanced at Domenico, who shrugged.

"Yes, it was a joke," said the judge. "Just breaking the ice here."

"Understood, Your Honor," said Domenico. "I'm Domenico Falco, here on behalf of the petitioner." He turned and identified everyone seated behind him. The hospital attorney did the same.

"All righty then," Rucker said, "let's make sure I understand why I gave up my regular rendezvous at the man salon. It appears we have an abandoned newborn."

Domenico shot to his feet. "Your Honor, doesn't apply in this case. The baby was delivered during an emergency home birth and brought—"

"To the Humboldt Division Regional Care Center in New Hope, yes," the judge said. "I can see that. Sit down, Mr. Falco. We'll split hairs another time." He paused. "And much as I'm tempted by another witticism, I understand the gravity of this situation. The infant has been medically determined to be less than seventy-two hours old. The hospital has accepted physical custody of the child, is that correct, Ms. Wasco?" he asked the hospital attorney.

"Yes, Your Honor."

"And the birth mother is now at the hospital as well? Maternal testing has been done?"

"Yes, Your Honor." Wendy Wasco referred to the detailed statements from everyone who had been present, including Reese. It felt strange to hear her own words being quoted aloud. In the report, she had followed hospital procedure to the letter, evaluating and admitting the baby while the authorities were called.

"The next step will be for the county department to assume temporary custody of her as an abandoned child," Judge Rucker added.

Domenico was on his feet again. "We respectfully ask you to hold that action in abeyance and remand the case to the district court. Hannah Stoltz, the birth mother, is making a claim of parental rights."

"And doing so after the fact," the judge pointed out. "Let's not forget that."

"The birth occurred at home in an emergency situation. A home, I should point out, lacking in telephone service. There is absolutely no indication of abuse, neglect, or misconduct."

"And yet the newborn was left in the safe haven box," the judge pointed out.

Domenico referred to the statement Hannah had made after Reese had brought her to the hospital. "Hannah delivered the baby alone in an emergency home birth. Since she was in no shape to travel and had no means of transport, her brother took the baby to the safe haven box at the medical center. I would argue she made a responsible decision on behalf of the baby's well-being." Domenico spoke directly to the judge, painting a picture of a young, frightened girl in a state of unbearable pain and panic, and a young boy simply following instructions.

There were questions—*Why didn't Hannah alert an adult in the household?*

As an unmarried woman in a strict religious community, she was understandably reluctant to publicize her condition.

Why didn't Jonah make a 911 call from the community phone box?

I can't speak to Jonah's state of mind.

The judge set aside the papers. "Jonah, can you explain why you left the baby and didn't speak with anyone about what you were doing?"

He stood up, and Reese saw the moment Rucker noticed his mechanical arm for the first time. Jonah cleared his throat, tipped up his chin, and looked the man in the eye. "They save people at the hospital," he said simply. "I know that for a true fact. There's a special box that opens outside the hospital. Once the baby's inside and you close it, a silent alarm sounds and the box locks. That way, you know the baby's safe."

And you claim she will not be terminating her parental rights?

Absolutely not, Your Honor. Hannah is in the patient care unit at the hospital now. She very much wants to bond with her little girl and bring her home.

"The birth mother is a minor," the judge pointed out. "Her parents are deceased." He looked at Caleb. "You're her guardian, then?"

Reese held her breath. Caleb never, ever lied.

"I've been looking after Hannah and Jonah ever since my brother and his wife were killed. Hannah has my support, one hundred percent."

Rucker sighed loudly. "There are elements of this situation that I find troubling. At this time, we have many more questions and issues to be resolved."

"Per statute," said Domenico, "Hannah has sixty days to reclaim her child by filing a petition in court."

"In that case, does the filing mean she's admitting to relinquishing the newborn? Because if so, then that contradicts your claim that there was an emergency home birth."

Shit. Reese tensed every muscle in her body. It was a trap with no exit.

"I'm reluctant to proceed until we have more clarity as to the birth mother's state of mind and intention."

Reese held her breath. She felt everyone around her doing the same.

A door at the rear of the courtroom creaked, and when it opened, a barrage of camera flashes leaked from the hallway into the courtroom. Reese turned to see Hannah walking up the aisle.

Caleb jumped up and rushed to help her to a seat. Hannah spoke to him quietly and remained standing. Her face was pale, her movements wobbly, but her gaze as she faced the judge was rock steady.

"Your Honor, my name is Hannah Stoltz. May I speak?"

Domenico started to say something, but the judge waved him silent. "Let's hear from the young lady."

Hannah's clothes were rumpled, her bonnet strings loose. She held her hands knotted together in front of her skirt. "I got myself in trouble," she said, "and I was afraid to say anything, so I kept it a secret. What happened, it's no one's fault but my own. And Jonah, he was just trying to help by making sure my baby went to a safe place. My brother knows that a hospital is that place. I truly believed in my heart she would be better off with another family, because in our community, an unwed mother is a cause of great shame."

Watching Hannah—humble, brave, vulnerable—Reese clenched her jaw until it hurt. She'd learned so much, working among the people here. She'd come to value the deep connections of family and community that defined their way of life. Now she couldn't suppress a hot jolt of anger. The closed society was toxic to Hannah, driving her to hide a pregnancy and abandon a baby. As a physician, Reese was obligated to respect a patient's beliefs without judgment. As a woman, she wasn't sure that was possible.

"Something happened the next morning," Hannah said to the judge. She turned slightly to indicate Reese. "When I went to the hospital and held my baby in my arms, I realized she's more than a responsibility. She's my very soul, and I must keep her no matter what punishment and shame I'll have to face. I named her Sarah Jane Stoltz, and she's my very own child, and I love her with every beat of my heart. I aim to be her mother."

No one said a word. The judge stared at Hannah, his face inscrutable. "You came here on your own from the hospital?"

"I was not on my own. I came in a taxi."

The inscrutable face softened. "You got yourself to the hearing, then."

"They said I didn't have to be here but I had to come. I want everyone to know I'm ready to take care of my daughter."

"You mentioned facing a punishment," the judge said. "Can you explain what you mean?"

Hannah cleared her throat, then swallowed. "I will be called on to confess and repent before the elders in our community, and I'll be put under the Bann. Those who've been baptized into the church will shun me so they won't be tainted by my shame."

Reese felt a fresh wave of anger. Being a new mother was hard for anyone. Being shunned would add a layer of difficulty no girl should have to face. She tensed, preparing to get to her feet, to speak up, to do something. Domenico gave an almost imperceptible shake of his head.

At the same moment, Caleb stood up. "My name is Caleb Stoltz," he said. "I'd like to speak on behalf of my niece, Hannah. Ever since her parents died I've raised her over in Middle Grove, the way her parents wanted her raised. Hannah's a good girl, hardworking and good to her family and friends. She'll be good to her baby, and she'll live under my roof for as long as she needs me."

Reese stopped breathing. It seemed everyone else did, too, as the judge stared at Caleb for several silent seconds. Then he said, "So you won't take part in the shunning?"

A tic leaped in Caleb's jaw. "I'm not obliged to, as I've not been baptized into the faith."

Another long pause. The judge addressed the hospital lawyer. "There's a lot to consider in this situation," he said. "DCFS will conduct a child protective investigation and a home study, and their recommendations will be submitted to the district court. In the meantime, Ms. Stoltz is to be taken back to the hospital and allowed to bond with her baby. I'm granting temporary custody to Hannah Stoltz on the condition that she resides at her family residence. I order that a social worker will monitor the situation to make sure the baby is receiving proper care until such time as the district court rules on the petition."

The gavel came down with a decisive thud.

22

Reese stared at the email message on her screen. Her finger hovered over the Delete button to dismiss the note, which came with an information attachment. But her gaze snagged on some key phrases—*unexpected opening, combined program, med-ped. Palm Springs. Riverside, California.*

"Jesus Christ, Mom," she murmured, suspecting her mother's hand was behind the invitation to apply for the special program. Okay, maybe just a peek. She opened the attachment. To her surprise, the referral had not come from her mother at all, but from Dr. Jimenez of Mercy Heights. He'd attached a note: *This is a rare opportunity for an elite program. Give it due consideration.* She read the document with an undeniable tingle of interest. It was everything a resident could dream of in one program— internal medicine and pediatrics—two specialties that would allow her to take care of patients for their whole lives.

Mose came into the kitchen and sat down next to her. "Your coffee is getting cold."

Wordlessly, she turned the laptop screen so he could see it. He was silent for a few minutes. Then he took off his spectacles and set them on the table. "This sounds like the opportunity of a lifetime."

"Yes." Damn it all to hell. She didn't want to want this. Yes, she did. That was undeniable. Still, she didn't want to be tempted by something that would take her far away.

"It's a rare chance." He folded his arms and looked directly at her. "More than we can offer here. If you decide to pursue it, I'll support you."

"You think I should."

Mose was nothing if not plainspoken. "I think the decision is up to you."

The incident with Hannah had shaken Reese's confidence along with her standing with her preceptor. She had been subjected to an inquiry by the hospital. As her program directors, Mose and Penelope had conducted an inquiry of their own. By failing to disclose her hunch about the baby's birth mother, she had wandered into a gray area of protocol. Although her actions were not specifically in violation of policy and practice, she'd allowed a personal situation to intrude on her judgment. Or had she?

Yes, she was obligated to turn the girl in, to subject her to interrogation and a physical examination, but in that moment, she believed—no, she *knew*—that the invasive actions would shatter the fragile teenager.

She stared at the screen a moment longer. One finger hovered over Delete, and another over Save.

She hadn't seen Caleb in a week—an exhausting, stressful, eventful week. And unlike most guys, he didn't call or send text messages or email. Their relationship was tenuous, stretched taut between unbearable yearning and immovable obstacles. And despite this, he was the first person she wanted to talk to about the decision she had to make. He had somehow become the best friend she'd ever had, but she was losing him. What she felt was more than the chemistry that blazed like the sun every time he was near. It was also that unexpected, settled calm she'd always sensed in his presence, practically from the first moment they'd met. She had no idea where that came from, but it was as palpable and undeniable as her physical passion for him.

She drove to Middle Grove in the evening, hoping to find him at home. Slowing down to make way for the occasional buggy or pedestrian, she took in the purity of the rural landscape, untainted by billboards, flashing signs, or even phone and electrical lines. The macadam lane took her past a farm stand selling brown eggs and whirligigs from the adjacent wood shop. Behind a horse-drawn cart, a rusty contraption plucked corn stalks from the ground and fanned them onto a cart bed. At the edge of town, a baseball game was in progress, the action gilded by the setting sun. Families watched the action from quilts spread on the ground. No one had their face in a phone. No one was tweeting. They were just . . . being. In moments like this, she understood on the deepest level the appeal of living Plain.

At the Stoltz farm, she spied Caleb walking toward the horse barn carrying two galvanized pails. His silhouette against the evening sky sketched a lonely picture. Though he never complained, she knew there was too much weighing on him. He worked all the time, pulled between his job at Grantham Farm and working the farm, and now looking after Hannah and her newborn.

Following their discharge from the hospital, Hannah and the baby were home under strict conditions imposed by the court, and those conditions included support from Caleb. Now he had not two, but three children to raise according to the promise he'd made to his brother. *She'll live under my roof for as long as she needs me*, Caleb had told the judge. That could mean years, Reese realized. Decades, even. What did that mean to a man who had once tried to leave the community?

The barn was warm with the scents of sweet feed, oats, and hay, and she could hear Caleb murmuring to the horses. He came out of a stall, still speaking in a friendly patter. She could not look at him without wanting to touch him. He made her weak in the knees, painfully uncertain in a way she'd never been before.

He turned to look at her, and a stillness came over him. After a few seconds, after an eternity, he said, "Reese. It's good to see you."

That was all it took to send her running into his arms. He enfolded her in a big, protective embrace, and for the first time in a week, she felt balanced and calm. Inhaling his evocative odor of man and horse, she placed her cheek against his heart. "How are Hannah and the baby doing?" she asked.

"A house call, is it?" he asked, a smile in his voice as he let go of her.

"A social call," Reese admitted. "Caleb . . ."

He took a cloth from his pocket and wiped off his hands, gazing down at her thoughtfully. "She's shunned," he said.

"I'm sorry. It must have been horrible for her."

"She had to confess on her knees before the elders. I thought she would faint dead away of humiliation. The church elders want her to marry Aaron Graber. The boy himself has no interest in taking responsibility but has said he's willing. Hannah, now, she's refusing to consider it. For my father, this is a fate worse than death—having an unwed mother in the family. The bishop even suggested the baby could be adopted by a family in another district, but Hannah won't hear of it. I won't either."

Reese's stomach knotted. "I simply don't get the point of shunning."

He studied her for a moment. "No. You wouldn't. It's a ritual to remind the wayward of their sin."

"How is she supposed to function—let alone thrive—without a support system?"

"I'm her support system."

"She's lucky to have you. But she needs more." Reese thought about all he did for Jonah and Hannah, for his miserable father and all their neighbors. He'd even been willing to marry Rebecca Zook, thinking it was a way to get her to accept treatment. "Caleb, you can't save everyone."

"No, that's your job."

It was the first time Reese had heard an edge of anger in his voice. She bit back a retort. "I'd like to see her."

"She's in the house."

They didn't speak as they walked together to the farmhouse. Twilight hovered across the hilltops, etching the broken silhouettes against the darkening sky. Reese stepped inside, pausing to let her eyes adjust. Hannah sat in a wooden rocking chair, holding the baby in nursing position. At the opposite end of the room, Asa Stoltz sat at a rough-hewn table, reading one of his German papers by the soft glow of a lantern. Across the table from him, Jonah was reading a book. Jubilee lay at his feet, and her tail thumped gently against the floor.

Just for a moment, the scene resembled a family in a tableau of contentment, at peace with each other, cocooned in their world. Then Asa looked up at her and Caleb. He said something in German, dismissed Reese with a glare, and went back to his reading. He had the ability to chill a whole room. Caleb had once told her that Asa had never remarried because he'd never divorced his wife. He was too proud to admit defeat, and local women knew he was mean.

She went over to Hannah and pulled a stool up next to her. "How is little Sarah?" she asked, leaning forward to peer at the bundle.

Hannah moved the thin, wispy blanket aside. She'd opened her top and stuck the fastening pins in her shoulder cape. The baby was nursing, the curve of her tiny cheek echoing the shape of Hannah's pale breast. "You can see for yourself," she said quietly. "Everyone else does."

Reese tried to imagine the crushing pressure of the social workers. "She looks wonderful. How are you feeling?"

"How do you think? I had to make my confession before the whole community. Everyone who's been baptized into the faith shuns me, including my own grandfather. When Alma and the other quilters come over, they bring food and do the washing, but they never say a word to me. I'm a ghost."

"I'm sorry," Reese said. She hadn't thought this through—encouraging Hannah to keep the baby. *What did I do to this poor girl?* she wondered, imagining what it would be like for the baby to grow up this way. Maybe she'd overstepped, recklessly plunging into a world she didn't understand.

"You should have left things alone."

"You don't mean that. Look at your precious child."

Hannah's face softened as she gazed down at Sarah. "One day, she'll be old enough to understand that I did a terrible sin, and she'll be ashamed of me."

"That's not how it works."

"That's exactly how it works." Hannah didn't look at Reese. Though she didn't move, the girl withdrew, talking only to the infant in a soft, nonsensical patter, keeping everything else away and slowly slipping into the baby, living inside it as it had once lived inside her.

"I want to help," Reese said. "Tell me how I can help."

"I have the help I need from Caleb." She absently rubbed her thumb across the baby's forehead. "He doesn't speak of love. It's just something he does. Something he *is*. Love is the something he does while other folks sit around talking about it."

Reese understood this completely. What wouldn't she give for a love like that? Change her future? Alter her life's plans? Submit to a different sort of shunning?

Hannah kept whispering to the baby as she finished nursing. Then she stood and padded on bare feet to the stairs. "I'm putting Sarah down," she said. "Good night, everyone." She added something in German to Asa, but he didn't react. Then she went up the stairs, the only sound the creak of the wood beneath her bare feet.

Asa closed his book with a snap and got up, walking out through the back door. Caleb followed him, and Reese could hear them speaking in tense, urgent tones.

"What are you reading?" she asked Jonah, hoping to distract him and dissolve the worried frown from his face.

He held up the book—*Theodore Boone: The Activist*. "Domenico gave me some more of these books by John Grisham when he found out how much I like them."

"That looks really good. Domenico thinks you're quite a guy."

Asa spat something loudly in German, and Jonah winced. His face turned pale, his expression stony.

Reese's throat felt thick with emotion. "Is your arm doing all right?"

He shrugged his shoulders. "I need to practice more. Grandfather thinks the robotic arm is too modern. He and Caleb fuss about it all the time."

"I'm sorry about that, too. Do *you* think it's too modern?"

Another shrug. "I'm just a kid. I don't get to say." He reached over and made an expression of deep concentration. The arm grasped the handle of the lantern, and he picked it up.

"Hey, that's pretty good," Reese said. "I think if you like it, you should keep practicing."

"Yah, okay. I'm going upstairs to finish my book. Good night, Reese."

She smoothed her hand over the top of his head and placed a kiss there, inhaling the little-boy smell, something like dry leaves and puppy dog. He went to the stairs, Jubilee following at his heels.

She found Caleb alone in the darkened yard. "You're dealing with so much," she said, touching his arm. "I want to help."

"You've been a great help to us," he said, "in many ways. But now with Hannah and the baby, it's all too much. It's best you step away, Reese."

Her heart skipped a beat. "What are you saying? How is any of this my fault?"

"None of it is your fault. I caused it. I became so caught up with you and all the English ways, I failed my own family."

"Good God, you haven't failed anyone or anything. If not for you—"

"Reese. I understand what you're saying. I wanted to believe our lives could be different somehow. That's a dream, though. It's best we accept that it's over now."

"I don't want it to be over. I'd miss you too much," she whispered and rose up on tiptoe to kiss him.

He felt stiff and hesitant, already distancing himself.

"Caleb? What's the matter?"

"We have to stop," he said, his voice quiet and firm. "We never should have started . . . this."

Her breath caught in her throat. "Is it about what happened to Hannah?"

"It's about everything. But, yes, that is the catalyst. The wake-up call."

"What does our relationship have to do with Hannah's situation?" she asked, feeling her heart splinter.

"I had a duty to Hannah. A duty to my brother. And I failed."

"Because of us?"

"Because of *me*. You're all I think about, when I need to be thinking of so many other matters."

"See, when you say things like that, it makes me want this to go on forever." It was the closest she'd coming to telling Caleb she loved him. It was clear that he didn't want to hear it, though. He was eating himself up with guilt.

"Forever is an absolute term," he said.

"I know that." She paused, letting the words sink in, wondering if he realized what she was implying. Now was not the time for that discussion, though. "Listen," she said, "Hannah is wonderful. So is the baby. So is Jonah. You can't look at them and call yourself a failure."

"Let's consider all this wonderfulness. Jonah spends his time reading books he gets from your lawyer friend, Domenico, and hiding from the other kids at school, because they give him trouble. Hannah is watched like a freak by social workers from the county who follow her every move, clear down to the way she pegs out the washing to dry."

"That's temporary. Assuming she makes good choices for her child—and it appears that she's doing fine so far—then the monitoring will end. Then you and I—"

"We can't have the same future. It's just not possible. We'll never belong in the same world together, and it's too painful to keep trying to make it so."

A heavy ache surged in her chest. Losing him would be like losing a part of herself. "What's painful is you pushing me away."

He looked around the darkened landscape. "This is where I belong."

"And I can never be part of it." The heavy truth of it sank deep into her.

"I'm sorry. This will not get easier, Reese. My focus has to be on my brother's children, and now the baby. You once said you wanted a grand passion. A grand life. You deserve exactly that. You deserve everything I can't give you. You deserve all the opportunities before you— here or any other place in the world. I'd only be holding you back."

The night breeze stirred the clouds, and a glimmer of moonlight swept across the quiet yard. She could see his face in the faint light, the flash of his eyes, the face she adored. *Those lips*, she thought. Never to feel them again, never to breathe in his scent. She wanted to be with him in every way—the weight of him on top of her, his warm breath in her ear.

"I'll always be grateful that I knew you, Reese. That you let me into your heart."

Then let me keep you there.

It was a church Sunday, and for Jonah's sake, Caleb had sat through the droning opening sermon and main sermon, the unison hymns printed in the Ausbund. He tried to forget the day Hannah's name was announced so everyone would know to impose the shunning upon her to avoid being in a state of sin.

The expression of pain and shame on her face haunted him still, made him question his promise to his brother.

John would not have wanted this for Hannah, surely. The irony was, Hannah had always been such a good Amish girl, accepting baptism, practicing Plain ways as though called to do so. Even without the guidance of a mother, she had embraced the ideals held dear by the people of Middle Grove.

He let himself in the house and Jubilee greeted him with a swishing tail. "Where are the girls?" he asked the dog. "Hannah, are you there?" He looked up and down the hallway, then went to her room. Her market basket was gone, along with the usual clothes on the wall hooks. The stillness and the absence of all her personal things tweaked his awareness with unmistakable certainty. An old memory reared up from when he was a little boy, of his mother's empty room after she'd left.

A cold ball of fear tightened in his gut. Where would Hannah have gone? To find Reese, maybe? Doubtful. Reese would have brought her straight back to Caleb. Despite their painful goodbye, he knew Reese wasn't spiteful.

He clattered down the stairs and sprinted to the horse barn. Minutes later he was on the road to town, urging the black Morgan to a gallop. There was no Sunday bus from the junction, so he guessed Hannah would try to make her way to the main depot—a long walk, but the three-hour church service had given her plenty of time.

He tethered the horse at the mercantile, now busy with Sunday tourists. None of the Amish were at work, but Mr. Jolly was English, and a friend, particularly since Hannah's quilts were in such high demand. "I need to borrow your car," Caleb said. "It's urgent."

He tried not to panic as he drove to the Martz station five miles past the junction. There were a few buses parked in the bays, their destinations on display— Philadelphia, Newark, Allentown. He walked among the molded plastic benches in the waiting room but didn't see Hannah there. Maybe she'd already boarded a bus.

He strode to a door marked PASSENGERS ONLY.

"Ticket, please," said an attendant.

"I'm not traveling. I'm looking for someone," Caleb said. "A young woman with a baby."

"Sorry, can't let you through without a ticket."

Caleb clenched his jaw. He heard the diesel rumble of an engine starting up. "It's urgent."

The attendant studied him, taking in Caleb's broadfall trousers and plain jacket. Then he glanced over at a kiosk marked SECURITY. "You need a ticket," he said.

Caleb pivoted, intending to buy a ticket, any ticket, when he nearly collided with a woman behind him. She didn't say anything but gestured toward the restrooms across the way. As he approached the entrance, he heard Sarah's goat-bleat hunger cry. The knot of ice in his gut melted.

"Hannah," he said, heading into the restroom. It was marked LADIES, but he didn't care. His niece stood at a plastic drop-down changing table, fastening a clean diaper on the baby. "Hannah, what can you be thinking? I was scared to death when I got home to an empty house."

Her face turned pale, but she didn't pause as she swaddled Sarah and picked her up. "I'm not coming home," she said simply.

"You don't have a choice."

The woman who had tipped him off came into the restroom. "Is everything all right here?"

Caleb held his breath. Hannah could make trouble if she told the woman she didn't want to go with Caleb. Runaway Amish weren't uncommon in the area, and local folks kept an eye out.

Hannah looked at Caleb, and he could see the thought

behind her eyes. "Don't do this," he said in German. "If the social workers find out, you could lose Sarah for good."

She hesitated a beat longer. Then she turned to the woman. "I'm all right," she said.

"Come and sit," Caleb said, picking up her basket. As they left the room, he nodded a thank-you to the woman. He led Hannah to a bench off to the side. "Running away is not the answer," he said to her.

"It's the only answer," she stated. "I'm going to Sarasota."

Where Caleb's mother now lived. Hannah didn't even know her, but she knew about the Sarasota Express, a bus service popular with the Amish.

"It's not permitted," he pointed out. "If you violate the order of the court—"

"Then what? Will it be worse than the shunning? Worse than having the Grabers telling me how bad I am because I won't marry Aaron?" She hugged the baby to her chest, her small hands curving around the bundle. "I can't stay in Middle Grove. Everyone will be better off if Sarah and I simply disappear."

He didn't blame her for yearning to escape. He studied her face, so soft and young, the image of her mother. She'd endured the misery from the shunning and the intrusive visits from the child welfare workers. He felt rotten for not doing more to ease her heart. "I'm sorry, *liebling*. It's been hard, neh? And you've been truly brave and strong. What a fine mem you are to Sarah."

"I'm not strong," she said. "I'm not brave. I'm scared all the time, and all I want is to be gone." Her delicate hands shook as she lowered the infant to the crook of her elbow and gazed into her face. "I don't want to be Plain," she said. "I don't think I ever wanted that."

Caleb felt a jolt of shock. Never had he heard her utter

a word about the issue. He'd assumed she was content in Middle Grove, her parents' daughter to the core. She'd accepted baptism. "That's a very big statement to make," he said.

"It's a very big wish," she replied, still studying her daughter's face.

Caleb came home to a ruckus. He pulled Mr. Jolly's car up to the house to let Hannah and the baby out. Then he planned to return the car to its owner, but as he helped Hannah up the porch steps, he heard yelling.

"Go sit," he said. "I'll be right back."

At the barn, the buggy lay at an odd angle. The horse was pacing in agitation in the paddock. Asa was with Jonah, yelling about something. Jubilee pranced around, barking.

As he got closer, Caleb could hear his father berating the boy in German. ". . . do such a careless thing. The front axle is broken now, thanks to you."

"I said I was sorry," Jonah retorted.

"Sorry won't fix the buggy. So careless! And on the Lord's day. Get over here, boy."

That tone and those words raised long-buried memories. The thin whooshing sound of a leather strap sent him running. Red-faced with fury, Asa held the thick strap high as he advanced on Jonah.

Caleb grabbed the strap from his father's hand and flung it as far away as he could. "This stops now," he said. "Stay away from the boy."

"He's old enough to drive the buggy, he's old enough to take his punishment like a man."

Caleb flashed on another memory, not of Jonah but of himself, young and cowering, his big brother charging in and grabbing the weapon—what had it been? A rake handle, he recalled—from their father's hand. This was what John had done all those years ago. John had stood up to their father in order to protect Caleb.

Holding his father in his burning gaze, Caleb spoke to Jonah. "Go to the house and help your sister," he said quietly. "*Now*."

Jonah scampered away, the dog at his heels. Asa glared at Caleb. "The boy insisted on driving the buggy. Even though I warned him, he took a corner too hard. He has to learn, and you're too soft to teach him."

Caleb struggled to hold his temper in check. Reese had wanted to know the real reason he'd sent her away. It wasn't because he was distracted by her. It was because this was his life. How could he possibly bring anyone into a situation like this? "He'll learn nothing from you except cruelty and fear," he said.

"Nonsense. He's old enough to accept the consequences of disobedience and carelessness. It's the way I was raised, and my forebears, and all the others in our brotherhood."

"I won't debate that with you," Caleb said. "Your brotherhood—"

"—is the one thing that keeps our community strong." Asa surveyed the broken buggy. "Submission and obedience allow us to live in our faith, and our ways must be preserved. Discipline is the way we protect our faith, keep our family close, and prepare ourselves for heaven."

"Your brotherhood keeps its back turned when men like you are cruel to little boys. That's not preparing you for heaven. If anything, it's preparing *you* for eternal damnation."

Asa flung off the comment with a wave of his hand. "What is cruel is you putting his salvation at risk by

bringing the modern world into our home. That arm is
an abomination."

"That arm is allowing Jonah to live a normal life,"
Caleb said. "You can keep your face turned away from
the world, but I never could, and neither will Jonah or
Hannah."

"I was too soft on you, then, or you wouldn't speak to
me so disrespectfully. I wish I'd taught you better to be
humble and respect our traditions—"

"You nearly ruined John with your 'teaching,'" Caleb
spat. "Or don't you remember that he tried to take his
own life?"

"I didn't make your brother jump off that bridge," Asa
said. "That was the devil's work, and God's miracle that
he survived and came into the faith. You leave Jonah to
me, and he, too, will come around."

"Jonah's my concern now. I won't have you abusing
him. I won't let you make him so crazy he tries to kill
himself like John did."

Asa caught his breath, and his eyes flared with anger.
"You have no say in the matter. I am Jonah's guardian,
and I will assert my rights."

"I've been reading up on guardianship." Caleb walked
into the shadowy barn and went to his work area, furnished with a desk and a lantern. Picking up a printed
sheet, he read, "'The job of the guardian is to ensure the
child's safety and well-being.' You're failing Jonah."

"I'm just getting started with Jonah. You know we
don't hold with using the courts, but I will if you push me."

"Consider yourself pushed, then. Bring it on."

"I'll go to the judge. I am the legal guardian of these
children, not you. And I decree that they will abide by my
rules, not yours."

Caleb called his bluff. "Do what you must. And I will

do the same." He took out the court papers Domenico had drawn up. "I was not going to bring this up on a Sunday, but you might as well know. I'm transferring guardianship to me. You can try to fight this, but you won't win."

"It's a terrible thing, stealing those children away from me, their own grandfather. I forbid it."

"You won't be able to stop me." The lawyer had been less certain, but Caleb hoped the case wouldn't end up in front of a judge. For some reason, he remembered the day he'd been pulled over for speeding, when Reese had told him he should make up some story to avoid getting a ticket. He'd told her then that he wouldn't lie. Now he realized he'd been living a lie for a long time. He couldn't lie to get out of a speeding ticket, but he could lie to live a life he didn't want.

His father slapped the papers away, scattering them to the floor. It was probably as close as he would come to admitting defeat. "You're just like your mother."

"No, I'm not. John was like our mother. And he was too good for this world."

"You can't take his children away from their family home. He wanted them raised Plain."

"He wanted them raised in a house filled with love. And they will be."

"When you walk away, there's no chance of heaven." Asa's face was mottled, his eyes narrowed and flinty. "Think about being in hell. Just think about it."

"I *am* in hell," Caleb said and walked outside to fix the buggy.

In the morning, Caleb gathered up the last of his things. Hannah and Jonah were already in the taxi, waiting in front of the house.

He looked around the kitchen, dim and quiet except for the incessant ticking of the wall clock. He felt like a man without a place in the world. His brother had been murdered by outsiders, yet now he was about to become an outsider too.

He'd barely slept the night before, his mind filled with questions and doubts. What Asa said was true—John had wanted his children to be raised Plain. But Caleb knew in his heart that John would have wanted his kids to be happy above all else. Maybe the best way to honor his brother was to set his kids free and let them go their own way. Living Plain should be a daily joy, not a daily burden.

While putting his belongings in a rucksack before dawn, he'd come across a *Himmelsbrief*—heaven's letters—a book that had belonged to John. When Caleb was little, he used to see his brother up late at his studies, his face bathed in lamp glow. "I was so mad at you, John, when you tried to take your own life. I yelled at you, wanted to know how you could leave me. I understand now. And honestly, you were always my hero," Caleb had whispered last night, looking at the few papers stuck between the pages of the book. Lists of verb declensions and painstaking penmanship practice: *Whoever carries this book with him is safe from all his enemies, visible or invisible; and whoever has this book with him cannot die without the holy corpse of Jesus Christ, nor drown in any water, nor burn up in any fire, nor can any unjust sentence be passed upon him. So help me.*

On the handwritten page was a pencil drawing of a rocket ship, blasting through the clouds into the heavens. Caleb had tucked the page into a pocket of his rucksack.

The sound of a footstep drew him back to the present. His father came into the kitchen, wearing his work clothes and a dour expression. "It's a terrible thing you're doing," he said. "You'll live to regret it."

Caleb drew a long, steadying breath. It was the Amish way to forgive and let go. "I forgive you," he said.

His father slapped his hands down on the kitchen table. "And what is it you think needs forgiveness?"

It would take hours to enumerate everything, so Caleb said, "I forgive the beatings and belittlings, the harsh words and isolation. Only you know in your heart what made you treat your wife and your sons that way. I'll never understand your cruelty, but I do forgive you. And now I'm letting you go." He placed a card on the table. "That's where you can find me. Goodbye, Asa Stoltz."

Asa turned away, presenting his back. Caleb walked out the door, out into the jewel-bright autumn day. He glanced up at the sky, so blue this morning that it made his eyes ache. The silver flash of a jet streaked overhead.

23

Reese discovered that gardening helped her think. With her hands in the soil and the sun on her back, she let her mind wander. After hours at the hospital or clinics, bent over reports or seeing patients, the strenuous physical work helped her clear her head. Sometimes she became too enmeshed in her work. The doctor-patient relationship was an awkward dance between distance and intimacy, and she hadn't quite mastered the steps. Knowing someone's medical history was not the same as knowing their personal history. Yet when you knew the details of someone's sexual habits, you probably knew more about them than their closest family did.

The crackling autumn afternoon suited her mood— brisk and bright. Although the vegetables and fruits and flowers had been harvested, there was still plenty of work to be done in the garden. She dug into the soil with a broad iron rake, working the teeth through the fibrous residue of squash and tomato plants and the long curly tangle left behind by the just-harvested pie pumpkins. After loosening a section of soil, she added mulch from a wheelbarrow, breathing in the damp, fecund scent of the earth.

As she worked, a shadow fell over her from behind. She straightened up and turned, feeling a jolt of surprise. "Dad. What are you doing here?"

Her father smiled. "I felt like seeing my girl, so I jumped in the car and drove up here."

"That's . . . wow. So un-Dad-like." She peeled off her gloves and gave him a hug. "I'm a mess," she said.

"You look wonderful."

"So do you." He looked as handsome and slender as ever in jeans and a Princeton sweatshirt. "Where's Mom?"

He shrugged. "She had a thing. A fund-raiser. I weaseled out of it." He picked up the rake. "Can I help?"

She narrowed her eyes in suspicion. "Who are you, and what have you done with my father?"

"Okay. I deserved that." He picked up the rake and started on a row of spent cucumber vines.

She watched him for a moment, then worked at his side, putting the debris into a bin for the compost heap. "I've missed you," she said without breaking the rhythm of their work. "And Mom. More than you know. I wish you were more a part of my life."

"We feel the same way, baby," he said. "Let's not do that anymore."

As they worked together, she told him about her job—the changing array of patients she saw during each shift, the moments of success and the awful failures, the asthma study that was taking shape and being reviewed for special funding. Then she talked about her life—learning to embroider and to make jam, her volunteer work with migrant laborers at the Latino Living Center.

"So it's good, then. This residency."

She was quiet, smoothing the mulch over the soil. For the first time, she felt she was living life on her own terms and making choices for herself, not to please her parents or fulfill someone else's expectations. It was a powerful, liberating feeling, but there were challenges. Without her parents advising her, she was on her own, and sometimes doubts crept in. "Another option came up—an opening for a med-ped program in California."

He fell still, listening as she explained the situation. "Is this something you want?"

She smiled. "I was expecting you to say 'you should' or 'of course you will,' or—"

"Is that what I do?"

"Pretty much, yeah. Thank you for not doing that now."

More moments of silence. Then her father asked, "And your friend Caleb?"

Her friend. She couldn't talk about him without feeling a terrible ache. He wasn't her friend. He wasn't anything, and it felt so terribly wrong. Instead of moving past that chapter in her life, she missed him more and more each day. She remembered looking into his eyes and seeing her whole world in there, in him, in the deep, sweet connection they had.

A few weeks after they'd parted ways, her period had been late. For one soaring moment, she'd felt nothing but joy, imagining herself going to Middle Grove to tell him she was pregnant. That, of course, had created a tidal wave of panic, followed by a reality check. When the pregnancy test turned up negative, she'd been relieved. Sort of. But sort of not.

For a long time, she had been fighting against the new world Caleb had presented to her. A part of her was still entangled with her work and her parents. The incident with Hannah had brought Caleb's world up sharply against hers, throwing off the safeness of the world she thought she inhabited. "I'm not quite ready to talk about that," she said quietly.

He simply nodded and kept working. After spending her whole life planning and executing those plans, Reese was ready to do something different. Something spontaneous. Reconnecting with her father was an unexpected breath of fresh air.

In a curious way, both she and Caleb had been shaped—and perhaps damaged—by trying to live up to the expectations of their parents and the world around them. Now she was realizing her independence and faced with shaping her own future. She'd been doing right by her patients, and by everyone else, but not by herself. In the deepest part of her soul, she couldn't imagine living without Caleb. Yet he had been firm in his conviction that he couldn't see a way to be with her.

She had people around her—good people—but the relationships didn't have the depth and authenticity she'd found with Caleb. Sometimes she didn't actually know why she wanted to be with him. Yet her thoughts kept drifting to him. She couldn't forget the expression on his face when he'd said goodbye. She couldn't keep herself from believing it didn't have to be that way. But every time she tried to imagine the compromises each would have to make, it seemed impossible. Time was running out to make a decision about the program in California. An amazing opportunity. A new beginning. And an ending to the incredible, messy, heartbreaking, life-altering time here.

After her father left, she went inside to clean up, scrubbing the garden soil from her hands and fingernails. In her room, her gaze fell on the sampler cloth from Rebecca Zook. Rebecca had embroidered a single letter— W—and then the thread trailed off to nothing.

Passing her hand over the soft cloth, she folded it up and placed it on the nightstand. Maybe one day she would finish it.

Caleb hung a clock in the kitchen and touched the pendulum. The quiet rhythm ticked into the silence. "How's that, Jubilee?" he asked the dog, knowing she would thump her tail in approval.

They had settled into the new place on the premises of Grantham Farm, in the largest of the workers' residences. It was plain, but not Amish Plain. He and the kids now lived in a cottage with electric lighting and running water, hot showers whenever they wanted, and music playing on the radio.

"Let's get that layabout up and ready for school," he said to the dog, opening the door to Jonah's small room.

Watching the boy greet his dog with a sleepy smile, Caleb had no regrets about leaving the community. He had to believe John would understand. Asa would always be Asa; he would never change. In Middle Grove, the brotherhood to which he was so loyal would observe Plain ways, practice humility, be stewards of the land, and reject anything that got in the way of faith.

Caleb had been born and raised Amish, but his faith was not automatic. He couldn't force it. Instead, he needed to find it. Or not. Could be he just needed to live his life. Could be he had found his own kind of faith right here, right now. It was real and tangible, made of the things he could see and touch and feel deep in his heart—the peace and contentment that came from seeing the brush of sunshine on a little boy's cheek just before he awakened in the morning. The sound of a young mother singing a lullaby. The laughter of a growing baby as the dog frisked around her. These were the things the world was made of—everyday blessings, delivered in moments, not homilies.

You can't save everybody. Sometimes, Reese's words came back to haunt him. Sometimes, he thought about the vast emptiness in his life that only she could fill. During one of Jonah's arm appointments, the boy had asked

Mose about her, voicing the question Caleb couldn't bring himself to ask.

"She's going to California," Mose had said. "Got an invitation to a special program that'll make her an even better doctor than she already is."

Caleb knew she'd suffered a crisis of confidence after the Hannah incident. Reese had questioned her own actions and judgment. Maybe she'd decided life here wasn't for her after all.

You can't save everybody.

He felt terrible about having flung the bitter words at her. And the words weren't merely bitter, but wrong. He wished Reese could see Hannah now. Then she'd know. She'd realize that her actions the morning Sarah Jane was born *had* saved everyone.

He sang along with the radio while he fixed breakfast. What a luxury to use a toaster. The charred shingles of the past were a distant memory.

Jubilee gave a sharp bark—an alert. Caleb stepped outside. Visitors to Grantham were rare.

To his astonishment, Reese's car was parked on the gravel drive. She got out and came toward him, looking to his eyes like the risen sun. "Hey, stranger," she said.

"I thought you were going to California," he said.

"I thought you were staying in Middle Grove," she said.

"It appears we were both mistaken." His heart tried to beat its way out of his chest. He couldn't hold off another second. He hauled her into his arms, stunned by how much he wanted her. He held her so close, there was no room for doubt, none at all. She nestled there and then lifted her face and kissed him, so softly.

"I was going to say we need to talk," she said, giving him a smile he'd never seen before, her eyes filled with hope. Gently extricating herself from his embrace, she added, "But maybe I'll just give you this instead. It's a sampler cloth. I've been practicing my embroidery."

Mystified, he took the wispy cloth from her. In the few seconds it took to unfold the cloth, he thought about how deeply he loved her, with every beat of his heart. It was a breathless, heartaching love, a feeling he had carried around practically from the first moment they'd met. Reese was a leap into the unknown, and he'd realized that from the very start. He couldn't say how or when it had happened, this bond between them. It transcended both their worlds, pulling their hearts together, powerful and undeniable.

He looked down at the sampler she'd handed him. There was a message, painstakingly stitched into the cloth: *Will you marry me?*

Epilogue

The day I left you at the safe haven, I had no way of seeing the life before me. That came later. It came from watching and listening, having lots of big thinks, as your mama would say. It came from knowing I had the love of Caleb and Reese, from observing their commitment to each other, and seeing the respect they have for each other's beliefs.

They married in a civil ceremony attended by the few friends who had not taken sides in the drama. We all moved to a town deeper in the Poconos, close to the hospital where Reese worked. I attended public school for the first time. Hannah sold her quilts to collectors and took classes at community college. That's where she met Wesley, the man you call your dad.

Reese built a busy practice amid farmers and townspeople and published papers on asthma research. And had two babies of her own.

As a family, we had adventures those in the Amish community might only dream about—flying in planes, going to the seashore, skiing in the mountains. But the greatest adventure, I can tell you, is simply life itself.

It was years before I learned the truth about the guardianship issue. Caleb knew his father. He knew Asa would not pursue us beyond Middle Grove. But I always knew I was the reason for us leaving. Or if not the reason, then the catalyst.

In the Amish community, the focus was on all the things I couldn't do because of the accident. But it's a funny thing about loss. It can be balanced by gain. I gained connections from the love and support I found after the accident. When we left Middle Grove, I focused instead on the things I could do—hold you in my lap and read you a story. Run a four-minute mile. Play chess with my uncle. Go to law school. Become a child advocacy lawyer.

You were the start of that, Sarah Jane. Leaving you on the night you were born was an act of desperation, one that gives me chills to this day when I realize what I put at risk. I'll always remember that night, and the place where it all happened. It will always be a place in my heart, a place in the middle. Middle Grove. And one day, I'll take you there. One day.

I'll always be grateful we were given a second chance with you. There are those in the Amish community who regard us even now as a fallen family, but I don't see anyone falling. Reclaiming you and moving on was an affirmation, and an acknowledgment that the world is waiting. Just waiting to be found.

Acknowledgments

Thanks to Dan Mallory for being there at the beginning, and to Rachel Kahan for being there at the end. The remarkable team of professionals at William Morrow Books—Lynn Grady, Liate Stehlik, Tavia Kowalchuk, Lauren Truskowski, Kathy Gordon—for their dedication, creativity, energy, and spirit. Meg Ruley and Annelise Robey of the Jane Rotrosen Agency are, as always, pillars of strength, humor, and professionalism. For guiding me and my readers through the social media labyrinth, I am eternally grateful for Cindy Peters.

I'm grateful to my fellow writers—Elsa Watson, Sheila Roberts, Lois Faye Dyer, Kate Breslin, and Anjali Banerjee—for reading and discussing early drafts. I'm also grateful to Ed Aleks, a law enforcement professional, for helpful technical advice.

Thanks to Laura Cherkas and Laurie McGee for thorough and thoughtful copy editing and to Marilyn Rowe for proofreading.

My husband, Jerry Gundersen, will see his name on this page, and he will know exactly why I'm so grateful to him.